OVERCOME by impatience, Fox shoved Tanner down on the blanket and climbed on top of him.

"I don't mean to sound bossy, or maybe I do, but it's time to stop this blathering and start, well, you know."

His eyes sparkled and he wore the expression that came over him when he was trying not to laugh.

She narrowed her eyes and tried to find the anger that helped her through her vulnerable moments. "I mean, that's why we came here, isn't it?"

"Are we running behind schedule?"

Her cheeks heated. Sitting up, he leaned forward and kissed the tip of her nose. "I like the way you're wearing your hair tonight. Piled on top of your head. You have beautiful hair." After kissing her lightly on the mouth, a tease, he removed her hairpins and waves of red hair tumbled to her shoulder then spilled down her back almost to her waist.

"Like silk," he murmured.

The heated look in his eyes stifled Fox's laugh. Her throat went dry and hot and she felt the first tremor of what she suspected would soon erupt into an earthquake deep inside. Fox felt his hand cupping the back of her head, buried in her hair. She had never felt a man's tongue before but did so now and a jolt of lightning scorched through her body. He tasted of smoke and coffee and something sweet, and she wanted more of him . . .

Also by Maggie Osborne

SHOTGUN WEDDING
PRAIRIE MOON
THE BRIDE OF WILLOW CREEK
I DO, I DO, I DO
SILVER LINING

FOXFIRE BRIDE

A Novel

MAGGIE OSBORNE

BALLANTINE BOOKS • NEW YORK

An Ivy Book
Published by The Random House Publishing Group

Copyright © 2004 by Maggie Osborne

All rights reserved under International and Pan-American Copyright Conventions. Published in the United States by Ivy Books, an imprint of The Random House Publishing Group, a division of Random House, Inc., New York, and simultaneously in Canada by Random House of Canada Limited, Toronto.

Ivy Books and colophon are trademarks of Random House, Inc.

ISBN 0-7394-4726-2

Manufactured in the United States of America

To George.
They've all been love letters to you, cowboy.

ACKNOWLEDGMENTS

The names Norwood and Barbara Robb were generously
offered by their auction-winning owners. Excelsior and
I are grateful to the Robbs for their charity
and their good humor.

CHAPTER 1

THE ice wasn't good this year. Ordinarily the lake froze to a depth of eight or ten inches, but this winter had been unusually warm. Frustrated and worried, Fox sat on a rock, smoking and scowling at the fringe of thin ice circling the lakeshore. She had some decisions to make.

"We haven't cut enough ice to fill half the shed and winter is almost over," she said to Peaches. Peaches wore a thick flannel shirt beneath his overalls. This time last year they had both worn heavy coats, scarves, and hats with fur earflaps.

"We'll get by."

Sometimes Peaches's relentless optimism was exactly what Fox needed. Other times optimism made her want to bash him over the head with a block of ice. This was one of the bashing times.

"Once summer comes, it'll take us about three weeks to sell the ice." She jerked a thumb over her shoulder toward the ice shed. "And then what?"

"We ain't the only cutters with no ice. Nobody going to have ice this year. That ice is going to fetch a pretty price."

That was true. Fox smoked and watched the sun sparkling on the water in the center of a lake that should have been frozen solid. Raising the price on the ice they had already cut might see one person through the season, but not both of them.

She had a feeling that fate was gathering force, getting ready to kick her in the fanny. That the ice wouldn't be profitable this year was a nudge.

"You could go back to doing what you're good at doing. Me? I can always pick up work," Peaches said.

Fox swiveled to study his brown face. Deep lines scored a grid on his cheeks. His hair was more white than dark. "How old are you? Seventy?"

"I don't know how old I am," he said with a shrug. "Doesn't matter as long as I can work."

He had a point there. And unless his rhumitiz was acting up, Peaches could work rings around anyone else Fox knew, including herself. But a seventy-year-old man shouldn't be looking for work. A seventy-year-old man should be able to sit on the porch if he had a mind to, and do nothing at all.

"I've been thinking about a lot of things," she said, fixing her gaze on a distant peak.

"I know it, and I don't like it when you start thinking deep." Standing, Peaches examined a line of clouds building to the north. "Looks like a storm coming in," he said hopefully. "I swear it feels colder already."

"I'm thinking how I just gave up on everything when DeBeck shot me and put me out of business. And I'm thinking about Hobbs Jennings and how he stole my whole life and I haven't done a fricking thing about it. Mostly I'm thinking about revenge. DeBeck died before I could kill him and there's a lesson in that. So I'm thinking about killing Jennings before he up and dies on his own." Thinking was too mild a word. Brooding and obsessing were closer to the truth.

"You can't change the past, Missy." Peaches's voice softened like it always did when he was worried about her. His big hand came down on her shoulder and squeezed. "You can only change the future."

"I'm thinking about taking my half of the ice money, whatever it is, and going to Denver. Hobbs Jennings's future is the one I want to change." She had almost made up her mind. All she needed was a sign that she was thinking right.

Over supper, Peaches brought the subject around again. "We might as well talk about it. So, let's say you go to Denver."

"All right, let's say that." Tilting her biscuit toward the lantern, she buttered the surface. She didn't like a blob of butter in the middle like some people she could name. The butter should be neatly spread to the rim.

"And let's say you find Mr. Jennings and you shoot the bastard and kill him. Then what?" He put a scoop of butter in the center of his biscuit just like she knew he would. "The law will arrest you and hang your butt. So what did you achieve?"

"Jennings would be dead. He would have paid for what he did."

"But you'd be dead, too."

"Now why can't you butter your biscuit right? You end up with a couple of dry bites and one bite that's pure grease!"

"If you want to talk manners, Missy, I done told you a hundred times that refined folks don't hold the handle of their fork in their fist. Here's how you're supposed to hold it."

"And I done told you a hundred times that me and refinement don't fall within spitting distance." It could have been different. That she wasn't refined was the fault of Hobbs Jennings. And that thought circled her back to brooding about fulfilling her vow, to find Jennings and put a bullet in his thieving heart.

After they washed up the supper dishes, Fox stepped outside for a smoke. The cabin was small, and they had agreed not to stink it up with cigar smoke. While she waited for Peaches to set up the chessboard, she thought about walking away from the cabin, the lake, the ice business, and Peaches. Peaches was the sticking point.

Fox had known him since she was six or seven. They had run away from her mother's cousin when Fox was twelve. There'd been some gaps, but by and large they'd been together for almost twenty years. Peaches had taught her pretty near everything she knew that was worth knowing. What he couldn't teach her, like reading and woman things, he'd made sure she learned from someone else. And some things she'd learned herself.

Her biggest learning experience had come when she'd run off again when she was seventeen, leaving Peaches behind. At the time she hadn't known that seventeen-year-olds, particularly women, didn't set off alone to find the goldfields in the mountains west of what was now Denver. That had been some trip, all right. The memory curved her lips in a smile. She'd gotten half frozen, half broiled, half starved, and was hopelessly lost about a hundred times. She had talked her way in and then out of Indian camps, had shot a mountain man with rape on his mind, had killed two bears and enough deer and rabbits to keep her alive.

Newspapers all over the territories had printed articles about her journey, which had launched her into the scouting business. She'd found a livelihood that had worked just fine until DeBeck shot her in the leg. After that, she'd fetched up in Carson City, gimping around and waiting for her leg to heal.

"Remember that day we met up again?" She'd gone into Jack's Bar and discovered Peaches sweeping the place. It was like coming home. "You were still mad that I'd run off in the middle of reading you one of Charlie Dickens's novels."

"I ain't got over it yet," he said, grinning as she came back to the table. "You're black this time."

It didn't matter which color she played, he always beat her. "How long have we been sitting on the side of this mountain just drifting and waiting for something that never comes?"

" 'Bout three years, I guess. That's a long time to brood, Missy."

"Is that what you think I've been doing?" It was as good an explanation as any.

"I know that's changing. I know you're going to go to Denver. Probably knew 'fore you did." He studied the board. "You want some company on the ride east?"

"Could you stand to see me hanged?" She studied the board, too.

"Might not happen. Might be you'll stop living in the past and start making yourself a future. Might happen before we get to Denver."

It would be like old times, her and Peaches on the road. But she was smarter now, wiser to the ways of the world. If Peaches was with her when she shot Hobbs Jennings, even if she shot him in front of a dozen witnesses, everyone would swear the black man was the killer before they'd believe a white woman had pulled the trigger.

"You can't be with me when I shoot Jennings. You have to agree to that or I'm leaving you here."

"We'll cross that bridge when we get there. I'm going."

There was no point arguing now. They'd have about twelve hundred miles to work out details.

When Fox opened the door in the morning, snow swirled into the cabin on a blast of frigid wind. She and Peaches slapped hands, then carried their coffee out to the lake to watch the snowflakes melt into the water. The pine trees looked like they'd been dipped in vanilla frosting and smelled sharp and tangy the way Fox thought green ought to smell. "Now if it would just stay this cold for another two weeks!"

But it didn't. The new ice was gone in three days.

Fox stood in her shirtsleeves, not needing a coat, and frowned at the stacks of ice blocks that filled about a third of the shed. The shed was protected from the sun by pines and aspen, and she had insulated the ice blocks with straw. There was no melt water on the floor of the shed, but if the weather got much warmer, there would be.

"Company's coming," Peaches called.

Picking up the shotgun that leaned against the inside of the door, Fox stepped outside the shed. At least it was still colder inside the shed than outside. Peaches lowered his wood-chopping ax and they both waited for the man they could see glimpses of as he wove through the trees.

The horse was quality, not blowing and heaving at this altitude. The rider looked to be quality, too, judging from his leather hat and wool jacket. He was clean-shaven, which set him apart and marked him as a city man, possibly from the east.

"Hello the cabin," he called, much later than he should have, which made Fox think he was damned lucky he hadn't been shot long before now.

"Come on in," she answered.

He rode into the clearing and tipped his hat to her then looked toward the lake. "Nice view you got here."

"What's your business, mister?"

Once he'd admired the lake and the peaks, he examined the cabin and shed, then swung his gaze from Fox to Peaches and back again.

"I'm looking for Fox." His eyes stopped on Peaches. "Would that be you?"

"That would be me," Fox said, swinging up the shotgun so he could see it. "What do you want?"

Surprise tightened his jaw and he stared at her, then an irritated frown pulled his brow and he swore under his breath. "I beg your pardon, ma'am. I suspect some boys in town were having a bit of fun at my expense."

"Is that so." She kept her gaze narrow and hard, ready for anything. He wasn't wearing a gun, didn't pack a rifle scabbard. And since he didn't sport a beard, she could see that he had one of those craggy angular faces that could flash from pleasant to threatening in a heartbeat. "And who are you?"

"Matthew Tanner." He took off his hat and nodded, revealing shoulder-length reddish brown hair. Clean shiny hair, which also set him apart from the miners, prospectors, and general grub bags who seemed to gravitate to this part of the territory. "I'll be on my way, but first, I wonder if I could trouble you for a cup of water?"

"I'll get it." Peaches set down his ax and headed toward the lake with a bucket. He wouldn't have left the clearing if he'd smelled one iota of trouble on Matthew Tanner. Peaches's judgment was good enough for Fox.

She leaned the shotgun against the shed wall. "Might as well get down and stretch your legs."

"Thank you."

He turned out to be as tall as she'd guessed he would be. Maybe six feet. At least a head taller than she was. "So why were you looking for me?"

"It's a mistake." Eyes the color of old wood examined her. "I need a scout. Some men in Carson City said Fox was the best scout in the territory. Directed me up here."

"Well," she said, walking around him, sizing him up, "those boys weren't wrong. Except I gave up scouting after I got shot."

He was one damned fine-looking man. Built like a wedge of muscle and sinew, not an ounce of fat on him. Wide shoulders, buttocks made for long days in a saddle. His jawline announced he was stubborn, but what man wasn't? The lines of his face saved him from being handsome, but not from being attractive. Fox felt a tug deep inside that she would have sworn was long dead.

"I didn't want the aggravation that one of my competitors was giving me. So I decided to go into a different business. But you coming up here is like fate paying a call. I've been thinking about going back to work."

His smile turned into a stare. "You really are a scout?" After a minute he walked around her, doing his own sizing up, inspecting her work boots, trousers, poncho, and raggedy hat.

Fox experienced an insane urge to tuck up her hair and scrub her face with her hanky. Scowling, she gave him stare for stare.

"Listen, when I was taking parties east, I was the best there is," she snapped. "You don't have to be a fricking man to find your way from here to there, so you can stop looking so amazed. Where do you want to go?"

"Denver."

The word rocked her back on her heels. Peaches heard, too. He stopped on the path so abruptly that water slopped from the bucket. His eyes widened and swung toward Fox.

"Well, hell," she said uneasily, slapping her hat against her thigh. Destiny had just kicked her in the pants. "You can get to Denver without a scout. Just head up to South Park in Wyoming, cross the divide, and turn south."

"That's the route I took coming out here, but I need to get home by a faster, more direct way." He ladled water out of the bucket and thanked Peaches.

"You can cross the divide through Wyoming, or you can go south and pick up the Sante Fe trail. If you try it as the crow flies, you'll have to cross several—I'm saying several—mountain ranges. That's not smart. And trouble and setbacks could end up costing more time than if you'd taken either of the tested routes."

"But it could take less time."

"It could. But that's not how it usually happens."

His gaze hardened. "The truth . . . have you taken the direct route before?"

"The truth?" The hair on the back of her neck bristled. "Listen, mister." She jabbed a finger on his chest, making him step backward. "I don't lie. There's not much about me to hang my pride on, but honesty is one of those things." She stared up at him, her eyes glittering. "Yes, I've done the direct route. Several times. And each time was a fricking disaster. You hear me? People died, people got hurt. Go up through Wyoming." Turning on her heel, she went into the cabin and slammed the door.

Who the hell was Matthew Tanner to ride into her yard and question her honesty? Who did he think he was, anyway? Pacing, she returned to the window and peered out in time to see Tanner following Peaches down to the lake. All right, now what was Peaches doing? A fresh wave of anger burned through her.

It took several minutes before she calmed down enough to ask the real questions. Why was she so angry? No answer popped to mind. Why in the world should it matter that Tanner was disappointed that she was a woman or that he wondered if she was as good as she claimed? No answer popped to mind. And it wasn't unreasonable for him to want to know if she'd previously made the trek since he would have to trust her judgment and he'd be paying her.

Fox stamped across the floor to the small mirror over the

sink. She seldom looked in a mirror because mirrors never reflected the face she expected to see. The face she expected was the happy round face of a child, not the plain lived-in face of an adult or the sharp suspicious eyes that said keep away.

She peered into the glass trying to see whatever Matthew Tanner had seen when he looked at her. Wild red hair coming out of the knot on top of her head. No, not red. Auburn. Auburn sounded more refined, not that she cared a whit for refinement. At least her face was clean. And she wasn't missing any teeth, which was a miracle because Fox had probably been in as many fights as a man her age would have been. Matthew Tanner wasn't missing any teeth either, she recalled.

He was looking for a scout to lead him to Denver.

She stared at herself in the mirror. How did the old saying go? Be careful what you wish for, it might come true. And sure enough, here was the chance she'd been telling Peaches she wanted. If she took on Matthew Tanner, he'd pay her to go where she wanted to go anyway. She'd reach Denver with money in her pocket. Biting her lip, she walked back to the window and peered outside. What were he and Peaches saying to each other?

"All right." Jamming her hat on her head, she pulled open the door and strode down the path. "You're still here," she said, walking past the rock Peaches and Tanner sat on.

"We're talking about the war," Tanner said, standing as if a lady had entered the room.

"Mr. Tanner thinks slavery will be abolished. I'll be a free man."

Fox laughed and turned around. "Peaches Hernandez, if you were ever a slave, I sure never heard about it."

"Well, I coulda been," he said, smiling. "Just luck that I wasn't."

Matthew Tanner listened as if he were trying to figure out their relationship. When she turned a cool gaze on his face, he nodded once then cleared his throat. "I'm not making an offer, but are you interested in leading a small party to Denver by the direct route?"

"First, there is no direct route. We won't be following an established trail, we'd be picking our way along, hit and miss. Second, I have a lucrative business here." From the corner of her eye, she saw Peaches suck in his cheeks, saw him roll his eyes toward the sky. "Me and Peaches, we're ice cutters. We store the ice over there, then drive it down to Carson and sell it for a pretty penny when the weather gets warm. If I leave, I'd be walking away from a pile of money."

Tanner scanned the ice-free lake and raised an eyebrow. "So to lure you away from large profits, I'd have to pay you a fortune, is that it?" His jaw set in a line and he studied her face. "What's the going rate?"

"You pay for all provisions, and provide a good horse for me and Peaches and pack animals that I approve. You pay any expenses we encounter on the road. And you pay me one hundred and fifty dollars a month, figuring at least three months. You pay half up front, half when I drag your butt into Denver. There's an extra charge for every person in the party beyond five. If you take an established route, no one cares if your party numbers two or two hundred. If you go direct with me, we go with a small party that can move fast if it has to."

"Your man goes, too?"

"Peaches is his own man, not mine. We'll need a wrangler, and that'll be Peaches. You pay him a hundred a month."

She had stacked all the expenses on him and upped the going rate by half again. From the looks of him, he could afford whatever she chose to charge. But the primary reason she gouged him was to discover how far fate was going to push her.

"One more thing," she said, standing close enough that she could smell leather and horse and a whiff of perspiration. "You and your party take your orders from me. If I say we don't go through a particular valley, we don't go through it, no questions asked. If I say we have to ride around a gully, then you and everyone else rides around it. If I say we don't ford a river, no horse gets its feet wet. If I say we go across, we go, whether or not anyone agrees. You understand? If I'm responsible for your lives, then I'm in charge. If you or anyone else in your party objects to taking orders from a woman, then find yourself another scout."

He nodded slowly. "You've given me a lot to think about."

Which was a polite way of saying that he intended to scrape the earth and try to turn up another scout. That was fine with Fox. If she was going to Denver, it would be a whole lot less aggravating to go alone and take the relatively easy route up through Wyoming.

"One thing," Tanner said before he walked away. "There's some urgency involved. How soon could you get under way?"

Fox pursed her lips. "We'll have to sell the ice. As warm as it's been, we could probably sell it now instead of waiting for summer. Probably. That might take a week."

"Suppose someone bought all your ice and you didn't have to deal with selling it. How soon?"

"The minute you give the go-ahead, me and Peaches will ride to Carson City and start arranging provisions and looking at animals. I'd say we could ride out of Carson in three days."

"You can guarantee we'll get to Denver in three months?"

"Mister, I can't guarantee anything. All I can tell you is that I'll try like hell to get you there."

Hands fisted on her hips, Fox watched Tanner return to the clearing, mount, and ride toward the trees. He waved before he disappeared, but she didn't wave back.

"What did you learn about him while you were talking?"

Peaches stood and pressed his hands against the small of his back. "He probably comes from money, judging from his boots, his clothing, and the way he speaks. He's got the east in his voice. No strong ties there, though, or he'd be chomping to get into a Union uniform."

Most of the time Fox forgot there was a war going on. The only sign she'd noticed was a heavy influx of miners as the gold and silver mines went into twenty-four-hour production. The government would buy whatever the mines produced. But out here, unless a body was in the mining industry, the war didn't have much of an effect.

She thought of something else over a supper of potatoes and dried fish. "Tanner was mighty pale, didn't you think? Like he doesn't spend a lot of time in the sun even though he sat his horse well."

"Miners are pale, if that's what you're thinking. I hate dried fish."

"I don't make him for a miner. Too well dressed, too much authority, clean fingernails. Did you see his face when I talked about being in charge? That didn't set well. He's used to making decisions and giving orders." She shoved a fork at the fish. "I don't like fish either."

"Then why do we have to eat it?"

"Because we spent all that time last summer drying fish for nights like this when we don't have a rabbit."

"You should be ashamed of yourself, Missy, charging that man thieving rates."

Fox grinned around a mouthful of limp carrots grown last summer. "He doesn't have to hire me."

"He will," Peaches predicted, looking at her across the table. "After Mr. Tanner checks you against what else is available, he'll be back."

"I'm more or less planning on it." All Fox had to do was think Jennings's name and a familiar burn flamed inside. Jennings had stolen her life. If it wasn't for him, she wouldn't consider leading a bunch of greenhorns on a long dangerous trek that was going to be a whole lot of trouble. She wouldn't be here in this cabin, wearing men's clothing and eating with her fist wrapped around her fork. If it wasn't for Jennings, she wouldn't be trying to think of one good reason to get up every morning and go on living.

"I have to do this, Peaches," she said in a low voice. "I'm almost sure Jennings is still in Denver. I heard that he owns several mines in this area, but his company is still based in Denver. I need to accomplish one good thing in my life, and that would be killing Jennings. He has to pay for what he did."

"Well, the good news is that you're moving again. Going to get off this mountain. Who knows what you'll find out there? Might find something better than revenge."

"There's nothing better than revenge. I just wish I'd done it sooner."

Peaches pressed his lips together and cleared the table. "We're playing checkers tonight. You're the red chips."

CHAPTER 2

*B*Y morning Fox had made up her mind. Shortly before dawn, she and Peaches loaded the wagon with as many ice blocks as the horse could pull, then headed down the mountain to Carson City.

To call Carson a city expressed breathtaking optimism. On the other hand, the little town had boomed in the three years since the Comstock Lode had put the Nevada Territory on the map. Carson wanted to be the town where the Comstock miners and supervisors spent their pay.

Before they reached the outskirts Fox and Peaches changed places on the wagon seat since Peaches didn't believe it was right or decent for a woman to drive while a man rode passenger. It was an argument that Fox was never going to win.

While they were stopped, she nailed a sign to each side of the wagon slats: Ice for Sale.

"I guess we'll find out if it's been warm enough to create a market," she said, climbing up on the passenger side.

Peaches chose a circuitous route down dusty streets past a hodgepodge of tents, lean-tos, shacks, and tidy homes that would have fit comfortably into a real city. By the time he turned south on Curry Street, half the ice had been sold.

"The hotel will buy the rest," Peaches predicted.

"Hold back a block or two for the bar." A squint toward the sun told Fox it was near midday. "Drop me at the General Store," she said, patting her vest pockets to find her list. "I'll make sure McGurty has the provisions we need, then I'll see if

Whitfield has any horses worth what he'll try to charge me. How about you and me meet up at Jack's Bar about four o'clock."

"I'm thinking we should be on the road no later than four thirty," he said, lowering his head and giving her a look from beneath his eyebrows that said, I mean it. "So don't get social and don't go looking for a fight. I don't want to be sitting in Jack's Bar at midnight."

Tanner thought he spotted Fox striding into the General Store, but when she didn't emerge after a few minutes, he decided he'd been mistaken. That didn't surprise him since his eyes were red and stinging from riding all morning in a dusty breeze. What irritated him more than sore eyes was wasting a day that he didn't have to spare.

While he waited for the bank to assemble his request, he considered the scouts he had interviewed. The most recent had occurred this morning at a shack built on a low rise surrounded by blowing sand. The man Tanner had ridden six miles to interview impressed him as being as shifty as the ground swirling around the bare boards of his place.

The teller returned to the cage and cleared his throat, blinking curiously behind his spectacles. "We've accommodated your requirements, Mr. Tanner."

"Thank you. The St. Charles Hotel is expecting delivery." On the way out, he stopped by the president's office to express gratitude for everything that had been done to meet his needs, namely a relay of riders sent to Reno to dispatch and receive telegrams from Denver.

After he'd confirmed that the St. Charles manager had locked the bags in the hotel's vault, Tanner ordered a whiskey sent to his room, then changed out of his dusty riding togs into evening attire suitable for an at-home supper at the home of John Manning, with whom he'd been working at the Gallows Mine.

He had a few hours before he was due to arrive at Manning's house; a walk might clear his mind. Everything was in place for the journey except the scout. He had to make a decision. No sooner had he thought the words than he spotted Peaches Hernandez driving an empty wagon south on Curry Street. The bed was wet and there were for-sale signs on the side slats.

So he hadn't been mistaken about noticing Fox. He hailed the wagon and asked where she was, then walked toward the trading corral next to the smithy.

She wasn't hard to spot, not with that fiery hair. She stood nose to nose with Harry Whitfield, the only horse trader in town. Leaning forward from the waist, she slapped her hat against her thigh, looking mad enough to chew nails.

"That's it," she shouted, shoving her hat on her head. "My client isn't going to pay one hundred dollars for a scrawny bag of bones! That's robbery, you bastard. And the mules." She flung a hand toward the animals in the corral. "Bow-backed with one hoof in the grave! Eighty dollars? Ha! Only if every other animal in the territory drops dead in the next hour." Spinning on her heel, she walked into Tanner. It occurred to him that the collision was like two rocks smacking together. No give in either of them.

Fox shoved back from his chest and raised a flushed face. "I'm glad you're here. You won't believe what this thief is trying to charge you for those horses! Look at 'em. I never saw such sorry specimens." She threw a glare over her shoulder and shouted at Whitfield. "You think about it and come up with a better price, a discount for volume, say, or I'm heading up to Gold Canyon to see what Pinky Borden can offer. I'll stop by in the morning for your final offer. On my way to Gold Canyon."

She watched Whitfield stomp toward the smithy then gave Tanner a push toward the corral. "We're going to buy those two mustangs," she said, speaking in a low voice and pointing out the horses after making sure Whitfield was not watching them. "A California mustang doesn't look like much, but they all have sure feet and endurance and can go a long way on a sip of water." She squinted up at him. "I'm making some assumptions here."

"You sure as hell are."

"I'm assuming we only need horses for me and Peaches. I'm assuming you'll ride the big bay you rode up to my place. Correct?"

"You're assuming I'm going to hire you."

"Of course you are. By now you know I'm the only credible choice you have. The real question is, Do I want to spend three months with you? We need to get that settled." Tilting her head back, she measured the sun's progress. "I'm meeting Peaches at Jack's Bar in a few minutes. You should come, too. We got things to discuss before this is a deal." Drawing back, she looked him up and down before she took off down the street. "My, my, look at you. Aren't we fancy."

Tanner crossed his arms on the top rail of the corral and studied the horses she'd pointed out. Then he considered the mules. At once he saw that she'd chosen the best animals in the lot. He hoped she was as competent in all other areas because it appeared that he'd hired her. With luck, he wouldn't regret it.

She was the only woman in Jack's Bar who wasn't wearing a skimpy costume and carrying a serving tray. Nobody paid her and Peaches a lick of attention so Tanner figured they came here often.

"Whiskey," he said to the bartender who was chipping at a block of ice that still had bits of straw frozen on the surface.

"He's paying for us, too," Fox said, pointing her thumb at Tanner before she turned to face him. "I dropped a list of provisions at the General Store so McGurty knows what we need. But I can't figure quantities until I know how many are in our party."

"You, Mr. Hernandez, me, and two other men."

"Fine. I'll firm up the order. When do you want to leave?"

"As soon as possible. Will the day after tomorrow give you enough time to put things together?"

"I told you it would," she said, frowning. "Do the two other men have their own horses?"

"They have horses and gear. So do I." He could almost see her ticking items off a mental list. "I'm not going to buy your ice."

"Buying our ice was part of the deal." Stiffening, she narrowed her eyes.

Tanner called her attention to the bartender who had returned to his ice pick and the block of ice, then he pointed to the frozen chunks in his whiskey glass, which he'd gotten without asking. He didn't like ice in his whiskey. "You don't get to sell the same ice twice, not if I'm one of the buyers." Over her shoulder, he watched Peaches suck in a smile and look at the ceiling.

"We only sold a small part! I'll be busy tomorrow working on your requirements, and I won't have time to sell the rest. The remaining ice is going to melt if I go off with you. That's a lot of money turning into water. I figure you owe us!"

"Maybe so, maybe not. Regardless, I'm not going to pay you for the ice."

"Well, what about that horse out there hitched to the wagon? I'm trading it to Whitfield for a credit on your animals."

"You keep the horse you trade for," he said with a shrug. "Aside from the ice, the deal you offered is acceptable."

Stretching his imagination, he tried to visualize what she'd look like if she were a traditional woman. But he couldn't do it. First, her clothing was loose enough that it was impossible to guess what kind of body she had under an oversized rough shirt and a vest that would have been too large for him. Then her face was tanned and her cheeks and lips chapped by cold winds. Finally, she had that mass of wild red hair and not enough hairpins to hold it in place. He doubted that she'd had a ladylike coiffure in years.

On the positive side of the scale, she had well-shaped eyebrows that were a shade darker than her hair. Her eyes were frosty but of an intriguing color that would appear blue in some lights, gray in others. Lips were something Tanner usually noticed, so he noted that Fox had a well-defined upper lip and a lower lip full enough to form a perfect pout. The thought made him smile. This wasn't a woman who did much pouting.

"Who are the men coming with us?" She tossed back her whiskey and motioned to the bartender to bring another.

"Does it matter?"

"I suppose not," she said after a minute. "As long as they keep up and understand who's in charge."

Her nose was neither too large nor too small. The same could be said of her forehead. When she turned to say something to Peaches, Tanner admired a clean sharp profile. If he'd been pressed to describe her, he would have said she was a handsome woman, but few would notice since she was so unconventional in all other ways. A casual observer would see only the odd clothing, the unkempt hair, and the ready-to-fight challenge in her eyes.

"Did you say something?" he asked when he realized she was staring back at him with an expectant expression.

"Tell me about you. I need to decide if I can stand you."

A humorless smile twitched his lips. "You have to like your clients to take their money?"

"I have to not detest them. I have to be able to stand their company for a long period of time." She was serious.

"I'm a mining engineer," he said, suddenly irritated.

"What exactly is a mining engineer?"

"I design mines, and inspect existing operations. I look for ways to improve safety, check the equipment, suggest methods to make the mine more efficient and profitable."

One eyebrow lifted and she nodded slowly. "And you like doing that?"

Did he? Spending most of his life in an office or underground was not what he'd planned. Frowning, he studied her face. "For the moment."

"Where's home? Here in Carson, or at the other end, in Denver? Or someplace else entirely?"

"I have a house in Denver. The company I work for is headquartered there, although the company owns mines in the Sierras, the Rockies, and in Utah. I go where the company sends me."

She sat up straight and stared. "You wouldn't happen to work for Jennings Mining and Mercantile, do you?"

"Yes." He hadn't realized that JM&M wielded enough presence in the area that someone like Fox would recognize the company.

She met Peaches's gaze in the back-bar mirror, then dragged a hand down her face. "Damn all," she murmured before she pulled back her shoulders and released a breath. "We're almost finished. Do you read books? Play chess or checkers?"

"What in the world does that have to do with going to Denver?"

"Would you say you're a patient man? Willing to carry your share of the load?"

He'd had enough nonsense. "I'm willing to pay you to lead my party to Denver," he said in a terse voice. "Do you want the job or not?"

"All right," she said after a minute. "We've got a deal. Me and Peaches will meet you tomorrow to buy the horses and provisions. We'll leave at dawn the following day."

Peaches put down his glass and wiped his mouth. "We got to be going. Thank you for the whiskey, Mr. Tanner."

"You don't have to thank him," Fox snapped, "he's not doing us any favor. Part of the deal is that he pays our expenses."

"I done taught you better than that, Missy. If you want to have style, you got to have manners. Can't have the one without the other."

"Who said I wanted style? Damn all, Peaches."

"I know what you're thinking before you even think it."

Tanner didn't hear her response because the door swung shut behind them, cutting off whatever she might have replied. After checking the time, he ordered another whiskey.

"Do Miss Fox and Mr. Hernandez come in here often?"

"Miss Fox?" The bartender smiled. "Never heard her called that before."

The bartender moved to the far end of the bar, signaling he wouldn't be drawn into a conversation. Tanner stretched his neck against his hand and flexed his shoulders. All in all, a frustrating start to the day had ended better than expected.

Throughout the evening with John Manning and his wife, Tanner's thoughts continually strayed toward Fox. If he'd had more time, perhaps he could have located a more conventional guide. He suspected there would be occasions when Hanratty and Brown would object to taking orders from a woman.

And he recalled his surprise and then irritation when he discovered Fox negotiating with Harry Whitfield. His first thought had been if he was going to pay for those horses and own them, then he'd damned well do his own bargaining.

Yes, there were going to be moments when taking orders from a woman wasn't going to sit well at all. He'd have to remind himself, and Hanratty and Brown, that Fox was the expert, she had the experience and the knowledge and following her lead was part of the bargain.

The next day he met with Hanratty and Brown, told them when and where to meet the following morning. Afterward he had a shave and a haircut, then shipped his belongings to Denver except for the items he'd need on the journey. He ran into Fox and Peaches outside the St. Charles, looking pleased with themselves.

"It's been a good morning so far," Peaches said by way of a greeting. He smiled broadly, displaying perfect white teeth.

"That's a fact," Fox said, swinging down off the wagon. "We sold another load of ice, and Whitfield has agreed to meet our terms." A satisfied smile lightened her expression. "Peaches is taking the horse and wagon to Whitfield right now. We had to throw in the wagon, but that's all right."

"The cabin's closed up," Peaches added. "I reckon we're ready to go."

Tanner nodded. "You've got everything in hand. It doesn't sound like you need me, so I'll—"

"We need your money," Fox said, pulling a list from beneath her poncho. "You should stop by the General Store and pay McGurty for the provisions, then pay Whitfield for the animals. Then go to the bathhouse and pay them. And me and Peaches want our up-front money anytime today that you want to pay it." She gave him a long measuring stare as if challenging him to prove he could produce the funds.

He planted his feet in the dusty road and looked down at her. "What's this about paying the bathhouse. What for?"

"Well, for me and Peaches to have a bath, what do you think? I figure we should start out clean. We aren't going to have another decent hot-water bath for a long time." Her gaze skimmed his close shave and shorter hair. "Looks like you had the same idea yourself. Now, when are you planning to pay us?"

"Right now," he said after a minute, reaching for the pouch inside his jacket.

"Not here," Fox said between her teeth. Grabbing his arm, she gave him a tug toward the lobby of the St. Charles. Inside, she looked around then led him behind a tall leafy plant growing out of a massive urn. "It's not smart to go flashing money around," she said, rolling her eyes like she couldn't believe what a rube he was.

"And you don't think two people hiding behind a plant will occasion any comment?" She was the strangest woman he'd ever met. Acutely aware that everyone in the lobby had watched her drag him behind the urn, he quickly counted eleven twenty-dollar gold pieces into her palm and one ten-dollar piece. "That's yours, half of three months' pay up front, and here's—"

"I'm not taking Peaches's money." The glare deepened. "You can pay Peaches when you catch up with him at Harry Whitfield's." She closed her fist around the coins then opened her palm again. "You gave me five dollars too much."

"That's for the bathhouse."

"It won't cost anywhere near five dollars."

Tanner swore under his breath. She could find an argument in the simplest statement. "Keep the change. I'll see you at daybreak tomorrow."

She followed him around the urn and back to the street. "You'll see me before that, at the General Store. It's going to take time to check all the provisions against my list, and I want to persuade McGurty to let us use his back lot as a staging area."

"I have some things to take care of. I'm sure you'll be finished before I get to the General Store." He wasn't going near the store until he was certain she was gone. He'd had enough aggravation for one day. "If you'll excuse me, I'm going to Whitfield's to pay for the animals."

Fox stood on the boardwalk and watched him stride down the street. He had good manners, she'd give him that, but it was beginning to look as if he was moody and possibly ill-humored. There was nothing worse on a long trek than temperamental companions. And she hadn't met the other two yet, whoever they were. Well, if the worst happened, she didn't have to spend time with them. She had Peaches, and Peaches was always good company.

Checking the provisions went more smoothly than she'd anticipated, and the new gear was in order. As she ticked the items off her list, she silently calculated how she would pack everything and how best to distribute the load among the mules. She had everything figured out before she met Peaches at the bathhouse.

"We want the works," she told the attendant. "Shave, haircut, and bath for him; shampoo and bath for me—and we want all the extras, the good-smelling stuff. We want private rooms and sandwiches and whiskey." With a flourish she counted out four dollars then headed toward the women's side of the building.

It felt good to walk past the communal bathing pool, which had a light scum floating on the surface, and enter one of the private rooms. Fox had only enjoyed a private bathing room one other time in her whole life.

An attendant had gone ahead and laid out towels that didn't look as if they'd already been used, had lit the lamps and set out fancy scented soap, a pot of face cream, and tooth powder.

"Food, drinks, and hot water are on the way," the attendant announced cheerfully. "There's a dish where you can put your hairpins. Clothes go on those hooks over there. I'll be back before you've finished creaming your face."

Fox had never in her life creamed her face. She opened the pot and sniffed the contents. The scent made her think of mountain junipers. Well, why not? Maybe her face was starving for cream. She didn't know about that kind of thing.

After undressing, she wrapped herself in one of the wonderful towels, then covered her hair before she slathered the cream on her face. A light tingling rose in the chapped areas.

When she was finally settled in steaming scented water, sandwiches on the small table beside her, a whiskey in one hand and a cigar in the other, she closed her eyes, sighed, and gave herself up to true luxury.

And she wondered where Matthew Tanner was right now. What were the "other things" he had to do today? Was there someone to whom he needed to bid farewell? Did he have some work to finish before he left?

A frown wrinkled her brow. She'd nearly choked on her whiskey when Tanner mentioned that he worked for Hobbs Jennings. For a moment she'd heard a roaring in her ears, fate shouting to make sure she was paying attention. After that it didn't matter how Tanner answered her questions. Any niggling doubt had fled her mind.

Relaxing, she blew a smoke ring through the rising steam then swallowed a sip of whiskey. Matthew Tanner. If Fox had lived the life she was supposed to have lived, if she'd been the woman she was supposed to have been, Matthew Tanner was a man she might have set her cap for.

She thought about that, letting herself daydream fairy-tale fantasies until her bathwater cooled. Then she sighed. She hated it when she let herself dream of might-have-beens. That kind of dream left her feeling inadequate and depressed.

After she wiped the cream off her face, she looked into a mirror. Maybe her cheeks appeared less red and raw. Maybe. She couldn't really tell.

What the hell difference did it make, anyway? Matthew Tanner was never going to pay her any attention. And she didn't want him to. Business and pleasure didn't mix.

By the time Tanner arrived at the staging area, minutes before dawn, Fox and Peaches had loaded the panniers and strapped them on the mules. The mustangs that Tanner had bought yesterday were saddled and waiting. Holding a tin cup of coffee, Fox stood to one side, sizing up Cutter Hanratty and Jubal Brown and running her eyes over the mules.

"I guess you met the boys," Tanner said, leading a mule up to the trains. Fox had put three mules in one train, two in the other.

"What's this?" she asked, incredulous. Angry and disbe-

lieving, she strode forward to stare at his mule. "We have all
the mules we need. Besides, we agreed that *I* would select the
animals!"

"We needed one more," Tanner said, moving his mule up
behind the short train. As the sky brightened, he studied the
method she'd used to tether the mules. Excellent. If one balked,
the twine lead would break and the other mules wouldn't be
pulled over.

"The hell we do," she snapped, following him. Without a
by-your-leave, she untied one side of the tarp, raised it, and
stared at the load underneath. For a long minute she frowned,
not recognizing what she was looking at. Then she said, "Oh
my Lord. You're packing bags of money! Good God."

Hanratty stepped forward, but Tanner waved him back.
There had never been any realistic hope that Fox wouldn't learn
what he was carrying. "It's gold coins," Tanner said in a low
voice, tying the mule into the short train.

Fox looked around as the sun popped over the horizon.
"Did you steal this money?" she demanded, stepping close so
no one could hear her furious whisper.

The question offended him. "It's my money."

"All right, let's suppose I believe that. But actually, it doesn't
matter, because you aren't taking bags of money on this trip!"
Spinning, she opened the tarp on the far side. "Four bags total.
Damn it. What were you thinking? This is flat unacceptable."

"The money is the whole purpose of this trip."

She looked around again, glared at Hanratty, Brown, and
Peaches, then leaned in close. "This money is going to paint big
targets on our backs. Don't you understand that? Every outlaw
in the territory will be looking for us. It's too dangerous."

"Nobody knows about the money except the people standing right here. And I've taken precautions. Hanratty and Brown
are here for the sole purpose of guarding the money."

"Don't tell me that no one knows about this." Now she had
her fists on her hips and was leaning up on her tiptoes to look
him in the eye. "A bank teller knows. Probably others in the
bank. The Carson bank is too small to keep this many coins on
hand, so a telegraph operator knows. Whoever guarded the
money until the bank picked it up knows this money went to
Carson. It's too early for the bank to be open, so you probably
kept the coins in the hotel vault. Whoever opened the vault for
you knows. If each of those people tells one other person . . . a

whole lot of people know you are moving a whole lot of money. Exactly how much money did you think you were going to take through the wilderness?"

"Fifty thousand dollars." Opening his jacket, he reached for the telegram.

"Oh Christ." She turned in a full circle, then looked up at him, shaking her head. "I won't do it, Tanner. Either you take that mule back to the bank, or you find yourself a new scout. I'm not crazy enough to beg outlaws to come get us."

"The money goes with us."

"Then I quit."

"Read this first," he said, putting the telegram in her hand. Turning, he faced east, not knowing how she would respond.

She read aloud, anger clipping her tone. "If you want to see your father again bring fifty thousand in coin to Denver stop. Arrive by May first or your old man dies stop."

Tanner heard her draw a long breath before she swore and then read the telegram again, the anger draining out of her voice.

"Somebody's kidnapped your father," she said, frowning at the money mule. "Have you checked to make sure this isn't a hoax?"

"It's not a hoax." He turned and studied her face. She was no longer spitting mad, but she wasn't happy. He couldn't tell what she was thinking. "You read the telegram. If I don't get this money to Denver, my father dies."

Without saying anything more, she walked to the edge of the staging area, folded her arms across her chest and turned her face in the direction of the rising sun. When she took her hat off and slapped it against her thigh, the sun lit her long braid like a column of flame.

"Peaches?"

When Peaches joined her, they both stood with arms across their chests, staring at the sky. Tanner smoked and waited, watching them, wondering if he could find Denver on his own.

Finally he heard her say, "It's his daddy. I'd do the same thing." Watched Peaches nod then murmur, "We got to go."

"All right," she said, walking back to the horses and mules. "Move the money mule to the middle of the train." Her gaze swept Tanner and his guards. "That money is your responsibility, not mine. You hear me, boys? If there's trouble because of this, that's your problem, not mine and not Mr. Hernandez's."

"Thank you," Tanner said quietly. He folded the telegram back into his inside pocket. There was no reason to keep it, but he did and he read it over and over.

"We've got seventy-one days," Fox said, squinting into the sun. "With luck, we can make Denver with a little time to spare. Depends on how things go."

"Are your parents alive?" Tanner asked, curious as to why she had capitulated so easily.

"Both dead. A long time ago." She glanced toward Peaches who was mounted and waiting. "Me and Peaches will lead the trains for the first few days while you boys get used to the saddle, then we'll trade off. We'll make it a short day today, only go as far as Gold Canyon. It'll take a while to establish a routine for setting up camp."

After Hanratty and Brown finished moving the money mule to the middle of the train, Fox stood beside it, eyeing the tarp.

"You really believe outlaws will follow us?" Tanner asked, swinging up on the big bay. He made sure his bedroll was tied down, checked his canteen and rifle scabbard.

"Oh yeah." Shifting, she narrowed her gaze on Hanratty and Brown, watching them step into their saddles. "That gold is going to be trouble. How well do you know your guards?"

"I trust them," he said coolly.

"Well, then." Fox gave him a nod before she swung up on her mustang. After adjusting the rope trailing back to the three mules she would lead, she touched her heels to the mustang's flanks. "Let's go."

It didn't surprise Tanner that she sat a horse like she'd been born in a saddle or that she made leading a mule train look easy. It did surprise him though to admit how much he trusted this small angry woman. He glanced ahead at the red and gold braid dropping down the back of her shapeless poncho. He'd be following that flaming braid for over a thousand miles.

He just hoped to God that she was right when she said she could get him to Denver before May first.

CHAPTER 3

*F*OX set a moderate but steady pace. She'd promised Tanner short days until he and his guards grew accustomed to all day in the saddle, but in truth it had also been a while since Fox or Peaches had spent eight or ten hours on a horse. She suspected she'd feel the effects before they stopped for the night, but right now she experienced the exhilaration of getting under way.

Starting out was the best part of any journey. At this point the company was pleasant and cordial, men and animals were whole and healthy, anticipation and optimism wafted on the breeze. Anything could happen in the weeks ahead, good or bad.

But packing gold fell on the bad side, Fox thought, frowning. Every few minutes she battled an urge to look over her shoulder and make sure the money mule hadn't bolted or been stolen.

"Could be that nothing bad will happen," Peaches suggested when they stopped beside the river for a late lunch. Cupping his hands around a coffee mug, he glanced toward a clump of bare cottonwoods where Tanner and his men were eating bread and cheese and talking. "You're thinking everyone out there knows about the gold and is busy figuring out how to steal it." When Fox nodded glumly, he smiled. "Now me, I share Mr. Tanner's opinion. I'm thinking that bank teller, and the hotel manager, and whoever else, is honest and upright and has already forgotten about the gold."

"Right. Just what we need, more fricking optimism." Fox rolled her eyes like she did when he started seeing roses among the weeds. "How are you doing?" she asked after a minute, pulling her gaze away from Matthew Tanner. Tanner's tall figure and commanding stance drew her attention like a magnet. Which irritated the hell out of her. "Holding up all right? I can tell one of the guards to lead the second train if your shoulder is bothering you. And it seems to me you're coughing a lot."

"Now, Missy, are you going to be fussing over me during this whole trip?" His eyes narrowed. "Why aren't you wearing the sun protection I mixed up for you?"

"I forgot. I'll wear it tomorrow."

Now that she wasn't worrying about growing ice, she could enjoy the sun on her face and the warm breeze blowing down the valley. It was nice to reacquaint herself with the music of a river. Nice to watch the animals grazing next to the trail and hear the murmur of men's voices. At this moment, it was hard to believe that revenge was her motive for being here.

Once they remounted, Tanner rode up beside her. "I figure we're about a mile off the stage road, starting to climb toward the cut up to the Comstock. So far, I could have led this expedition."

"You're right." She slid him a sidelong look from beneath the brim of her old hat. He looked good on the big bay horse, riding easy and loose. But he looked good whatever he was doing—sitting, standing, walking. "But you don't know where we should cut south, or where the best campsites are or how to find the water holes."

His smile relaxed, almost a tease. "That's when I start getting my money's worth." They rode a mile in silence before he said, "I'm obliged that you changed your mind about traveling with the gold."

"I get pissy every time I think about it, but there isn't a real choice. If I had a father, I'd do the same thing."

Fox didn't remember her father, and over time the memories of her mother had faded. Only vague impressions remained, mostly of a sick room and the terrible grief closing her throat. But she remembered her stepfather. Him, she would never forget.

"I guess your mother is gone, or the kidnappers would have approached her."

"My mother died shortly after I was born," Tanner said. "I have no memory of her."

"And your father never remarried?" These questions pushed the limits of what was acceptable, but she couldn't stop herself.

"My father married again years later, but his second wife died less than a year after the wedding. I never met the woman."

"How old were you then?" Fox's face flamed. Silently she commanded herself to stop asking personal questions before he got the idea that she was interested in him.

"I was about ten or eleven. In school back east."

At least he had a father. Fox thought it must be good to have someone who cared no matter what a person did. She had Peaches, but she would have given anything to have a real mother and father, too.

When she turned her head, Tanner had dropped back behind the mules. Seems he didn't welcome personal questions. That's what going to school in the east did for a person, installed a reserve. In the west, folks didn't stand on formality, they wanted to know who was talking to them and that required questions. But once the basics were known, it was live and let live. Or maybe she was looking for an excuse to justify her curiosity.

They rode into Gold Canyon about three in the afternoon. The town was one of the oldest in the territory, strung out along a tight valley near the river. The racket from the mills servicing the Comstock would have driven Fox mad if she'd had to live here—the noise and the lack of sunlight. The dreary town was already in shadow.

As the town pump was the primary source of rumor and gossip, they paused there to refill canteens and stretch their legs. Fox used the opportunity to ask questions. She didn't like the answers.

Thinking about the news, she led Tanner's party down the main street and continued out of town, past a few small farms and out to the edge of the desert. The campsite she wanted was still there, nestled beside the river in a copse of tall cottonwoods.

After she swung down off the mustang, Fox flexed her knees, feeling the pull along the insides of her thighs. She'd be stiff in the morning.

"All right, let's get organized." Peaches knew what to do, she didn't worry about him. "Lay out your bedrolls, then we need someone to fetch water, someone to get a fire started, and someone to cook supper. You gentlemen work it out among yourselves as to who does what. I'll help Mr. Hernandez unload the mules and I'll find our supper fixings."

She'd just tied her horse to one of the trees when she heard Cutter Hanratty snarl, "Touch that mule, mister, and you're a dead man."

Whirling, Fox grasped the situation in a flash. Peaches was on one side of the money mule and Hanratty stood on the other side, a gun pointing at Peaches's chest.

Moving fast she came up on Hanratty's side, then slipped between him and the mule. The bags of coins pushed at her back, she felt the barrel of Hanratty's gun drop to her stomach.

And she suspected Hanratty felt the tip of her knife pressed against his side, just above the waist of his trousers.

"Put the gun down, right now." Her voice shook with fury. "You don't pull a gun on anyone in this party, understand?" Leaning forward, she let the knife press hard enough that he glanced down and swore.

"Nobody touches the gold."

"It's Mr. Hernandez's job to care for the animals and pack and unpack them." The gun didn't waver and neither did her knife. They stood close enough that Fox smelled him, could see little bubbles of spit at the corners of his mouth.

He bared his teeth. "Tanner didn't say nobody except Mr. Hernandez touches the gold. He said nobody."

"It appears I was shortsighted," Tanner said. His hand came down on Hanratty's shoulder and he spun him around, shoving down the hand with the gun. "I trust Mr. Hernandez to unload the coins. And I trust anyone here who wants to help him." His gaze locked on Hanratty's. "Stow the weapon, Cutter. Right now."

Peaches released a long low breath then threw up the tarp and studied the lumpy bank bags as if nothing had happened. "Where you want me to put these?"

"Put them near my bedroll and cover them with my saddle."

"Don't you ever do something like that again," Fox said to Hanratty, speaking between her teeth.

Hanratty moved backward and made a show of shoving the gun into a hip holster. "I was just doing my job. No harm done."

Fox studied his small eyes and rough, stubbled face. "And I was just doing my job. No harm done." But she was mistaken. A small dot of blood appeared on Hanratty's shirt above his waist. She'd either scratched or jabbed him. "Sorry."

Hanratty pulled up his shirt and stared at a small puncture

in disbelief. "Well, goddamn," he said, turning to show Jubal Brown the drop of blood on his skin. "She knifed me!"

"You ain't never going to live that down," Brown said with a grin. They both stared at Fox like they were just seeing her. "Ma'am, that was the bravest, stupidest thing I ever saw anyone do. You know how many men this man has shot down?"

"I don't give a rat's ass," Fox said, returning their stares. "Just don't go shooting anyone in this party." They kept staring at her like she'd grown a foot taller. "Whichever one of you is going to cook tonight, get going."

"Looks like you're the cook," Hanratty said to Jubal Brown. "I can't do it, I'm wounded."

It took forty-five minutes longer than it should have to set up camp and get the coffee and some steaks on the fire. They would get quicker and more efficient in the next few days as the group established a routine.

Fox washed the supper plates in the river and stacked them near the fire for breakfast. As with any good campsite, the coffeepot stayed over the coals and everyone had retained his cup. It pleased her that none of the men brought out a whiskey bottle. If they had a bottle, they were saving it for a special occasion. That augured well for the trip.

They sat in a ring around the fire pit, drinking coffee, not talking much as the sun dropped below the horizon in a burst of deep blue and gold. Immediately Fox felt the temperature plummet. With the warm days they'd been having, it was easy to forget that February was usually a cold month.

Jubal Brown tossed back his coffee then lit a cigar. "Might as well get this over with. Find out where everyone stands. Union or Confederate."

Fox was astounded. "I didn't imagine anyone out here cared about that."

"Most don't, but I'm on my way home to Georgia where I plan to join up." Brown's chin jutted forward. "My family don't own any slaves, so that part of it ain't important to me. What's important is the states should have the right to secede. The South shouldn't have to be part of a Union if we don't want to be."

"It's hard to grasp that Nevada is lobbying to become a state and join the Union, while the South is fighting to withdraw." Fox shook her head and watched one of the coals flare into a puff of flame. "I guess I don't have an opinion on this except to say I don't believe people should own people."

Tanner looked straight at Jubal Brown. "I'm for the Union."

Brown nodded slowly, and his mouth pursed, but he didn't comment.

Next they turned toward Hanratty. "Hell, I don't care who wins." He shrugged. "That fight is thousands of miles from here. It don't touch me."

"What's your opinion?" Fox asked Peaches.

"Well now, I have to agree with Mr. Brown," Peaches said after a minute. Fox's eyebrows lifted in surprise. "Nobody should be forced to be where they don't want to be."

"How can you favor the Confederacy? They own slaves in the South!"

"Mr. Brown's family doesn't. Eventually slavery will collapse no matter who wins the war. How can the Confederates fight for free will and then deny it to their servants? You have to believe in the basic goodness and decency of all people."

"That's a noble sentiment, Mr. Hernandez, but I think you're wrong." Leaning forward, Tanner refilled his cup from the pot above the coals. "It's not that simple. The Southern economy is built around cheap labor. If slavery is abolished, the economy will likely collapse. I don't see the South willingly bringing themselves to that kind of disaster."

Jubal Brown covered a yawn. "Seems we got two Rebels, one Yankee, one undecided, and one don't-care." He thought a minute. "Doesn't look like much of an issue. You're taking the first watch, right?" he asked Hanratty. "Or is your wound troubling you too much to work? The wound you got when a woman knifed you."

Hanratty's smile didn't reach his eyes. "I think I can manage." Picking up his rifle, he stood and scanned the perimeter of the campsite. "Just for the sake of curiosity, ma'am, how many men have you knifed?"

"Not as many as I've shot. I've got a medical kit if you think your wound needs attention." If Hanratty wanted to pretend his small puncture was significant, she was willing to go along, but not without a broad hint of sarcasm.

Not bothering to reply, Hanratty moved beyond the fire's light and slipped among the trees.

"Reckon I'll be turning in right after I rub some of that horse liniment on my shoulder," Peaches said, rising.

"Do you want me to do it for you?"

"I'm telling you, stop fussing. It's just a touch of rhumitiz."

Muttering he headed into the darkness toward the tether line, leaving Fox and Tanner beside the fire.

"Well? What do you think?" Fox asked, putting some distance between them. They were almost shoulder to shoulder and she didn't like the odd way his proximity made her feel. Sort of like she'd eaten something that made her stomach churn. "About the trip so far."

"We've only gone twelve miles, and it took a couple of hours longer than it should have."

"You can't hurry mules. If you try, you're likely to have a train wreck. It's always going to feel as if we didn't cover as much ground as we should have."

"I'm not criticizing, just noticing." When he turned his head, the firelight painted his craggy face in gold and shadow. "All in all, I'd say the first day went well. My guard didn't kill my scout, and my scout didn't kill my guard. We had steak for supper." A shrug and a smile lifted his expression. "Brown was right, you know. What you did was brave and stupid."

"Maybe," she said, gazing at the dying fire. "But Peaches and me, we've been together off and on for twenty years. That old man is the closest thing I've got to family. He took care of me for a lot of years. Now it's my turn to look out for him." In this light Tanner's eyes looked almost amber. Not that she cared. She didn't know why she had even noticed.

When Tanner didn't say anything, Fox continued talking. "I figure Hanratty and Brown are just this side of the law. Very likely they cross back and forth over the line."

A flicker of amusement crossed Tanner's expression. "Why would you say that?"

She met his glance before she pushed to her feet. "A man doesn't hire a preacher to guard his gold. You hire somebody who's used to shooting first and asking questions later."

Tanner stood, too. "Tough as shoe leather, aren't you, Miss Fox?"

"Miss Fox?" She smiled. "And tough? Life could have worked out differently, but it didn't. So, yes. I'm plenty tough, Mr. Tanner. That's what's kept me alive. By the way, we're going to pick up the pace tomorrow. There's been some trouble with the Paiutes so I want to get to Fort Churchill. That's about a thirty mile ride."

"Thirty miles," Tanner repeated, staring down at her. "More than twice today's distance."

"I know. I said we'd take it slow for a few days. But it's smarter to spend tomorrow night under shelter rather than sleeping in the open." Annoyance thinned her voice. "Why do you keep looking at my hair? Is there something wrong with it?"

"Not at all. Your hair is a beautiful gold and red, particularly in the firelight. And a braid suits you."

Compliments cut the ground out from under her and left her with hot cheeks and speechless. Flustered, she walked away from him abruptly, calling good night over her shoulder.

For a time it appeared she was too rattlebrained to find her bedroll. When she did, she swore for a minute, then pulled off her boots and was folding back the blankets when she discovered the gloves.

"Peaches? Are you asleep? What's this?"

"It's gloves filled with bacon grease. You wear them while you're sleeping. Rub a little of that grease on your cheeks and lips, too. Just in case."

The dilemma she'd been discussing with Peaches was how to present herself when she shot Hobbs Jennings. If Fox killed Jennings looking like she did now, as herself, no one would care about her. The newspapers would dismiss her as an aberration, a wild woman, and they wouldn't wonder about her reason. But if she killed him looking like herself, Jennings would see how differently her life had unfolded from what it should have been. Jennings would see what he'd done to her and he'd be sorry.

On the other hand, if she transformed herself into a conventional young lady, even a young lady with rough edges, the newspapers wouldn't dismiss her as easily. They would clamor to know why a respectable young miss had killed a prosperous businessman, thereby giving her the opportunity to tell everyone what a thieving bastard Hobbs Jennings was. She wanted the truth about him in print. The difficulty with this option was that if she looked like a respectable young lady, it wouldn't appear that Jennings had injured her as much as he had. Maybe she wouldn't even be believed.

"I don't know," she said, holding the gloves to her nose and sniffing. Not too bad. The grease hadn't turned rancid.

"We have talked this subject into the ground, Missy." Fox heard a yawn. "You should give yourself a choice. Avoid the sun. Soften up your hands and face. I'm going to sleep now so don't go talking anymore."

"Avoid the sun," Fox muttered. Like that was possible.

"Wear the sun protection lotion I fixed up for you."

Peaches's advice about providing herself a genuine choice made sense. She thrust her hands into the gloves and made a face as grease oozed around her fingers and up under her fingernails. She suspected that trying to smooth her cheeks and hands would be about as effective as trying to pretty up a goat by trimming its hooves, but she guessed she'd give it a try.

Tossing her braid over her shoulder, she eased down into her bedroll and closed her eyes. Matthew Tanner sure did look good on a horse. He rode with his hat pulled down to shade his face, and one wrist resting lightly on the saddle horn. He looked like a man who had fifty thousand dollars to spare. Which was to say, he was as far out of reach to someone like Fox as the most distant star.

But he thought her hair was a beautiful color. If that didn't beat all. She never would have imagined that any part of her would look beautiful to a man like Matthew Tanner.

Tanner heated river water over the fire then shaved standing in front of a mirror he'd hung from a tree branch. Neither Hanratty nor Brown bothered with a razor. This was fine with Tanner. The rougher and more disreputable they looked, the less inclined anyone would be to challenge their party.

He'd wondered if Fox would seek privacy for her morning ablutions, but she didn't. She went about washing her face at the river and then brushing out her hair and replaiting it in a no-nonsense manner that suggested she wasn't aware or didn't care that all the men watched her with sidelong glances.

But of course she was aware. By now Tanner knew Fox was alert to everything happening around her. For that matter so was everyone else in the group. This created a sense of tension, but also enhanced security. It wasn't likely that anything would take them by surprise.

After breakfast, Fox announced they had a long hard day ahead and explained the reason. "Ordinarily the Paiutes don't attack without cause, but apparently they bushwhacked a rancher's cabin and killed the whole family. Rather than tempt fate, we'll ride past Miller's Station and go on to Fort Churchill."

"Who's to say the rancher didn't give them cause?" Hanratty asked, tossing out the remains of his coffee.

Jubal Brown frowned. "The soldiers at Fort Churchill, are they Union or Confederate?"

Fox gave him a long stare. "They're Indian fighters, Mr. Brown."

Tanner stepped up beside her. "Strictly speaking, the soldiers are Union since they're paid by the government. But they aren't fighting your war."

Brown's lips twisted and for an instant Tanner saw the killer beneath the good-old-boy facade. Cutter Hanratty looked like the gun-for-hire that he was. But in Tanner's opinion, Brown was equally dangerous, or more so, because his plain open face and apparent good humor lulled one into forgetting that his reputation was more ruthless than Hanratty's.

Peaches broke an uncomfortable silence. "With your permission, Mr. Tanner, I'd like to put a pannier on the money mule and stow the gold inside. I think it'll be more secure and less likely to shift and spook the mule."

"Less conspicuous, too," Fox offered.

They were correct, Tanner thought, irritated that he hadn't noticed himself. All the mules but his were piled high with supplies. The money mule had a thin lumpy cargo hidden beneath a tarp, and stuck out like the proverbial sore thumb.

Once the adjustments were made, they rode out onto land that became increasingly dry and barren as the day progressed. The river cut through endless expanses of winter brown sagebrush and grass, the riverbank shrubbery offering the only hint of green in a rolling landscape of beige and brown.

When the mules weren't kicking up clouds of chilly dust, Tanner could see Fox's braid swaying against the back of her poncho like an arrow pointing forward.

He'd heard of women like Fox, but he hadn't met such a person before. Undoubtedly that accounted for an interest bordering on fascination. She didn't behave like any woman he'd ever known, which made her appealing in a way that puzzled him.

It occurred to him that his father would be appalled if he knew that Tanner found himself drawn to a woman like Fox, which wasn't surprising as he'd never lived up to his father's expectations. Somehow he always fell short of the mark. He'd believed that he would stop caring about disappointing his father once he achieved adulthood, but it hadn't worked that way. His father still expected the impossible, and Tanner was still far from perfect.

His frown settled on the money mule. He hoped his father

knew he was coming with the gold. This time he wouldn't disappoint. But he'd believed that before.

He didn't realize that Fox had dropped back beside him until he felt the heat of the mustang and she shouted his name.

"Sorry," he said, imagining the scent of bacon.

"Do you think the kidnappers will mistreat your father?" she asked, squinting against a swirl of dust.

"I don't know if he's still alive." His hands tightened around the reins. If the bastards killed his father, he'd spend the rest of his life hunting them down. Whatever they'd done to his father, he would do the same to them and more.

"We'll get there in time. A few long days like this one will put us ahead of schedule." She slid him a look, a flash of blue then gone. "If you can see through the dust, that's Fort Churchill up ahead. They'll send someone out to check on who we are, and I'll request permission to camp within the fort tonight. My question is this: Is Jubal Brown going to be a problem?"

He'd been asking himself the same question. "I'll speak to him."

"Better you than me."

"Right after the noon break, I thought I saw movement on the hill to the north of us. Did you see anything?"

"Paiutes," she said before she urged the mustang into a trot and returned to the head of the line.

Tanner scanned the horizon looking for anything that moved and found nothing. Looking ahead he noticed that Hanratty was leading Fox's string of mules. She rode up beside him, said something, then shrugged and moved ahead, leaving Hanratty with the mules. Tanner almost laughed. He doubted many men, let alone women, had pulled a knife on Cutter Hanratty.

When Tanner spotted the rooftops and adobe walls of the fort, he urged the bay forward, trotting up beside Fox as he noticed a half dozen men riding toward them, kicking up a long coil of dust.

She looked surprised. "I can handle this. It's my job."

"It's my party," he said in a pleasant voice. There were some responsibilities he was not willing to abdicate. "Everyone here answers to me," he added, watching a frown clamp her mouth and forehead.

"All right," she said in a tight voice, her gaze on the uniformed men riding toward them. "Some things you might like to know. The fort occupies about a thousand acres spread out on both sides of the river. Usually there are between fifteen hundred and two thousand men garrisoned here. The camp is teetotalist and they don't allow cards or gambling."

When the soldiers were within hailing distance, Tanner rode forward, hearing Fox behind him. Two of the soldiers kept an eye on Hanratty, Brown, and Peaches while Tanner introduced himself and Fox.

"Haven't seen you in a while," Captain Brightman said to Fox, giving her a smile. "I heard you quit scouting."

"I'm back at it." She wiped dust from her forehead. "I've been seeing Paiutes off and on all day. They didn't come close, just showed themselves then vanished."

"You heard they killed the Watson family? Damned shame."

Tanner interrupted the chat. "We request permission to camp within the walls, Captain. We have our own provisions."

"Permission granted, Mr. Tanner. You can also graze your animals near the river." To Fox he added, "We don't expect more trouble with the Paiutes, but we didn't expect the Watson incident. It's a long ride but if you're continuing east, I'd suggest you head for the Carson Sink station tomorrow. Best not camp in the open right now."

Tanner rode toward the fort with the soldiers, irritated that Fox and Captain Brightman fell back, talking like old friends. Maybe they were for all he knew. Once he heard her laugh and he ground his teeth together, not certain why her laughter would annoy him, but it did.

Once through adobe walls, he could see the fort was a village unto itself, with several adobe buildings stacked on stone foundations. There were corrals, a smithy, a laundry, and general store, everything needed to be self-sufficient. Outside the walls, aspen and cottonwood grew near the riverbanks, but inside the fort the trees had been cut. The compound would be hot as hell in the summer, but there was nothing to impede the view.

Captain Brightman pointed, indicating a large haystack not far from a ditch that brought water from the river. "You can camp over there. I assume Fox informed you of the basic rules we expect visitors to abide by? Good." He turned to Fox. "My wife is visiting. You're welcome to join us for supper, I'm sure she would enjoy meeting you."

A half smile formed on Fox's lips and she turned aside. "Thank you, but I didn't bring any lady go-to-supper clothes." When Brightman assured her that she could come as she was, she shook her head. "We're still a new group," she said, scanning the mules moving past her toward the haystack. "I have my hands full here."

After Brightman and the soldier rode off, Tanner gave her a look of annoyance. "You can go to supper with your friend, for Christ's sake. I think we can muddle through one evening without you." It offended him that she had indicated otherwise.

"I don't want to go," she said, watching Brightman and his men skirt the parade grounds. Her eyes were an unreadable gray blue. "I don't get on well with regular ladies. The minute I left, Brightman's wife would laugh at me. She'd make jokes about how I held my fork, and how I sat, and me wearing trousers."

"You know her?"

Fox shook her head. "I don't have to know her. That's just how it is." She rode past him to help Peaches with the mules.

Tanner looked after her, the anger leaving him as swiftly as it had come. "I'll be damned," he murmured. She wasn't afraid to step in front of a gunslinger itching to squeeze a trigger, but she was afraid of an officer's wife who was probably small and delicate and about as threatening as a kitten, whose only weapon was ridicule.

CHAPTER 4

*F*OX woke with a start in the cold hour before dawn, blinking and straining to see through a moonless darkness. When she spotted a man-shaped shadow walking through the camp, pausing to peer at bedrolls, she jumped to her feet and leveled her rifle.

"You better be Hanratty or Brown, mister, or you're dead."

"Corporal Hansen here, ma'am. Captain Brightman sent me."

Hansen approached, easing past the snores rattling out of Peaches's bedroll. Before the soldier reached her, Matthew Tanner appeared beside Fox, holding a Colt in his right hand.

"Where's Hanratty and Brown? Why the hell didn't they hear this soldier before he was inside our camp?"

Fox was also interested in the answer to that question. "What do you want?" she snapped at Corporal Hansen.

"We've got two of your men in the garrison brig. Captain Brightman said you should fetch them and head out." Hansen spoke to the space between Fox and Tanner, not knowing who he should address. "I'll take you there."

Fox pulled on her boots then looked toward the other bedrolls. If Peaches woke and found no one in camp, he wouldn't know what to make of it. But she hated to wake him before time. Peaches was a man who needed his sleep. Hell, what was she thinking? Peaches would sleep through the final judgment, he wasn't going to wake before someone gave him a shake or the camp bugle sounded.

"Why are my men in the brig?" Tanner asked as they

neared the torches placed at the corners of the parade ground. His stride was long and angry.

"Captain Brightman is waiting, sir. He'll explain."

"I want to know now, Corporal."

"There was a fight, sir," Corporal Hansen explained reluctantly. "A dozen soldiers are injured or in jail." He opened the door of the only building fronting the dirt street that was blazing with light at this hour.

There was no friendliness in Brightman's eyes. He turned from speaking to a man with a ring of keys at his waist and scanned Fox and Tanner.

"I'll let you have them, but this is a favor, Fox." He stared at her. "I want you out of here by first light. If these two men are with you the next time you ride this way, keep on riding. Don't stop here."

"What happened?" Tanner demanded, glancing toward the sound of shouts and cursing coming from the corridor of cells behind Brightman.

"A member of the watch discovered your men involved in an illegal poker game with some idiot soldiers. Very likely the watch would have broken up the game and let it go at that, but one of your men demanded to know where my men's sympathies lie regarding the war back east and he didn't like the answers. All hell broke loose. The barracks nearby heard the fracas and joined in. I've got ten men back there," he jerked his thumb over his shoulder, "and three in the infirmary."

Tanner pressed his lips together and knots ran up his jaw.

"If everyone hadn't removed their weapons before the poker game, we'd have bodies to deal with." Brightman nodded at his jailer. "Bring out the civilians."

"Do we owe you for any damage?" Fox asked.

"Just get packed and get moving." Captain Brightman stepped past her and outside, letting the door slam behind him.

It was hard to say who looked worse when Hanratty and Brown came into the office, blinking at the light. They had black eyes, split lips, bloodied knuckles.

Jubal Brown gazed down at his shirt, now fit for a ragbag or a bonfire. "Nosebleed," he said by way of explanation.

"Damn," Hanratty muttered, gingerly touching his swollen eyes then skimming a finger over his lower lip and wincing.

Tanner accepted their gun belts from the jailer then walked

out the door, waiting for them in the street. When they emerged, he turned on them with a coldly furious expression.

"You not only abused the fort's hospitality, you left our camp unguarded. Give me one good reason why I shouldn't fire your butts right now."

"Where in hell would your"—Hanratty peered up and down the dark street—"cargo be safer than in the middle of an armed garrison? Didn't seem to us like there'd be any harm in taking the night off."

"You've only worked two days," Fox said in disgust. "But you need a night off?"

"We figured it would be a long time before we'd get another one," Brown said, rubbing a shoulder. "We didn't think we were doing anything wrong."

"You swore to Mr. Tanner that you could deal with sleeping among Union soldiers."

"Well, I was wrong, now wasn't I?" A glitter came into Brown's eyes, and Fox stepped backward, frowning. Jubal Brown had impressed her as the weaker of the two men, but she sensed she'd made a mistake. For a minute he looked dangerous and crazy.

"Go on back to the camp," Tanner said after Jubal averted his gaze. "Start packing up." He gave Fox a glance that told her to remain behind. "What do you think?" he asked when Hanratty and Brown moved away in the darkness. "My instinct is to leave them and go on alone, but that would create problems of a different kind."

Fox scuffed her boot in the dirt. "If we didn't have the cargo," she, too, looked uneasily up and down the deserted street, "I'd say leave them behind."

Tanner glared at a point somewhere above her head. "They disobeyed. They broke the fort's rules. They instigated a fight."

"If you fire their butts, then we've got two angry and resentful gunslingers who know about the cargo," Fox said slowly. "Who's to say they wouldn't come after us themselves?"

His glare lowered and settled on her face. "I'm thinking the same thing."

"It's your call." Whenever he looked at her, Fox felt her stomach roll over and her mouth go twitchy. She started thinking about how handsome he was, and how long it had been since she'd been with a man. Sighing, she tilted her head, checked the sky, and guessed they had less than an hour before first light.

Tanner fell into step beside her. "Much as I'd like to leave those two behind, we'll keep them a while longer. See if anything else happens. Are you comfortable with that?"

That Tanner involved her in the decision both surprised and pleased her. When Tanner had insisted on riding out to meet Captain Brightman she had wondered if they were going to bump heads over who was in charge of what.

"I'll decide the route," she said, feeling her way on this issue. "You decide personnel questions."

"Someone is cooking breakfast," Tanner commented as they walked into the chaos that accompanied breaking camp. "I smell bacon."

Fox was glad he couldn't see her face as she rubbed her hands on her trousers. He was smelling her. "Not in our camp. We'll skip breakfast and settle for an early lunch."

Peaches was awake and loading the mules; she passed him on her way to the ditch to wash the bacon grease off her hands and cheeks. He lifted an eyebrow and Fox murmured, "I'll tell you the story later."

Without the gold, they could have dispensed with Hanratty and Brown. But they had the gold. Fox suspected this wouldn't be the only time she would regret those gold coins.

Forty minutes later she led them out of the adobe walls surrounding the fort, ignoring the growl in her stomach.

At midday Fox signaled a brief stop, urging the party to grab something quick to eat and allowing the animals to graze although there wasn't much forage among the clumps of sagebrush.

When everyone had slaked their hunger on biscuits and ham and cheese, and had gulped down cups of scalding coffee, Fox addressed the company.

"I'm sure you've noticed that we're being followed." Peaches nodded, but the others hid expressions of surprise by squinting at the low hills rolling away from the river. "I don't know if it's the same group of Paiutes tracking us, or if it's different groups."

Tanner took a spyglass from his saddlebags and scanned the horizon. "I see them." He handed the glass to Cutter Hanratty. "Will they attack?"

Fox shrugged. "All I can say is they haven't yet. We're about four hours from the Carson Sink. It was a pony express station before they shut down the express. That's where I want to camp tonight. In the meantime, if the Paiutes decide to take us on, we'll spot them coming long before they reach us. The groups I'm seeing are no more than eight or ten strong, so I'd say we're about an even match." She tossed out the remainder of her coffee. "Let's go. And keep up the pace."

Swinging into the saddle, she suppressed a groan. Her fanny was saddle sore and her thigh muscles ached like blazes. Two long days were showing how soft she'd become during her time cutting ice. And if Fox was stiff and aching, she figured the others were, too. But the men would never complain as long as she didn't. Hanratty and Brown, maybe even Tanner, would rather step into quicksand than let a woman best them.

"The situation can't be too bad if you're smiling," Tanner said, trotting up beside her. The sun blazed high and hot, and he'd removed his jacket, riding in a vest and his shirtsleeves. From the look of it, he'd have a sunburn on his arms and face before they called it a day. When she said as much, he shrugged. "I spend most of my life inside or down in a mine shaft. The sun feels good. I doubt it's possible to ride out here for any length of time without getting a burn."

He was right about that. There wasn't a scrap of shade along this stretch, and nothing much grew near the river. White patches of desert alkali had begun to appear more frequently.

"How serious is the threat of an Indian attack?"

"Hard to say," Fox answered, trying to recall if she'd put on Peaches's sunburn protection. "Brightman's troops are looking for the warriors who slaughtered the Watson family. The investigation keeps the Indians resentful and angry. If they get themselves worked up enough . . . there could be more incidents."

"And we could be one of them," Tanner said, scanning the hilltops. Frowning, he slapped his reins against his thigh. "How in the hell do you see that far? You must have eyes like an eagle."

This was the second compliment he'd given her and Fox didn't know what to make of it. At least she thought it was a compliment. It seemed to her that eagle-eyed was a good thing to be. But she couldn't think of anything to say back to him.

"Have you been in an Indian fight before?"

Relief dropped her shoulders. Now she had something to

say. "A few times. All the tribes have horses and guns now, but ammunition is difficult to get so they don't do much practice shooting. Unless an Indian is almost on top of his target, he's likely to miss his shot. But if they use bow and arrows, well, that's a different story."

They had left the fort in a hurry and Tanner hadn't shaved this morning. Fox noticed the dark shadow of stubble and thought he might look good wearing a beard. On the other hand, she preferred clean-shaven men.

She wondered if Tanner realized that even with a hint of the east in his voice and even wearing quality boots and clothing, he was as formidable a figure as Hanratty and Brown. And no one looking at the three men together would mistake who was the boss. Hanratty and Brown both depended on weapons to establish authority, but Tanner managed the same thing in the way he carried himself and in the confidence and superiority he exuded.

Some might label him arrogant in the way he took charge of matters or even the cocky way he tilted his hat, but Fox liked arrogant men. She didn't like men who mumble-fumbled over making a decision, or who were content to follow rather than lead. Of course, arrogant men could be hard to get along with since they had an annoying propensity to believe they were always right.

"Do you think someone will try to steal your gold?"

He turned his head to meet her gaze. "No, I don't."

There was proof of what she'd been thinking. Reason and argument would not convince him that he was wrong. He was going to have to learn the hard way. She hoped she was wrong, but she didn't think so. Maybe that thinking made her a little arrogant, too.

"See those trees ahead? That would be the station. There'll be good forage for the animals since the station is between a lake and the river. The grass is more abundant there than out here." Slowly she scanned the hilltops. "Looks like the day is going to end well." In fact it was impossible to tell. But if Fox were a Paiute she'd attack out here instead of letting the targets get within thick adobe walls. She figured her Indian concerns were over for the day.

The station was small, large enough to house ten men maybe, but not comfortably. Adobe walls enclosed a frame house and a corral.

"There's something eerie about deserted places," Tanner remarked as they rode into the enclosure.

Fox glanced at him in surprise. She'd been thinking the same thing. Already the house appeared derelict. One corner of the roof sagged and bricks had fallen from the chimney.

"The pony express went out of business only four months ago," Fox said, eyeing the house. Nature was harsh out here. It didn't take long for heat and cold and blowing sand to leech the life out of creatures and structures.

A quick inspection showed the house had been stripped clean of furnishings and anything useful. An odor of grease and smoke lingered in the walls.

Fox stood on the stoop examining the enclosure and concluded they'd be more comfortable outside than inside the house. She turned her head toward the adobe corral where the men were unloading the mules, about to call to them when an arrow chunked into the wall of the house. That the shaft missed her by only a foot was a matter of luck. If the Indians could have seen her over the walls, they would have been more accurate.

Swearing, she jumped off the stoop and hit the ground running toward the corral where her rifle was still in the scabbard hanging from her saddle.

"Indians!"

The men looked up as an arrow sailed over the wall and pierced the pannier on the money mule.

Fox swore. "See those platforms with the ladders against them?" The ledges jutting from the adobe near the top of the walls provided a view and firing site. "Scatter. I want one of you on each side of the enclosure."

Before she'd finished speaking, she had her rifle and ammunition and was running toward the front of the enclosure. Tanner was on her heels as she scaled the ladder and kneeled next to the wall. The sun was sinking but the adobe was still warm to the touch.

Below them, Fox heard shouts and laughter and whoops and thudding hooves as the Indians charged the wooden gate and fired arrows into the rough-cut logs.

"You know what that sounds like?" She let her voice trail and listened. "Kids. Just fooling around." She flashed Tanner a glance of irritation. "Cover me, but don't shoot anyone unless you have to."

He was in midprotest when she stood and stared over the wall. Sure enough, six young Paiutes painted like warriors were having a grand time. The oldest couldn't have been more than maybe fifteen.

"Hey," she shouted, feeling the ever-present anger rise in her chest and tighten her throat.

Tanner rose alongside her, leveling his rifle. "What the hell are you doing?"

"You go on home before you get yourself killed," Fox shouted in Paiute. Smiles wiped clean, the boys looked up at her dumbstruck, as if a tree had spoken in their language. "Arrows don't stand a chance beside rifles. Watch this." Raising her rifle, she put a bullet into a post out on the desert about thirty yards from the gate. The next shot went into the ground twelve inches from the oldest boy's feet. They got the point of the demonstration. The oldest boy fired one last defiant arrow into the gate, then hopped on his pony and they all rode toward the hills.

"You could have gotten yourself killed, standing up like that." Tanner's craggy face pulled into an expression of anger and exasperation.

"They were kids."

"Kids with weapons. What did you say to them?"

Fox dropped down the ladder. "I told them they looked real cute in their paint."

"Well, hell. Looks like we missed all the excitement," Hanratty said, coming across the compound. "I wouldn't have minded taking me an Indian scalp."

Fox rounded on him and poked him hard in the chest with her finger. "Listen and hear me good, Hanratty. You, too, Brown. You don't fire at *anyone* until or unless I tell you to. That means Indians, whites, soldiers, or each other. It's clear that you don't know squat about the situation out here, so walk softly." Furious with the anger that seemed to erupt whenever an excuse arose, she glared up into Hanratty's tight expression. "White men don't take scalps, Hanratty."

"Some do."

"You're right," she said, curling her lip in disgust. "Let me rephrase this. Decent white men don't take scalps. Now let's set up camp."

After supper, no one went immediately to his bedroll. It had been a long tedious day, but the incident with the Indians left everyone too charged up and restless to sleep.

For a time Peaches played soft plaintive songs on his harmonica, then Jubal Brown told a tall tale about camping in the
Georgia woods with an uncle when it started to rain frogs.

"Little pale frogs about this long," he finished, holding his
fingers apart about two inches.

"I'll bet you believe in fairies, too," Hanratty said, hunching closer to the fire pit. "Cold tonight."

For several minutes Fox had been aware of Tanner regarding her across the fire with an intent expression. When he
turned his full attention on something or someone, it was like
nothing else existed. A tiny shiver ran up Fox's spine and she
wet her lips.

"Where did you learn to speak Paiute?" he asked softly.

The question caused her gaze to sharpen. More often than
not, she was asked where she had learned to speak Indian. But
Tanner either knew or guessed that while the Indian nations
shared some words in common, they each had their own language.

"The first time I crossed country to Denver, it took me a
year. I spent some time with the Paiutes, the Shoshone, and the
Utes, and learned to speak to them." Modesty wasn't one of her
virtues so she didn't shrug off her accomplishment. "I'm good
with languages."

"You speak Indian?" Brown asked, sounding impressed.

Fox looked pained. "I can speak to Paiutes, Shoshones, and
Utes. If an Apache shows up, we're in trouble."

"Say something in Indian," Hanratty said.

The firelight made both men look worse than they had in
daylight. Deep shadow darkened black swollen eyes, while a
burst of flame made cuts and scrapes appear livid.

"If you had an Indian name, it would be Mean and Ugly,"
Fox said, speaking Shoshone. From the corner of her eye, she
saw Peaches smile. He knew just enough to catch the drift of
what she'd said. She winked at him.

"What did you say?" Hanratty demanded, looking from
Fox to Peaches.

She stood and stretched. "I said it's been a long day and tomorrow will be, too. We'll go as far as the Sand Springs station."

In the morning they all inspected the arrows driven into the
gate as they rode out of the adobe enclosure. Fox was glad that
Hanratty hadn't been on the platform overlooking the front or

there would have been some dead Paiute kids. Hanratty and Brown were hard men to like.

"We were lucky yesterday," Tanner said, riding up beside her leading Peaches's string of mules. When Fox lifted an eyebrow, he shrugged. "Mr. Hernandez didn't complain, but I could see his shoulder is troubling him."

Just when Fox thought she had Tanner figured, he did something or said something that showed her how wrong she was. She had decided he preferred to remain aloof, wanted to draw a line between himself and his employees. Now here he was doing Peaches's work, leading a string of mules.

"If Hanratty or Brown had been on the platform we were on . . ."

Fox's eyes widened. This wasn't the first time he'd said the same thing she was thinking. What did that mean? Anything? When she slid him a glance, his expression was tight.

"You're carrying a lot of money," she said in case he was having second thoughts about hiring guards. Defending Hanratty and Brown wasn't a comfortable position, but Fox suspected the time would come when she'd be glad to have two extra guns present. "They're keeping up, doing their share of the work."

Tanner gave her an unreadable look then squinted against the grains of sand blowing on a sharp breeze. "How long will we be camping in abandoned pony express stations?"

"Until we reach Utah territory. Then the pony express stations turn north and we continue east."

"It's a smart choice." He spoke slowly as if he'd given the matter some thought. "If we'd been in the open last night, things might have gone differently."

"You aren't complaining that you're not getting your money's worth? That you could have found the stations on your own?" She wasn't sure if she was teasing or not.

"I'm getting my money's worth," he said firmly. A smile curved his lips. "Left to my own devices, I could wander around out here for days looking for the next station."

Fox laughed. "I doubt that, but it's nice of you to say so."

Tanner had weighty matters on his mind and it didn't surprise her that he seldom smiled. When he did, his face softened and his mouth relaxed. Those occasional smiles made Fox's scalp tingle and her mouth go dry, which annoyed her no end.

During the next two days, whenever the hours in the saddle turned dull and tedious, she tried to pin down what it was about Matthew Tanner that caused her body to respond in rebellious ways that she didn't welcome.

He was a different sort of man than she usually encountered. Better educated, better dressed, more mannerly. Confident enough that he could ask questions if he didn't know something. And he was willing to stand back and recognize Fox's expertise without appearing that it cost him anything to do so.

Moreover, Tanner seemed wealthy and his father even more so. Whenever Fox tried to grasp how much money fifty thousand dollars actually was, her brain froze. Last night she'd given Peaches a hand moving the coins, slinging a bag over her shoulder and wincing at the weight. The bags weighed almost twenty-five pounds apiece. Never in her life had Fox expected to handle that much money or know a man worth that much.

But the strange breathlessness that came over her when Tanner stood too near had nothing to do with money or education or manners. She suspected the reason was more about wide shoulders and sunburned hands and a lean muscled body and an intensity that sent shivers up her spine.

Which meant that she was as shallow as a pot lid, she thought with a sigh.

CHAPTER 5

*I*N the morning Tanner could see his breath hanging in the chill air in front of his shaving mirror. Here at this altitude the nights were frigid and dawn sparkled across ground and boulders rimed with frost. Sound and scent sharpened in the cold air, and grits, fried ham, and strong coffee had never smelled as good.

After toweling his face, Tanner adjusted his collar and buttoned his shirt, pulled up his braces—or suspenders, as they called them out here—and donned his jacket. The heat of the campfire on his face and hands was welcome as he ate, the food as hot and delicious as he'd anticipated.

"Whoever made the coffee this morning—it's especially good."

Peaches flashed a white-toothed smile. "Coffee's my specialty."

"It was cold last night," he said to Fox who sat staring into the fire with a surly expression. "Did you sleep well?"

"I hate people who are cheerful in the morning," she muttered, flicking him a glance and then glaring at Peaches.

"This is the best time of the day," Peaches said with a laugh.

"The hell it is," Jubal Brown snapped. "You can say that only because you weren't up and down all night trading off the watch." Smothering a yawn, he reached for more coffee.

Morning might not be Fox's favorite time, but Tanner noticed that she had washed her face, braided her hair for the day, and she had already helped Peaches load the mules.

"I'm getting the idea that Nevada is a succession of mountain ranges separated by long bowl-shaped valleys. Is that correct?"

"You have to have conversation in the morning." For a minute he didn't think she would say any more, then she sighed. "If you crumpled a piece of paper that's what Nevada looks like. A succession of north/south ranges and valleys." Tilting her head, she squinted at the sky. "It's time to get moving. We'll lose a couple of hours when we reach the valley."

There wasn't much forage in the mountains, merely a few dry tufts between rock outcroppings. To satisfy the horses and mules, they would have to let them graze in the broad valley below. At this time of year the grass wasn't abundant even on the valley floors.

Today the descent was gradual and relatively noneventful, with only one narrow cut through substantial rock walls that looked difficult for Fox and Peaches to negotiate since they were leading the mules. Their expertise was a pleasure to watch.

And then a cool enjoyable morning erupted into chaos quicker than Tanner would have believed possible. One moment he was gazing out at the wide bowl-shaped valley below, thinking it would be an easy crossing, the next minute he heard Fox and Peaches shouting and swearing.

Tanner watched it happen. The second mule in Fox's string balked at the incline. In rapid succession the twine broke between the mules as it was supposed to in a dangerous situation. Then the lead mule jerked the rope out of Fox's hand and her string was free and running toward the valley. In an eyeblink the string Peaches led also broke free and also trotted toward the valley floor. The mules reached the valley in time to scatter in all directions before Tanner and the others came off the mountainside and reined up hard.

Fox swore for a full minute then shook her head at Peaches. "Damn it! Any idea what spooked them?"

"Not a notion. Oh Lordy, look at that."

Tanner followed Peaches's frown and watched the money mule lie down and roll in the distant valley grass, then do it again.

Fox pulled her fingers down her throat. "She's trying to scrape off her load."

The mule succeeded. The top pack busted loose and dropped, but that wasn't the worst of it. When the mule pushed to her feet and trotted farther down the valley, gold coins bounced out of the pannier.

Not trusting his eyes, Tanner grabbed the spyglass from his saddlebags. Son of a bitch. The pannier and one of the bank bags had been pierced by the Indian boy's arrow. He knew about that. The hole had seemed harmless enough for the last couple of days, but it hadn't withstood the mule's rolling. The spyglass revealed that the hole was now a tear and leaking gold coins with every step the mule took.

"All right," Fox said after a minute. By now Tanner knew that she slapped her thigh with her hat when she was angry and frustrated. Sun blazed on her hair. "You and your men go after the money mule," she said to Tanner. "Me and Peaches will chase down the other five. If you finish first, come and give us a hand. Are you happy with that plan?"

At the moment he wasn't happy about anything. The damned mule was scattering twenty-dollar gold pieces over a wide area. "Let's get the mule first," he ordered Hanratty and Brown, "then we'll pick up the coins."

It took them forty-five minutes to corner and capture the money mule, and would have been impossible, in Tanner's opinion, if there hadn't been three of them doing it. At the end of the chase he was hot, sweating, and had decided that he'd never hated an animal as much as he hated that mule.

"I'd shoot the damned thing," Hanratty said, wiping his forehead with his bandanna, "except she'd figure out a way to get my gun before I could pull the fricking trigger."

Brown nodded. "My daddy had a mule. She was smarter than all the horses put together."

Tanner could believe it. Sliding to the ground, he approached the mule and took a close look at the pannier. The frame was busted. The tear in the canvas side panel had lengthened to eight inches. There were gold coins scattered over several acres.

He was thinking about shooting the mule himself when Fox rode up and swung off her mustang. "I'll stake her right here," she said, passing him with a hammer and a metal spike. "Peaches will collect her once he gets the others settled down."

"You and Peaches caught the other five?" Tanner asked, struggling to keep his voice level. After he spotted the mules about a half mile away, he turned back to Fox. It would never have occurred to him to carry a hammer and metal spikes in his saddlebags.

"Peaches is chasing down the last of them. The others are staked with enough rope to allow grazing."

For the first time it registered on Tanner that she was wearing glasses with blue lenses to protect her eyes from the sunlight. As hard as he tried he couldn't recall if she'd worn the glasses yesterday. What he wanted to know more than that was how she and Peaches had caught five mules while he, Hanratty, and Brown were making fools of themselves chasing one. He decided he didn't want to know badly enough to ask.

She took off the glasses and scanned the valley searching for sunlight bouncing off gold. It wasn't hard to spot. "There's no easy way to do this," she said finally. "I'll get some pots and then we'll all go treasure hunting." She gave Tanner a shrug. "Meanwhile, you might want to stitch up that tear."

"I suppose you've got a needle and thread in there, too," he said, watching her stow the hammer in her saddlebags.

She produced a heavy needle and thin cord, gave them to him, then rode off to fetch containers for the coins. He narrowed his eyes and watched her fiery braid swinging across the back of her poncho.

"Nothing I hate more than an uppity woman," Hanratty said. To underscore the point he spit on the ground then wiped his mouth with the back of his hand.

Brown took a swig from his canteen. "What you hate is getting bested by a woman. I didn't see you catching five mules."

"I'm getting tired of your mouth," Hanratty snarled, swinging off his horse. He started toward Jubal Brown.

Tanner stepped in front of him. "Not while you're on my payroll." A challenge flickered in Hanratty's stare then receded. "If you two want a piece of each other, fine." Tanner addressed them both. "But you wait until this money is safely delivered in Denver."

In silence they waited for Fox to return with containers. When everyone had a pot, Tanner took off his jacket and rolled up his shirtsleeves, then started the overwhelming job of picking up coins. After twenty minutes he wished for a blast of the morning's cold air. There was no shade on the valley floor, nothing to block the sun. After an hour, he was soaked with sweat.

Once during the next two hours he looked over at Fox and discovered she'd removed her heavy poncho and opened her collar. Sitting back on his heels, he took his canteen from around his neck and stared at her as he took a long swallow of warm water.

Underneath the poncho she'd worn an overlarge shirt. What she probably didn't know was that the shirt was thin enough that the sunlight behind her made a silhouette of her body against the side Tanner faced.

He sucked in a soft breath. She was bending, reaching to pick up a coin, and he saw the shadowy outline of heavy breasts and a slender waist. His throat closed and he had to remind himself to exhale.

It wasn't decent to take advantage of a situation she was unaware of. Turning his head, he blinked unseeing at a coin caught among short branches of sage. For some reason he had expected Fox to be smallbreasted. It was an electric jolt to discover otherwise.

He picked up the coin and dropped it inside the Dutch oven he carried. For five entire minutes he managed not to look at her, then he swore quietly and turned his head.

This time she was kneeling, wiping sweat from her face and throat with the long tail of the shirt. When she spotted him watching, she raised an eyebrow then smiled and returned to picking up coins.

When she smiled her whole face brightened, and to Tanner's astonishment he realized she might have been beautiful if fate had given her an easier life. Instead, she hid beneath shapeless clothing and a cantankerous expression guaranteed to repel rather than attract.

Certainly she made no attempt to be particularly agreeable. She didn't address Hanratty or Brown unless they spoke to her first. And twice now she had stood up and moved when she found herself seated next to Tanner. The only person whose company she sought was Peaches. Every night before turning in, she spent a few minutes reviewing the day with Peaches. Occasionally Tanner heard her laugh, once her voice had been sharp and angry.

Bending to pick a coin out of the dirt, he frowned and decided he was spending entirely too much time thinking about his scout.

Distances were deceiving out here, but Fox judged the valley stretched between twelve and fifteen miles wide. If they set out now, well past midday, they would have to camp in the open or travel in the dark to reach the foothills of the next range.

Chewing over the problem, she considered the pots of coins set out on the ground. "Do you need to count them?"

"If the bags contained the same number of coins, each would hold six hundred and twenty-five coins," Tanner said. "But the only way to know if the coins were evenly dispersed would be to count each bag." He shaded his eyes and gazed toward the next range on the far side of the valley. "It would take too long to count all the bags, but I do need to count the coins out of the broken bag."

The money was the purpose of the journey. "All right," Fox said, her decision made. "We'll camp here. The animals could stand to graze, and you'll have the rest of the afternoon to count." Turning to Jubal Brown, she waved her hand over the ground. "There's too much brush to risk an open fire so one of you needs to dig a pit, and Peaches could use a hand unpacking the mules."

"I'll dig a pit," Brown agreed, "but I didn't sign on to tote and haul supplies."

Fox bared her teeth. "You signed on to get this money to Denver. That means doing whatever it takes. Right now it takes unloading those mules."

"Then you do it yourself." The tight crazy light came into his eyes. "I'm not taking orders from a woman, and I'm not going to do a Negro's work for him."

Fox stared at Brown but spoke to Tanner. "We're going to have trouble here." From the corner of her eye she saw Tanner start toward them, but she held up a hand. "It's my problem and I'll take care of it." She considered Brown for a moment. "Are you going to do what you signed on to do?"

"I'm going to have a nap."

"I don't think so." Making a fist, Fox punched him in the stomach hard enough that he'd have a bruise. Stepping back, she watched with a cold eye as he doubled over. "When you're finished bellyaching, give Peaches a hand. Or else . . . I'll knock your teeth out." She turned to Tanner, and was tempted to smile at the astonishment pinching his expression. "You need any help counting those coins?"

His gaze slipped past her to Brown who was bent over swearing, much to Hanratty's amusement. "I could use some help, yes."

She turned over a water bucket and sat on it, her eyes a stormy gray. "I think it'll go faster if one of us counts and one of us runs a tally. Would you rather count or tally?"

Before he could answer, Brown stomped up to the pots of coins. "You saw what she did!" He sent Fox a murderous glance. "Ain't you going to do something about it?"

"What would you like me to do?" To Fox's satisfaction, Tanner's voice was cold and unsympathetic. But this wasn't his fight.

She stepped between the two men. "You and me, and Hanratty and Peaches, we're the hired help. All of us. Not three of us with you being the exception. All of us. That means we share the work."

"That means you follow the lady's orders, Brown." Hanratty's grin curved the lower part of his face. "When she cracks the whip, you jump, boy."

"Shut up, Hanratty." Fox scowled at him. "But you do follow my orders. You knew that going in. You also know what needs to be done to set up camp. At this point I shouldn't have to tell anyone what to do. You should be able to see that a job needs doing and then pitch in and do it. Now get busy, or get out. Leave." To Tanner she added, "I'll get some paper. You count, I'll keep track."

Before she returned to the pots of coins, she made sure Hanratty and Brown had moved to assist Peaches. Neither of them worked with any speed, but they were doing it. For a long moment she held Jubal Brown's stare, then she walked back to where Tanner waited by the pots.

"I think we need to talk," Tanner said. Sunlight slanted across the valley, turning his eyes an amber color that made Fox think of good whiskey. She could have used a drink right now.

"Let's get these coins counted and stowed, then we can talk."

They counted all the coins from the broken bag and came up with a total of 622. "If you're right about how many coins should be in here, we're short three coins," Fox said, inspecting the mended bag. If she'd done the job, she would have used a patch instead of just stitching the rip. "We can fetch the others and go out there and look for them."

Tanner scanned the broad valley floor then swept off his hat and ran his fingers through his hair. "Three coins amount to sixty dollars. I'll add three coins to this bag before I give it to the kidnappers."

Sixty dollars was a small fortune in Fox's view. "If it took until dark to find the missing coins, it would still be good pay for the effort."

"I'm willing to pay sixty dollars not to have to spend another two hours searching dirt and sagebrush."

"It's your money," she said, twitching a shoulder. The coins were counted, camp set up, the animals peacefully grazing. She could relax. Taking a cigar from her shirt pocket, she lit it and sighed with pleasure. "What did you want to talk about?"

"You've knifed one of my guards, and beat up the other." Tanner also lit a cigar, one that smelled a lot better than hers did. Fox wondered what he'd paid for his. "You aren't making friends on this trip."

"I have a friend. I don't need more," she said, glancing toward Peaches who was repacking what they wouldn't need tonight. "Besides, I only jabbed Hanratty, I didn't knife him, and I only punched Brown, I didn't beat him up."

Tanner exhaled and watched the breeze dissipate the smoke. "These are dangerous men, Fox. It isn't wise to, begging your pardon, piss them off."

"If I lose control of this expedition, we might as well turn around right now and call it quits. I need to gain their respect even if it means, begging your pardon, pissing them off." That was, in fact, what had to happen before they would respect her. "I know what I'm doing. This isn't my first experience with men like Hanratty and Brown."

A silence opened between them before Tanner spoke again. "You're a remarkable woman."

Her eyebrows soared in surprise. "Why? Because I smoke and cuss and know how to find east?"

"That's part of it," he said.

She held his gaze until she felt her cheeks grow hot, then she stubbed out her cigar, stood up, and dusted her hands together. "Well, we've still got a few hours of daylight, so I think I'll take your advice and mend some fences and build some respect."

She hoped to hell that she wasn't about to make a huge mistake.

"This is a damned fool idea," Tanner snapped, offering Peaches a cigar.

"Don't mind if I do and thank you." Peaches sniffed the cigar, smiled, then bit off the end and accepted a light. "Don't worry, Captain. Missy knows what she's doing. She wouldn't have suggested a competition if she didn't think she could win."

Right now an enthusiastic argument ensued among Fox, Hanratty, and Brown over how far out to place the targets. Tanner's instinct was to interfere and prohibit the shooting match. He didn't see anything good coming out of this.

Once the distance was decided upon, Hanratty paced up the valley, counting off yards.

"Are you sure you don't want to compete?" Fox asked, joining them. She took a puff off of Peaches's cigar.

Peaches held up his hands. "You know I couldn't hit the side of that mountain if you gave me ten tries."

Tanner shook his head. "Whatever's going on here, it's between you and them."

"Then you can referee." She dangled her arms and shook her fingers. "Best shot out of two tries. If the shooter misses on both shots, he's out. We'll start in ten minutes."

Hanratty and Brown used the time to have a smoke. Fox paced up and down, muttering and stamping her feet.

"What is she doing?" Tanner asked Peaches.

"She's getting mad. Making herself furious."

"Why?"

"If she don't get mad, Captain, she'll get scared." Peaches shrugged as if the answer was obvious.

The idea that Fox was not totally fearless startled him. And touched him on a level he couldn't have explained.

"All right, let's go. Come on, Tanner." Red-faced and cold-eyed, Fox strode up to the line Brown had dug in the dirt with his boot. "Get out of my way. I'll shoot first."

"The hell you will," Hanratty protested. "We'll flip a coin." He turned to Tanner. "You got a coin?"

No one laughed as Tanner produced a twenty-dollar gold piece. "You and Brown," he said. They didn't look happy, but both nodded and he spun the coin in the air, caught it, and slapped it on the back of his hand.

"Tails," Hanratty said.

"Tails it is. Now you and Fox."

This time it came up heads and Hanratty won again. He smirked at Fox, knowing he had first chance to intimidate her and Brown. The losers swore and stepped back from the line.

Hanratty had raised his rifle and was about to squeeze the trigger when Fox said, "Wait."

"What the hell are you trying to pull?"

"Just wondered if you boys want to make this a little more interesting. I've got ten dollars that says I win."

"The hell."

The men looked at each other then reached in their pockets. Everyone gave ten dollars to Tanner for safekeeping.

"Now shut up." Hanratty glared at Fox before he shouldered his rifle. The old skillet that Peaches had contributed fell off the tree stump. "Got it on the first shot."

Brown narrowed his eyes. "Maybe it fell off by itself. Someone should go check." He didn't look at Peaches but it was clear who he meant.

"I'll do it." When Peaches reached the target area, he held up the skillet and shouted. "He got it." He reset the skillet as Fox stepped up to the line.

"And I got it with one shot," Hanratty boasted.

Fox fired before he finished speaking, and the skillet flew backward. She stepped away from the line without waiting for Peaches to verify the shot. "Your turn," she snapped at Brown.

He, too, hit the skillet with one shot.

"Move the target back," Fox called to Peaches, then resumed pacing and muttering and building steam under her hat.

This time it took Hanratty two shots to hit the skillet. Fox and Brown scored with one shot, and Peaches moved the target farther back. Impressed, Tanner was glad he'd had the sense not to participate.

No one spoke as Hanratty stepped up to the line. He gave Fox a thoughtful look then sighted in and fired. The skillet jumped off the stump and Peaches hurried forward to reset it.

Fox fired and missed, swore, slapped her hat against her thigh, then knocked the skillet off with her second shot. Tanner released a breath he hadn't realized he was holding. Brown also hit on his second shot.

Peaches moved the target to a distance that looked to Tanner as if it would be impossible to hit.

Hanratty hit it on the second shot. Fox hit on the first shot. Jubal Brown missed both shots.

"You're out," Fox said.

Brown looked angry enough to tear something apart. But

when Hanratty stepped up to shoot, he turned and walked away.

Peaches moved the target twice more before dusk settled and Tanner decided it was time to halt the competition. He moved up to the line. "At this point it's no longer a shooting contest, it's more of an eyesight contest with some luck thrown in. I declare the competition a tie between Hanratty and Fox." Both protested vigorously, but Tanner held his ground. "It'll be full dark in a few minutes. Time for supper." He divided the money between them. "That was impressive shooting," he said, meaning it. "Congratulations to you both."

No one had much to say during a three-B supper—bacon, beans, and biscuits—but Tanner noticed Hanratty and Brown scarcely glanced at their plates. Both of them stared at Fox with hard expressionless faces. It occurred to Tanner that she had made the same point with them as she'd made with the Indian boys.

"How did you learn to shoot like that?" Brown asked over coffee.

Fox didn't look up from scrubbing the plates with sand. "The same way you learned. Lots of practice." The noise of the fire popping and sand scraping tin was the only sound for a full minute, then Fox looked up and smiled. "Want to go again tomorrow? With pistols?"

Hanratty and Brown laughed and Tanner felt the tension evaporate. The remainder of the evening passed quickly in talk of rifles, specifically a Sharps, versus pistols, particularly a Colt repeater, stories of various target shoots, and what weapons were reputed to be favored by famous outlaws and lawmen. For the first time since the journey began, Fox stayed at the fire with the men and they actually asked her opinion and listened when she responded.

Before Tanner called it a night and rolled out his bedding, he took Fox aside, needing to satisfy his curiosity. "What would you have done if you'd lost the contest?"

Her eyelids flickered, then her chin came up in a gesture of bravado. "I never considered that possibility."

"Consider it now."

Peaches had banked the coals in the fire pit. There wasn't enough light to see her expression. All he could make out was the pale oval of her face and the line of her throat. Imagination filled in blue eyes and a full shapely mouth.

"I wouldn't have lost. Good night, Mr. Tanner."

He sat beside the fire pit another five minutes, thinking about the day. Most of the events centered around Fox, her direction, her expertise, her assistance, her skills.

This was a unique situation for Tanner. In his world of design and mines, others looked to him for direction, expertise, and skill. He was as good in his field as Fox was in hers. For reasons he could not have explained, he regretted that Fox would never see him in his natural role as he was seeing her in hers.

The thought made him smile and shake his head. Ordinarily he didn't feel a need to impress a woman or court her admiration. But he'd never met a woman like Fox.

CHAPTER 6

*T*HEY spent a chill frosty night at altitude in the Shoshone mountains. In the morning, after crossing a rough divide, the company descended to a canyon that housed the deserted remains of a pony express station. Indians or settlers had stripped the station to the stone foundation. Here the well was dry, and if Fox hadn't earlier ordered everyone to carry extra water, there would have been no coffee for supper or breakfast.

The following day stretched long and tedious, skirting house-size rock formations before crossing the Reese River. The water level was low at this time of year and the mules plodded across without incident, but Hanratty's mount balked at entering the water.

He tried shouting, then spurring the animal, and finally jumped to the ground and attempted to lead the agitated horse down the bank. The horse reared and foam bubbled on his lips, his eyes rolled.

Red-faced and angry, Hanratty cussed and pulled on the reins, river water washing over his boots.

Before Fox could hand off the mules and start back across, she saw Tanner ride up to Hanratty and insist that Hanratty take Tanner's horse across. Words were exchanged then Hanratty swung up on Tanner's bay and ran it across the shallow river.

Curious, Fox pulled her hat down against the sun and watched to see what Tanner would do. First, he led Hanratty's horse away from the water, talking softly. Continuing to murmur, he stroked the horse's neck until the animal was calm.

Then Tanner tied his bandanna around the horse's head and eyes before he led the horse into the water and walked it across the river.

"Hell, I could have done that," Hanratty swore.

"Yeah, but you didn't." Jubal Brown smirked.

Once the men were on their own mounts and the company moving again, Fox turned in beside Tanner. "How'd you know what to do back there?"

"Mules are used in the mines to haul the ore carts. Occasionally something spooks them and they balk." He turned his head to look at her. "This strikes me as being in the category of asking how you know where north is."

"Sorry," she said with a smile. "I didn't mean to sound as if I'm surprised." But she had been, a little.

And that wasn't fair. None of the men were the greenhorns Fox had expected, and that included Tanner. It hadn't been necessary to instruct anyone how to dig a fire pit or how to fold a bedroll efficiently. Even Tanner took his turn cooking and served up a meal as competently as Fox could have done.

As if he'd read her mind, he said, "I've spent a lot of time in the wilderness looking for Jennings's mines." His eyebrow lifted. "Did you think you were going to nursemaid a novice?"

"The thought crossed my mind."

Her mustang shifted to avoid a rock, pushing her leg against Tanner's. Lightning flashed up to her thigh and her cheeks heated. Damn it. What was it about this man that turned her into a quivering adolescent? He gave her a look that made her mouth go dry. Her leg brushed his and suddenly a fire ignited in her stomach.

"You make me mad," she said, scowling at his broad shoulders and open collar.

"Really? How's that?"

"I don't know. You just do." Touching her heels to the mustang's sides she trotted away from him, her face still hot.

On the positive side, Tanner's mention of Jennings was exactly what Fox needed. She hadn't spent as much time planning her revenge as she had expected she would. Worse, some days she forgot to apply Peaches's sun protection, and sometimes she simply didn't feel like sleeping with her hands immersed in bacon grease. If she was going to have the choices she wanted, she needed to focus more on Jennings and stick to her beauty routine.

Riding up next to Jubal Brown, she extended her hand for the mule's lead rope. "Thanks for spelling me. I'll take them now."

"I don't mind leading them a while longer."

Well, well. Hiding a smile, Fox stayed beside him. "So you're going home to join the war."

"Might as well. Seems I've worn out my welcome in the west."

Meaning the law was after him. Fox nodded, wondering how old he was. Twenty? Twenty-five? Some men weren't destined to die of old age.

"Do you really believe it somehow demeans you to assist Mr. Hernandez?"

"He's a Negro."

"He's an old man with rhumitiz and a cough."

"If he can't handle the job, he should have stayed home."

"It that were true, he would agree. But it isn't true. Mr. Hernandez and I both believe he can handle the job. The thing is, we're a team here, Brown. If one of us could use a helping hand, the rest of us have an obligation to offer that hand."

"I'm doing it, ain't I? So why are you chewing on me?"

"Because I'm sorry you made me punch you," Fox said, fixing her gaze ahead. "Some times that's the only way to get a man's attention."

"I can think of other ways a woman can get a man's attention."

She gave him a look cold enough to wipe the grin off his lips. "You best forget that I'm a woman, Mr. Brown, or you could get yourself shot or knifed."

"I just meant—"

"I know what you meant, and you can keep those kind of remarks to yourself."

Riding forward, she slowed near Hanratty. "Is everything all right?"

"Why wouldn't it be?"

Damn all. Every man in the group had a burr under his butt today. "Have you seen anything that might be Indians?"

"Are you fixing to give me another lecture about our noble red brothers?"

Fox strove for patience. "Outside of me, you have the best eyesight in the company. I'm just asking if you've seen anything."

"I've seen some antelope, a couple of rabbits, and a coyote."

"All right," she said, narrowing her eyelids down to slits. Leaning forward, she prepared to ride ahead where she could be alone and away from surly men.

Hanratty reached out and touched her arm. "Tell me something."

"I've seen some rabbits myself, and a couple of deer."

A grin broke across his whiskery face. "I ain't seen any Indians. I did see two men about two miles that way." He tilted his head south. "Riding the same direction as us, only traveling light and moving fast."

"I saw them, too. So what do you want to know?"

"Does Tanner think me and Jubal Brown stole the missing gold pieces?"

Fox hadn't seen that one coming. She stared at him. "There wasn't a hint that Tanner thought the coins were stolen. He appeared to believe like I did that we overlooked the missing coins when we searched. It would be easy to do. They were scattered over a wide area."

Hanratty nodded and pulled down his hat brim.

Fox didn't ask if he or Brown had stolen the coins. That was the kind of question that got a person killed. Surely neither of them were that stupid. She drew a long breath, inhaling the scents of sage and grass, man and horse.

"We're looking for a lake. Should be over that next rise."

"I'm going to ride ahead and kill something." When Fox raised her eyebrows, Hanratty added, "For supper."

"I wouldn't say no to a couple of fat rabbits."

She watched him gallop east, kicking up coils of sandy dust. Maybe they all needed a hard ride and a chase to soothe tempers sharpened by the daily tedium and by having to live in close quarters with other loners like themselves. Tomorrow or the next day, Fox would send Brown out by himself. Tanner, too.

She mentioned the idea to Tanner after they had set up camp between the lake and a small meadow where the grass was lush and starting to turn green. The horses and mules had found heaven.

"I wouldn't mind doing some exploring on my own," Tanner commented, taking in the scenery. "This is beautiful country."

"You don't think every range looks the same?"

They climbed one mountain range, searched for the pass, then dropped down to a valley, climbed the next range, dropped down to a valley. Fox had made the journey enough times to see and recognize shapes or faces in rocks and peaks, and the valleys were subtly different, each with its own character. But to most people, particularly to people like Tanner who hadn't grown up in the west, the ranges and valleys usually looked monotonously alike.

"Why did you ask that?" Tanner gazed at her with an intense expression that made Fox half believe that her emotions were writ large across her forehead. "Do you think each range looks like the next one?"

"Well, no," she said, frowning. Once again she had asked him a question that was turning out to be a mistake. And feeling agitated and dumb because of it. "But I thought you might."

Annoyance quirked his mouth before he turned to study the mountains rising in front of them. "Is there mining nearby?"

"As a matter of fact I'm planning to stay in a mining camp tomorrow night." She almost asked how he had guessed, then remembered that he was a mining engineer and managed to save herself an embarrassment. "How long have you worked for J M and M?"

"Fifteen years. A lot longer than I expected to."

Fox gazed into her coffee cup and inhaled the scent of roasting rabbit wafting from the campfire behind them. Supper must be almost ready. "What do you think of your boss? Mr. Jennings?"

"I like him." Tanner finished his coffee. "He runs a fair and honest operation."

That was not what Fox had expected to hear. "Now that surprises me. I heard Hobbs Jennings is a no good thieving son of a bitch."

Tanner turned to face her and she noticed that the paleness of working underground had vanished, replaced by a weathered tan that deepened every day. The polish had rubbed off his boots, and his trousers were as dusty as his jacket. He was starting to look more like Fox preferred a man to look, only much more handsome.

A frown pulled his eyebrows. "Where did you hear that?"

She shrugged. "Here and there."

"Hobbs Jennings pays a higher wage than other mine owners, and he takes care of a miner's family if the miner is killed or injured on the job. He's concerned about efficiency and profit, but he's also concerned about safety. Many owners aren't."

Irritated, Fox started toward the campfire. "Saint Hobbs? I don't believe it. You just don't know him well enough."

"And you do?"

She heard the puzzlement in his voice and realized she'd said more than she should have. Planting her fists on her hips, she considered the rabbits spitted above the fire. "My mouth is watering."

It was Peaches's turn to cook. "Thanks to Mr. Hanratty, we're goin' to have a feast. I've got corn bread making, too."

They had stopped early to let the animals graze. They'd have a couple hours of daylight after eating. "Are you up for chess?"

"Best ask if you're up to getting your butt whipped."

Fox smiled. "Someday I'll beat you."

"And someday the moon is gonna fall right out of the sky."

The rabbit tasted as delicious as it had smelled, and Peaches's corn bread melted in the mouth in buttersoaked goodness. Midway through the meal Fox noticed Peaches staring at her with what he called his "significant look." When he had her attention, he rolled his eyes toward Tanner's plate. It took a minute for Fox to understand what Peaches wanted her to notice. When she did, she inspected Hanratty and Brown, too.

Hanratty, Brown, and Fox ate with their forks clutched in their fists. Tanner used his utensils the way Peaches insisted refined folks did. If Tanner noticed how Fox ate, and of course he must have by now, he would place her in the same class as Hanratty and Brown. Fox might have a background lacking in the social graces, but she considered herself head and shoulders above the likes of Hanratty and Brown.

Frowning, feeling like she was putting on airs, she switched her fork in her hand. She hoped Tanner would notice that she was no longer eating like Hanratty and Brown.

"I believe I know Hobbs Jennings as well as anyone in the company," Tanner stated after they'd eaten.

Fox kept her gaze fixed on the chessboard Peaches was setting up. Peaches flicked her a glance when he heard Jennings's name.

When she didn't respond, Tanner cleaned his throat. "You're implying that you know someone who's been with J M and M longer than I have and you believe he knows Jennings better than I do."

"This person has known Jennings much longer than you

have." Fox spoke reluctantly, mentally kicking herself for bungling things.

"Can you tell me his name?"

"No." Sitting on the grass, Fox studied the chessboard as if she'd never played the game before. "You open," she said to Peaches.

"Damn it, Fox, you're irritating the hell out of me."

"Then go away so me and Peaches can play chess in peace."

"What exactly did this person tell you about Hobbs Jennings?"

Finally she looked up at him. "Jennings is your boss and I can see why you'd be loyal to him. Let's leave it at that."

For a moment he held her gaze, then he turned and walked toward Hanratty and Brown, taking a cigar from his vest pocket.

"I made a mistake and I know it," Fox said to Peaches, "so don't say anything."

"I believe the sun protection is working. The bacon grease and remembering to wear your riding gloves is helping your hands, too."

"Are my cheeks still chapped?" She knew her lips were, but they were gradually getting smoother.

"Not as bad as when we left Carson City."

In an eyeblink, Peaches took a bishop and one of her knights. Fox stared at the board in disbelief. "How did you do that?"

"You aren't paying attention, Missy." He withdrew a cigar from the pocket of his overalls and Fox recognized the band around it. "You got other things on your mind."

"That's one of Tanner's cigars."

"It is. Me and Mr. Tanner been getting acquainted." Peaches drew on the cigar and closed his eyes in pleasure. Then he captured one of Fox's rooks. "That man knows a bit about everything."

"He never offered me one of his fancy cigars."

"That's probably because he doesn't think to. I doubt Mr. Tanner knows many ladies who smoke."

"But that means he thinks of me as a lady. Nobody thinks . . ." Biting her lip, she blinked down at the board. Did Matthew Tanner think of her as a lady? No, he couldn't possibly. But he might be thinking of her as a woman.

What did he see when he looked at her? Right now he'd see

her sitting Indian-style on the dry grass, covered from neck to knees in her old poncho, her hair dusty and in need of a wash. Tendrils had pulled loose and floated around her cheeks. She suspected she was beginning to smell as ripe as the men.

"What kind of things do you and Tanner talk about?" She took another of Peaches's pawns, no triumph in it.

"We talk about everything and nothing. About the war and how it might go, about development moving west, about the Indian problems. He knows the names of the stars and the names of different kinds of rocks. He's read all the books we have."

Why couldn't Fox talk to Tanner about those things? Instead, her mouth went dry and all her social talk blew away like grains of sand on a wind. She ended up asking him personal questions that annoyed him, or babbled about weather and scenery, and usually finished by putting her foot in her mouth.

"Does he ever ask about me?" Sighing, she watched Peaches mount an attack on her queen. The game was turning into a rout.

"Every now and then."

"What kind of questions?" She kept her head down.

"Like when did you and me hook up? Did I teach you to read and write and do sums, or did you go to school? That kind of thing."

Heat burned on her cheeks. "How do you answer?"

He pounced on her queen. This would be one of the shortest games they had played. "I answer without any details. Don't volunteer anything."

"Does he ever offer any information about himself?"

"Not much. I know he's plenty worried about his pa. I have an idea his pa expects a lot out of him. Maybe more than he can give. Maybe more than anyone could give."

Fox raised her head. "What's that mean?"

"I 'spect it means Mr. Tanner can't ever please his pa. Probably means he feels he's always disappointing his father."

Fox sat back and thought about that. Not having parents, she knew she cherished an idealized view of the parent/child relationship. In her vision, both parties gave and received unconditional love even though Fox suspected there was no such thing as unconditional love.

Turning her head, she watched Tanner talking to Hanratty and Brown. They stood near the bedrolls, smoking, occasionally laughing. All a person had to do was look at Matthew Tanner to know he was the kind of man who did the right thing, a man whose word was as good as a contract, a man with duty and loyalty at the core of his character. She could not visualize him failing at anything.

It occurred to Fox that if there was anything worse than having no father, it might be having a father you could never please, a father who looked at you with disappointment.

"Your butt is whipped."

When she jerked her attention back to the board, Peaches's men had captured her king. Fox swore as he picked up the pieces and stacked them back in the box. "Sorry," she apologized. "I didn't give you much of a game." A flash came into her eyes. "Why do you care if Tanner knows the name of the stars? It was you who showed me the Big Dipper and how to find the North Star. You already know the names of the stars."

"A few," Peaches agreed. "But not like Mr. Tanner does. He knows constellations."

"You do, too."

"Not as many as Mr. Tanner knows."

"Peaches Hernandez," her eyes came down in slits. "are you trying to make Tanner look good in my eyes?"

"I 'spect he already does, Missy."

Part of Tanner's job was to judge the mood of the miners and listen for complaints as he traveled among the JM&M holdings. Hobbs Jennings did not want to be the last to know about a problem brewing in his mines. He wanted to know quickly, while there was time to solve any difficulty.

Not everyone regarded Hobbs Jennings with the loyalty and affection Tanner did, but in fifteen years Tanner had never heard Jennings referred to as a thieving son of a bitch. It was troubling to think such an individual was out there, probably working for the company. A man holding such strong negative feelings would be trouble sooner or later. At the least, he would breed discontent around him, at worst an insurrection could develop.

The dust opened ahead and for an instant he glimpsed Fox's long red braid, saw her glance back at the string of mules she led. He could argue all day and she would never reveal the name of the man who believed Hobbs Jennings was a thieving son of a bitch. He bit down on his back teeth as the dust closed around her. Stubbornness was not an attractive trait in a woman. But then, Fox had a multitude of traits that most people would condemn.

While he waited for another sight of her straight back and long braid, he considered the qualities he liked about her. She was self-reliant, that was obvious. Fate could plunk her down anywhere and Fox would survive and thrive. Her self-reliance went hand in hand with her independence. Fox made her own decisions, went her own way, and she didn't appear to care what anyone else thought. That in itself made her vastly different from the women Tanner had known.

She had a temper, but she was undoubtedly the bravest woman he'd met. And the most foolhardy and reckless, he thought, recalling how she'd punched Jubal Brown and doubled him over. She was lucky that Brown hadn't retaliated in kind, although Tanner suspected Fox had been ready for that possibility. Until he'd observed Fox in action, Tanner would have said with utter conviction that it was unthinkable for a woman to effectively incapacitate a man.

"Speak of the devil," he said softly as Fox rode toward him, turned, and came up on his right. She'd handed off the mules to Hanratty.

"There's a decision you need to make."

Leaning closer, he examined her face. "You have something on your cheeks and forehead." Something that gave her skin a yellowish tint.

She pursed her lips and he didn't know if she intended to respond. Finally she released a sigh. "It's Peaches's formula to prevent sunburn. I was doing fine with something he makes called Sesame Milk, but this morning he insisted I try this one. It's a mixture of egg yolk and honey and some other stuff that Peaches keeps secret."

The revelation that Fox used beauty treatments stunned him.

"I guess you think it's stupid to smear glop on my face to avoid sunburn."

"I've never known a woman who welcomed a sunburn." There weren't many trees out here in the Nevada wilderness. The cedars, pine, and junipers weren't shade trees by any stretch of the imagination. The only shade a person had was the brim of his hat, and that was seldom enough to block the sun entirely.

"I don't mind a little bit of tan, but I don't want to get

much darker than I am now," she said, glaring between her horse's ears.

Right now her face had a golden glow that made her eyes seem more blue than gray. Tanner doubted Fox would ever have the milky white skin decreed by fashion. She would always have a touch of sun-gold on her skin and rose on her cheekbones. To Tanner's eyes, her vivid coloring made her more attractive than any milk-skinned woman he could think of.

"I didn't come here to discuss my fricking face," she said as if the subject made her angry.

"What did you want to ask me?" Talking to Fox was like walking across a field with buried traps ready to spring shut.

"I have a reason for not wanting to arrive in Denver with darkly tanned skin." Her chin came up and the flash in her eyes dared him to comment. "I'm not wearing egg yolk on my face out of vanity."

"There's nothing wrong with a little vanity." He had no idea what to say on this subject.

"I want to talk to you about the mining camp up ahead."

Thank God. Mining camps were something he knew about.

"I think we should stay two nights at the camp, but that's a decision you need to make."

Instantly he thought of the deadline given him by the kidnappers. "Why do you want to stay two nights?"

"We haven't had a rest in ten days. The animals could use a free day and so could all of us. There's a washhouse in the camp and a couple of rough eating spots, but the fare is better than cooking in the wild. And there's one or two oversized tents designated as saloons."

Everything Tanner owned needed washing, and the entire company smelled of horse, smoke, and sweat. She was right about the animals needing a day without the weight of saddles or packs.

"We're making good time," Fox added. "Wasting a day shouldn't affect our overall schedule."

The saloons concerned him. As far as Tanner was aware, Hanratty and Brown had obeyed his instructions about carrying no liquor on this journey, but neither had been happy about the prohibition. How much attraction would the saloons exert?

"All right," he reluctantly agreed.

"Good." Fox gave him a short nod. "We're packing tents. We'll set up on the outskirts of the camp."

At the midday break, Tanner spoke to Hanratty and Brown. "Drunk men don't make effective guards."

"That seems harsh, to deny us a chance to cut up a little."

It wasn't surprising that it was Brown who protested.

Hanratty focused on the money mule. "I agree that drunk ain't professional, but two drinks don't make a man drunk. How about that? We don't leave our cargo at the same time, and we don't have more than two drinks?"

"That's acceptable," Tanner agreed, speaking slowly. "But if you two leave the gold unguarded for one minute, you're fired. If either of you come back to camp drunk, you're fired. That's if I don't shoot you first. Is that understood?"

"Damn." Jubal's eyes sparkled. "First thing I want is a bath and a shave. They got any women in the camp?"

They rode into the mining camp in midafternoon. One of the first things Tanner noticed was three or four rough-looking women dressed in men's clothing. One led a mule packed high with prospector's provisions. Another moved tent to tent, selling pies out of a wheelbarrow. By comparison, Fox appeared the essence of femininity, he thought with a smile. Unlike these women, Fox had not cut her magnificent hair, her skin was tanned but smooth and clear. Seeing her from the back, swaying in her saddle, no one would mistake her for a male.

The camp was located along a river valley about a mile west of the steep canyon where most of the mining took place. Tanner's experienced eye noticed an abundance of native granite, and more important the quartz ledges that signaled the possibility of silver. He made a mental note to mention this spot to Hobbs Jennings as worthy of investigation and possible investment.

Dropping his gaze, he frowned at the money mule. At Fort Churchill he'd felt reasonably comfortable taking the gold into a populated area. But every soul in this camp was here for one reason only. To find gold or silver. If anyone suspected what was riding at the bottom of the money mule's pack . . .

Fox chose a site at the far east side of the camp where the grass wasn't grazed out. After studying the sky she instructed Peaches to unpack the tents.

"Already done it, Missy." Peaches nodded to a pile of canvas and poles. "Goin' to snow, I'd say." He covered a cough and complained about the congestion he couldn't seem to shake. "Glad we ain't heading up around that canyon. I'd hate to get stuck in the mountains in a blizzard."

Newcomers attracted attention and Tanner noted they had drawn their share of interest. The residents of the small tent village would wonder if they were passing through or if more competition had arrived.

"Stick to the plan," he instructed Hanratty and Brown. "One of you always in camp. But don't be obvious about it. No sense advertising the fact that you're hired guards or that we're carrying something that requires guarding."

"We aren't stupid," Hanratty said. He spit on the ground next to the tent he had erected. "I'll take the first watch. The rest of you can go where you will." He gave Jubal Brown a long stare. "You be back here in three hours at the latest, or there'll be consequences."

Brown's smirk suggested he didn't much care, but he nodded agreement before setting off immediately toward the tinny music drifting out of a long saloon tent.

"I'll keep Mr. Hanratty company," Peaches decided, setting up the coffeepot. "I think I'd rather visit the washhouse tomorrow. I suspect I'll be craving heat come morning. The temperature's dropping by the minute. Do you play chess?" he asked Hanratty.

"I'd rather play poker."

"Not my preference. Checkers?"

Tanner left them to sort out their entertainment and checked on the gold coins. The bags were covered by a saddle blanket beneath his saddle. They seemed safe enough, especially with Hanratty facing them.

"Well," he said to Fox, gazing down at her. "I think I'll buy one of those pies that woman is selling and eat it during a long soak at the washhouse. Are you heading that way?"

She kept her gaze on the animals, tethered to a line long enough to allow ample grazing. "I was thinking about it." She slid him a look. "Thinking about a pie, too."

"I see this coming. You want me to buy you a pie."

"And we should bring one back to Peaches. I never saw a man like pies the way Peaches does. Especially if it turns out to be a dried apple pie."

"I have an idea that you want me to pay for your bath, too."

Her chin lifted. "Well, you did agree to pay all expenses." When she turned, her eyes sparkled with the pleasure of taking advantage of him. "Hey, Hanratty," she called. "Do you like pies? Seems that Mr. Tanner is in a generous mood."

"I like pies well enough." Hanratty watched Peaches set up the checkerboard. "I always play black, I don't like the red pieces."

Restraining a smile, Tanner fell into step beside her. "It occurs to me that it pleasures you to spend my money."

"That it does," she said, holding out her poncho and inspecting it. "Laundry is also a legitimate expense."

They didn't speak again until after Tanner had paid the washhouse attendant. "I guess I'll see you later." He'd never taken a female to a washhouse before, hadn't realized how awkward such an intimacy would feel. Circles of color rose in Fox's cheeks, then she gave him a half wave like she was having troubling thoughts, too. Frowning, he watched her pause in the doorway of the women's side and stare at him over her shoulder before she stepped inside.

Two things struck him once he was settled in a steaming tub. He'd forgotten to buy the pies, and Fox was naked on the other side of the wall. Hunger tightened his stomach, but it wasn't hunger for a pie.

He supposed it was human nature for a man to be drawn to the wrong woman. Maybe that explained his growing feelings for Fox. Unlikely attractions had been happening since mankind inhabited caves.

No matter how much he thought about it, Tanner could not completely account for why he was so powerfully attracted. It explained nothing to say that Fox was different from the ladies he ordinarily encountered. And his interest ran deeper than simple lust, although lust was certainly present and strong. He'd spent a lot of hours remembering the sun shining through her shirt and casting her full breasts in silhouette.

Fox amused him, annoyed him, roused feelings of respect and admiration and irritation.

And she was totally wrong for a man born into money and prominence, educated in the east, and expected to marry within his own social class. Having spent a lifetime failing to measure up to his father's expectations, Tanner had long ago decided that when it came time to choose a wife, he would restrict his courtship to young ladies his father approved. His relationship with his father was awkward enough without adding a wife who also didn't measure up.

For a long moment he gazed at the washhouse wall separating the men's side from the women's side. There could be no possible future with Fox, and he respected her too much to engage in a short-term dalliance, assuming she was even willing.

Brooding, he shouted at the attendant to bring him some whiskey.

On the women's side, Fox eased into water hot enough to turn her skin bright pink. Once she was settled, she listened for any sounds from the men's side but didn't hear anything.

The idea of Tanner sitting bare-butt naked in a tub not ten feet away made her feel peculiar inside. She liked men with hair on their chests and legs and wondered how it was with Tanner. Lord. Picturing him sent a quiver down her spine.

"Oh, stop it," she snapped, feeling exasperated. Every thought of Tanner was a thought wasted. Worse, thinking about him made her feel inadequate. He was the king on the chessboard, and she was a lowly pawn. The two didn't usually come in contact.

If Tanner did happen to take an interest, Fox had no illusions as to what that meant. His interest would last only as long as the journey. Knowing that she would be temporary in his life . . . if she submitted what would that make her? She knew damned well what it would make her.

Well, most likely she was just woolgathering. Matthew Tanner wasn't drawn to someone like her. And she had better sense than to let some man usc hcr for a few weeks then toss her away.

Still . . . she wondered if he had hair on his chest and legs. And the future didn't matter because her future was a hangman's rope.

"Damn it."

After a while she summoned the courage to pick up the hand mirror on a table next to the tub. Disappointment tugged her lips. As usual, she didn't look like she expected to look.

But she decided, after a thorough inspection, she looked better than she had the last time she'd peered into a mirror. Her cheeks didn't appear as red and raw, and her lips weren't peeling. Peaches's sun protection must be working because she wasn't burned and didn't appear as tanned as she ordinarily did after nearly two weeks in the sun.

But she would never be a beauty, she decided, frowning into the mirror. Her mouth was too wide, her brows too dark. She was too strong-featured. Her skin would never be cream-colored, she had freckles, and she didn't know how to create a fancy hairdo. She wasn't dainty and graceful, had no idea how to form a come-hither look or a pretty pout. She would rather have set her boots on fire than force herself into a corset.

Putting down the mirror, she lit a cigar and blew smoke at the wall separating the women from the men. A sigh of resignation dropped her shoulders.

For the first time in her life, Fox wished she was beautiful, wished it with all her heart.

CHAPTER 7

*T*ANNER waited until Fox emerged from the women's side, her fiery hair plaited into a wet braid and smelling of coarse soap. Silently he decided that she didn't need whatever beauty routine she practiced. A freshly scrubbed face suited her.

She arched an eyebrow. "I thought you'd be gone by now."

"I promised you a pie," he reminded her as they headed toward the grassy lane that served as a street. "Or . . ." He recalled her tossing back a whiskey at Jack's Bar in Carson. "Would you prefer a drink?"

"What is this, a test? I don't drink when I'm working." This time she sent him a glare. "Seems like you should know that."

Actually, he did. "Just thought I'd ask."

Deliberately, Tanner maintained an arm's length between them. Considering the heated images he'd been having mere minutes ago, avoiding any accidental brush against her seemed a prudent choice.

Determined not to think about Fox's soapy clean skin, he turned his attention to the camp. There wasn't much to see. One mining camp was the same as another, a ramshackle collection of tents and campfires surrounding a central area that contained the essentials. A couple of saloons, an outfitting store, a spot for the assayer, and usually a sectioned tent for a handful of whores.

Miners also were much the same, sometimes dreamers, sometimes desperate, never pleased to see newcomers arrive at the pickings.

No one offered a greeting as he and Fox walked through the camp. Even the pie lady regarded them suspiciously. "Staying or passing through?" she asked, wiping her hands on a pair of mended trousers. When she learned they weren't staying, her expression eased. "Then I'll take a dollar off the price of a pie. You can have one for fifty cents."

"It's robbery at thirty cents," Fox sniffed, "but that's all we'll pay."

"If it wasn't the end of the day, I'd spit on you and send you off with your belly growling." The pie lady looked Fox up and down with interest. "But it's time to go home and fix supper so I'll give you a pie for thirty-five cents."

"Thirty, not a penny more."

"I'm glad you're not staying," the pie lady said to Fox. To Tanner's surprise, the two women smiled at each other.

After Tanner paid for four small pies, he and Fox leaned up against a hitching post to eat theirs, watching the western sky flare into twilight streaks of gold, silver, and purple. This was a land of big skies that left a man feeling exposed and smaller than he'd felt himself to be.

"Mine's sour cream and raisin," Fox said. "What did you get?"

Tanner watched her run her tongue over her upper lip, licking at a fleck of filling. He swallowed and made himself look back at the sky. "I've got dried peach."

"Peach! No wonder the pie lady charged the earth. Dried peaches are hard to come by, and expensive, too."

"Can you make pies?" he asked curiously. A woman who could speak Paiute and outshoot a man didn't strike him as a woman who would be content to stand in a hot kitchen and stir up a pie.

She pressed her lips together and red circles appeared on her cheeks. "No," she said finally, apparently hating to admit it. "I can cook ordinary things, but nothing fancy. The only baking I do is make biscuits."

"Sounds like that's good enough."

"It'd be nice to have a pie or a cake once in a while, but Peaches doesn't know how to bake so I don't either." Her chin came up. "I could learn. There's nothing I can't learn. I've just never felt a hankering to learn baking."

They finished the pies in silence then Tanner wiped his

hands on his bandanna. "It's getting dark." And a sharp chill blew on the breeze. Peaches might be right about snow tonight. Tanner picked up the pies for Peaches and Hanratty and turned toward their campsite.

Fox yawned. "That bath made me sleepy. I think I'll turn in early and sleep in tomorrow until after dawn."

They had reached the far edge of the mining camp, where Tanner expected their site to be when he realized it was dark ahead. "Didn't we leave a fire burning?"

"Of course. We always have a fire in camp." Tanner felt her stiffen beside him then peer forward into the deepening darkness. "Something's wrong."

Twilight had faded into night. They should have spotted the welcome flames of their campfire. Dropping the pies, Tanner pulled his pistol and moved forward without making noise. Fox silently came up beside him. They both slowed as they approached the perimeter of the camp, straining to see what kind of problem they were rushing into.

"It's been ransacked," Fox murmured.

Tanner swore. There was enough light to see that their tents had been kicked down. The mule packs were opened and the contents scattered on the ground. Items of clothing tumbled in the breeze. A bag of flour had broken and he smelled vinegar. Striding forward, he moved directly to where he'd left his saddle covering the bank bags. His saddle had been tossed aside and the bags of gold coins were gone. Shock and rage dimmed the muffled sounds behind him.

"Wait until I get a fire going," Fox snapped. The garbled noises sounded frantic. "It appears you've been there awhile, a few more minutes won't kill you."

Swinging around, Tanner's narrow gaze settled on the two figures on the ground, Hanratty and Peaches, tied hand and foot and gagged. Once Fox had the fire going, flames popped from the fire pit and their faces came into focus. Tanner read resignation in Peaches's black eyes, embarrassment and fury on Hanratty's stony expression.

He ripped a dirty bandanna away from Hanratty's mouth. "What the hell happened here?"

Tight-lipped and squinty-eyed, Fox cut the ropes binding their hands and ankles. Both men stood rubbing their arms and stamping their feet to restart circulation. Fox leveled a furious stare at Peaches. "You're not the guard, I'm not mad at you. Saddle Tanner's bay and my mustang." She spun toward Hanratty. "You, I'd like to shoot."

When Hanratty finished swearing, he met Tanner's icy stare. "There were two of them. Could be the two men who passed us yesterday. They hallooed the camp, came up smiling and friendly, then pulled guns." He rubbed his mouth with the back of his hand. "You can figure the rest. They knew what they were looking for, though. Didn't take anything except the gold and a mule to carry it."

"Where's Brown?"

"The bastard hasn't come back." Hanratty spit and his fists opened and closed.

"I'm guessing they headed west," Fox said as Peaches led the horses up out of the darkness. "Is that right?"

"I didn't see them leave," Hanratty said, rubbing a knot on his forehead.

"They headed west," Peaches confirmed. "Didn't go back through the camp, just lit out from here." He talked while he saddled the horses, describing the thieves. "You'll know 'em when you see 'em. Both are on the small side."

Hanratty swore and looked around for his pistol.

"Both wearing mustaches. One of them is youngish, the other is older and has a scar across here." Peaches drew a line with his finger from eyebrow to jaw. "One's riding a black with a white blaze, the other's riding a dappled gray. They took the mule named Jackie."

"What the hell is this?" Hanratty strode up to the horses then scowled at Peaches. "That isn't my horse."

"You're staying here," Fox said, looking through items of clothing strewn around the campsite. She made a small sound when she found her heavy coat and shrugged into it.

"The hell!"

"You heard what she said." Tanner found his own coat and thrust his arms into the sleeves. His dark eyes glittered in the firelight. "You better hope I recover the gold, Hanratty." Glancing up, he studied a sliver of moon and a bank of black clouds blotting the sky to the northwest. With limited light and a storm coming, progress would be slow. Swearing, he checked his rifle and pistol, watched Fox do the same.

"Better take bedrolls," she said briskly. "We don't know how long this will take."

Tanner knew she was right but he'd been burning to take off from the minute he saw the gold was missing. Impatient, he kicked through the mess littering the ground until he found his bedroll. While he strapped it behind his saddle, he noticed Peaches stuffing cheese and bread and jerky into Fox's saddlebags. He shoved kindling into Tanner's bags. Then Peaches handed them both canteens as they swung into their saddles.

"Be careful," he said to Fox, looking up at her and patting her knee. "There's not enough moonlight to rush this, and you're going to lose the moon in about two hours. I'm guessing the snow will be light, but I've been wrong before."

Tanner told himself he was taking off in two minutes with or without her.

"Don't worry." Fox leaned to touch Peaches's face with the fingers of her gloves, then she adjusted the scarf around her throat. "They aren't traveling fast, not with a mule. And they probably think we won't chase after them tonight because of the storm coming in. We'll get the gold back, Tanner."

Tanner flicked a glance at Hanratty who stood leaning over the fire, his body rigid, staring into the flames. "We'd better."

They rode into the darkness, trotting when Tanner wanted to gallop. "It's too dangerous. There isn't enough light," Fox said as if she'd read his mind. "Plus we can hold this pace longer than we could hold a hard run."

The bowl stretching between the ranges before them opened like a dark void. It seemed impossible that they would ever find two men and a mule in the vast expanse. They didn't even know for certain that the thieves had headed west.

After a few miles, Fox came in close and shouted over the rising wind. She'd guessed his thoughts again. "It's more logical for them to head back west than to try for Salt Lake City. Salt Lake is too far away. You'll see. We'll spot them as soon as it starts to snow."

"That doesn't make sense," Tanner said sharply, pulling his scarf up to cover his chin. The temperature was dropping by the minute but he hardly felt the cold. Fury heated his blood.

"They won't build a fire if they think there's a chance we're after them. We'd see it from miles off. Once it starts snowing, they'll want a fire badly enough to convince themselves that nobody would be fool enough to ride out here in a storm. Plus they'll think the snow hides the fire, which isn't true."

Tanner reined to a halt. Fox trotted past him, pulled up and came back. He waited until she was near enough to hear him over the wind. "I didn't ask you to come. If you want to go back to camp, head on out."

"Why do you think I want to go back?" Genuine puzzlement roughened her voice.

"You said only a fool would ride out here in a storm."

He couldn't see her expression, but he heard the smile in her answer. "That's right. We're a couple of fools who are going to surprise those bastards and get your gold back. Did you feel that?" She brushed a glove across her cheek. "It's starting to snow."

Clouds sailed across the sliver of moon, pitching them into tarry blackness. Tanner hoped to hell that his horse could see better than he could.

Slowly they rode forward, letting the horses pick their way along. The snow felt like a thin fall, but the darkness was so complete that Tanner couldn't be certain. Almost an hour later, he heard Fox give a low shout.

"Look to your right. Do you see that glow?"

He didn't see a damned thing except snow falling past his hat brim. But if she was right, they could easily have ridden past the thieves if the thieves hadn't built a fire. They corrected direction and angled north. Now the snow swirled into his face, sticking to his lashes and brows, but within minutes he, too, spotted a glow through the flakes.

"How far away are they?"

"Not far. I'd guess not more than a mile. How do you want to handle this?"

He'd been thinking about that. "They didn't kill Hanratty and Peaches . . ."

"Because shots would have brought the rest of the camp running to our site."

"I agree. That's the only reason Peaches and Hanratty are alive. We'll give the bastards an opportunity to walk away with their lives, but I doubt they'll take it." He tried to see Fox through the snow and darkness. "You cover me while I walk into their camp. If it's them, I'll take my money. If they object . . ."

"They'll object," Fox stated flatly.

"I know you told Hanratty and Brown that you'd shot a man before. Is that true?"

"Damn it, Tanner. I don't lie." He felt the heat of her anger sweep through the snowflakes. "This is not a good time to make me mad."

"I had to ask." He'd be placing his life in her hands, depending on her to back him up. After a moment's reflection, he decided he would rather have Fox behind him than Hanratty or Brown.

Within minutes of drawing closer he heard voices, another few minutes shaped the voices into words. He glanced toward Fox but didn't speak, wondering if she heard what he did. Two voices, no more.

She nodded then pointed to the ground before she swung out of her saddle, holding her rifle. Quickly, she peeled off her gloves and stuffed them into her coat pocket. Tanner did the same. Apparently she trusted the horses not to run off in the storm.

Bending, they moved forward, progressing from one clump of sage to the next, finally pausing behind a snow-draped tangle of dead brush. The men's voices were clear now, planning tomorrow's route, complaining that the mule slowed them down. Tanner would have known it was them by their conversation even if he hadn't glimpsed the man with the scar.

He stood up straight, letting rage tighten his muscles on a sweep through his body. Letting himself feel the cold inside his mind. Before he stepped forward, he touched Fox's cheek with his fingertips and gazed into her eyes through the falling snow. Their stare held until she brought the rifle up and settled the stock against her shoulder, then Tanner nodded and strode into the outlaws' camp.

He must have looked like an apparition walking out of the snow and wind, his face stony, a gun in his hand.

"Goddamn!" One of the men started badly enough to spill hot coffee on his thigh. "Who the hell are you?"

"It's him," the other one said, jumping to his feet.

Wind tossed the hissing flames in the fire pit, throwing an uncertain light. But it was enough that Tanner spotted the bags of gold.

"I've come for my money," he said, speaking through his teeth. "Put down your weapons and step back and no one will get hurt." They wouldn't, he knew that, but giving them the chance would make remembering easier.

"Look out," the scarred man shouted. "There's another one out there." Both men reached for the pistols on their hips and gunfire exploded.

When the smoke cleared, Tanner ran a swift mental check and decided he hadn't been hit. Both of the outlaws lay sprawled on the ground.

Fox strode into the campsite and kicked the men's guns away from their bodies. "Just in case," she said, gazing down at them. "Bastards!"

"Are they dead?"

"Oh yeah."

The bags were all present. Tanner noticed a type of knot he hadn't seen before, so the thieves had opened one of the bags. The idea of searching a dead man's pockets was repugnant, but not as irksome as counting to discover if all the coins in the opened bag were accounted for. Walking around the fire, he knelt beside one of the bodies and started going through the man's pockets. When he looked for Fox, he saw her holding the thieves saddlebags toward the firelight, looking inside.

"Find anything interesting?" he asked when he'd finished his search.

"One of them is named Alfie Hinton. Don't know which one. One of them saved a Wanted Poster—no drawing of a likeness on it—but the name on the poster is Russell Borden. Either of those names sound familiar to you?" She wiped snow from her cheeks and gazed up at him.

"Alfie Hinton," he repeated slowly. One of the men had recognized Tanner the instant he walked into the camp. "Alfie Hinton. It'll come to me."

"Did you find anything?"

He jingled some coins in his pocket. "Six twenty-dollar gold pieces. I'm betting they're mine." When he raised his head, he noticed Fox had wiped her cheek, leaving a red smear behind. "You're bleeding."

"Am I?" Frowning, she ran her fingertips over her face, throat, and ears. "Damn all! They shot my earlobe!" She looked up at Tanner in astonishment. "I felt something warm trickling on my neck and cheek, but I thought it was melting snow. Those bastards!"

Kneeling beside her, Tanner tilted the left side of her face to the firelight. A bullet had notched the outer edge of her earlobe. He stared at the curved notch without really seeing it, instead he pictured what would have happened if the bullet had been an inch or two closer to her face. Certainly she would have been disfigured, most likely she'd now be dead.

"I'm sorry," he said, his voice gruff.

"What for? You didn't shoot me." She pressed her bandanna against her ear, pulled it back to look at the blood, then held it over her ear again. "I'd say I came out pretty well. Whichever one of them shot me is dead and all I've got is a little cut on my ear."

"It's more than a little cut, there's a piece missing." It surprised him that she wasn't crying from pain or vanity. "Doesn't it hurt?"

"It's starting to," she said, grimacing. "A piece missing, huh? But a small piece, right?"

"Yes."

She felt beneath the bandanna. "Well, it's not too bad," she said finally. "I never cared much about matching earlobes anyhow."

Since it was *her* earlobe, Tanner cared. If someone had to get shot, it should have been him. It was his gold, his father, his problem. Removing his hat, he shook off the snow, then pulled a hand through his hair and swore. This was his fault.

"I think the bleeding's stopped." Fox stood and pushed the bloody bandanna into her coat pocket before she pulled on her gloves. "Let's drag those thieving bastards out of the campsite, then we'll find out if they made decent coffee."

Tanner tried to see her ear through the snow and poor light. Damn it. He was paying Hanratty and Brown to face down any thieves, but it was Fox who got shot.

"Or would you rather ride off about a hundred feet and set up a camp of our own?" Fox asked. "Personally, I'm tired and hungry. Ready for something hot to drink. I don't see the sense in abandoning a perfectly good campsite that's already set up."

He didn't either. The only reason he hadn't made the same suggestion was that he'd thought she might object.

In that uncanny way she had, she seemed to read his thoughts again. "I pride myself on being a practical woman, Mr. Tanner." A thin smile and a shrug finished her declaration.

"Practical women are a blessing." It was possible he even knew another one besides Fox.

Working together they dragged the two thieves away from the campsite. If he found a shovel in camp, Tanner would bury them in the morning. While Tanner brought their horses into the light and removed the saddles and bags, Fox returned to rummaging through the thieves' goods.

"I found a tent. Just one, but it will provide some shelter." Holding the thieves' blankets to the firelight, she examined them for rips and lice then nodded satisfaction before she set up the tent.

Occasionally habit kicked in with a display of manners and Tanner's immediate instinct was to assist her, but he checked the impulse. Whenever he rose when she came to the fire or extended a hand to help her mount or dismount or tried to take over her chores, his reward was a scowl or an eyebrow arched in offense.

Still, he was uncomfortable standing aside and letting a woman erect a tent, no matter how willing or how efficient she might be. His gaze sharpened—it was a small tent, a one-man tent. His mouth tightened as he considered the long night ahead. Fox would take the tent, of course, and he would roll out his blankets near the fire. With luck the wind wouldn't bend the fire to set his blankets aflame, and hopefully he wouldn't get buried in snow.

When Fox joined him at the fire, she handed him one of the thieves' blankets and he followed her example by wrapping the blanket over his hat and around his body. Once they were settled, sitting on a fallen log, he gave her half of the bread and cheese that Peaches had packed, and a strip of jerky. "Their coffee was awful. I made a new batch." Flames licked the bottom of a rusted pot.

They didn't talk while they ate, watching the snow hiss into the fire. Now that he had the gold safely in his possession, Tanner could let himself think about the disaster that would have resulted had they failed to recover the ransom money. His stomach tightened and his eyes narrowed into slits. His father's life depended on getting this gold to Denver.

He poured coffee into cups that Fox had washed out with the snow starting to pile on the ground. "Are you warm enough?" he asked.

"Hell no. Are you? I'm half frozen, but with the wind so high I'm afraid to move closer to the fire." She cupped her gloves around her cup. "Well? Are you going to say it?"

"Say what?"

"That I was right and you were wrong about someone trying to steal the gold."

Fox might not be fragile or dainty, but she was like all other women he'd known in wanting the pleasure of hearing him say he was wrong.

"You were right," he said finally, speaking through his teeth. "Satisfied?"

She grinned at him. "Actually, I'd rather that you'd been right."

"I figured it out. Alfie Hinton was a desk clerk at the St. Charles hotel in Carson. I kept the gold overnight in the hotel's vault. Apparently the manager was indiscreet." He drew a breath of cold air. "As you predicted."

"Are you going to keep Hanratty on the payroll?"

Tanner swallowed a sip of scalding coffee. "He's not the first man to get jumped by bandits," he said eventually. Shifting, he tried to see her face, but the blanket draped over her hat concealed most of her profile.

She nodded slowly. "Stealing the gold from one man, one woman, and an old man with rhumitiz would be as easy as picking seeds out of a melon. There's no way around it—we need Hanratty and Brown."

"It's more dangerous to fire them than to keep them." Which was a problem without a solution.

She nodded, her gaze on the wind-tossed flames. "Maybe Hanratty was humiliated enough over this incident that he won't let it happen again."

The snow appeared to be thicker. Like most spring snows, the flakes were fat and wet, accumulating quickly. Right now it seemed an eon ago that Tanner had been soaking in a steamy tub. The same thought must have occurred to Fox, but she hadn't voiced a complaint.

"Why don't you go ahead and crawl into the tent? Get some sleep." Sleep was the best healing agent Tanner knew. Moreover, she'd planned to turn in early if he remembered correctly. "Fox? You were marvelous tonight." He knew that he hadn't shot both of the outlaws. She'd done her part. "Thank you for coming with me, and I'm sorry as hell that you got shot."

"No thanks necessary," she said, her voice sounding peculiar as it did every time he complimented her. "And it was only a nick. Well, all right, a small chunk that I'll never miss." Raising her cup, she swallowed the last of her coffee before she moved the pot away from the flames. "We'll save the rest for morning. Damn, it's cold." Standing, she pulled the blanket around her and stamped her feet, then she headed toward the tent. "Are you coming?"

"You take the tent. I'll sleep out here"—as soon as he found his bedroll. He hadn't seen it since he took off the saddles.

"Don't be foolish. I put your blankets in the tent."

CHAPTER 8

*F*OX and Tanner quickly discovered the tent was too narrow for them both to lie on their backs. Fox rolled on her side, which brought her nose within two inches of the tent wall. The canvas smelled dank and musty, as if the tent had been put away wet.

Tanner shifted and hunched and finally spooned around her. When Fox gasped and went rigid, he said close to her ear, "This position gives us the most room and will probably be the warmest." After an awkward silence, he added, "But if you'd prefer, I can take my blankets outside and—"

"I told you I'm a practical woman," Fox answered, staring at the tent wall inches from her face. This position was closer to comfortable than anything else they had tried, but . . .

Layers of clothing and blankets bunched between them, nevertheless she could have sworn that she felt every muscle of Tanner's torso. She told herself that was impossible. Then Tanner's gloved hand slipped around the waist of her coat.

"I don't know where else to put it," he explained, sounding irritated.

Through her blankets and his, Fox could feel his knees curved up against hers. His arm was around her in a loose embrace. She licked her lips and swallowed. It had been a couple of years since she had been this intimate with a man.

"There's just no easy way to stuff two people into a one-man tent," she muttered. But he was right about this position being warm. The instant Tanner had curled around her, a wave of heat shot through her body.

"We wouldn't have this problem if I'd brought Hanratty with me."

Because one or both of the men would have slept out in the snow. "Now that I think about it, I just assumed I'd be the one to go. It's my job to get you and the gold to Denver."

"You have a habit of making assumptions."

His warm breath on the back of her neck made her feel dizzy. "I probably should have asked what you wanted before I sent Peaches off to fetch the horses."

"Actually, I was glad to have you along. Until now."

"I know what you mean." She assumed he meant having to share the tent. After a minute she asked, "Is my braid right in your face?"

"It must be off to the side."

His arm tightened around her, pulling her closer into his body, as if he were settling in for sleep. Her fanny cupped up tight against his privates and that was enough to widen Fox's eyes. Every nerve tingled and suddenly she couldn't stop talking.

"Have you ever noticed how everything gets silent when it snows, but even so you think you can hear it falling?" Lord she was babbling, but babble was better than wondering what might be going on with his privates.

"I've noticed," he said, the sound of a smile in his voice. "Is your ear hurting?"

"It smarts a bit," she admitted. "But it isn't too bad." That was also true. "Breaking a leg hurt a lot worse. Knife cuts and burns hurt, too. What's the worst injury you ever had?"

If something was stirring down there in his private region, she suspected Tanner would be embarrassed. If nothing was going on with his privates while they were pressed up against her fanny, then she would be humiliated. Unfortunately, the layer of blankets between them made it impossible to judge what was or was not going on with Tanner's privates.

"The worst injury? Some friends and I were racing gigs. We were young enough and had enough brandy in us to think racing at night wasn't stupid. My rig slid out on a curve, pulled the horse down, and we rolled into a ravine." He was silent a moment. "I broke my collarbone, an ankle, my arm. The worst of it was the horse had to be put down because of my foolishness."

"That's bad," Fox agreed. Putting down a horse was tragic. "Were you ever in a mine cave-in?" She didn't move, not an inch. If she so much as wiggled, he might interpret it as an invitation. Tanner was a gentleman, but in a circumstance like this, misunderstandings could arise—so to speak.

"I've been in a couple of cave-ins. They're heartstopping events."

"Were you injured?"

"I was lucky both times. Do you want to turn the other direction?"

"This is fine. Unless you . . ."

"I'm fine, too.

Actually, lying curled up in his arms was kind of nice. It occurred to Fox that there was no other place she wanted to be at this minute. They were protected from the wind and snow. Matthew Tanner's large hard body spooned around her, his breath flowed warm on her skin. If she cared to, she could pretend that he wanted to be in the tent with her, could imagine that he, too, was having heated thoughts.

"Did you tell me if you were married?" she asked, wondering exactly how compromising this situation was and if the tension she felt should be even worse.

"I've never been married. Damn it, I think my left arm is going to sleep." After he'd shifted and jostled and done something or other, he settled down again.

"So why haven't you married? Seems like you're about the right age. You appear to have money and a decent job." Wind buffeted the tent walls sending waves of musty odor toward Fox's nostrils. She would rather have had her nose pressed to Tanner's neck, inhaling his nice soapy bathhouse scent.

"The only woman I came close to considering was too flamboyant for my father to accept. I thought you were sleepy."

"I was, but now I'm wide awake." She shrugged and instantly regretted it hoping he wouldn't interpret the movement as a subtle hint that she might be open to more. Damn. She wished she knew the condition of his privates so she'd know where she stood. "What does that mean, she was flamboyant?"

"On another subject, why won't you tell me who called Hobbs Jennings a thieving son of a bitch?"

"Why is it important for your father to accept your wife? It's you who has to live with her, not him."

"You're not going to tell me, are you?" An exasperated sigh feathered warm air across Fox's cheek. "First, my father sacrificed a lot for me. I owe him. Second, if I married, my wife and I would probably live with my father."

"That's a terrible plan!" Fox pushed up and tried to glare over her shoulder, but couldn't turn far enough and it was too black inside the tent for him to have seen a scowl anyway. "Your wife married you, not you and your father. You should not make her live in your father's house!"

"Fox, I'm often in the field for months at a time. I won't worry about her if I know she's with my father and taken care of."

"So you'll make *her* miserable because *you* don't want to worry? You selfish bastard!" This time she did manage to sit up and stare down through the darkness.

"That's not it at all, and why do you assume she'd be miserable? She shouldn't have to live by herself for months on end."

"The hell. I'll wager that she prefers to live by herself. You ought to know that every woman deserves her own house and so does your poor wife! And she should not have to play nursemaid to your judgmental father!" God only knew what his father would think about someone like her. Fox would horrify him right down to his toes.

"I didn't say my wife had to play nursemaid," Tanner objected angrily. He managed to sit up, too. "But I don't think she should be expected to take on the responsibility of running a house by herself."

"Oh, so now you're saying this poor woman is too stupid to pay whatever vendors she uses? Or the household help? She can't manage her own house?"

"Damn it! I did not say she was stupid."

"Well, you certainly implied it." Furious on behalf of his wife, she jabbed him in the chest with a finger. "I don't know why she married you! You've denied her a home, foisted her off on your father, gone off and deserted her, and now you're calling her stupid! I'm not staying in this tent one more minute with someone as selfish and indifferent as you are!"

Flinging back her blankets, Fox crawled out of the tent into the snowstorm. Swearing, she realized she'd have to crawl back into the tent to retrieve her hat. Before the thought was fully formed, her hat came sailing out of the flap and landed near her boots. "Thank you," she shouted, jamming the hat on her head. This small act of consideration changed nothing. He was still mistreating his wife.

Except . . .

"Fox?"

When she saw him striding toward her through the falling snow, Fox dropped her forehead into her hand and sucked in a long breath of cold damp air.

He stopped in front of her and planted his fists on his hips. Leaning forward, he glared at her through a veil of snowflakes. "What the hell is going on here? I don't have a wife. I am probably never going to have a wife. I for sure as hell don't want a wife."

"But if you did . . . ," she said weakly. There was no leg to stand on here. "Are you sure about not having a wife?" For a few crazy moments, his wife had seemed so real.

Tanner threw out his hands. "If I did have a wife, I'd want her and my father to like and enjoy each other. Now I don't see anything wrong or unusual about that. These two people would be the only family I have and it's important that they approve of each other and share a mutual respect." He leaned down until they were nearly nose to nose. "Now that's all I'm going to say on the subject of wives."

"There's still the problem of making her live with your father." Fox stared into his eyes, determined not to look away first.

"I am not going to argue about a nonexistent wife who I assure you would be delighted to live with my father." Tanner stared back at her, standing so close that she felt his breath flowing over her lips.

Later she couldn't remember who was first to make the muffled snorting sound of suppressed laughter, but it was contagious. In a moment, they were both laughing like loons, falling on each other, wiping their eyes and laughing until Fox's ribs ached.

"Never in my life have I had such an idiotic argument," Tanner said when he could speak.

"That makes two of us. Lord, my sides hurt from laughing." And she was cold without Tanner wrapped around her. Even so, she was glad to be out of the tent and away from the tension of lying in his arms. Pulling a stick from the pile of dead brush, Fox poked at the coals in the fire pit and fed in twigs and branches until she had the fire blazing again. "I apologize. I think I started that argument. Shall I put the coffeepot back on the fire?"

"Might as well," he said, stepping forward to warm his hands. "I don't think we're going to get much sleep tonight."

Good. She'd feared that he might want to give the tent another try.

They sat on the fallen log, wrapped in blankets with their shoulders pressed together, watching the flames struggle against the falling snow. Fox thought the storm was letting up some, but she couldn't be sure.

"You said your father made sacrifices for you . . . what kind of sacrifices?"

"He wasn't always wealthy," Tanner said after a lengthy hesitation. "It must have been difficult for him to keep me in a private school during the years before he made his fortune. He's never explained exactly what sacrifices were necessary, but it's clear that he made some unpleasant compromises."

"If he did, then education must be important to him." Fox would have given anything to have a formal education. If she ever had a child, she guessed she'd do what Tanner's father had done. She'd make whatever sacrifices were necessary to give her child the best education possible. But of course she would never have children. Her future ended in Denver at the bottom of a rope.

"Absolutely." Tanner smiled at the coffeepot. "But my grades were never good enough. And I didn't appreciate the educational opportunity of touring Europe, not enough to please my father. I had an idea that he sometimes regretted those sacrifices."

Hearing a flatness in his voice, Fox slid him a sidelong glance. "What did he want you to do with all that education?"

"I think he expected me to become an influential and prosperous financier. If not that, then accept a position in the business end of his company."

"You didn't want a position in your father's company?" Fox asked, taking her arms out from under the blanket to reach for the coffeepot. "Why not?"

Tanner held out his cup and took his time answering. "I like working in the field. In fact, I'd rather do something that kept me outside all day. I detest office work. The business side is made up of meetings and paperwork."

"I guess I understand that," Fox said, nodding.

"Eventually I'll get out of engineering. Hunt fossils, maybe. How about you? Is scouting something you always wanted? Something you see yourself continuing to do?"

She almost laughed. What would Tanner think if she confided that she was going to Denver to kill a man? His boss, in fact. He'd be appalled and think she was crazy.

She held a swallow of coffee on her tongue, considering how to answer. "I'm good at scouting," she said finally, "but it's not something a person would want to do forever. This will be my last trip across these mountains and valleys."

"And then what? We talked about a wife for me, is there a future husband waiting in the wings for you?"

Startled, she turned her head to look at him and then laughed. "Now what kind of man would want to marry a woman like me? A man doesn't want a woman who can out-shoot him, outdrink him, outcuss him, and who hasn't worn a corset but twice in her life and who'd rather wear trousers than lady clothes."

"You're not doing yourself justice, Fox." His gaze slipped to her mouth and lingered. "You're a handsome woman, unique and admirable."

As always, compliments made her scowl and feel uncomfortable. She turned her face back to the wavering fire as the conversation dried up between them.

He was partly right, but mostly wrong in what he'd said. There might be a man out there who would marry a woman like her. But he'd be a man living on the fringe, like Cutter Hanratty maybe. He wouldn't be an educated upstanding man like Matthew Tanner. And there was the problem. She'd never been drawn to the men who could accept her as she was. No, the men who set her juices flowing were the men she might have attracted if she'd lived the life that Jennings stole from her. Men so far beyond reach that it hurt to think about.

They finished the coffee and then it was time to make a decision. Brew up another pot or climb back into the cramped tent.

"More coffee?" Fox shifted the choice to him.

Tanner hesitated then nodded.

And Fox wondered what that meant. Did he wish to avoid returning to the tent because his privates responded to her? And that made him uncomfortable? Or was the tent too small for him to find a comfortable position? Did her neck smell peculiar? Was she talking so much that he couldn't get to sleep? She sort of hoped the reason had to do with his privates.

On the other hand, she felt enormously relieved. Why torture herself when she didn't have to?

"It's going to be a long night," she remarked, building up the fire. Cold and uncomfortable. "So," she said, settling back on the log and leaning lightly against his shoulder. "Show me the constellations. Peaches says you know constellations he's never heard of."

"Excuse me?" A shine of amusement twinkled in his eyes. "It's still snowing in case you haven't noticed."

"It's starting to thin out some." She let a smile twitch her lips. "Besides, Peaches claims you're good enough that you could point out constellations on a cloudy night."

He laughed then extended his arm through the falling snow, pointing at the sky. "The Big Dipper should be about there."

Fox leaned her head against his shoulder and sighted up his arm. "I know about the Big Dipper. Show me one I don't know."

"How about Cassiopeia?"

"That sounds sort of familiar, but if so I've forgotten. Show me where it is and tell me about it."

At some point before dawn, the snow stopped and Fox fell asleep sitting in front of the fire with her head on Tanner's wide shoulder, her head full of imagined stars and the very real man who slipped his arm around her waist.

Even if Tanner had found a shovel in the outlaws' camp, the ground was frozen and digging two graves would have been difficult and time consuming. Instead, he and Fox collected stones and covered the outlaws' bodies as best they could.

"Do you have any objection to turning their horses loose?" Fox asked him. "Or do you want to take them back to the mining camp?"

The animals were young and in good condition. They would probably fetch a decent price. But Tanner also knew Nevada was home to herds of wild horses. "Set them free."

Fox slapped the thieves' horses on the rump and watched them trot down the snowy valley. "Is there anything you want here?"

Tanner scanned the tent and the thieves' saddles and saddlebags. "Just my gold." He secured the bags on the mule's back, then swung up on the bay. Fox was already mounted and waiting, smothering a yawn.

They held the horses and mule to a steady pace, glad when the sun topped the mountains and climbed a clear sky. By early afternoon when they rode into their camp at the mining site, the sun had burned off all but the snow lying in shadowed patches.

Hanratty and Brown watched them ride in, relief easing their expressions when they spotted Jackie the mule.

Beaming, Peaches came forward to take the animals. "Knew you'd find those bastards," he said to Fox. Then he spotted the blood on her coat and a frown flew to her ear. "While I'm taking care of the horses, you find my doctor kit."

"All I need is some sleep."

After giving his reins to Peaches, Tanner studied his guards coldly. Both men looked as mauled as they had after the fight at Fort Churchill. Cuts, knuckle scrapes, and Jubal Brown had a black eye. From the looks of them, Brown had taken the worst of it.

"No thanks to either of you, we retrieved the cargo." Hanratty and Brown started to talk at once, but Tanner held up a hand. "From now on, you both stay with the cargo. No more going into any town we camp near. No more taking turns for some time off. You were hired as guards and that is your only concern. So far I don't see either of you taking that responsibility as seriously as I'm paying you to."

"Anybody can be jumped by bandits," Hanratty insisted hotly. He turned a stare on Jubal Brown. "If you'd come back when you were supposed to, things would have gone differently."

"Oh yeah?" Brown sneered. "Are you claiming that you would have stayed here and refused your turn up at the saloons?"

"Do you want another beating?" Hanratty threatened with a snarl. "If you do, I'm ready."

Tanner gazed at them with disgust. "If you've changed your mind about this job, or if it's too much for you, you can both leave right now. If you stay, I expect you to earn your pay." His eyes glittered. "That means this cargo never leaves your sight. Do you both understand that?"

They stared at him, angry, embarrassed by the incident, resentful.

"I need a wash," Jubal Brown said. "What am I supposed to do? Take the cargo with me to the washhouse?"

Tanner bit down on his back teeth. "You can have your wash." He saw Hanratty still staring and realized the conditions he'd set were too restrictive. "Both of you need a wash.

Hanratty goes first. When a reason arises that absolutely requires one of you to leave the campsite, you may do so if Fox or myself is here to take your place. There should be a least two men guarding the cargo at all times. Mr. Hernandez is not a guard."

Later, after having a bite to eat and after watching Peaches wash and treat Fox's ear before she crawled into her small tent, Tanner realized he'd lumped her in as one of the two "men" authorized to guard the gold.

As he knew, she was anything but a man. Frowning, he sipped his coffee and stared at her tent. Logic insisted it was only his imagination, but he could swear that he'd felt the rounded fullness of her breasts through the material of her heavy coat. And the blankets between them had not prevented a painful erection when her fanny moved up against him. He didn't know if she'd been oblivious to the situation, or if she'd noticed but was determined to politely ignore his loss of control.

One thing he did know: Holding Fox in his arms, smelling the soapy warm scent of her skin, had lifted his fascination for her to another degree. Underneath that rough exterior was a woman in hiding and she had seized his imagination.

Jubal Brown sidled over and sat down beside him, holding out a cigar. "The man I won these off of said they came all the way from New York City."

"Thank you." Tanner lit the cigar, nodded, then waited to hear what was on Brown's mind.

"She's missing part of her ear," Brown said, tilting his chin toward Fox's tent. "She get shot?"

Tanner nodded, his jaw stiff. "It wouldn't have happened if you and Hanratty had done your job."

"How much of a Yankee are you?"

"I'm not part of your war, Brown. I'm not even very interested in it. Whatever happens is going to happen a couple thousand miles from here."

"But you sympathize with the Union."

"I'd hate to see this land broken into two countries. If that happens, the west will probably form a separate country, too. I think that's wrong. I think America will be stronger as one country."

"But you don't believe that enough to put on a uniform and fight."

Tanner's eyes narrowed and his mouth went hard. "The

Union needs gold and silver to finance this war. Keeping the mines working is my contribution."

Brown blew a smoke ring in the direction of Tanner's saddle. "Getting paid pretty well for that contribution, seems to me."

"If you're trying to say something, just say it."

"I want to know the truth about that gold." Brown's voice went low and coarse. " 'Cause what you said about finances is true. Both sides need every cent they can get. It occurs to me that fifty thousand dollars would buy a lot of Union horses and uniforms."

"You think I'm taking this gold to Denver to give it to the Union?" His smile didn't reach his eyes. "I almost wish that were true. But it isn't. The gold is ransom money."

"That's what you say . . ."

Standing, Tanner flipped the cigar away and gave Jubal Brown a cold glance. "If you can't trust my word, then walk out of here right now." Not looking back, he moved closer to the fire and sat on a stump across from Peaches. "How bad was her ear?"

"Not too bad. Folks don't need earlobes anyway. Don't serve any purpose that I can think of." Peaches smiled down at the saddle blanket he was mending. "I take it those two outlaws aren't going to steal any more gold?"

"You take it right." Tanner helped himself to the coffee on the fire, hoping it would keep him awake until dark. "What happened between Hanratty and Brown?"

"Mr. Hanratty was not pleased by the robbery or by being left behind. When Mr. Brown returned to camp, there was a discussion over who was to blame for the turn of events." Peaches lifted the blanket to his mouth and bit off the thread. "After the fight, Mr. Hanratty went into town, if you can call it that, and didn't return until this morning. In a way, I'm glad the fight happened. It's been coming."

Tanner agreed. Maybe now the two would settle down and stop sniping at each other. If they stayed on the job. "Do you think either of them will quit?" he asked Peaches curiously.

"Mr. Brown will stay because he's heading east anyway. Mr. Hanratty will stay because he isn't going to allow Mr. Brown to look like the better man."

Those were Tanner's thoughts in a nutshell. "How are you feeling?"

The old man's head jerked upward and Tanner wondered if

he'd offered offense. "I'm fine," Peaches said shortly. "Why wouldn't I be?"

"You look tired. And the chest congestion isn't clearing up." Until today, Tanner had tended to forget Peaches's age, but today Peaches appeared less vigorous than he ordinarily did.

" 'Course I'm tired, after being up most of the night worrying." Peaches turned his head toward Fox's tent.

"There wasn't much to worry about. Those outlaws didn't stand a chance. One of them got off a wild shot as he went down, but aside from that Fox was never really in danger." He put a shine on the story for Peaches, but not by much.

Peaches met his eyes. "I wasn't worried about outlaws, Mr. Tanner."

"Then what?"

Peaches didn't speak for a full minute. "If you look at her or listen to her, you'd think nothing could ever pierce that armor. You'd think there's nothing inside her that's soft enough to crack or break. But you'd be wrong."

Tanner's brow lifted. He hadn't anticipated this.

"A man like you, I 'spect you're used to sophisticated ladies with enough experience to recognize the difference between flattery and courting. I 'spect you're used to enjoying a woman and walking away without a backward glance. I 'spect you never have to worry 'bout killing a woman inside her mind. And that's fine . . . as long as you stick to professional ladies or experienced ladies of your own kind."

Tanner stared. Peaches was warning him away from Fox, reminding him that Fox wasn't his kind, telling him not to break her heart or some such thing.

"Put your mind at ease, Mr. Hernandez," he said gruffly. "I admire and respect Fox but that's as far as it goes."

"I'm not worried about your side of it."

There was nothing to say to that, so he walked out to check on the horses and mules.

Something had changed last night. The result was he and Fox were easier, more comfortable with each other. Yes, he'd had that moment in the tent of wanting her, but there was more to last night than the strong sexual acceleration.

Still, he believed he understood what Peaches was saying. Fox really wasn't his kind of woman, he couldn't argue that point. Leaning against the side of her mustang, he shook his head and smiled, imagining himself introducing Fox to his father. His father would be shocked. The society his father moved in would never accept Fox into their midst. She would be a scandal.

Tanner couldn't possibly pursue Fox for anything more than a brief trip-long fancy. And that wasn't fair to her, he understood that without Peaches having to raise the point. Regrettably, Fox wasn't suitable for anything more.

The problem was he hadn't been drawn this strongly to any woman, ever. The women he might be expected to wed were pale shadows, and he'd thought so before he met Fox. Now that he knew Fox existed, he couldn't conceive of himself spending an evening in bland conversation with a pastel creature who stood ready to faint at the sight of a blood drop or at the hint of a body part.

So where did that leave him? Bored with his own kind, as Peaches phrased it, and aware that the unique and interesting and challenging women were totally unsuitable for a man of his background and family.

A man like Matthew Tanner didn't bring home a woman who could shoot an outlaw dead, then calmly sit down and drink the outlaw's coffee and sleep in his tent.

He shook his head and kicked at the dirt. Fox was some kind of woman, all right. Unfortunately, they lived in different worlds.

CHAPTER 9

No one was happy.

The fistfight between Hanratty and Brown did not settle their competitiveness as Fox had hoped it might. If anything, they both seemed determined to needle each other more than before. Even Peaches the eternal optimist seemed to have a bee in his bonnet about something. He'd kept to himself the past two nights, turning aside any offers for chess or checkers. When Fox caught him watching her, his expression was sober and concerned but he wouldn't explain himself even after she badgered him to tell her why he was looking at her like he was worried that she was getting sick.

The biggest puzzle was Tanner. Fox had returned from their raid on the outlaws feeling as if she and Tanner had forged a new understanding. They had argued; they had laughed. They had each let their guard down. They had communicated in a manner they had been unable to do before. She'd returned to their campsite feeling comfortable with and about Matthew Tanner, and she had liked that feeling as much as she liked remembering his arm pulling her in close to his body.

By the next morning everything had changed. And that stung. Fox had expected their camaraderie to continue. She had expected to enjoy Tanner's company on the trail. But it didn't happen that way.

Granted, Fox was not good company immediately after waking, but until now Tanner had tried to be. Yet the last two mornings he'd been as surly and unapproachable as Fox.

On this stretch of terrain the going was hard. Steep canyons blocked their path and narrow passes appeared that demanded single-file travel. There were, however, valleys and plateaus where Fox could have ridden beside Tanner for a bit of conversation had he been willing. To her surprise, he'd been cool and unwelcoming. At the midday break he spent the hour with Hanratty and Brown, ignoring Fox as if he'd forgotten she was present. In the evenings he sat close to the firelight, withdrawing into a book and turning aside any attempts at conversation.

On the third night out of the mining camp, Fox halted early enough to allow Hanratty to hunt for fresh meat. Before he rode out, he tossed Jubal Brown a triumphant smirk.

"How come you sent him?" Brown inquired, swinging off his horse and glaring after the coil of dust that followed Hanratty. "Is it because I got eliminated from the shooting contest? I was just having a bad day."

"You'd complain if I sent you, and you'd complain if I didn't," Fox snapped, handing Peaches her reins. She would like to have sent Brown off to gather piñon nuts, to get him out of camp and away from her, but it was too early in the year for nuts. "Do you think you could get a fire started without grousing about it?"

At this altitude the sun felt thin and weak. Drifts of snow lingered under rock overhangs and vegetation was sparse. On the positive side, the spring Fox remembered was running and the water was clear and as sweet as any they'd had so far.

"Thank you," she said, extending her hands to the fire that Brown finally coaxed to life. God forbid he should start the coffee. "Remind me," she said, her lips pulling down. "How many servants did you have when you were growing up?"

"No sense getting pissy at me because you've had a falling out with your gentleman friend."

Fox wanted to punch the sly smile off his face for the sheer pleasure of hitting someone. Right now, Jubal Brown was the someone she most wanted to hit.

Taking her time, she poured water from a bucket into the coffeepot, then added grounds. "I don't know what the hell you're talking about so just shut up." But of course she did. And it made her angrier to learn she wasn't the only one to notice Tanner's coolness.

Lifting her head, she scanned the campsite and finally spotted Tanner helping Peaches unload the mules. The sight irritated her. Tanner should have put Brown to the task rather than doing it himself.

"Who's cooking tonight?" Brown crossed his arms over his chest and adjusted his back against his saddle. His hat brim was pulled low and Fox couldn't see his eyes.

"I think it's my turn." Peeling onions and potatoes would give her something to occupy her hands other than mending, which she'd told herself she needed to do soon. She'd noticed a couple of loose buttons and a tear in her favorite shirt. "So don't talk to me. I don't like to talk while I'm cooking."

"Tell me what you're going to cook, then I'll shut up."

"I'll cook whatever Hanratty brings back." While she waited she could start peeling the onions and potatoes, and rolling out some biscuits.

"Seems we're making good time the last few days," Peaches remarked, settling down nearby to repair Tanner's bridle.

Fox didn't see where Tanner had gone. "I was glad to find this campsite, it's been a while since I was here last. We'd have lost time if I'd wound up a bit north at the alkali flats."

"I swear I don't know how you do it, Missy, but somehow you manage to find the passes that will save us from having to cross the summits of some mighty tall peaks. How high are we now? About eight thousand feet? That's as high as I want to go."

Fox scraped the peelings into a pile that she would bury later along with any leavings from supper. "All right, what's on your mind?"

Peaches blinked innocently. "What makes you think I got anything on my mind?"

"You don't pass out compliments unless it's to soften up a person for something that person isn't going to like to hear." She pressed the open end of a coffee cup on the biscuit dough she'd rolled out, then slapped the round on a baking sheet. "So?"

Late afternoon sunlight slanted over the peaks behind them, shimmering in a last burst of light and warmth. Fox remembered Peaches looking glossy and vigorous in this kind of light, but today his skin looked dull and the wrinkles seemed more prominent.

"Hey, old man," she said in a soft voice. "How are you feeling?"

A frown of indignation tugged his eyebrows. "I'm at the

top of the cream, Missy. Not a thing wrong here that a good night's sleep won't cure."

"Then I hope you catch a good night's sleep," she said after a minute. Before she let herself go down for the night, she always checked on Peaches, and thus far she hadn't noticed that he'd experienced any problem going to sleep. She studied the tone of his skin and the slope of his shoulders and decided that one of the younger men would lead Peaches's string of mules for a few days. "So what's on your mind? Why've you been looking at me like you're seeing something no one else does?"

"Well, you know I don't agree with what you're planning to do when we reach Denver." He held the bridle closer to his eyes and squinted. "And you know I was hoping something would happen on this journey to change your mind."

Fox rolled her eyes toward the sky. "I bought you spectacles not two months ago. And I know I packed them in your saddlebags. Now, why aren't you wearing them?"

"Has anything happened to change your mind about what you're planning to do in Denver?"

"No." As soon as she finished rolling out the biscuits, she'd search for his spectacles.

"You sure about that, Missy?"

She knew what he was talking about and heat flooded her cheeks. Irritated, she flipped her braid over her shoulder. "Nothing's going on that a preacher couldn't watch."

"Uh huh." Lifting the hem of his shirt, he polished the bridle buckles. "Remember when we lived with your mother's cousin?"

"I wish I didn't, but I do." The only thing good about that experience had been meeting Peaches.

"Remember when Miz Wilson ordered you to stir up a cake or a batch of cookies? And then when they were baked, you weren't allowed to eat any."

Fox dusted flour off her hands. "What's the point of this?"

"It hurts to touch, smell, and work with something you can't have. Remember?"

She met his level gaze and held it for a long moment. "Just once I'd like to have something that I really want," she said in a low voice. "I don't want it forever and all time, I know that's beyond reach. But just for a little while . . ."

"Would one bite of the cookie have satisfied you? Or would learning how it tasted have made not having more even worse?"

Tanner returned to camp, examining a chunk of rock in his hand. Looking up, he nodded at them then headed toward the tents they had set up to make the night a little warmer.

"I don't know," Fox whispered, watching the way he walked, the swing of his hips and shoulders. "I just know I want this cookie even if it's only a small taste."

Peaches pushed to his feet and looked down at the bridle, then he sighed and squeezed Fox's shoulder before he left to check on the horses and mules.

When she lowered her hand from her forehead, she spotted Jubal Brown watching from beneath his hat brim. "Were you eavesdropping?"

Grinning, he raised both hands. "Will you give me a beating if I say yes?"

Fox tried to remember exactly what she and Peaches had said. Nothing specific that she could recall.

"Don't worry," he said, his grin widening. "I was dozing until a minute ago. All I heard was something about cookies. Are you going to bake cookies?" He sounded hopeful.

"You could have heard every word for all I care." A shrug punctuated the lie. She wished Hanratty would come back so she could get supper over with and crawl into her tent. Her energy seemed lowest at altitude.

"You don't like me much, do you?"

Fox glanced at him, but didn't answer.

"Is it because I'm a Confederate?"

"I told you. The war isn't real to me."

"Are you mad because the gold got stolen? That was Hanratty's fault, not mine."

Fox rocked back on her heels and examined him. Long, lean, and good-looking in a rough unpolished way. Two days of not shaving had given him a thin beard that made him appear a bit older. Fox had to remind herself he was a killer with the morals of a slug.

"I'd like you better if you complained less and helped out more."

"You'd like me better if I was rich and had the manners of a duke." Settling back against the saddle, he tugged his hat brim back down over his eyes. " 'Course if I was a rich duke, I'd stop watching your butt and go find me a fancy lady wearing silk and dripping perfume."

"Did I mention coarse and vulgar?" Fox snapped. "I'd like you marginally better if you displayed even a hint of manners."

"Like you're accustomed to fine manners."

Grinding her teeth together, Fox flicked a glance at Tanner's tent, then cut the potatoes into small pieces and dropped them and the onions into a pot of spring water that she hung over the fire. Maybe she didn't know chapter and verse about manners, but she could appreciate someone who did.

"Do you think Tanner's pa really got himself kidnapped?"

Fox's head jerked up in surprise. Brown's face was covered by his hat and she couldn't see his expression. "Why on earth would you ask such a peculiar question?"

"Maybe we're enduring all this aggravation for a whole different reason altogether."

"Such as?" She had no idea what he was implying.

"Tanner's a Union man, ain't he?"

She considered his comment and the direction it pointed. "Forget it. If Tanner wanted to send money to the Union, it would have been closer to take the gold to San Francisco. He could have been there and back by now."

"Maybe there's some reason he has to take the gold to Denver."

"That doesn't make sense."

"And it doesn't make sense that kidnappers would hold his pa for three fricking months. If I was the kidnapper I wouldn't mess with some old guy for three months. I'd shoot him and be done with it."

Fox glanced toward Tanner's tent and lowered her voice. "I hope not, but maybe that's what's happened. Tanner will pay the ransom but his father is dead."

Jubal Brown thumbed up his hat. "If the old man is dead, then why wait three months for the money? If it was me, I'd send a telegram saying I had the old man, wire fifty thousand within a week or the old man dies. And I'd shoot him anyway. But the whole thing would be over in a week. Not strung out for months."

Fox wished he hadn't put this idea in her head. Biting her lips, she frowned at Tanner's tent, seeing him sitting inside studying the rock he'd brought back. Would he use his father to cover some other reason for taking the gold to Denver?

"Well, it's not you who kidnapped Tanner's father. Obviously, the men who did kidnap him have their reasons for doing it this way. It's probably safer for them than putting their names in a telegram."

Brown made a sound of disgust. "They wouldn't use their real names."

"Even so." She was glad to spot Hanratty riding toward camp with a small deer draped over his horse's rump. "I have no reason to disbelieve what Tanner's told us. As far as I'm concerned, that's the end of it."

But she wondered. And all through supper, she watched Tanner holding his platter of hot venison apart from the rest of them, asking herself if he might have lied about his father being kidnapped.

Along about midnight, she stopped staring at the peak of her tent and decided Brown's suspicion was nonsense. Matthew Tanner was an honorable man. But what if . . . ?

His reason spoke to his character. If he was pushing to reach Denver to rescue his father, then he was admirable, a devoted son, a man of loyalty whom one could trust. If he had lied about his father and the gold was for the war effort or some other secretive thing, then Tanner was a liar, a deceiver, and without conscience about using his father to gain undeserved sympathy.

That was not possible.

Shifting on her side, she heaved a sigh. She longed for Matthew Tanner's touch, burned for him. But he was avoiding her. She didn't like it much, but the thought occurred to her that she might have to take matters into her own hands.

The next few days were uneventful. By now crossing creeks and ascending or descending treacherous slopes had become as routine as setting up camp in the evenings. It was cold on the peaks, warmer in the valleys. One day a heavy morning snow turned into cold rain by afternoon and they rode hunched over, grinding their teeth and enduring the misery. But by and large they had been lucky with weather.

Hanratty and Brown complained of boredom and the sameness of peaks, valleys, and overarching sky. Tanner suspected the two would have been lost in half a day as they clearly lacked the keen eye for landmarks that Fox possessed.

So far, Fox had stumbled only once, leading them to the edge of a deep, steep-sided gully that the animals couldn't cross. As a result, they'd lost several hours to the necessity of riding around the gully. Otherwise, she had been on target. In the morning she generally announced where they were heading and how long she estimated it would take, and then she unerringly led them to the campsite she'd selected.

Tanner would have liked to ask how long it had been since she'd previously taken the direct route, and what landmarks did she key off of. Did she remember the route in total, or did she recall the terrain as the bowls and peaks unrolled before her?

But Peaches's words had stuck in his mind. He admired Fox enough that he didn't wish to take any advantage that might cause her grief at the end of the journey.

So he'd kept his distance, curtly turning aside any approach she made. That wasn't easy because it wasn't what he wanted.

Right now he sat beside the campfire, brooding and watching her brush out her hair with the same intensity as he'd watched her wash her face and throat. Every evening she went through these woman routines, and every evening they fascinated him. Before she crawled into her bedroll, she'd rub something on her face and then she'd sniff her bedtime gloves with a pinched expression before she put them on and settled down for sleep.

That was another thing he wished he could ask. Why did she wear gloves to sleep in?

"Mr. Tanner?" Peaches asked for the second time. "Would you be interested in a game of checkers?"

The other men had their backs to Fox and didn't see her brushing out long wavy lengths of auburn hair. But Tanner understood that Peaches knew what he was watching.

"Not tonight, thanks." Standing, he stretched his neck against his hand and examined the sky in the fading light. There were no clouds, just a slice of moon. "I think I'll take one of the lanterns to my tent and read a while."

Spring rains often came at night and they had decided to accept the aggravation of setting up the tents rather than risk waking up soaking wet.

Crawling inside, he lay on top of his bedroll with the lantern positioned above his shoulder, his head propped on a couple of the bank bags. He'd just opened the book he was reading when Fox shouted outside his tent flap.

"Get out of that tent!"

He burst outside in one fluid motion, his gun ready in his

hand. "What's happened?" A swift glance around the site didn't reveal anything amiss. The men drinking coffee at the fire smiled. Smirked was more like it. Except for Peaches, who watched Fox with a frown.

The last glow of sunlight lit her face, still rosy from a wash with cold spring water. Tonight her eyes were more gray than blue, but throwing off sparks like two rocks struck together.

"I've had enough. We need to talk." She scowled and jerked her thumb toward the men at the campfire. "Not around them. In private." Without waiting for a response, she stomped off toward a stand of juniper.

Tanner noticed the sway of her poncho skimming the top of her fanny, but her long braid wasn't moving much. This meant that she held her neck rigid, which in turn meant that she was angry.

Not liking the situation, he followed her around the juniper until the men at the fire were blocked from sight. And he reminded himself that Fox's anger was often puffed up to conceal a streak of vulnerability.

"What's on your mind?"

She didn't let him finish the question before she was up on tiptoe, hands on hips, speaking inches from his face.

"You can ignore me if you want to, and I don't give a damn. But it's eating my liver that I got myself shot in your service and you don't have the decency to inquire how I'm feeling or healing." She pointed a finger at her earlobe.

"Mr. Hernandez has kept me informed." It looked to him as if her earlobe was healing nicely, the edges knitting together. There was a small half circle of missing lobe, but the wound seemed on the mend.

"Didn't it occur to you that maybe *I'd* like to know that you were at least a little interested in the welfare of an employee who gave up an earlobe in an effort to recover *your* gold?"

Referring to herself as an employee startled him as he didn't think of her that way. "Mr. Hernandez assures me that he's been dosing you with preventatives against fever and further that he believes you're now beyond the danger point. He also reports there is no sign of infection. Is that true?"

She narrowed flashing eyes. "Yes," she said finally. "But my ear could have gotten infected and I could have died from fever."

"But you didn't."

"No thanks to any concern on your part!"

He saw it now. She'd induced the anger so he wouldn't guess that his apparent indifference cut her. As the worst of the storm seemed to have passed, he cautiously removed a cigar from his waistcoat pocket and offered it to her. After a hesitation she accepted, and they smoked in silence, gazing at the stars appearing overhead.

"I apologize for not seeming to care about the loss of your earlobe," Tanner said, exhaling a stream of smoke. "I assure you that was and is not the case. I'm deeply grateful and indebted to you for your valor and sacrifice in recovering the gold. And I'm sorry that you got shot."

"Are you poking fun at me?" she asked suspiciously.

"Not at all." He felt her waiting. Felt the closeness and night heat of her body. She had replaited her hair, but the image of her brush sweeping through long silky strands stayed in his mind. He frowned and gazed into the distance. "I've been keeping to myself because it seems best for all concerned." That was the question she wanted answered, but damn it, men were not good at this sort of thing.

"I'd say 'all concerned' means you and me," she said after a minute. "So why is it 'best' that we ignore each other?"

He examined the glowing end of his cigar, glad it was dark. "I'm attracted to you, Fox." He cleared his throat. "Once or twice I've had a fancy that perhaps you might be attracted to me, too." She didn't confirm or deny his guess. "It strikes me that mistakes could happen. Circumstances might lead to a situation that couldn't end well."

"I guess I know what you're referring to," she said, speaking slowly.

"Then you'll understand why I've kept some distance rather than make an uncomfortable situation more difficult."

She shifted and he could have sworn that he smelled bacon. It seemed a strange time of night for the men at the campfire to be frying bacon, but they must have been.

"I enjoyed that night in the outlaws' camp," she said finally. "Well, not all of it. Not getting my earlobe shot off, or freezing, but you understand what I mean. Don't you?"

He did. In years to come when he thought of this journey, that was one of the nights he would remember. He hoped by then he'd remember things about that night other than feeling the heat of her body curving into his, other than the warm sweet scent of her skin next to his nose.

"I liked being with you," she said in a voice so low that he had to lean to hear her. "Other than Peaches, there aren't many men I've laughed with."

The comment seemed odd and almost sad until it occurred to Tanner that he hadn't laughed with many women. Over time he had concluded that in general men and women were not amused by the same things. But that night in the outlaw camp he and Fox had laughed together and shared an intimacy that he'd been reluctant to admit.

"I liked being with you, too," he said. "That's the problem."

They stood shoulder to shoulder, smoking, looking into the darkness as if there were something to see out there. Even if there had been, Tanner wouldn't have noticed. His awareness was centered on the woman standing beside him, wondering where this talk was leading.

"Let me make sure I understand. You're keeping to yourself because talking to me and being near me would . . . what?"

This was the most awkward conversation he'd had. He wasn't accustomed to plainspoken women. On the one hand, plainspoken was refreshing. On the other hand, with subtlety and nuance, one didn't have to state the truth in bald terms.

"I don't want to spend this whole journey speculating about taking you to bed," he said, angry that she'd made him say it straight out.

"And when you talk to me, that's what you think about?" She sounded surprised and delighted.

Frowning, he tried to see her expression through the shadows. If he had spoken this bluntly to any other woman, she would have slapped his face and stormed away, never to speak to him again.

"This is not an appropriate conversation, and I apologize."

"Oh for God's sake." Fox dropped her cigar and ground it out under her boot heel. "We're making progress, so don't go hiding behind manners before we finish this."

People did hide behind manners, she was right. Thinking about it, he put out his cigar, too, then turned and clasped her shoulders.

"Listen to me, Fox. I think about you all the time, and that isn't good."

"Why not?"

"It could lead to taking advantage. That wouldn't be fair to you as I can't offer you a future." How blunt should he be? Knots ran up his jaw. "Our worlds are too different." She was smart. He didn't have to state that she wouldn't fit in society, wouldn't enjoy the restrictions his class placed on women.

"I know that."

His fingers tightened on her shoulders. "All I can offer is a trip-long romp." He let the stark words hang for a moment. "That is not honorable or right, and it isn't fair to you."

It crossed his mind that less than a foot separated them. If she stepped forward, she would be in his arms. Instantly his stomach tightened.

She stiffened beneath his hands on her shoulders. "First, I know what my future is going to be and that's what I want, so you don't have to worry about me and the future. You aren't part of my plans. Second, you don't get to decide what's fair or right for me, Tanner. That's *my* decision. Third, you're offering a chance to scratch a temporary itch. Well, maybe I'm feeling that itch, too."

It took a moment, but it dawned on him that Fox was rejecting his argument. In fact, she appeared to encourage the idea of a temporary liaison. "Good Lord," he said softly, straining to see the pale oval of her face.

"I'll say it right out," she whispered. "I wouldn't mind you pursuing me."

He had to make certain that she understood. "If we embark on . . ." What could he call it? "A liaison, we both have to accept that it ends when we arrive in Denver. I can't offer anything permanent."

"Your daddy would never approve."

He heard the smile in her voice but didn't share it. "No, I guess he wouldn't." He knew damned well his father wouldn't approve of Fox. That was not his primary reason for a temporary liaison, but it was there. "We can enjoy each other for the duration of the journey if you're agreeable, but that's all."

Surely there could be no misunderstanding. But he sounded cold and calculating, the way he imagined a womanizing cad operated. He was telling her that he was willing to use her on this trip, then toss her away when he reached Denver. Disgust rose in his throat and he dropped his hands from her shoulders and turned aside.

"This isn't right. Not for either of us." It was a struggle, but he managed to do the honorable thing, say the right words. "Let's forget this conversation and return to the fire."

"Now don't be a damned fool. We've just about got this deal negotiated. What about Hanratty and Brown? We're too small a party for them not to notice what's going on. That has to be addressed."

A laugh rolled out of his chest before he could stop it. That she believed they were negotiating the terms of an affair astonished him, until he realized that's exactly what they were doing. "There is absolutely no one like you," he said softly.

She stepped backward. "Don't go sweet-talking me until we get this worked out."

"Hanratty and Brown," he repeated, smiling in the darkness. "I don't give a damn what they think."

"Peaches will know, too," she said, dragging the words out.

"He won't approve. Does that upset you?" he asked curiously.

"Peaches is worried that I'll get hurt."

"I'm worried about that, too."

"Don't flatter yourself, mister."

Tanner imagined he saw her chin come up.

"Maybe it's you who'll get your heart broken, not me."

In an odd way, he thought, startled, she might be right. Not only was Fox a woman he could never have, but she represented a life Tanner would never know. Total independence and the freedom to live as she pleased, go where she pleased, do as she pleased without answering to anyone.

"Now, to summarize. I believe we've agreed that you'll stop keeping your distance, that you'll pursue and catch me. Is that correct?"

God help him. "That's correct."

"We will enjoy each other, as you put it, for the duration of the journey then part forever in Denver. No hard feelings on either side. Correct?"

"That's how it has to be."

"Good!" She thrust out her hand and Tanner gripped it before he realized what he was doing. "It's a bargain." Sounding pleased, she gave his hand a vigorous shake. "Let's go see if there's any coffee left."

They had shaken hands to seal their agreement to have an affair. Tanner looked down at his hand and shook his head, then followed the sway of her poncho around the stand of juniper and back to the campfire. Their love affair, if he could call it that, was off to a hand-shaking strange start.

Fox halted near the fire and narrowed her eyes on the men. "Me and Tanner are going to have us a liaison. If you have a problem with that, say so now."

And things were getting stranger. Tanner rolled his eyes, then looked at the men. They stared back at him with appraising glances.

"What exactly is a liaison?" Hanratty asked, shifting his gaze to Fox.

"You're a grown-up man, you ought to know." Fox sounded disgusted.

"Ah," Hanratty said, informing her that he was fooling with her. "That kind of liaison." He tilted his head. "Suppose I said I have a problem with that plan. What would you do?"

Tanner stepped up beside Fox. "I'd tell you to go to hell."

Jubal Brown laughed. "That's going to happen anyway." Standing, he stretched and looked toward the bedrolls. "I'm calling it a night."

"I think I'll turn in, too," Fox said, smothering a yawn. "It's going to be a long day tomorrow."

She looked up at Tanner and firelight softened her face. For the first time, he saw a flash of shyness and vulnerability in her eyes and his anger faded. Her instinct was correct. The men would have known, there was no point trying to make a secret of something that would be obvious.

She cleared her throat. "I feel like I ought to say something, but I don't know what to say." Looking flustered, she pressed her lips together then groped for his hand and gave him another vigorous handshake. "It's a deal. And I'm very pleased about our liaison."

He didn't know what to say either, particularly with an audience grinning and listening to every word. "I'm pleased, too," he muttered, feeling like an idiot.

Peaches was the last to leave the campfire. His black eyes bored holes in Tanner's forehead. "If you hurt her," he said softly, "I won't rest until you pay for it."

Then Peaches walked away leaving Tanner alone, looking into the dying flames.

He had just committed to a public love affair with a woman

he hadn't yet kissed. Hell, he didn't even know how they had gotten into the subject or agreed to have an affair. After a time, he tilted his head up to the stars and smiled. Fox was unlike any woman he had ever known. Why had he imagined that a liaison with her would follow an ordinary course?

CHAPTER 10

*F*ox guided the party southeast into and through the White Pine Mountains, climbing high above the sagebrush and scrub oak. Here pine and juniper grew in fragrant stands so thick that if she hadn't possessed an acute sense of direction, she could easily have lost the way and wandered aimlessly among dense branches and towering shadows.

The nights continued brittle and cold and her poncho felt good during the day, but Fox sniffed spring in the air. The melt had begun. Creeks that had been winter low and sluggish now swelled and tumbled in their beds, running dangerously fast.

Reining in beside a stream that most likely had been little more than a trickle as recently as a week ago, Fox studied rushing water that tossed and foamed, close to overflowing its banks.

It was possible they could get the animals across safely if no one made a mistake and luck favored them. Maybe. The odds seemed better that they'd lose a horse or a mule. If the money mule was swept downstream and the bank bags broke in the water, the gold would not be recoverable. Fox would never forgive herself.

"We'll head south, look for a shallow, calmer section."

"I think we can make it across," Tanner said, riding up beside her to examine the turbulent water. "Hanratty's horse might balk, but he hasn't lately. We'll manage."

Fox's expression went blank. "We're not going to cross here," she stated flatly.

Tanner met her stare and her heart sank. They were going to argue, and they would have a falling out before they ever got to the kissing and liaison part. Well, so be it. She wasn't going to risk the money mule to this stretch of water.

"Suppose I ride across first and test the currents."

Her chin came up. "You do that. But me and the mules are heading south until we find a safer crossing."

"Even if I show you that it's safe here?" He sounded irritated.

"I'm not willing to risk losing an animal or, at best, getting our supplies wet just so you can prove a point." She flicked a glance at his mouth then rode around him. "You agreed that I would make these decisions. I'm sorry to learn that you don't keep your word." Chew on that a while. She let him think about it while she informed the others that they'd follow the stream south, seeking a more acceptable crossing.

She half expected to turn her head and see Tanner riding on the far side of the stream, but he trotted up beside her.

"You're right," he said in a tight voice. "It was your decision to make."

"Damned straight."

"I keep my word."

"For a moment it sounded like you wouldn't."

"I still think we could have crossed back there. These detours cost time."

She stared. "These detours? This is only the third time we've been blocked! Besides, the way I make it we're right on schedule."

"And I'd like to stay on schedule."

They studied each other through narrowed eyes, then Fox kicked her mustang into a loose canter and rode ahead, fuming inside. They'd both been irritable for several days. This confrontation was merely the latest in a series of small set-tos.

She couldn't speak for Tanner, but she'd figured out why she was pissy and ready to bite off heads. Days ago they'd decided to have a liaison but so far nothing had happened. The disappointment was enough to make anyone itchy and irritable.

Oh, there were reasons, she conceded that. The pine forests required single-file travel that didn't allow for any banter that might be considered pursuit. And the temperature dropped like a stone at night making any thought of getting naked very unappealing. Nor did it sound exciting to roll around on the frozen ground wearing scarves and heavy clothing. Fully dressed and freezing was no way to begin a liaison.

But the delay in getting this liaison started was driving her crazy.

Every time she looked at Tanner, she imagined that sensual mouth moving slowly over her throat and body. She couldn't take her eyes off the way his trousers fit tight around his thighs and snugged up next to his butt. And when he stared at her across the fire at night, a tingle began in the pit of her stomach and shivered up her spine to the top of her scalp. Lord. If he could do that to her with a glance, she could hardly bear to imagine what he might do if they ever got to the liaison. Fox decided that no one had ever prayed for warm weather as fervently as she did every night. But so far to no avail.

"This looks passable," Peaches commented, coming up on her left side. Despite Peaches's protests, Fox had assigned Hanratty and Brown to trade off leading his string of mules. At the moment the men were leading her string, too.

"I don't know." The stream didn't appear as deep as the first site, but the water was white-tipped and running fast. A tree limb shot past in an eyeblink.

"This might be as good as it's going to get."

Fox had begun to think the same thing. She wasn't going to find an ideal safe crossing. "What's your guess? Three feet deep?"

"Probably less in some spots, more in others. On the positive side, the bank over there is about level with the water. The animals won't have to climb an incline to get out."

Trust Peaches to find something positive in a dismal situation. But he was right. Fox drew a long breath.

"All right," she said when the men brought up the mules.

Hanratty stared at the water and swore. Already his horse was dancing away from the bank's edge.

"This is probably as good as it's going to get. We need to know what we're dealing with, so I'll ride across and then come back."

Tanner frowned. "My bay is taller than your mustang. It makes sense for me to go first in case the water's deeper than we're guessing."

"I'm in charge here, Tanner. I take the risks. I cross first. Peaches, you make sure the loads are evenly distributed on the mules and tight. Brown, you help him. Hanratty, start thinking how you're going to get that paint across." She looked into Tanner's hard eyes then dug her heels against the mustang's flanks.

The instant the mustang plunged into the water, she knew it was going to be a struggle. Over the rush and low roar of the water, she heard rocks knocking into each other as the swift current rolled them along the bottom. If one of those rocks smashed against her horse's feet . . .

"Easy, boy. Take it slow. Nice and steady."

The mustang picked his way, stumbling once as the water rose to his belly and the current hit him broadside. Fox held on, giving the horse his head and trusting that he didn't want to be swept away any more than she did. Laying low over his neck, talking in his ear, she urged him forward. He stumbled a second time and she thought they'd both go down, but the mustang had heart and showed it.

He came out of the stream on the far side, snorting, tossing his head, and streaming water. Only now did Fox realize that her lower legs were wet and numb from the icy water. Her teeth chattered with cold and relief.

When her breath steadied, she looked across the mist thrown up by the turbulence and saw the men staring at her in silence. Peaches wore his oh-my-God look. Hanratty had his mouth open and so did Brown. Tanner jerked off his hat and pulled a hand down his face.

"I'm coming back across," Fox shouted.

A chorus of no's came back at her. "Stay where you are," Tanner yelled. The others nodded.

She would have ignored them except the mustang quivered beneath her thighs. He needed to rest and warm himself in the sun. Reluctantly, she agreed to stay put. After she staked the mustang in grassy sunlight, she returned to the low bank, stamping her feet to restore feeling. The noise of rushing water made it impossible to hear what the men were saying on the other side, but she could guess.

Peaches was taking the mules out of the tethers. Fox nodded, agreeing with the move. The mules shouldn't be tied to one another or they would all go if one lost its footing. Tanner and Brown were arguing, nose to nose, Hanratty had led his horse away from the water and stood beside him, stroking his neck.

Fox paced along the bank, watching debris go tossing by and wished she had a smoke. Wished she was on the other side giving orders and checking every detail.

When she looked up, Tanner, Brown, and Peaches had mounted. They talked among themselves, looked across at her and then it began.

Tanner and Peaches positioned their horses at the edge of the stream. Shouting and yelling, Hanratty and Brown drove the mules between Tanner and Peaches. When the first mule saw what lay ahead he started to balk, but momentum carried him forward and the mules behind pushed him into the racing water. Once the mules were in the stream, trying to swim and keep their heads above the surface, their packs swaying and wobbling, Tanner rode into the water on the up side of the mules, and Peaches entered on the down side.

At once the stream became a churning tossing mass of men and frightened animals. The water rushed up to the mules backs and they rolled wild eyes and fought to keep their footing against the current and tumbling rocks. Tanner and Peaches shouted them forward while struggling to control their own mounts.

One of the animals went down and Fox choked. She couldn't tell if it was the money mule. An instant later the mule got its feet beneath its body, thank God, its head reappeared and it continued scrambling toward the bank. The force of rushing water had pushed the animals downstream and Fox now saw they would emerge several yards from where she stood shouting encouragement.

She was trying to calculate whether the mules would be blocked by a thick growth of willows, so she wasn't facing the stream. Not until later did she learn that the current had flung one of mules against Peaches's horse, knocking the horse's feet out from under him. When Fox turned back to look, Peaches was in the water and his horse had swept past him, tumbling in the savage current. For one horrified instant her eyes met Peaches's and she saw him shout "no." Then the current pulled him under.

She knew Peaches had just told her not to enter the water in an act of heroic idiocy, and she had only to look at the flooding currents to know he was right. Feeling frantic and helpless, Fox screamed at Tanner, but he was fighting to keep the bay upright, trying not to crash into the swimming mules. He didn't hear. Christ! There wasn't time to get her horse. Running full out, Fox raced along the bank, knowing she couldn't keep up with the raging current, not knowing what she could do anyway. Ahead she saw Peaches's head break the water then disappear again. She couldn't reach him.

Gasping, choking with panic, Fox stopped and pressed a hand to her burning side. She couldn't breathe, couldn't think. Didn't register anything except that Peaches was drowning and she couldn't do a goddamned thing to save him. Shock and disbelief closed her throat.

A brown streak flashed past on the far bank but Fox didn't grasp the importance until Jubal Brown's horse shot into the water too far downstream to help.

No, she was wrong. He'd picked exactly the right place. When she understood what he would try to do, she ducked her head and ran hard, cursing the willows that snatched at her poncho, struggled to force breath into her scalding throat.

The hardest thing was not to shout, not to distract Brown when he needed every ounce of concentration plus more luck than any one man was entitled to. The worst thing was to be stuck on the bank instead of being in the stream herself.

She could see the water was deep here, racing fast, pouring over large rocks. Jubal Brown's horse fought the deadly current, eyes rolling, legs scrambling for footing beneath the turbulence.

Peaches's dark head broke the surface but Fox had no idea if he saw Brown or understood that Brown would try to catch him. There would be only one chance.

Heart in her mouth, dashing tears from her cheeks, Fox skidded to a halt, a prayer frozen on her lips. She saw Peaches tumbling in the water, his flannel shirt breaking the surface then vanishing. Saw Jubal turn his horse sideways, presenting the largest target but also exposing the horse to the full broadside force of the current.

Jubal's horse started to turn, pushed by the current, unable to hold his footing. Peaches would fly past him. Fox's breath stopped and her hands flew to her mouth.

Icy water splashed up on her as Tanner shot past and his horse plunged into the froth and foam. She hadn't heard him galloping down the bank.

Tanner had less than a minute to position his bay broadside

against the current, the same as Jubal was fighting to do, and then Peaches swept down on them.

Peaches crashed into the bay, knocking the horse off balance. But Tanner grabbed an arm. Peaches's momentum swung the big bay around and Fox screamed, certain the horse and Tanner would go down, too. And they might have if Jubal Brown hadn't caught hold of Peaches's other arm so they didn't lose him when Tanner let go to stay in his saddle as the bay stumbled and slipped, fighting to regain his footing.

Fox couldn't see Peaches in the melee. The men and horses battled the current, throwing up water and curses. She couldn't tell who had Peaches, or if they had him at all.

Plunging, eyes wild, the horses strained toward the bank. They came out breathing hard, streaming water, flesh quivering. Tanner and Jubal Brown each had one of Peaches's arms, dragging him out of the water between them.

He looked dead, limp-boned and head hanging. Fox tried to shout, but her throat was raw from screaming. By the time she reached them, the men had Peaches on the ground and were pounding his back. Gouts of water gushed from his mouth each time Tanner or Jubal leaned on him.

Fox paced in a circle, wringing her hands, dashing tears from her eyes, swearing, praying. When Peaches coughed and sputtered, she fell to her knees and covered her face. That cough was the sweetest sound she had ever heard.

"He's freezing." Tanner glanced up at her. "Get some dry clothing."

It would take a while. She'd have to find the mules then locate the mule carrying Peaches's things, and hope to hell Peaches's clothes had come through the crossing without getting soaked.

"Here." Stripping off her wool poncho, she tossed it to Jubal Brown. "Put this on him until I get back."

The mules were not scattered to hell and gone as Fox had expected. They were staked on tether lines in the sun. And Cutter Hanratty was walking toward a freshly dug fire pit carrying a stack of dry limbs and brush.

"Is he alive?"

Gasping for breath, Fox bent at the waist and pressed a hand against the stitch in her side. "Just barely." She'd run up the bank like the devil chased her. "He still has to survive being half frozen and beat to hell against the rocks." Her voice was a croak.

"I'll get some coffee going then I'll ride south, see if I can find his horse and get his saddlebags. I don't expect the horse to be alive though."

"Thank you."

She noticed the money mule had come through intact and she didn't see any leaking coins. That was a blessing. And she found the right pack on the second try, pulling out a coat, shirt, trousers, long underwear, and Peaches's second pair of socks and boots. He'd wrapped his clothing in oilcloth, it wasn't even damp.

Hanratty rode up beside her and extended a hand. Fox swung up behind him and let him ride her back to the site beside the river.

Tanner and Brown had stripped off their shirts to use as towels before they dropped Fox's poncho over Peaches's head. When Fox slid off Hanratty's horse, the two men were walking Peaches up and down the bank. Dragging him was more like it.

Peaches was ashen gray, his lips bluish purple. He shivered uncontrollably and his teeth chattered. He looked at Fox, tried to say something then just shook his head and closed his eyes.

"Keep walking, old man." Jubal Brown pulled Peaches's arm tighter around his neck, taking on more of Peaches's weight.

Tanner had an arm around Peaches's waist. "I know it hurts to walk, but we need to get your circulation flowing again."

"You'll warm up if you move."

"One foot in front of the other. That's right. Now again."

Feeling helpless and useless, Fox walked beside them. "How badly hurt is he?"

"Mr. Hernandez is one big walking bruise," Tanner said, keeping his gaze on Peaches's face. "Maybe a sprained ankle. Hard to tell. We'll know more when he warms up enough to feel pain. Dozens of small cuts and scrapes."

Fox's poncho was long enough to cover Peaches's butt. From there his legs were bare down to his wet boots. "Maybe we should get him into dry clothing," she said, anxiety making her voice even hoarser.

"In a few minutes." Tanner threw her a glance. "If you want to be useful, catch our horses and take them back to camp. I assume we have a camp going by now. Get the saddles off. Do what you can to unpack the mules. Check and see if any of the animals are cut and in need of doctoring."

Fox nodded, glad to have something to do, angry that she'd lost charge. "He'll live, won't he?"

Jubal Brown tossed her a thin smile over Peaches's head. "This old man is tougher than rawhide. I would have bet every coin we're carrying that he wouldn't come out of that stream alive."

Tanner agreed. "He'll hurt like hell for a few days, but unless he takes a fever, he should make it."

"Thank God." Fox swayed on her feet.

It suddenly struck her that the last person she would have counted on to rescue Peaches had been the first into the river. Jubal Brown hadn't hesitated. He'd seen Peaches pulled under and had acted instantaneously. And if Jubal hadn't been in the river when and where he was, Tanner couldn't have known where Peaches was or where to make a stand. Without Jubal Brown . . . her eyes widened and a shudder rippled down her spine.

"Thank you," she whispered when Jubal looked at her. He shrugged, adjusted Peaches's arm and urged Peaches forward.

Fox stood like she'd taken root, staring at the men and chewing over the fact that Jubal Brown had saved Peaches's life.

"If you want to say thanks," Brown called over his shoulder, "find me and Tanner some dry clothes, too."

She'd been so anxious about Peaches that she hadn't thought about Tanner and Jubal Brown also being wet and cold, but both wore trousers soaked up to their crotches with icy water.

Up to their crotches. Her gaze dropped to the bottom of Tanner's butt and she was glad she wasn't facing him or she would have embarrassed herself. It was bad enough that she'd taken a long hard look at his bare chest and shoulders.

Matthew Tanner was a man who looked as good without his shirt and waistcoat as he did wearing them. His skin was tight over muscles that suggested he'd swung a pickax in his time and moved heavy rocks. Broad shoulders tapered down to a lean waist that looked as hard as a board. And he had dark hair on his chest. This was a matter that Fox felt particular about. Too much chest hair was a tad revolting. Too little chest hair made the man look unfinished, as if he'd quit growing before he should have. But the amount of hair on Tanner's chest was just right. She was glad to discover this as she'd been a bit anxious about the chest hair issue.

Jubal Brown, on the other hand, looked better in his shirt. A naked chest and arms made him look puny, too skinny and bony, and Fox could have counted the few hairs on his chest.

And she was a flaming idiot to stand here comparing bare chests when there was so much to do. Whirling, she rushed back to camp. Before she did anything else, she'd find Peaches's doctor kit and steep tansy herb in whiskey. He'd have whiskey in the doctor kit because there were so many medical uses, like this one for fever. The whiskey would help with chills, too.

While she worked, she whispered a prayer of gratitude. She couldn't imagine life without Peaches, he'd been her family and her friend for as long as she could remember.

Tanner sat where he could see into Peaches's tent. Fox had squeezed in beside the old man and held his hand. Earlier, she had insisted on feeding him bean soup thickened with crumbled biscuits, which had set off an argument. But Fox had won, patiently spooning soup into Peaches's mouth. Tanner suspected Peaches would rather have had more of the medicinal whiskey than beans and biscuits. Right now, Tanner could have used a drink himself.

At the end of a turbulent day, a good horse was dead, a good man had almost died, three mules had serious cuts, and Jubal Brown's horse was favoring the left front leg.

"I don't think it's serious," Brown said when Tanner inquired. "He probably stepped hard on a rock and bruised the pad. He isn't cut and nothing's broken."

"We'll stay here a couple of days," Tanner decided. "Give Mr. Hernandez and the animals a chance to rest and heal."

They were into range country now, with spring grass painting the ground a tender green. The animals could use a day or so of unhurried grazing and Peaches needed time to regain his strength. All Tanner had to do was try like hell to ignore the clock ticking in his head, counting off the days.

"Makes no never mind to me," Brown said, yawning hugely. "I wouldn't say no to a day or two of nothing but dozing and eating."

Tanner studied the surface of his coffee then looked up. "I'm obliged for what you did today."

"You sound surprised."

"I guess I am."

"You thought I'd let a black man die?" Standing, Brown stretched and pulled back his shoulders. "We need him to pack and unpack the mules."

Clenching his jaw, Tanner watched Jubal Brown saunter toward his tent. Some men were beyond understanding.

"You interested in some checkers?" Hanratty eased down on the grass beside him.

"Not tonight." Tanner looked toward Peaches's tent, wondering what Fox was saying that had made her smile. When she smiled, her face relaxed and she looked younger and softer.

"Interesting woman, that one," Hanratty said, nodding toward the tent. "I knew one like her once. Up north. Problem with women like her, they got no future. The woman I knew got herself hanged for rustling cattle. She didn't need those cattle. It was like she looked ahead and saw nothing, so she decided to let the law make it so."

Tanner couldn't guess where Hanratty intended to take this conversation, but he didn't want to hear it. Standing, he walked away from the fire, following purple shadows that lengthened as the sun slipped down the western curve of the sky.

He lit a smoke and studied the horses and mules, focusing particularly on the animals that had sustained injuries. Today had shocked him. Aside from the outlaws at the mining camp, the journey had been demanding but not unduly so. Tanner had let himself be lulled into forgetting this was a dangerous trek. They'd been fortunate so far.

"You have another of those cigars?"

"Yes." He hadn't heard her come up behind him.

"Thank you. What were you thinking about so hard?"

"I was thinking about you and how you've steered us clear of routes that could have been a lot more dangerous."

She glanced at him and arched an eyebrow. "I told you from the start this wouldn't be easy."

"How is Mr. Hernandez feeling?"

"He's stiff and sore, smashed up some, but there's no sign of fever, thank God. He's sleeping now." Tilting her head back, she blew a smoke ring into the evening air. "Peaches taught me how to make smoke rings. Peaches taught me everything I know that's worth knowing."

"He's a good man." During their time together, Tanner had

come to respect Peaches Hernandez and enjoy his company. "I've encroached on your authority. I told Hanratty and Brown that we'd spend a couple of days here."

"That would have been my decision, too." She formed another smoke ring. "But don't make that kind of decision again without consulting me first, or we're going to have trouble."

Tanner smiled. One thing he liked about Fox, he always knew where he stood. She didn't mince words, didn't cloak her opinions in polite wrappings.

"There's something I have to say." She flipped her braid over her shoulder like she did when she was uncomfortable. "This is the slowest start to a liaison I ever heard of. I don't want to rush you along, but it would be helpful to know when you plan to begin the pursuit part."

He'd been pondering this question himself. "The terrain hasn't been conducive to much of a pursuit."

"I agree. Until today it hasn't."

"And it's been cold at night."

"The weather should get better now that we've come down into range country. It shouldn't be nearly as cold."

"Mostly I haven't figured out how to ensure some privacy." Men didn't pursue a woman in public. Courting, if that's what they intended to do, was a private matter. He didn't want to say something to Fox then hear it parroted back to him the next day from Hanratty or Brown.

"There's no real privacy on a trek of this kind," Fox stated flatly. "We'll have to make do."

He was reaching that conclusion.

"It's not like they don't expect us to want to be alone. We told them we're going to have a liaison."

"Well then." As casually as he could, he slipped an arm around her shoulder. Ordinarily he thought of Fox as tall, but actually she was a small woman. When she stood beside him, the top of her head rose just above his shoulder. And he usually thought of her as substantial under her poncho, but touching her suggested small bones in keeping with her height. In fact, Tanner had no real notion of how she would look stripped of her oversized clothing. Thinking about it caused a stirring between his legs.

Fox adjusted herself under his arm and leaned slightly against his body. "I think we should shorten the pursuit part and get right to the liaison part. What do you think?"

Her hair had the clean fresh scent of river water overlaid by a warm musky scent that was hers alone.

"I'm willing to jump ahead to the liaison part," he said in a husky voice, wondering what she would do if he kissed the top of her head.

"I need to know a couple of days before the liaison so I can start putting Peaches's softening lotion on my fanny."

"What?"

"That's not part of my usual beauty routine. I didn't think about it until right now."

He stared down at her. "You want to put lotion on—"

"On my fanny. In case you . . . you know . . . grab me there."

Instantly he had a full-blown and painful erection. Easing her away from his body, he tried to think of something to say. "That's considerate. I can imagine some grabbing taking place." Jesus. He could imagine every detail. He cleared his throat. "So. There's such an item as fanny-softening lotion?"

"I don't know, actually." She dropped her cigar and stepped on it. "Until recently, my only beauty routine was a regular bath and hair wash. I'll ask Peaches about it, but I'm guessing the same old bacon grease I'm using on my face and hands will do for my fanny."

"You use . . ." Suddenly the smell of bacon was explained. He was glad she couldn't see the huge grin that spread across his lower face. "I'll tell you what. When we get to Denver, I'll buy you the biggest bottle of face and body lotion that I can find. As a parting gift." Her silence told him that he'd erred by mentioning parting.

"That's not necessary," she said finally. "Once we get to Denver, I won't need any lotions."

So the whole business of rubbing bacon grease on her face and hands was for his benefit. A sense of unease settled in his chest.

"No, I haven't expanded my beauty routine for your sake," she said, sounding angry. "I have reasons that don't have a damned thing to do with you." She started to walk away then came back. "We've decided to start immediately on a brief pursuit, correct?"

"That's my understanding."

"Good."

As he watched the sway of her hips moving away from him,

three thoughts entered his head. She could read his mind. He didn't believe that the bacon grease was not for his sake. And he wanted her more than he'd ever wanted any woman.

Matthew Tanner had made up his mind that he was just the man to tame this unusual woman.

CHAPTER 11

"IF I play one more game of chess, my head is going to explode." Fox rubbed her temples. "You couldn't let me win just once, could you."

"Now, Missy, you wouldn't like that. When the time comes that you beat me, you'll be glad the win is real."

"How are you feeling?"

"Stiff and sore. Mighty glad for the sun. Good enough that we don't need to lose another day on my account."

Fox didn't attempt to conceal a long hard examination. The swelling on Peaches's forehead and the left side of his face had diminished some. His cuts had scabbed over nicely, and she was no longer anxious that a fever would get him. But she knew he wasn't feeling up to snuff because he let her fuss over him. Peaches hadn't objected when she went to the trouble of cooking fried eggs just as he liked them instead of scrambling as usual. And he'd let her wash his clothes. That concession both amazed and worried her.

"You'll have to ride one of the mules," she said, wishing there was more spark in his eyes. "We can get rid of some things, redistribute the rest among the other mules." The ordeal in icy river water had worsened his congestion. She didn't like the sound of his cough.

Peaches nodded, turning a wooden knight in his hand. "I think Rebecca would be best for riding."

"We'll get you another horse as soon as it's possible."

"I've been thinking."

"Damn, I hate that as much as you hate it when I do some thinking."

They smiled at each other then Peaches said, "I was thinking about what my last request would have been if I'd had a chance to make one."

Fox's smile vanished. "I don't want to talk about that kind of thing, so stop right there."

"My deathbed request would be that you forget about killing Hobbs Jennings."

"Damn it, Peaches, that's not fair! I'm not going to promise that and you know it."

"You would deny a man's deathbed wish? Now, Missy, that ain't right."

She slammed the chess pieces into the box. "If you asked that of me on your deathbed, I'd want you to die in peace so I'd lie to you and make the promise. Is that what you want? Me going to hell for lying to a man on his fricking deathbed?"

"I don't want you getting yourself hanged over something that happened a long long time ago."

"I'm still paying for what Hobbs Jennings did to me. Every single damned day. Look over there." She nodded toward the willows where Tanner sat in the shade cleaning his pistols. "No matter what happens here," she smacked her fist against her heart, "me and Tanner agree to part ways in Denver. We both know I can't fit into his world. But I could have if Jennings hadn't stolen my inheritance!"

With her inheritance, she would have grown up in the same rarified world as Tanner. She wouldn't have to remind herself how to hold a fork, fancy manners would come automatically. She would own pretty lady clothes and know how to wear them right and be comfortable in them. She'd know how to talk to men like Tanner, would know what interested people of culture and refinement.

"Things are what they are," Peaches said quietly. "Killing Jennings ain't going to turn back the clock and put things right. Killing him isn't going to change anything except how long you live."

"I know it's too late to change anything," she said, standing and pulling her hat brim down to shade her eyes from the sun. "What I want is punishment. I want him to pay for stealing my mother's money and for throwing me away and robbing my future." She couldn't bear to look at Tanner, so she stared down at the chessboard on the short range grass. "Don't go asking me not to kill Hobbs Jennings on your deathbed."

"Deathbed requests aren't supposed to be easy. That's the whole point. If the request was an easy one, a person wouldn't have to wait for his deathbed to ask."

Fox looked around for Hanratty and signaled him to come and play checkers with Peaches. When Hanratty ambled toward them, she shoved on her blue sunglasses then wandered toward the laundered clothes she'd draped over the willows to dry in the sun.

"I've been waiting for you to finish your chess game," Tanner said, sighting down the clean barrel of his pistol.

"I didn't see you there," she said, as if she wasn't practically standing on his shirttail. She looked down at the array of weapons lined up near where he was sitting. "That's my rifle."

"I cleaned it for you." When she didn't say anything, Tanner squinted up at her, sunlight sharpening the craggy angles of his face. "This is part of my pursuit."

"Oh. Well then, I suppose it's all right." She thought a minute. "But don't get in the habit of messing with my belongings."

"I also picked you some flowers." He held out a bouquet.

Frowning, Fox considered the blossoms. She didn't know diddle about flowers. A rose she would have recognized, but these were tiny pink blooms and a spiky blue thing that she'd seen for years but had never given a thought to.

"Cleaning my rifle would have been enough." She didn't know what to do with the wildflowers.

"It seemed two gifts were appropriate for an accelerated pursuit." A smile curved his mouth. "And I have something else for you." Standing, he pointed to the ground. "Sit down, I'll just be a minute."

Fox looked back at the camp. No one lingered near the fire, it was too hot today. Hanratty and Peaches sat with heads bent over the checkerboard. Jubal Brown was out on the range among the animals, checking cuts and scrapes.

A huge white sky curved overhead. Spring sunshine spilled across the range tinting an awakening earth in tones of gold and green. The smell of sun-dried laundry drifted from the willows, and a drone of insects hovered above the splash and spray of rushing water.

Fox sank to the ground and folded her legs Indian-style, appreciating a perfect day warm with the promise of pursuit. On a day like this, something good ought to happen.

Tanner emerged from the willows carrying a jar with string tied around the lid. "Ice water," he said, smiling in triumph. "Or almost. The jar's been in the stream for two hours."

Laughing with pleasure, Fox took the cup he poured and tasted, holding the cold water on her tongue. "Wonderful!"

Tanner handed her a handkerchief. "It's clean."

"Thanks." After dipping the handkerchief in her cup, she pressed the cold cloth to her face. "Oh Lord. That feels so good. But I don't have anything for you."

"I don't expect anything. I'm the one doing the pursuing."

"I've been thinking about that. How long does the pursuing part go on?"

"It can continue for years," he said with a smile.

"Years?" There were things in the refined world that, in honesty, Fox had to admit she didn't cotton to. Women were not allowed to drink liquor, smoke, or cuss for instance. And now there was this business about courtships going on for years. "We don't have years." According to Fox's calculations, they had a few days more than two months before they rode into Denver. "We're getting off to a slow start as it is."

"We're on an accelerated schedule." He cleared his throat. "May I say you look particularly lovely today, Miss Fox?"

She stared then fell back on the range grass, laughing. "My braid's unraveling, I'm sweaty, and my clothes are sticking to me. My boots haven't seen a lick of polish since we left Carson City." She smiled up at the sky. "But I'm liking this so far. Say something else."

"Your hair is a beautiful sun-kissed red, and you have adorable ears." He grinned at her.

"My hair's a mess, and one of my ears is missing a bullet-size chunk!"

"I am particularly enchanted by the dew on your swanlike throat."

"It's sweat!" Laughing helplessly, she rolled over and pressed her forehead against the grass. "Swanlike throat, my fanny."

"Speaking of which . . . how is the fanny beautification project progressing?"

Something very like a giggle slipped out of her mouth, shocking her. "I haven't been working at it very long, but it feels like everything is improving nicely." Now that she'd added more area to grease, she must reek of bacon. "I hope you like the smell of bacon."

"Actually," he looked up at the sky as if he was considering. "I'm beginning to find the scent of bacon very arousing."

"I don't know if I believe that, but it's nice of you to say so." At this moment, Fox would have given the earth to own a bottle of perfume. She sat up and smiled. "I think I like this silly talk."

Oh Lord, he was handsome, sitting there with sun glowing on his jaw and on the arrow of skin inside his opened collar. He was tan now, his face and hands darker than hers. Which meant that Peaches's sun protection salve was working. But she forgot about that as she sank into the golden brown of his eyes. She could have stared into his eyes for the rest of the day without speaking another word. No man had ever looked at her quite like Tanner did, as if fascination lay in the curve of her cheek, as if mystery sparkled in her eyes and interesting whispers waited just inside her lips.

Tanner poured more cold water into their cups. "Tell me about you. Start at the beginning." When Fox arched a dubious eyebrow, he smiled again. "Learning about each other is part of the pursuit."

Well, he was the expert when it came to the rules of pursuit. Fox wet her lips and tried to concentrate on something besides the way he held his mouth, with just a sliver of teeth showing. "The beginning. I was born in San Francisco."

He looked up. "I was born in San Francisco."

"Really?" Delight widened her eyes. They had something in common after all. And since Tanner was only a couple of years older than Fox, they must have been in San Francisco at the same time. Surely that meant something significant. "Did your family live in the city?"

Tanner nodded. "On one of the hills overlooking the bay."

"We did, too! I wish I could recall the address, but I was too young. I don't remember. I wonder if we lived close to each other." He didn't dispute her claim, but she saw a blink of doubt. "I know. You're thinking your family was rich and mine wasn't. We wouldn't have lived in the same area."

"The houses on the hills are very large," he said gently.

"So was ours." Her chin came up. "What you don't know is that my real father was a man of substance. He was in ship-

ping. He died when I was little and I don't remember him."
Tanner's expression was polite. He didn't believe her father had
been rich. Fox drew a breath and continued, wishing they
hadn't gotten into this subject. "When my mother remarried,
we moved to a house that was even bigger than the first one."
She stared, daring him to say anything. "That's the truth. There
were servants, too. In both houses."

"That's pleasant," he said after a long pause.

"I'm telling you, my mother inherited a lot of money from
my father. It was a fortune."

"I see."

But he didn't believe. "And she already had money from her
parents. My mother was filthy rich."

Tanner's gaze ran slowly from her raggedy hat to the frizz
of unraveling braid to her floppy oversized shirt to the men's
trousers cinched at the waist with a length of thin rope and then
to her old scuffed boots. "Are you going to tell me that you
have a fortune stashed in a bank somewhere?"

"No."

His doubt set her anger on fire, because now she had to explain. She wished she had a big glass of whiskey to help her address an area she didn't like to talk about. Unable to stay
seated, she pushed to her feet and stepped over the row of
weapons that Tanner had cleaned.

"I should have inherited a fortune, but I didn't, even though
my mother left her money to me with my stepfather as my
guardian. But my stinking thieving stepfather didn't want to
manage someone else's money, he wanted my mother's fortune
all for himself. So, the day my mother died, my stepfather sent
me to my mother's cousin, and he announced that both my
mother and I had perished. With me dead, he inherited my
mother's money."

Tanner frowned, squinting up into the sun. "That's theft.
Why didn't the authorities arrest him?"

"No one knew what he'd done. I was six years old. I didn't
know he had announced that I was dead, too. All I knew was
that I had to go live with my mother's cousin, Maude Wilson.
My stepfather told Mrs. Wilson that my mother had appointed
her as my guardian. He also told her there was no money left.
All the cousin got was me."

She could hardly bear to spit out the words. The spring day
disappeared and what she saw was a little girl standing on a

porch with her heart pounding and a stern angry woman staring down at her.

Tanner stood and slipped an arm around her waist. "Let's go for a walk."

His hand burned through the material of her shirt, as hot as an iron. A crazy notion entered her mind that if she raised her shirt, she'd see the mark of five fingers scorched on her skin. And if he raised his hand two inches, his thumb would brush the side of her breast. Her knees went weak and she stumbled.

"My life was easier than yours." They walked beside the stream, skirting the willows, stopping occasionally to look at the flooding stream. "My father sent me to Boston when I was ten. He was preparing to remarry and decided it was a good time for me to visit my uncle. I lived there during the school years. At any rate, I didn't see my father during his second marriage. Didn't see him again until after the woman died. I spent that summer in San Francisco."

"Were you ever hungry?" Fox asked curiously. "Did you ever worry about getting shoes that fit?" She doubted it, but asked anyway.

"No." His hand tightened on her waist. "I've had a privileged life. Which I took for granted until I became an adult and saw more of the world."

Fox tried to imagine the opulence and plenty that lay behind his words, but her imagination didn't stretch that far.

"My mother's cousin had a houseful of children of her own. The last thing she needed was an orphan on her doorstep. She provided the basics, but it wasn't in her to do better."

There was no point mentioning that Fox had been little more than a servant in her cousin's house. That kind of detail sounded like whining.

"But I met Peaches there," she said, brightening, trying hard to focus. His hand, hot on her waist made it hard to think. "Finding Peaches was the best thing that ever happened to me."

"He worked for Mrs. Wilson?"

Fox nodded. "She was a widow. Needed a man on the place to fix and take care of things. Me and Peaches took to each other just like that." She snapped her fingers. "Mrs. Wilson didn't care if Peaches paid the neighbor to teach me to read or that he showed me how to sharpen scissors and hammer a nail. When I was with Peaches, she didn't have me underfoot, didn't have to think about me." Fox smiled, remembering. "I followed Peaches around like a shadow."

"And at some point you and Peaches ran away?"

"I'm tired of talking about this." Tanner didn't need to know all her history, at least not at once. And he certainly didn't need to know her stepfather's name. Fox still planned to learn more about Hobbs Jennings from Tanner. They turned back toward the campsite. "I'd rather know when the liaison is going to start."

Since the men were watching them, Tanner dropped his hand away from her waist and pulled back his shoulders. "Usually that decision is up to the woman involved."

Fox decided the rule was sensible. "All right. The pursuit has been very nice and I've enjoyed it. Especially the cold water and silly talk." Heat came up in her cheeks. "But I'm ready to be caught now."

"A one-day pursuit seems a trifle brief," he said, smiling.

"You cleaning my rifle tipped me over the edge." A bald-faced lie. She had been ready for the liaison to begin the first night they talked about it. Maybe she'd been ready from the moment she first saw him. "Since we're going to stay here one more day, I think the liaison should begin tomorrow night. That is, if you agree."

Fox had found a pool branching off the stream where there was no current. She could have a bath and a hair wash to start the liaison off on the right note. It was important not to smell like a side of bacon.

Tanner cleared his throat but he still sounded gruff when he spoke. "Tomorrow night is agreeable. I'll find a place that provides some privacy."

"Good." It seemed to her that the men stared at them as if they knew what Tanner and Fox were discussing. "Well, then. Tomorrow night." Every drop of conversation evaporated and she couldn't think of another thing to say.

"I'm looking forward to it." Tanner's gaze settled on her lips and Fox felt like a wave of hot molasses slid down the inside of her body. Lord, Lord. When his eyes turned that intense shade of golden brown wild fantasies galloped through her mind.

After running the tip of her tongue over her lips, she rubbed the end of her braid across her palm. For the first time since she'd met Tanner, she couldn't think of an easy and natural way to part.

"You should go away now." Damn. That didn't sound right. Too abrupt. "Good-bye."

Ducking her head, she walked away, her legs feeling wooden and awkward. People didn't say good-bye when they were only moving a few feet away. What was she thinking of? There was something about getting moony over a man that turned women stupid. She shook her head in disgust and narrowed a look on Hanratty and Brown. It would be good if one of them did something that required her to punch them. Right now she could use a reminder that she was not a pile of mush.

Angry at herself she stalked over to the awning that Hanratty had set up for shade. "I'm warning you right now. If you even look at me funny, I'm going to tear your liver out and cook it for breakfast."

"What the hell?" He lowered the shirt he was mending and stared.

"You too," she said to Jubal Brown. He yawned and settled back against his saddle. "I'd just love to kick your ribs in."

"Tanner would do us all a favor if he'd hurry up this courtship and get to the main event." Jubal opened one eye and looked at her then rolled to the side to avoid Fox's boot.

"You going to beat me up, too?" Peaches called.

She scowled at his grin. "I might."

Without another word, she stormed off to collect her laundry from the willows.

The instant Fox finished washing the supper plates at the edge of the stream, she caught Tanner's eye and jerked her head toward the horses and mules. He caught up to her a minute later.

"I need to talk to you about . . . you know . . . tomorrow night."

"Have you changed your mind?"

There was enough disappointment in his tone to boost her spirts. "No, but I'm worried about a couple of things."

Tanner ran a hand down the bay's flank. "Like what?"

"Well . . ." She patted the bay's neck, wishing it was dark but the days were stretching longer. "Here we are planning a liaison but we've never even kissed." She darted a look at him then focused on the bay's big brown eye. "What if we get to the liaison and discover that we hate kissing each other? What if we're standing there, ready to start the liaison and then find out there's no spark between us?"

Tanner took a step toward her, but Fox lifted her palm. "No, don't come kissing on me now. I'd feel like I'd begged a kiss out of you and that would make me mad."

An eyebrow arched and he studied her, his gaze settling on her lips. "Then how do you propose we remedy the problem?"

His stare made her mouth feel twitchy and stiff. "You're supposed to know that. You're the one in charge of the pursuit."

"I'm not going to hate kissing you, Fox."

"You can't say that. You might."

"All right, I'll think about the problem. What else?"

Damn. This kind of thing wasn't easy to discuss. "Well, I was wondering . . ." She addressed her remarks to the horse. "You aren't expecting a virgin are you?" Before he could answer, she rushed on. "Because there was this man about six years ago. He and I—"

"You don't have to explain anything."

Her cheeks felt as if they'd caught fire and she couldn't look at him. "It only happened twice. The first time was awful." Closing her eyes, she shook her head. "The second time was to find out if it would still be awful, and it was."

"Fox . . ."

"No, listen. You and me . . ." She stared into the bay's eye. "It's going to be awful, I know that. At least for me, I'm just not good at this. Maybe it's better for men, I don't know. Anyway. I'm not a virgin, but I'm also not experienced, so don't expect too much."

"I won't."

She could swear he sounded amused but when she swung toward him with a glare, he appeared serious.

"All right then. I just thought you should know." Lifting her chin, she marched past him. "If you plan to kiss me first, and I think that should happen before we go any further, it should seem natural. Like we didn't talk about it and I didn't have to ask you."

On the way to her tent, she stopped at the fire where the men were drinking coffee and smoking. "We'll stay one more night at this camp."

"I told you not to lose another day on my account," Peaches said, looking tired and guilty.

"The animals will be in better shape after another day's rest." She squeezed his shoulder on her way past.

It was too early to crawl into her tent, but Fox craved solitude. Finding moments alone on a cross-country journey was not easy and she counted every opportunity as precious. Stretching out, she pretended to read in case anyone glanced inside. But first, she checked the spot where she'd buried the flowers Tanner gave her. She hadn't known what to do with them. It wasn't like she carried a vase in her saddlebags. But it seemed the height of ingratitude to throw them away, so she'd hidden the flowers by burying them.

Holding her book on her chest, she stared up at the peaked roof of her tent and thought about all she had to accomplish tomorrow. She'd do her work first. Check the animals. Get the packs ready to go. Decide on the route. Then she'd go to the pool she had discovered and have a bath and a hair wash. Eat supper, if she could swallow anything knowing what was about to happen. And then Tanner would probably ask if she'd like to take a walk. Then he would do the test kiss. And if the test kiss was successful . . .

Anticipation shivered through her body, although she couldn't have said why. Her only previous experience had been embarrassing and awkward, and uncomfortable enough that Fox hadn't been interested in repeating the experiment until now. Why she was so eager for a liaison with Tanner puzzled her.

She knew about sex and it was nothing to get excited about. The only good part was the anticipation. During the anticipation, it was easy to forget that the sex part was fast, frustrating, and plain awful.

On the other hand, if her plans unfolded the way she hoped they did, Hobbs Jennings would die and she'd be swinging from a rope shortly after they arrived in Denver. If she was going to grab something good for herself, she'd better do it now.

And Tanner was a good thing.

Tanner hadn't needed the reminder that he and Fox had not kissed. Very likely he'd been thinking about kissing her longer than she'd been thinking about kissing. Until recently, he hadn't known if his kiss would be welcome. Once he learned that obstacle didn't exist, privacy became an issue.

After tucking away his shaving gear, he studied the sky. No clouds marred the high blue curve, but he'd keep checking. Rain would cause an unacceptable delay for tonight's plans as would another spring snowstorm. Fortunately, that didn't seem likely. Out here on the range, the days were hot and the nights cool but not unpleasantly so, as the nights had been at altitude.

Running a hand down his jaw, he decided he'd shave again before tonight. He'd bathe in the stream, and wear the clothing he'd washed yesterday. Last night he'd polished his boots, that was done. Shortly after dawn, he'd discovered a perfect place for privacy. Throughout the morning, he would take blankets and pillows to the spot he'd found inside a thick growth of willows and grass.

Gazing across the campsite, he observed the morning routines of the others. When he and Fox disappeared after supper, the men would know what was happening. That was awkward, but he didn't see a way around it.

At first he didn't spot Fox, then he saw her crawling out of her tent, carrying a towel and a cake of soap. His eyes narrowed and his jaw tightened. Tonight he would discover what treasures lay hidden beneath her oversized clothes. But the truth was, he liked the look of her regardless. Watching her now, he realized he usually forgot how small she was because she walked tall, her carriage graceful but brimming with purpose.

Ordinarily she dressed her hair in a braid that swung down her back, but once or twice she'd pinned it up under her hat in a careless knot. Tanner had wanted to remove the pins and catch the weight of that silken mass in his hands. He'd always had a weakness for red hair, although he couldn't have said why. Red-haired women, and he hadn't known many, seemed more vivid and alive. Certainly that description matched Fox, he thought with a smile.

He couldn't name one other woman he knew who spoke as frankly or as bluntly as she did. Instead of censuring this trait as unfeminine or objectionable, he'd discovered that he admired her directness. For the first time in his life, he knew what a woman was thinking because Fox was willing to speak her thoughts straight out.

And he applauded her fearless independence. Liked the confidence that allowed her to accept the responsibility for this journey and believe she was the best person to lead the way.

Finally, he loved the mystery in her eyes and the way they changed color with her moods. By now he knew gray eyes signaled an impending storm. Blue eyes stated that all was well in her world.

When she lifted a smile to the sunlight, the sight of her took his breath away. Tanner experienced an uneasy suspicion that for the rest of his life he would compare every woman he met to Fox. Frowning, he watched her move away from the camp, heading south along the stream bank.

It was time to settle the doubts about kissing. He couldn't wait another minute.

Fox didn't hear Tanner following until he was right behind her. Turning, she smiled and raised her towel and soap. "I'm going to—"

"Not a word."

The intense focus in his eyes and expression made her stomach drop to the ground. Suddenly her mouth went dry. Oh Lord. This was it. He was going to kiss her.

Tanner took the towel and soap out of her shaking hands, then raked a glance over her face, settling on her mouth. He dropped the towel and soap and took her by the hand, leading her around an old cottonwood.

He leaned her up against the trunk, then stepped forward, pinning her there with his lower body. Fox stared, wide-eyed, feeling his instant hard erection against her lower belly. Her breath caught and a shiver started between her legs and shot to the top of her head. Her scalp felt too small and her throat burned.

"Tanner . . ."

Her whisper ended on a gasp as his hands slipped beneath her shirttail and opened on the bare skin just above her waist. Her eyes closed and the breath rushed out of her as his thumbs caressed her, almost but not quite brushing the bottom slope of her breasts. It was that almost-but-not-quite that made her feel crazy inside.

She tried to move, unable to stay still, but his hips held her against the tree. What she accomplished was to rock herself against his erection, which caused a damp explosion between her legs. "Oh Lord."

When she trembled beneath his palms, he raised a hand to her face and gently cupped her chin, stroking the outline of her lips with his thumb. Fox dared a glance upward and read the hard intent in his eyes, which had darkened to a deep brown that was almost black.

When his mouth came down on hers, the shock of firm heat rippled down her spine. Her arms hung loose at her sides, she couldn't move. Her lips parted slightly and Tanner seized the opportunity to explore her mouth with his tongue, leaving fire and tingling where his tongue touched. He claimed her with tongue and lips, ravaged her, made love to her.

When he finally stepped back, releasing her, Fox stared wide-eyed, then she slid to the ground as if her bones had dissolved. She sprawled at the base of the tree, limp, her head spinning, her lips swollen and hot.

By the time she regained her senses, Tanner had gone.

Pushing to her feet, Fox blinked at the tree, then, moving in a daze, she stumbled back to the range to collect her towel and soap.

My Lord. She touched trembling fingertips to her lips.

There definitely was a spark between them. She absolutely was not going to hate kissing him.

CHAPTER 12

*I*T was the longest day of her life. Fox continually frowned at the sky, positive the sun refused to move.

She completed her chores in record time. Spit-shined her boots. Pinned and repinned her hair a half dozen times. Asked Peaches if he knew a recipe for lotion that didn't involve bacon grease. Something sweet-smelling would be preferable, but unfortunately, Peaches lacked the ingredients to concoct anything immediately. Then she considered the matter of clothes.

What did a person wear to a liaison? Probably nothing that Fox owned. Taking her saddlebags into her tent, she examined her meager collection of travel duds. The pantaloons that she wore under her trousers were plain white cotton with no trim. The same description fit her chemise. Her unders didn't boast a scrap of lace to excite a man's imagination.

Sighing, she turned her attention to her trousers. She could choose between black, brown, and gray trousers. Topped by one of three plain white linen shirts that would have fit a large man. The only items with any style were two overlarge waistcoats, one that was dull as toast for everyday wear and one with a fancy pattern for wearing to town.

She suspected that a liaison should begin with the woman wearing a flowing lacy night shift that swirled around her hips and ankles. But Fox had never owned such an item.

Sighing heavily, she frowned at the clothing strewn around the inside of her tent. Very likely it didn't matter what she wore since she wouldn't be wearing it long.

This thought led to a consideration of her body. Was she

too fat, too skinny, too short, or too tall? She had no idea what Tanner preferred. Would he be aroused or disappointed to discover that she had full breasts and hips? Did he fancy soft fleshy women or firm women with strong arms and thighs? And there was the freckle question. Like most redheaded women, a spray of freckles dusted her nose and cheeks, and dotted her chest and shoulders. Would Tanner consider her freckles charming or would he view them as an unpleasant flaw?

Fox rolled her eyes. Lordy, she would be glad when this evening was over. She was driving herself crazy.

Just as she had predicted, when suppertime at last arrived she could hardly swallow a bite.

"Looks like I wasted my time making that rabbit extra tasty," Peaches commented, watching Fox push her food around her plate.

"Eat up," Jubal Brown advised. "You need your strength." He and Hanratty snickered until they looked at Tanner, then they fell silent and went back to eating.

Naturally the men had guessed that tonight was special. Fox and Tanner were both shiny clean and gussied up in their town clothes. Tanner's hair was slicked back and carefully parted and Fox wore hers brushed into a coil on top of her head. They might as well have worn signs around their necks announcing: The liaison begins tonight.

After eating, Tanner lit a cigar, displaying no hint of haste. When it didn't appear that he was going anywhere, Fox accepted a smoke, too. Inside she was quaking with impatience, but conceded it would be better to wait until the sun started to go down. At least another endless forty-five minutes.

Eventually Peaches suggested chess or checkers but there were no takers. After finishing his cigar, he fetched his harmonica and played a few slow sweet tunes. Fox fixed her gaze on distant mountain peaks and didn't look at anyone, especially Tanner. She feared if she glanced at Tanner, her nerves would jump out of her skin.

"Can't you play anything livelier?" Hanratty finally asked.

While Peaches considered the request, Tanner stood and extended a hand to Fox. He cleared his throat. "Would you care to take a walk?"

She considered the deepening orange and red spreading across the western horizon as if she were thinking it over before she accepted his hand and stood. "I believe I would." Her cheeks blazed as fiery as the sunset.

"I could use a walk, too," Jubal Brown said, grinning. "How about you, Hanratty? We'll join them."

"That's enough," Peaches admonished mildly. "You stay right here. I'll play you some dance tunes."

"Are you sure you want to miss the dancing?" Brown called as Fox and Tanner walked away from the fire.

"Even though I'm the one who told them, I hate it that they know," Fox said tightly. She could hear Peaches's harmonica and Hanratty and Brown laughing, but she and Tanner had walked out of earshot.

"They would have known anyway. You were right about secrets being impossible in a group this small."

"Are we going far?" Not being in control was almost as unnerving as knowing what was about to happen.

"A few more minutes."

Fox wet her lips and reminded herself to breathe when Tanner took her hand. As she still couldn't bring herself to look at him, she gazed up at the sky. "There's the evening star. You showed it to me when we were in the outlaws' camp."

He laughed. "Can you predict where the Big Dipper will appear?"

Of course she could. She wouldn't be much of a scout if she didn't have a sixth sense for direction. But she went all girly and told a rare lie. "I'm not sure," she said in a voice that didn't quite sound like her own. "Can you show me?"

Tanner lifted an arm and pointed at the sky. After drawing a breath, Fox stepped close enough that her cheek almost touched his shoulder and she sighted up his arm. The sky had darkened to deep indigo and a few faint stars had begun to appear.

But Fox saw nothing. Her full concentration centered on the inch between her back and Tanner's chest. The scent of soap and river lingered on his shirt, and she felt his breath stirring her hair when he lowered his head. She closed her eyes and prayed that her knees wouldn't collapse.

"Your hair smells like lemon and sunshine," he murmured, his voice husky. He wrapped his arms around her waist and pulled her against his body. For a moment he held her in a loose embrace, laying his cheek against the top of her head.

Then he gently turned her in his arms and tilted her mouth

up to his. Fox's heart lurched and a long sigh escaped her lips. This time his kiss was tender, unhurried. His hands lay light on her waist.

What surprised her was the absence of clutching. He didn't grab her fanny or breasts, didn't turn wild and go at her like there was a two-minute deadline to get this over with. Tanner kissed her as if kissing was a pleasurable end in itself.

Easing back, he gazed down then frowned. "Are you crying?"

"No," she said, blinking hard. She appreciated it so much that he didn't grab at her. "I don't cry."

Tanner examined her damp eyes in the faint starlight, then clasped her hand and led her toward a thick stand of willows not far from the riverbank. "Now if I can find the entrance." He lit a lucifer and held it high.

Someone—Tanner, of course—had cut the willows at ground level, creating an entry into the center of the tangle.

"Wait here for a moment."

Fox drew a deep breath and held it, listening to her heart slam against her rib cage. Even though she knew she was experiencing the best part right now, knew that the actual coming together would be a frustrating disappointment, some perverse corner of her mind felt an urgency to get on with it. She wanted to touch his naked chest and look at his thighs. Men had beautiful legs, long and muscled and strong.

A glow of light appeared deep within the growth of willows. Quickly Fox checked to see how far the light penetrated a thick growth of foliage. Relieved, she decided those back at camp wouldn't notice.

Tanner loomed before her and placed his big hands on her shoulders. "If you change your mind at any time . . . just say so."

His hands felt proprietary and possessive, which felt oddly reassuring. "I won't change my mind," Fox whispered.

He guided her into the entry far enough to discover the source of light was a lantern illuminating a small room that made Fox think of a nest. He'd cut the willows in a rough circle, and used the branches and leaves to cushion the ground. Over the branches, he'd spread blankets and a couple of pillows.

"It's wonderful," Fox murmured. The leafy scent of the willows rose around them and she could hear the river nearby. Tonight the rushing water tossed and splashed, creating music accompanied by crickets and the occasional bass of a frog.

"We have a jug of coffee and another of water." Tanner bent over a basket Fox hadn't noticed until now. "Mr. Hernandez made tarts out of dried apricots."

The basket and its contents startled her. When did he plan to eat tarts? Refined folks certainly didn't go about this sort of thing the way crude ordinary folks did. Fox was certain of that. In this situation, the men she knew would have been finished by now and headed to the saloon for a drink. They wouldn't have brought a picnic to dawdle over.

Tanner sat on the blanket and removed the jug of coffee. "Would you like a cup?"

"Might as well." Since nothing else was happening. Fox sat on the blanket facing him, and hoped the lantern light shining on her face made her look nice. Thanks to the bacon grease, her cheeks and lips were no longer chapped. She thought it might be possible that she could bear up under a light shining in her face.

"This should be wine," Tanner said, touching his cup to hers. "Something special and extravagant."

Fox wet her lips, growing more nervous by the minute. "I'd just as soon have coffee. Or, better yet, whiskey. Of course I've never had any wine that was special or extravagant."

He gazed at her, his smile moving slowly over her face. "To a memorable night."

"To a memorable night," she said, repeating the toast and wishing things would start getting memorable. "Are we going to eat the apricot tarts now?"

"If you like." His gaze moved to the open collar of her shirt.

"Actually, I'm wondering if maybe you changed your mind about this." When he lifted an eyebrow, she rushed on. "I mean, the coffee and the tarts . . . I thought we came here to, well, you know. I'm confused about whether you came here to, you know, or to have coffee and dessert."

Fox raised a hand to her forehead and silently cursed. She prided herself on being plainspoken, but she couldn't bring herself to say "have sex" or "make love." All she could manage was "you know."

Tanner caught her hand and brought it to his lips. "We're in no hurry, Fox. We have all night."

Well, my God. No one had ever kissed her fingertips, and she had never for a minute imagined that someone might. Or that she would like it. When he released her hand, she examined her fingertips then clasped her hand in her lap.

"I never met the likes of you," she said after a moment. Did he expect her to kiss his fingertips? She guessed she wouldn't mind. He had big, well-shaped hands that looked capable of whatever demands were placed on them.

"And I've never met anyone like you."

This was turning into a night of surprises. Fox could have sworn that she read admiration in his gaze. A wave of pleasure swept the surface of her skin.

"I don't suppose it's common for folks like you and me to get together like this." But then, she'd heard that opposites attract. That might explain the tension that sparked and flashed between them and the way she'd been drawn to him from the start.

"There's something in your story that I'm curious about."

Instantly a frown puckered her brow. The last thing she wanted to talk about tonight was her own history. "What is it?" She hoped he heard her reluctance.

"How did you discover what your stepfather had done?" Reaching for the jug, he poured more coffee into their cups. "And how old were you when you found out?"

A sigh lifted Fox's shoulders. "Me and Peaches ran away when I was a month short of thirteen. We just left one day and didn't go back. We lived by doing odd jobs in the mining camps. Sometimes we returned to San Francisco and worked on the wharves."

Dropping her head back, she looked up at the velvety sky. More stars had appeared. Their nest felt snug and hidden from the world.

"Not long after I turned seventeen we were in San Francisco, and one night I was reading the newspaper to Peaches and ran across an article about my stepfather. I recognized his name." The article had announced that wealthy entrepreneur Hobbs Jennings was moving his headquarters to Denver in the Colorado Territory. But she didn't tell Tanner that part.

"Go on." Tanner stretched out on the blanket and propped his head in his hand.

"I'll make this short. I was curious. Me and Peaches went to the newspaper office and spoke to the newsman who'd written the article. He knew all about my stepfather. Told us the tragic story how my stepfather's wife and daughter had died within a day of each other." Her lips thinned and she paused before going on. "Told us how my stepfather's inheritance was the beginning of a great fortune. He hadn't had much money of his own, not until he married my mother. But her money built him an empire."

"Did you go to the authorities?" Tanner's voice emerged stiff with anger.

Fox shrugged. "Do you think anyone would have believed me? A seventeen-year-old runaway traveling with a black man? Living hand to mouth?" She shook her head. "I tested my story on the newsman and he just laughed. Told me to think of some other scheme, that one wouldn't work. He didn't believe for a second that I was the long-lost daughter come back from the dead. He thought I was an adventuress posing as the true beneficiary of my mother's fortune."

The shock of discovering she'd been cheated had made her wild inside. "I went back to Mrs. Wilson's place, hoping maybe she had some proof I could use. My mother had written her a letter explaining that in the event of my mother's death, my stepfather would be my guardian and manage my fortune until I came of age. If my stepfather died before my mother, Mrs. Wilson was to become my guardian since she was the only other family I had, and Mrs. Wilson was to hire a bank to manage the money."

"But the letter no longer existed," Tanner guessed.

Fox nodded. "Mrs. Wilson had seen no reason to keep it. She believed my stepfather when he claimed the money was gone and he could not afford to raise me nor did he think it proper when I had blood family to do the job." A shrug twitched her shoulders. "So no proof existed. A year later Mrs. Wilson died. After that, there was no one but Peaches who could swear I was who I said I was. No one would have believed either of us."

Tanner moved up beside her and pulled her into his arms, stroking the rigid muscles along the valley of her spine. "I'm sorry, Fox. You got a raw deal."

She turned her face into his collar, inhaling the fresh soapy scent of his skin and noticing that he'd patted good smelling lotion on his jaw. Lord, Lord. There was nothing better than a good-smelling man.

"I don't know if it's any comfort, but I believe we all pay for our sins. If not in this life then the next." He tipped her face up to gaze into her eyes. "That bastard will pay for what he did."

She stared into his eyes shining in the light of the lantern. "Oh, I know he'll pay. There is no doubt about that." She would see to it by shooting a bullet into Hobbs Jennings's black heart.

She also knew that she'd had as much conversation as her nerves could stand. Overcome by impatience, she shoved Tanner down on the blanket and climbed on top of him.

"I don't mean to sound bossy, or maybe I do, but it's time to stop this blathering and start, well, you know."

His eyes sparkled and he wore the expression that came over him when he was trying not to laugh.

She narrowed her eyes and tried to find the anger that helped her through vulnerable moments. "I mean, that's why we came here, isn't it?"

"Are we running behind schedule?"

Her cheeks heated. "You're teasing."

Sitting up, he leaned forward to kiss the tip of her nose. "I like the way you're wearing your hair tonight. Piled on top of your head. You have beautiful hair."

"Oh. Silly talk." This was more like it. "I enjoy the silly talk. It's funny and nice." And it sounded like events were finally moving in the right direction.

After kissing her lightly on the mouth, a tease, he removed her hairpins and waves of red hair tumbled to her shoulders then spilled down her back almost to her waist. Fascinated, Tanner caught a long coil and rubbed it against his cheek.

"Like silk," he murmured.

The heated look in his eyes stifled Fox's laugh. Her throat went dry and hot and she felt the first tremor of what she suspected would soon erupt into an earthquake deep inside.

He guided her into his arms and kissed her deeply, letting the hunger grow and build in one heated kiss after another. Fox felt his hand cupping the back of her head, buried in her hair. She had never touched a man's tongue before but did so now, and a jolt of lightning scorched through her body. He tasted of smoke and coffee and something sweet, and she wanted more of him.

When they were both breathing raggedly, Tanner ran his hands over her shoulders, pushing her fancy waistcoat down her arms. Gazing into her eyes, he tossed it aside and opened the first button on her oversized shirt.

Fox swallowed. "I have freckles on me."

"I guessed as much," he murmured, his voice husky. His fingers brushed her breasts as he opened more buttons.

No one had undressed her since she was a child. The idea of it was strange. She felt like a lump sitting there, letting him open her shirt, and she didn't know what to do with her hands.

"Should I be unbuttoning your shirt, too?"

"If you like." Leaning, he kissed her throat as her collar fell away. Now the top of her chemise appeared and Fox would have traded ten years of her life for a bit of lace trim.

Seizing on the task, she unbuttoned his white shirt with trembling fingers, suddenly yearning for another glimpse of the hair on his chest. Once she had enough area exposed, she flattened her palm on his skin, drawing a sharp breath. The just-right hair on his chest felt softer than she had expected. And Lordy his skin was hot.

When he'd taken off her shirt, he gazed at her a long moment with an expression that told her he was not disappointed. Relief emboldened her and Fox pushed his shirt off of muscled shoulders and waited while he pulled his arms out of the sleeves. His skin was tight and his muscles well defined and hard. There was no give when she poked him with a finger.

She expected him to slip off her chemise, but instead he untied the thin rope at the waist of her trousers. When he started opening her trouser buttons, she felt dizzy and tingly all over.

Did she dare? She decided she did. With fingers that fumbled and stumbled, she managed to open his belt and unhook the top button on his trousers then she brushed his arousal and snatched her hands back with a gasp.

An embarrassed pink flared on her cheeks. A woman her age ought to be more experienced than this, shouldn't be as skittish and unnerved as she was feeling. She started to say so, but Tanner covered her mouth with a kiss and a flood of sensation made her forget everything but the hard pressure of his lips and his big hands on her bare shoulders. She felt the calluses on his palms, would have sworn that she felt his very fingerprints.

"Oh," she breathed when he released her, the air running out of her body. Tanner had now kissed her more times than she'd ever been kissed in her life. And his kisses had aroused a stronger response than any kiss she had previously experienced or dared to imagine. She stared into his dark eyes with surprise and confusion and waited to discover what amazing thing he would do next.

He brought her foot up between his legs and tugged on her boot, tossed it aside, then kissed her toes before he reached for her other foot.

He kissed her toes! Fox could not believe it. Her mouth fell open and she stared. This was the most erotic event that had ever happened to her. Who would even think of such a thing? Only Matthew Tanner. She was positive no other man had ever kissed a woman's toes, for God's sake. Holding her breath, hardly daring to move, she waited to see if he would do it again. And he did. He kissed the toes of her other foot and she dropped back on the blanket, blinking at the starry sky and thinking she would surely faint for the first time in her life.

She might have except then he tugged on her trousers and she was astonished to notice that her hips lifted of their own volition to help slide the trousers off and down her legs. And there she lay, sprawled on the blanket in her chemise and pantaloons, one thin layer of material away from being buck naked.

When she finally raised her head to see what he was doing, she sucked in a deep breath and held it until she thought her chest would explode. Tanner stood above her, naked as the day he was born, holding out a hand to her.

Fox had seen naked men, but in bits and pieces, never all at once. She had seen bare chests and bare butts. Had seen legs and had even glimpsed the working part between a man's thighs. But never on the same man at the same moment.

He was absolutely beautiful. Like the statues outside the library in San Francisco. The soft spill of lantern light glowed on his skin like the gloss on marble. His thighs were muscled and taut, his stomach rippled. Somehow he seemed larger than when he was dressed, a force of nature that made her feel small and vulnerable.

When her gaze dropped and she saw the rampant state of his arousal, a great weakness spread through her limbs and her bones melted. Oh Lordy.

Gently he drew her to her feet and into his arms where he proceeded to kiss her like she had never been kissed before. Deep hungry kisses that ignited her body and soul. Kisses that made her forget where they were and why, kisses that spun all thought out of her mind until she trembled with pure sensation. She hardly noticed when he drew her chemise over her head and dropped it, and it was she who pushed down her pantaloons and kicked out of them. She wanted, no needed, needed to feel skin against hot damp skin, needed to know the touch of him with no barrier between them. For the first time she wanted a man's hands on her body, raising shivers of anticipation with each stroke, each caress.

Locked in a kiss, they sank to their knees. Fox touched his hair, his face, his shoulders. She felt his chest hair on her breasts, felt the dampness of his skin and her own. And when he eased back to look at her, she felt an agony of embarrassment followed by a soaring elation of pride as she watched his expression tighten and heard him murmur hoarsely, "You are so beautiful. So perfect and beautiful."

She wasn't, but it thrilled her to hear him say the words.

Gently he cupped her full breasts and brushed his thumbs across nipples so hard they ached. Fox closed her eyes and arched her spine. Her head fell backward and a low moan issued from her lips. The earthquake gathered strength in her lower belly.

When she opened her eyes, they lay together on the blanket, and he stroked her, following the curve from breast to waist to hip. She trembled beneath his palm, opened her lips to his kisses and wanted him in a way she had never experienced. Felt a damp emptiness that yearned to be filled.

"Tanner, Tanner." His name burned on her lips and she writhed beneath his hands, her hair twisting across the blanket. "Please . . ."

As he rose over her, her fingers flew over his chest, tugged at his hips as her body lifted to meet his thrust. And a tiny scream of relief and ecstasy broke from her lips as he entered her.

Bracing on his arms, looking down at her, he moved slowly in long even strokes until Fox was wild beneath him, thrashing, lifting, urging him with hands and body. Only when she felt half out of her mind did he unleash his own hunger and urgency and increase the tempo, taking her higher and higher, building a tension that confused and almost frightened her in its intensity.

And then, when she thought she would surely explode, it seemed that she did, felt as if she soared outside herself, expanding toward the starry night then contracted back into herself. Weak and spent, she wrapped Tanner in an embrace as he collapsed above her and sank to the side, pulling her into his arms.

They lay together, panting for breath, slick and shiny with perspiration, grateful for the cool air rising from the river.

"Never in my whole life . . ." Fox whispered when she could speak. "I never even imagined . . ."

Tanner lifted a wet tendril from her cheek and smoothed back her hair. "You are wonderful."

She didn't know what to say. Something had happened to her that surpassed any effort to describe or explain. That such passion and rapture could exist between a man and a woman had never entered her thoughts. She would have laughed and dismissed outright any claim to such nonsense.

Rising on an elbow, Fox gazed down into Tanner's face, wishing she possessed the eloquence to tell him what a miracle he'd wrought and how awed she was by it. After a moment she gave up and simply said, "It wasn't awful."

Laughing, he pulled her into his arms and kissed her forehead, her nose, her lips, her chin. "Would you like some cold water?"

"I would crawl over loose shale for some cold water."

Fox sat up and was admiring the lantern light on his buttocks and thighs when they heard the first shots. Tanner spun toward the sound and they stared at each other.

Then Fox jumped to her feet and she and Tanner collided in a frenzy of searching for pants, shirts, boots. Tanner remembered to extinguish the lantern before they burst out of the willows and raced toward the campsite.

CHAPTER 13

꠱꠱꠱ ꠱꠱꠱ ꠱꠱꠱

As they raced toward the dust and confusion swirling over the campsite, Tanner spotted large dark forms running between him and the firelight. He and Fox were almost on top of the animals before he realized it was a herd of elk.

Shouting, he grabbed Fox's arm and spun her off to the side, concerned about the gunshots. Hanratty and Brown were trying to turn the elk away from the campsite, but the shots hadn't been effective. The question was which direction they were firing. Into the herd? Above the herd? Toward him and Fox?

"Elk," Fox gasped. Bending, she placed her hands on her knees and a curtain of loose hair swung forward to hide her face.

They waited as the animals, oddly silent for such big animals, ran through the camp. When the last one had rushed into the darkness and the bullets stopped flying, Tanner and Fox walked forward to inspect the damage.

The fire pit had been knocked asunder. Hanratty threw the camp's water supply on fingers of fire traveling out from the scattered stones. Brown beat at the flames with his saddle blanket. Once Tanner was certain the fire had been contained, he moved over the trampled ground and examined the destruction.

The tents were destroyed, stakes broken, the canvas torn and crushed into the ground. Hooves had gouged the saddles and ripped the leather in spots, but they still appeared serviceable. Foodstuffs littered the ground, and clothing. Several cooking pots were smashed beyond repair.

Gold coins glittered in the starlight, strewn across the camp and beyond.

Fox was first to speak. She pulled back her shoulders. "Is everyone all right? Any injuries?"

"Jesus." Hanratty stared at the damage. "It happened so fast. One minute we were just sitting here talking, and the next instant two hundred animals were all around us."

Jubal Brown pulled his hat out of the ground, examined the broken crown and brim, then threw it down in disgust. Stalking over to a carcass on the ground, he gave the dead animal a kick. "I wish I'd shot more of the bastards."

"Where's Peaches?"

"Right here, Missy." Peaches walked out of the darkness. "Our animals are all accounted for but agitated." He took a long look at the carcass. "Elk steaks tomorrow night."

Tanner found the bank bags near where his tent had stood. All but one of the bags had busted under the pounding of hooves. Everywhere he turned he saw flashes of gold. The enormity of the task ahead thinned his lips.

"Well," Fox said when everyone had looked his fill at the devastation. "Peaches, are you up to butchering that elk?"

"I guess so." He didn't sound happy about it.

"All right. Let's find the lanterns. Brown, you start cleaning up the camp. Hanratty, you help Tanner and me pick up coins."

"Now? In the dark?"

"It's going to take several hours to collect them and then do a count." She looked toward Tanner for confirmation, and he nodded. "We can't afford to lose another day, so we'll have to do it tonight." Everyone watched while she picked a torn sleeve off the ground, ripped off a strip and used it to tie back her hair. "Let's move."

Tanner found a Dutch oven and kneeled beside the broken bags. Many of the coins had clumped here and he started scooping them into the pot. As near as he could figure, 1,875 coins were somewhere on the ground. Grimly, he consulted his pocket watch.

"It's ten thirty-five," he said when Fox asked.

Their eyes met and held for an instant, then she nodded and walked away, a lantern in one hand, the dishpan in her other.

Tanner watched the swing of her hips and the wild tumble of red curls falling to her waist. For a moment his mouth went dry and he saw her in his mind, a lush hourglass figure of perfection. If ever there was a woman with no need to hide beneath oversized shapeless clothing, it was Fox.

He thought about her as he stuffed the Dutch oven with gold and began filling another large pot, digging out coins embedded in the ground.

Even if she hadn't told him so, he would have known she had limited experience with a man. And the man she'd mentioned had used her poorly. His mouth set in a line. The man had been a fool.

Fox was the most responsive woman Tanner had ever encountered. More responsive than professional women, less inhibited than the respectable kind. She was every man's dream. Beautiful, open, eager to please, wildly exciting in her enthusiasm. He felt an instant stirring remembering the firm touch of her skin and the musky fragrance of her arousal. Their time together had passed all too quickly.

At one in the morning, he and Hanratty and Fox walked through the camp one last time, holding their lanterns high, eyes on the ground. Hanratty found two coins they had missed, then they called it quits.

"The count will go faster if you and Jubal count some of the pots and Hanratty and I count the rest," Fox suggested, swiveling to work out the kinks in her back. The hours of bending to search for and pick up coins made one's back ache like blazes.

"You trust me to help with the count?" Jubal asked, covering a yawn.

Tanner's smile didn't reach his eyes. "I'll be watching."

They finished the coin count at a little after three in the morning. Tanner added the two sums and nodded wearily.

"We're missing thirteen coins." Fox reached for a lantern, but he shook his head. "We'll look again in the morning."

She sank back on the scorched grass and rubbed her eyes. "We found one thousand eight hundred and sixty-two. I wouldn't have believed it was possible."

"We're only missing two hundred and sixty dollars." Standing, Hanratty rubbed the small of his back and gazed across the camp, which Jubal had restored to loose order.

"Only?" Jubal asked. "Since when was two hundred and sixty dollars a piddly amount? You got a fortune you ain't mentioned?"

"Shut up. I'm going to find some blankets and go to sleep." Without a backward glance, Hanratty moved into the darkness. Smiling, Jubal Brown followed.

Fox scanned the pots of coins. "I'm too tired to think about what we'll do with these now that the bags are broken."

"Before Mr. Hernandez went to sleep, he sewed some new bags out of the tent canvas."

Fox's gaze softened and she nodded. "That's Peaches. Doing what needs to be done with no fuss about it." Lowering her head, she plucked at her shirttail. "Tonight was . . . you know, the part before the shots and the elk . . ."

Tanner put an arm around her, feeling the weariness in her shoulders. "You were wonderful."

"Was I?" Large blue eyes turned up to him. "Seems like you did everything and I just . . ."

He kissed her, slowly, deliberately, and smiled when she sighed. He rested his chin on top of her head. "Did I mention that the fanny project is a success?"

She laughed softly, snuggling into him.

"Do you have a name?"

"Fox."

"Other than Fox? Or is that the name your mother gave you?"

"I have a name," she admitted reluctantly. "But I'm not going to tell you. It's one of those lady names that was never meant for someone like me."

Someone like me. It pained him to hear her say that. She was smart, capable, self-sufficient. Beautiful, fearless, and honorable.

Long after Fox and the others were asleep, Tanner sat in the darkness, smoking beneath a canopy of stars. He thought about his father, awaiting rescue in the mountains above Denver. Thought about the unfinished mine design he'd left in Carson City. Mostly he thought about Fox.

It was going to be damned difficult to leave her when they reached Denver.

In the morning, they found eleven of the missing coins before Tanner decided it was more important to move on than to waste another hour searching for forty dollars. First, they had to wait for Peaches to mount his mule. Rebecca didn't take well to a saddle and threw him off twice.

Frowning, Fox watched Peaches push to his feet and straighten slowly. "Are you all right, old man?"

He grimaced and rubbed his hip. "I'm feeling my age."

Considering all he'd been through in the last couple of

days, Fox didn't doubt it. Once he was finally mounted and it appeared Rebecca wouldn't buck him off again, Peaches looked around for the rest of the mules.

"Jubal is leading your string today," Fox informed him. "I want you to take it easy." Peaches closed his eyes and nodded, and Fox's level of concern shot up a few notches. Today would be long, but thankfully, if she remembered correctly, the terrain was relatively level.

A wall of rock rose directly in front of them. Fox knew from hard experience that the Schell Creek Range was not passable. They would have to head south around it, climbing again in altitude. After a long hard examination of Peaches's color, not good, and his posture, slumped, she urged her mustang to the front and headed out, leading one of the mule strings.

The stopover had been costly. Peaches had taken a beating in the water, they had lost a horse and all the tents, a goodly amount of their food staples, some utensils, and clothing. And two gold coins.

Fox's back still ached and she wondered how many more times she could stand hours of bending and searching for the damned coins. As many times as she had to, she finally decided, her expression grim.

By noon the steady climb in altitude had carried them above the sagebrush and into an area of tall limestone formations that interested Tanner but no one else. Everyone bolted their midday food without conversation, tired and feeling the need to make up time.

That night they camped in a high meadow circled by rough granite peaks. "Go sit down," Fox ordered when she saw the lines in Peaches's face and his tight lips. "I'll unpack the mules and find what we need to make supper." Peaches nodded gratefully and sat, resting his bones against a tree trunk.

"It's cold again," Hanratty commented after a simple meal of biscuits and elk steaks. "Feels like it could snow."

"Are we close to a place where we can replace the tents?" Jubal Brown asked Fox.

"There's a settlement on the far edge of the desert that might have what we need." She couldn't say for certain. In this part of the country settlements might thrive, or they could vanish in less than six months. "If we put in some long days, we should get there in about a week."

"I think I'll call it a day," Peaches said, rising from the

ground with difficulty. "I'm stiff as a poker," he added, aware they all watched. "And coughing like a coyote. Nothing to worry over, just an aggravation."

Fox started to point out that the sun was still above the horizon, but bit her tongue. "Like you always told me, sleep is the best healer." Peaches rolled into his blankets and turned his face away from the fire. "I'm worried," Fox said in a low voice. The rattle in his chest wasn't going away nor were the coughing spells.

Abruptly, Tanner stood and gave her a long glance before he walked toward a grouping of pines. After a minute, feeling a rush of color in her cheeks, Fox followed. They stopped by the trees, in full view of the campfire. She noticed that Hanratty and Brown pretended not to watch.

Tanner handed her a cigar. "Mr. Hernandez needs bed rest."

"There's no place to get it." The thought drove her half mad.

"The second best choice would be to find a meadow with water and stay for a week." When she started to speak, he held up a hand. "But we can't do that."

"I know," she said in frustration and kicked her boot against the ground.

"I'm getting concerned about the time."

"We're almost into Mormon Territory. We'll pick up some time on the flat. But I know what you're saying," she added. "And Peaches would be the first to agree that we can't afford a week out of the schedule."

Frowning, Tanner gazed back at the fire. "The settlement you mentioned . . . could we leave Mr. Hernandez there to recuperate?"

"Leave Peaches behind?" Her chest tightened sharply and she ground the cigar out beneath her heel. "I can't do that, Tanner."

For a lengthy moment neither of them spoke. "Let's wait till we reach the settlement. Then, if Mr. Hernandez isn't feeling stronger, we can ask him what he wants to do."

It was a fair compromise, but Fox didn't like it. She nodded with reluctance. And then released a long slow breath as Tanner's fingertips stroked her cheek.

"There's something I need to say."

His skin took on a bronze cast in the flare of sunset, and his craggy features had softened. "Yes?" Fox asked, wetting her lips.

"I'd like to be with you every night." The rough pad of his thumb brushed across her lips. "I want you to understand that. I also want you to know that I respect you too much to be with you in conditions less than complete privacy."

She glanced again toward the fire and noticed Hanratty looking in their direction. Frowning, she nodded. "I agree." But she felt a twinge of heavy disappointment because she knew there weren't many opportunities ahead for the privacy they wanted.

"In the meantime . . ." Taking her hand, Tanner led her behind a thick-based pine and took her into his arms with a smile. "I don't see any harm in a quick kiss."

Thank heaven. She couldn't look at him or think about him without remembering the lantern light on his naked skin, without feeling a shiver of excitement when she recalled the wonder of exploding beneath him.

She lifted her mouth and experienced a deep weakness when his lips came down hard on hers. A flame kindled in the pit of her stomach and she wanted to lie with him again, longed to press herself along the strong length of his body.

Wrapping her arms around his waist, she laid her head on his chest and closed her eyes. "Tanner?" she whispered. "What we did last night . . . I liked it." Never had she expected to make such an admission. "The things you did . . . well, I never knew about all that." And she had never imagined a man could display enough control to make the evening last as he had with all the finger and toe kissing and the undressing. "Did we eat the apricot tarts? I can't remember."

His low laugh sounded near her ear. "I don't think so."

Rising on tiptoe, she kissed him with enough desire in her mouth and touch that she knew he felt it. "I sure hope we find some more willows soon," she murmured.

They continued east on the flanks of Wheeler Peak, winding among the twisted trunks of sharp-needled bristlecones. Fox had read that bristlecones could live hundreds of years and mentioned the fact to Hanratty, who led Peaches's string of mules today.

"Is that so." Not a flicker of interest enlivened his tight expression. "We ain't seen any Indians for a week."

So he'd noticed that the Indians kept their distance but were out there. "We're in Shoshone territory. The Shoshones won't bother us unless provoked."

"That's what they say about all Indians, and maybe sometimes it's even true."

Fox glanced at him. They had all lost weight on this journey and the loss showed on Hanratty's long face, drawing in his cheeks. Ordinarily Fox didn't notice, but he'd shaved this morning.

"How much desert are we going to have to cross?"

"We'll start seeing cactus as we come off altitude." Fox shrugged. "We've got some hot dusty days ahead. Why?"

"Just making conversation." He cleared his throat and watched a rabbit bolt through the tree trunks. "You know this thing with Tanner ain't going to end well for you."

Fox's head jerked up. "I don't recall asking for your opinion."

"I'm thinking about the ride back to Carson. Figured I'd go back with you and Mr. Hernandez. But you're going to be about as cheerful as a man whose been gut shot."

"I'm not going back to Carson City," she snapped and rode ahead. But the more she thought about his comment, the angrier she became.

After they stopped for the night and she'd seen to Peaches, she told Jubal to make supper. Then she pointed at Hanratty. "I want to talk to you."

Today's trek had taken them lower, back into the sagebrush, and Fox led him toward a large clump. When Hanratty caught up, she whirled and bounced her fist off his chest.

"What I do in my private time is none of your business!" She pushed her face up close to his so he could see the ice in her eyes. "But just in case you have the mistaken idea that it is, the end of this liaison with Tanner was decided before the liaison ever began. I know how things stand, and I'm agreed to it. That's the last comment I'm going to make, so don't go pushing into my affairs in the future."

Hanratty bit off the end of a cigar and spit it on the ground. "Tanner seems like one of us, but he ain't, Fox. And you eating like he does, and saying all the pretty-pleases and thank-yous ain't going to make you into one of his kind."

Embarrassment scalded her throat. She had hoped Tanner had noticed the improvement in her meal manners, but she hadn't given a thought to Hanratty and Brown or what they might make of the changes.

"It doesn't hurt a person to improve herself," she said in a flat voice.

"I don't know why, but I like you. I don't fancy the idea of you being the scratch for a rich man's temporary itch." Hanratty examined the end of his cigar, then walked away.

"What was that about?" Tanner asked when they took a walk after supper.

"Hanratty wants to join up with me and Peaches for the return trip." There was a lot she wasn't telling Tanner and didn't intend to. Realizing it didn't improve her mood.

Glumly, Fox scanned the landscape. There wasn't an inch of privacy to be had. The branches of the bristlecones were spaced far enough apart that she could have thrown a cat through them. There wasn't a hiding place even for a kiss. Damn it.

Hoping the men weren't watching, she let her hand brush against Tanner's. "I think we'll spend a day and a half at the settlement if it's still there," she said, considering. "We need to buy some things. Maybe they have a doctor for Peaches."

"Can we afford the time?"

"I think so."

"Would that settlement have a hotel?" Tanner asked, gazing at her mouth.

Her heart rolled in her chest and she swallowed hard. "They didn't the last time I was through but maybe they do now."

Talking to Hanratty had reminded her why she'd been so interested in this job in the first place. She had a goal. Tearing her thoughts from Tanner's mouth and the memory of his skilled hands, she plucked a sprig of sage and twirled it under her nose.

"If we can't, you know, I guess we'll have to just talk." She drew a long breath. "I expect you'll see your boss while you're in Denver . . ."

Tanner raised an eyebrow. "I hope to. Are you going to tell me again that Hobbs Jennings is a thieving bastard?"

"What kind of place is the J M and M office? Do you have a desk there?"

"I'm not the only mining engineer employed by the company. There are facilities provided when any of us are in town. Are you really interested in this?"

"So the building is large?"

"Not especially." Bending, he tried to see her expression.

"I suppose Jennings's office is plenty large."

"He owns the company."

"I guess that means he's surrounded by bodyguards."

"Just a secretary." Placing his hands on her shoulders, he turned her to face him. "What did you tell Hanratty? Will he join you for the return to Carson City?"

"I might hang around Denver." Tanner wouldn't understand the stupid joke she'd just made. She gave her head a shake. "Whatever I do, Hanratty won't be part of it."

"Whatever you do?" He sounded puzzled. "I assumed you'd head back."

"Now who's making assumptions? But don't you worry. I know the rules, and I won't be a problem for you."

Instantly he pulled back. "I never thought for a moment that you would be."

Reaching deep, Fox dredged up a smile as if she'd been teasing. Then, as the conversation had become uncomfortable she turned back toward camp. She didn't lie, but sometimes it was difficult to wiggle around the truth.

That night she lay in her bedroll staring at the cold stars and a shimmery half-moon, thinking about Hobbs Jennings. She hadn't imagined it would be possible to hate him more than she had for most of her life. But meeting Tanner made her hate Jennings so much that acid chewed at her throat and stomach. If Hobbs Jennings hadn't cheated her, she could have been the same kind as Tanner, and things might have ended differently between them.

Near dawn she tried to console herself with the knowledge that she'd learned some important information tonight. Hobbs Jennings didn't surround himself with bodyguards. Fox didn't need to fear that she'd be shot before she had a chance to kill him.

The wind blew for days, bitter at night and hot during the long dry afternoons. Sand sifted through clothing and bedrolls and into coffee and food. They crossed dry creek beds and rationed water. The two hilly ranges they crossed were sparsely vegetated and home to lean hungry coyotes that howled at night and kept the horses and mules in a state of agitation. Hanratty and Brown made sport out of shooting rattlesnakes and stringing the rattles around their necks as trophies.

After a week of miserable conditions, they camped near a salty playa that signaled Fox to turn north.

"We're a day's ride from the settlement," she announced wearily. Peaches had made a soupy stew out of the last of the elk. They all agreed the stew would have been tastier if it hadn't been laced with sandy grit. The biscuits were so sandy and hard on the teeth that only people too hungry to complain could eat them.

"Good." Peaches rubbed at the dust emphasizing the lines on his face. "Tell me there's a bathhouse there or a river nearby."

"The settlement's close to the Sevier River. But they should have a bathhouse." Fox flipped back her braid and watched with dull eyes as dust and sand showered across her shoulder. The men's hair was so dusty it appeared they had all gone a matted gray.

"Will reaching the settlement get us out of this fricking desert?" Jubal asked, making a face after a swallow of gritty coffee.

Fox nodded, aware that Tanner watched her. "The worst of it is behind us." The sand inside her clothing made her itch. They all scratched as if they had fleas. "Peaches? How are you feeling?"

"Stop asking every ten minutes."

The annoyed reply would have reassured her except he moved slowly and the damn cough persisted. For years Fox had teased by calling him an old man, but since his experience in the water, Peaches had genuinely looked old, and that scared her.

"Fox decided we'll stay two nights at the settlement," Tanner said, his gaze on her. "We can all use the rest."

So could the animals, who hadn't had their fill of food or water in days. And they needed to buy a horse for Peaches, and tents and provisions.

Shifting toward Hanratty and Brown, Tanner reminded them of his orders. "We have two guns in camp at all times." Hard eyes settled on Jubal Brown. "If you say you'll be gone for an hour and you don't return by then, don't bother to come back."

Jubal gave him a long sulky stare.

Leaning forward with his elbows on his knees, Hanratty gazed at the pile of dirty tin supper dishes. "If I never see another tumbleweed, it will be too soon."

Fox lacked the energy to scrub out the dishes, but it was her turn. God knew they had plenty of sand for the scouring. The damned stuff stuck to the sun lotion on her face, and she didn't care. Then she remembered Tanner and wiped her forehead and cheeks with her sleeve. When she looked at him, he managed a tired smile, then he collected the dishes and set to cleaning them. She offered a weak protest then let him wave it aside.

He was such a good man.

CHAPTER 14

THE hand-painted sign read: No Name, population 186.

Cattle could survive on the ranches spreading out from a small ramshackle town, but the grass was meager, growing in coarse tufts between thick sage. The small farms on the outskirts impressed Tanner as brave efforts displaying near unbelievable optimism. The farmers had cleared the sage from small patches that had begun to show green, but there wasn't enough growth to determine what crops were hoped for.

Still, he recognized the appeal of high mountain scenery and the shallow river that trickled past the edge of No Name. Aspen and narrow leaf cottonwoods offered shade, and wild roses trailed across backyards and fences.

At first glance the town seemed deserted, then he became aware of shouting and yelling. Fox led their party up the dirt street, following the sound of the commotion.

They arrived at a dirt field just outside of town where a stand had been erected for spectators. A long table displayed the remains of a covered-dish picnic. A group of men stood near an area set aside as a bar, drinking and pointing and yelling at the field. Kids and dogs chased each other around the spectator stand and down the sides of the field.

Reining up, Tanner pushed back his hat and studied the damnest baseball game he'd ever seen.

The cowboy at the plate was drunk and roaring obscenities at the pitcher who was one of the most amazing women Tanner had ever observed.

She was a tiny thing, barely five feet tall, but there was

nothing small about the fire in her flashing dark eyes, or the confidence with which she held the baseball and considered the cowboy. Tanner had an immediate impression that she could send the baseball streaking across the plate at exactly the spot where she wanted it to be. He suspected this woman could do any damned thing she set her mind to.

While she thought about her next pitch, ignoring the shouts from the stands, he took in the red silk dress she wore, cut short enough for running, and short enough to reveal a glimpse of matching red stockings above her boots. The bodice of the dress dipped low to display an impressive cleavage.

"My Lord," Hanratty said in a voice husky with admiration. "Even if that cowboy was dead sober, he wouldn't be looking at any baseball."

Tanner agreed. She was a striking woman even flushed from exertion and with her dark hair falling out of the fancy twist at the back of her head. It was the first time he'd seen a pitcher wearing feathers and rubies instead of a cap.

Eventually he noticed that the pitcher led an all female team. All the ladies wore shortened skirts for the game, and all wore necklines cut to exhibit their charms to advantage. The third baseman had hiked her skirt up at the waist, freeing her knees and showing off green stockings that seemed to be of particular interest to the umpire who had wandered off in her direction. The girl in the outfield clamped a cigar between her teeth and grinned at an exchange of shouted insults between a cowboy who'd made it to second base and the girl defending that position.

The girls on the female team appeared younger than the pitcher but none could hold a candle to her. Like everyone else in No Name today, Tanner couldn't keep his eyes off of her.

Dark eyes flashing, as full of fire as her red silk dress, she wound up and sent the ball flying across the plate.

"Strike two!"

The cowboy threw down his bat and went head to head with the umpire. "The hell it is!"

Tanner smiled and heard Hanratty laugh beside him. A ball game was exactly what they needed. Already he felt the weariness lifting from his shoulders.

"Howdy, travelers." A man broke from the crowd and ambled toward the road. "Ma'am."

Fox handed her string of mules to Peaches and the mustang danced forward. "I'm Fox, out of Carson City. That's Mr. Tanner, Mr. Hanratty, Mr. Brown, and Mr. Hernandez. We're passing through, heading to Denver. I didn't notice a hotel, so would anyone object to us camping near the river for a couple of nights?"

"You're welcome to stay as long as you like." The voice was friendly, but he looked them over carefully. "I'm Howard Lafferty, mayor of No Name, which ain't going to be the permanent name. That ain't been decided yet."

On the field, the umpire shouted "Ball three!" And a female voice yelled from the outfield, "He don't know what to do with two balls, let alone three." The crowd laughed and jeered.

"You can tie up over there," Lafferty suggested, pointing toward a hodgepodge of wagons and horses parked in the shade of several cottonwoods. "The vehicles will clear out after the game. Meanwhile, there's some food left, and beer if you're as thirsty as you look."

Fox hesitated, then glanced at her party's rapt expressions. "We're obliged. If you'll wait while we tie up, I have some questions about provisions. And is there a doctor in No Name?" At the moment Peaches was grinning toward the field, but an hour ago he'd had a coughing spell so prolonged that she'd feared he'd fall off his mule.

Lafferty followed them to the cottonwoods, talking to Fox, while Tanner thought about the gold. Hanratty and Brown would stay with the mules if he ordered them to, but they'd be sullen for days afterward.

"I'll stay with the animals," he said, watching Hanratty and Brown's expression lighten and eagerness flare in their eyes.

But Fox wouldn't hear of it. "Go watch the game. I'm not interested in baseball." As if any of them were interested in the actual game. She lifted her eyebrows at Howard Lafferty. "Who is the woman in the red dress?"

"That's Barbara Robb," Lafferty said. "Runs the best damned whorehouse east of San Francisco." His gaze scanned the men. "She's mighty particular and don't break her rules for no one. If you boys are interested in dropping by later, you'll have to go by the washhouse first for a tub and a shave."

"There's enough business in this settlement to sustain a whorehouse?" Tanner's brow arched in surprise.

"Son, there's several settlements out here. Miz Robb draws a clientele from a hundred miles in every direction. Without her, we wouldn't have a school or a stage coming in here once a month. We wouldn't have a library, such as it is, or a jail, which she put up the money for. This town would collapse in a week if Miz Robb moved on. That woman is amazing. She could organize a dogfight, she is that efficient."

"Does she, uh, entertain clients herself?" Hanratty asked, knocking the dust off his shoulders.

Lafferty looked shocked. "Absolutely not! If you mess with Miz Robb, you'll have to deal with her piano player. Norwood don't look like the type to take on a big man like you, but son he can outthink you in an eyeblink. He'll have you so tangled up in words that you won't be able to think straight. And by the time you sort it out, you'll be standing outside and your guns will have disappeared without you even noticing."

"That's a shame," Jubal Brown remarked, gazing at Miz Robb. "So which of us has to stay here with Fox?"

Fox responded before Tanner could. "I think we can relax the two-gun rule just this once." She flicked a glance at Tanner's scowl then spread her hands. "We just arrived so no one's had a chance to decide whether or not we're worth robbing. Which we're not," she added for Lafferty's benefit. "Plus our camp is going to be in full view of the field. I doubt I'll have any trouble. Bring the other string of mules over to the river, then you can all go have a beer and watch the game."

Tanner didn't like it, but he saw the sense in what she said. By the time he and the men reached the field, the ladies were at bat and had a runner on first base. A chalkboard read: Ranchers, 5; Whores, 3. He drew a beer and scanned a shaded enclosure looking for Barbara Robb, but didn't spot her. Then curiosity drew his gaze to the people crowded into the bleachers.

It was an interesting mix. Ranchers, farmers, shopkeepers, three Indians who sat apart, and four men dressed in staid black from hats to boots. Each of the men appeared to have three or four wives equally as dark and dour. Sipping his beer, Tanner watched the wives observing the children and dogs, refusing to look at the field.

This was not the first time Tanner had encountered Mormons, nor was it the first time their behavior had puzzled him.

Clearly they didn't approve of the ball game, yet they had stayed to watch.

He also spotted Howard Lafferty speaking to a gray-haired portly man sitting closer to the Indians than anyone else. After a moment, the gray-haired man picked up a bag and both men headed away from the field toward where Tanner had left Fox.

Beside him, Peaches sighed then put down his cup of beer. "I promised her if Mr. Lafferty found a doctor, I'd submit," he said before he, too, started across the dirt street, muttering under his breath.

Tanner turned back to the game, and this time he saw Barbara Robb speaking head to head with a lean, good-looking man who Tanner assumed was the piano player Lafferty had mentioned. He watched for a while, thinking about the lack of a hotel in No Name, beginning to see a solution and letting a plan form.

Frowning, the doctor wiped his hands on a damp cloth. "The news is bad, Mr. Hernandez. I'd say consumption."

Fox's hands flew to her mouth. "That's wrong," she protested. "He got dumped in the water and tumbled around. All he has is a cold and some bruises, and no wonder."

"I don't doubt it, but Mr. Hernandez also has consumption. Bloody cough, fatigue, pale . . . he needs total bed rest. Even then, at his age . . ."

Fox sat hard on a tree stump. "Total bed rest?" She had to admit that she'd never seen Peaches look so lackluster and tired. "Why didn't you tell me your cough was bloody, damn it?"

"Nothing to do about it, Missy." Peaches shrugged and buttoned his shirt. "I've already tried everything in our doctor kit."

"You seem like a sensible man, Mr. Hernandez. I strongly suggest you heed my advice." Tipping the hat up on his head, Doc Evans picked up his bag.

"What do I owe you?" Fox asked. Her own cheeks felt ashy and drawn.

"Fifty cents."

She was too shocked by Peaches's news to summon outrage at the fee. She paid without a murmur.

They didn't speak after the doctor returned to the ball game. Sipping the beers that Tanner had sent over to them, they sat on the ground in silence listening to the drone of insects and the shouts and cheers rising from the field across the road.

"What all did the doctor advise?"

"Nothing I plan on doing," Peaches said, leaning his head back against the wheel of someone's wagon.

"That's stupid. Tell me what he said."

Peaches opened his eyes. "Do you really think I'm going to stay here in some stranger's house in a strange bed while you go on to Denver?"

"I'll stay with you."

"No you won't. You hired on to do a job, and if I taught you right, you'll keep your word to Mr. Tanner. That means getting him and his gold to Denver. His daddy's life depends on it."

They stared at each other.

"I know about consumption. It killed my mother."

Peaches pushed to his feet. "No one lives forever. Now let's get this camp set up." A cough rumbled up to his throat and he coughed and choked until he was bent double and gasping. Before he shoved his handkerchief back into his pocket, Fox spied a flash of bright red blood.

"If you die, old man, I'm going to be so pissed."

He smiled. "So will I." When she started to argue, he wiped sweat from his forehead then held up a hand. "I'm not staying here in No Name and that's that."

"You can't rest on the road! Now you know that." Furious, she kicked the saddle covering the money bags.

"Missy?" Something in his voice made her look up. He opened his arms.

Fox flung herself at him and pressed her face into his neck, squeezing him tight. "I can't stand it," she whispered.

"I know."

She gave him a shake. "You better be there when I kill Hobbs Jennings! I'm counting on you."

"I'll be there." He stroked her back, gave her long braid a tug. "Unless you change your mind."

She smacked his back with her fist. "I'm not going to change my mind, so don't go planning that as your next death wish!" She forced herself to release him, trying to believe that he hadn't lost as much weight as it felt as if he had. "Doc Evans is just a small-town bum. What does he know anyway? You're going to get better, I'm sure of it."

"I am, too. Just going to take some time."

"I can finish up here," Fox said when she saw him eyeing the mule packs. "Why don't you go on ahead to the bathhouse? Have a nice long soak. It'll make you feel better."

Once Peaches was out of sight, moving slowly down the road, Fox went to the bank of the river, sat down, and pressed her forehead hard against her knees. Oh God, oh God. Please make him well again. I'll do anything you ask.

Supper came courtesy of No Name's leftover picnic, then Tanner dismissed Hanratty and Brown to have a bath and see the sights.

"Which consist of one saloon and the whorehouse, according to Howard Lafferty," Tanner explained to Fox after Hanratty and Brown had departed for the evening.

"Who won the game?" Fox nursed her coffee, wishing it was whiskey.

"The ranchers. By four runs." Tanner moved to sit beside her and slipped an arm around her waist. "What did the doctor say about Mr. Hernandez?"

Fox glanced toward Peaches's bedroll then laid her head on Tanner's shoulder. "You can't trust a doctor in a place this size. If he was worth a damn, he'd be working in a town where he could make some money."

"The news was bad?" He rubbed her back.

"Peaches is getting better every day," she said firmly. "As long as he can do his work there's nothing to worry about."

Tanner blew a smoke ring toward the moon. When she was ready, she'd tell him. "There's a horse for sale at the stables. I'll have a look at him tomorrow. Lafferty says the general store stocks most of the items we need."

"He told me the same thing," Fox said in a tired voice. "I've made a list." She pressed her face against his collar. "I'm sorry there isn't a hotel."

"I want to talk to you about that."

She'd washed her face in the river, but her hair still smelled of dust and her clothing was gritty. Tanner thought of the way most women fussed over a spot on their dresses and smiled. To his eyes, Fox was as appealing as any woman he'd ever met. Dusty or fresh out of a bath, she put other women in the shade. He wrapped his arms around her, feeling her breath warm on his neck.

"Talk away," she said.

"How would you feel about staying overnight in a whore-house?"

Drawing back, she looked at him, then laughed. "I've never been in a whorehouse, but I confess I've always been curious."

"I spoke to Barbara Robb. She'll rent us a room accessible by a back entrance. If you're willing," he added in a husky voice.

"I'm willing," she whispered, lifting her mouth for a kiss.

Tanner kissed her and electricity shot down to his toes. There was no explaining why one woman among all others set a man's blood on fire. No understanding why one woman felt right in his arms and no one else ever had.

He and Fox were different in background and tempera-ment, yet she reached him on a level where he hadn't been touched before. She could be the most irritating woman alive and an hour later give him a look that made his chest tighten and his mouth go dry. Her stubbornness made him crazy inside while the flashes of vulnerability raised an ache in his chest. He couldn't think of a woman whom he'd admired more.

"Do you worry about your father?" she asked after a while.

"Every day." The worst was wondering if his father ex-pected him to fail. That had been the pattern. Always Tanner sensed that his father felt surprised by Tanner's successes. In this case, he hoped to deliver the gold early and spare his father at least a few days of his ordeal.

"We'll get the gold there in time."

They sat quietly, holding each other, listening to the snores rising from Peaches's bedroll.

"I love that old man," Fox whispered.

"I know. I'm sure he'll be all right," Tanner said, trying to sound confident. He wasn't sure.

The next day was busy. Tanner bought the horse for Peaches while Fox arranged for tents and additional provisions. They both found time for a visit to the bathhouse. Peaches rubbed down all the animals and did some minor doctoring on a couple of the mules with long rests in between his chores. Hanratty and Brown packed the items Fox had purchased and nursed hangovers with pots of strong coffee. Having let off steam the night before neither groused about remaining in camp with the bags of gold.

As soon as darkness descended, Tanner escorted Fox to the whorehouse, a commanding three-story clapboard building on the edge of No Name. As he'd arranged, they entered by the back and didn't encounter anyone on their way up the stairs.

Once he closed the bedroom door, Fox spun into his arms and kissed him hard and thoroughly before he released her to look around. The room was small, crowded by a bed, a wooden side chair, and a low table holding a painted washbasin and the bottle of whiskey he had requested.

Fox hung her hat on the row of hooks and examined a framed painting of a bare-breasted woman lolling on a swing. Red flushed her cheeks and she turned away from the painting.

"Well," she said. "Here we are."

Smiling, Tanner added his hat beside hers and hung up his waistcoat. Then he picked her up and tossed her on the bed.

"What?" Surprise widened her eyes, then she laughed. "At least help me out of my boots first."

The awkwardness gone, he grabbed one of her feet and pulled off her boot, tossing it behind him, then caught her other foot. Golden light spilled from the globe beside the bed, bathing her face in soft tones of paleness and shadow, catching in her hair and making it shine.

"You're beautiful," he said, staring at her.

"No, I'm not." Dropping her head, she frowned at her bare toes.

"You are to me." Tonight her eyes were as blue as cornflowers, her lightly tanned skin as smooth as satin. He knew that under her oversized shirt and cinched-up male trousers was a lush abundance of curves. Experiencing an instant erection, he bit down on his back teeth and told himself not to hurry. They might not have another opportunity to enjoy a full night in a real bed.

"Are you going to kiss my toes?" she asked shyly, smiling down at her feet.

"I'm going to suck them right off your feet."

"Oh God." Clapping a hand to her chest, she pretended to swoon.

Sitting beside her, he untied the string at the end of her braid and gently pried apart the plaiting. A curtain of heavy silken hair spilled through his fingers, shimmering like flame, soft across his callused palms. When her braid was loosened, she leaned back against him with a sigh, and he felt her tremble as his arms came around her.

Sitting quietly pressed chest to back wasn't what he'd expected and the moment of tenderness surprised him. Suddenly Tanner wanted to tell her that he'd never felt this close to a woman or this comfortable. He'd never felt so possessive or so protective. Right now, he wished he could spread the world at her feet, wanted to give her all the things she had missed in life.

"What I really want is a glass of that whiskey," she said in the strange way she had of seeming to follow his thoughts. Then she laughed and turned to throw her arms around his neck. "Aren't you supposed to have whiskey in a whorehouse?"

"Later," he growled, fumbling with the buttons on the front of her shirt. He must have said what she wanted to hear because she lowered her head and smiled, then opened his shirt, doing it more quickly than he was managing to do with hers.

When she was naked, he drew a sharp breath. She had the form of a goddess. Full heavy breasts, a small waist, and flaring hips made for a man's pleasure. For a small woman, she had long strong legs, and ankles he could circle with his thumb and middle finger. A low groan rumbled out of his chest and he kissed her with desire powerful enough to rock him.

They fell back on the bed in a tangle of bodies, lips suddenly frantic and searching. Her stomach was flat and firm, the only softness her breasts rising to his touch.

She met him kiss for kiss, her hands flying from his face to his shoulders, pulling him closer, her body damp with the heat of passion.

Tanner kissed her throat, her breasts, tasting her and inhaling the unique scent of her skin and arousal. She tasted like soap and salt and sweetness, smelled faintly of bathhouse lotion and strongly female.

After brushing his palms across the buds of her nipples, he kissed and sucked until she moaned, twisting beneath him, plucking at his hair and shoulders with urgent hands. But he wouldn't be hurried. Stroking her waist and hips, he trailed kisses down her stomach, feeling her quiver beneath his lips.

"Tanner! What are you . . . ?"

Her words ended in a gasp as he found her center and circled his tongue in damp tangles of auburn. Trying to ignore an erection that had become painful with urgency, he kissed her, tasted her, made love to her until she exploded with a scream of wonder and amazement.

Only then did he move over her and thrust into the liquid heat of her. She gazed up at him with wide dazed eyes and touched his lips with shaking fingertips. Then her throat arched and she lifted her breasts, offering herself in total surrender.

Never had he known a woman like this one.

CHAPTER 15

*T*OO troubled in her mind to sleep, Fox pulled on her trousers and shirt, tied back her hair, and kissed Tanner's forehead without waking him. Closing the door quietly behind her, she stood for a moment in the hallway listening to the silence until she became aware of a piano playing softly down below. Descending the staircase, she followed the music until she emerged into a large deserted parlor.

Beautifully upholstered furniture formed conversation groupings that could be closed off by curtains if privacy demanded. Heavy Turkish carpets cushioned the floor, counterpointed by brilliantly polished brass spittoons and standing brass ashtrays. Large mirrors, which Fox ignored, and paintings depicting voluptuous women in various stages of undress adorned the walls. But Fox's primary impression was of the color red.

Red and gold wallpaper surrounded the room, and the upholstery ran through variations from deep maroon to pale rose. She decided the parlor was exactly how she had hoped a whorehouse would look, boasting luxurious man-size furniture, brass and gilt and crystal, and above all, red.

"What's your name?" The piano sat on a raised dais and the man quietly fingering the keys smiled at her. "I know a tune for every lady's name."

"It's Fox."

Compelling blue eyes sparkled in the light from the chandelier above. "That one I don't know. Do you like Stephen Foster's music?"

Fox had no idea who Stephen Foster was until the piano man teased "Jeanie with the Light Brown Hair" out of the keys, then she nodded. He wore a silver waistcoat over a white shirt with red garters to hold up his sleeves. At the ball game, a hat had shaded his face, but now Fox noticed threads of silver at his temples. He was a good-looking man.

"Can I help you?" a cool voice inquired.

Fox turned toward a table near the piano where Barbara Robb sat before a spread of ledgers and papers. Tonight she wore a silk wrapper in a color Fox hadn't seen before, a bright shimmery green. Norwood, the piano player, wore a gold ring on each hand, but Miz Robb had no need of jewelry. Even with her hair down and the paint scrubbed from her striking face she was beautiful.

"I couldn't sleep," Fox said, feeling foolish.

Miz Robb studied her, dark eyes missing nothing. Finally she nodded and beckoned Fox forward. "You're curious. Well, you should have come down sooner. There's nothing going on now."

Fox took the chair Miz Robb offered in front of the table. "Is running a whorehouse a good business?"

"Very good." Miz Robb pushed a glass and a whiskey bottle across the table. "Help yourself." She tilted her head. "What kind of lotion are you using?"

The woman was no fool. Having come in off the desert, Fox should have had a deep tan by now, and chapped lips and cheeks. "Bacon grease," she admitted. "And a concoction to protect from the sun."

"I'll give you something better than bacon grease." Barbara Robb made a face and touched her own sculpted cheekbones. "You don't strike me as the type of woman to be interested in face lotions . . ."

Fox swirled the whiskey in her glass and drew a breath. "In a few weeks I need to look like a respectable lady." She paused, then added hopefully. "You wouldn't know about that, would you?"

"I know more than you think." Miz Robb held up a hand and ticked down her fingers. "You stride. Don't. Take small steps. Don't drink or smoke. Don't cuss. Say 'oh my stars' instead of 'goddamn.' Always defer to men." Behind them, Fox heard Norwood laugh softly. "Never cross your knees, only your ankles. Cast your eyes down modestly. Don't raise your voice. Don't reveal your ankles or an inch of skin below your neck or above your wrists. And always always wear a corset."

"That's a lot of don'ts," Fox said, tossing back her whiskey.

Miz Robb shrugged and smothered a yawn. "The don'ts sum up respectability."

"Can I ask you something personal like?"

"Depends on what it is."

Fox cast a quick glance over her shoulder at Norwood, then lowered her voice. "Say there was a man. And when he looked at you, your heart slammed up against your ribs."

Miz Robb also glanced at the piano player.

"And say you felt like you wanted just one good thing in your life so you . . ." She spread her hands and felt her face turn crimson. "Well, you know."

"I expect I do." A smile twitched Miz Robb's lips.

"But there was no future there." Fox licked her lips and looked down at her lap. "Would it be better to take what you could for a short time, knowing it would hurt you bad at the end? Or would it be better to go on not having that good thing?"

"When life offers you a good thing, I say you take it."

Fox nodded slowly. "Even when you know it's going to damn near kill you when it's over?"

"Even then."

Leaving Tanner would hurt until she shot Hobbs Jennings and paid the price, but during that time it would hurt bad. "All right. I guess that's what I wanted to hear." She drew a deep breath. "Now let's say that you wanted that man never to forget you. Say you wanted him to remember you every time he looked at another woman, but say you didn't know much about, well, you know . . ."

Barbara Robb crooked a finger, beckoning Fox closer. Leaning forward until they were head to head, she started talking. Fox's eyes grew as wide as saucers. At the end, she fell back in her chair.

"I should do all *that*?" When Miz Robb nodded, Fox burst out laughing. "Good Lord!"

Near dawn she woke Tanner by circling his ear with her tongue. Then she ran her hand down his chest and belly until she found what she was seeking. Ducking her head under the covers, she slid down, down, giving him little nips along the way. And then she put Miz Robb's advice into action.

When they left the whorehouse two hours later, Tanner wore a stunned expression that made her laugh.

Fox hugged his arm close to her side and smiled up at him. "I never thought I'd say such a thing, but I just love doing this with you!"

From No Name they cut southeast and entered the mountains again. After a long day in the saddle, Fox found the valley that crossed the range they had entered. Here they tied up at Buttermilk Fort, built by Mormons and so named because of the buttermilk the Mormons offered travelers to refresh themselves.

"Thank you," Fox said to a smiling older woman even though Fox didn't like buttermilk. She made herself drink it down and returned the glass, wondering why the only women she noticed were of a certain age. Then it occurred to her that the younger women and wives stayed out of sight when a party of men came through. The way Hanratty and Brown were scanning the fort suggested that hiding the young women saved a great deal of unpleasantness.

"With all them wives, seems they could spare one or two for a night," Jubal Brown complained.

"You'll live," Fox snapped. "It's your turn to fix supper, by the way."

They'd chosen to camp outside the crowded small fort in a grassy meadow rife with wildflowers popping out of the ground.

"Where's Mr. Hernandez?" Tanner asked as they dismounted and worked the creaks out of shoulders and legs.

"Remember the hot springs we passed? I sent him back there. A hot soak will be good for those old bones." And maybe the steam would open up his chest and help him breathe better.

She had felt Tanner's stare all day and he was doing it again. He looked around to see where Hanratty and Brown were then brushed his fingertips across her cheek. "You were spectacular last night. I can't stop thinking about you."

"I want you to remember me," she admitted, feeling shy about the confession.

For a long moment their eyes held. "I'll never forget you," Tanner promised in a gruff voice.

The comment struck Fox with bittersweet force. Thanks in part to Barbara Robb, he wouldn't forget. But he'd also confirmed that nothing had changed, not that Fox expected it had.

They would say good-bye in Denver. She gave him a wobbly smile and walked away, fingering her shot-up earlobe.

Near dawn she came awake to the sound of gunshots and leaped out of her bedroll, snatching up her rifle. The shots came from the fort and she and the men ran through the darkness toward the gates, shouting to identify themselves. They took up an outside position beneath the men inside the fort firing above them.

"Shoshones," Fox said, sighting on one of the Indians racing past her at a gallop. In the dark and flying dust, she couldn't tell if she'd hit him.

"How do you know?" Tanner asked beside her, shouting over the explosions of gunfire.

"Glimpses of hair. Clothing. The way the horses are painted."

An hour later as a glow of dawn tinted the sky orange, the Indians rode away and slowly the dust settled. Four Shoshones sprawled on the ground. Fox lowered her rifle and stretched.

"Thank you for your help," a man said, stepping out of the gate. A look of disgust twisted his lips as he inspected the carnage. "Every few weeks they try to steal our cattle. Sometimes they get a few." He nudged his boot against an Indian's ribs. "Come inside and have some breakfast."

Fox thought of the long day ahead. "Thank you kindly, but we'll fix something quick at our own fire and be on our way."

The energy she'd felt at the start of the battle drained quickly, and her feet were dragging as she approached their camp. "Son of a bitch!"

One Indian was untying their animals and another had opened one of the bank bags and was fingering the coins. Hanratty's rifle swung up and the Indian trying to steal their mules hit the ground before Fox registered the sound of Hanratty's shot. Tanner and Jubal Brown both fired at the Indian with the bank bag. The Indian fell, but that wasn't what caught Fox's attention. The horses bolted and ran off in the early light, and coins flew out of the bank bag as the Indian went down.

Fox groaned and covered her eyes. They would lose time rounding up the horses, and she hoped Tanner wouldn't insist on a coin count. Regardless, they weren't going to get the early start she had hoped for.

"I'm starting to hate that gold," she said to Tanner, her eyes narrowed. "Hanratty? You and Brown catch the horses." Angry enough to feel that she could move a mountain, she gripped one of the dead Indians by the ankles and dragged him out of their camp.

"Missy?"

"What!"

"I think you better come back here." Peaches stood beside Tanner frowning at an arrow sticking out of Tanner's arm.

"Oh my God!" Skidding to a stop beside him, she inspected the wound. "When did this happen? Why didn't you say something?"

"At the fort, right before the Indians rode off." He spoke between his teeth, glaring down at the arrow. "Hurts like a son of a bitch."

When Fox looked around she saw Hanratty and Brown staring. They hadn't gone after the horses yet. "Someone needs to get this arrow out." She paused to see who would volunteer, but they all stared at her. Fox swore and pulled a hand down her face. "All right, the horses will keep. Brown, go back to the fort and see if they have anything stronger than buttermilk. Hanratty, make some bandages and an arm sling. Peaches, let's see what's in the doctor kit."

Peaches nodded. "We've got some laudanum, that'll help with the pain afterward, and we'll treat him for fever and infection."

The men dispersed and Fox pulled back her shoulders, reaching for Tanner. "This is going to hurt." In one strong motion, she ripped his bloody sleeve open to get a better look. Tanner winced and ground his teeth together, but didn't make a sound. "And this is going to hurt worse." She moved the arrow's shaft to see if the arrow rested against bone, and then felt the back of his arm.

This time he swore and sweat broke out on his forehead.

"Sit down."

He sat, holding his arm in his lap.

"There's two choices." She drew a breath. "We pull it out, in which case the wings on the arrowhead will tear up your flesh. This method almost always leads to infection and prolonged pain and poor healing, assuming you don't die. But it would be quicker. Or, we push the arrow through and pull it out the back of your arm. You still get chewed up but not as badly and the cuts are cleaner. It won't be fast, but that's the choice I recommend."

After prolonged muttering, Tanner gritted his teeth and squinted. "Push it through."

"Shall I do that before we pick up the coins or afterward?" she said to distract him. He almost appeared to be considering the question. In any case, he wasn't watching when Fox snapped off the arrow halfway up.

"Christ!"

"No sense pushing more through than we have to." Peaches dropped down beside her, opened the doctor kit and removed what they would require. "Thank you. I'll need my riding gloves and something to stuff inside for padding."

Brown returned as the sun edged over the mountains, looking disgusted. "Nothing but milk, buttermilk, or water."

Fox stared deep into Tanner's eyes. "Take a big slug of this laudanum." It wouldn't dull the pain as effectively as whiskey, but it would help. Taking scissors out of the kit, she cut away his sleeve and nodded at Hanratty when he appeared with bandages. "I'd rather one of you boys did this," she said in a low voice. Neither of them responded and she swore again. To Tanner she said, "We'll spend the day here. Sleep is the best thing for you."

"No." Knots ran up his jaw. "We've lost enough time. If you have to, tie me on my horse, but keep moving."

Fox pushed down a wave of squeamishness. Ordinarily she didn't wince at the sight of blood and considered herself as tough as any man in this sort of circumstance. But that was Tanner's blood soaking his shirt. And this was Tanner asking to be tied on his horse. She couldn't stand it that she'd have to hurt him to help him. Wetting her lips, she made herself stiffen her spine.

Next she lit a cigar and paced back and forth, working up the anger to see her through this. All she had to do was think about Hobbs Jennings and she was ready.

"All right, boys. You hold his arm, Hanratty. Brown, you and Peaches hold the rest of him and keep him steady." Again she met Tanner's gaze and apologized in advance for what she was about to do to him. "I'm sorry."

"Just do it," he said, turning his head away.

It wasn't easy. Before Fox finished, her hands and sleeves were drenched in blood, she was sweating and swearing, and Tanner had lost consciousness. But finally, thank God, the job was done.

Fox held up the bloody arrow, spit on the ground, then flung it as far as she could. Standing, she stretched cramped muscles before she washed her hands and face in the pan of water Peaches brought her. For a minute she closed her eyes and rubbed her temples.

"We'll let him sleep for an hour before we tie his butt into the saddle." Finally she remembered the gold. "I'll pick up coins. Somebody get coffee and breakfast going."

"You are one tough woman," Jubal Brown said. Admiration flickered in his gaze. "Sometime I'd like to hear your story."

"What I'd like is coffee." And a clean shirt.

"Does that sling suit you?" Hanratty asked, stepping away from Tanner's body.

"It looks good. Do you need help catching the horses?"

"They didn't go far." He considered her earlobe. "You sure you ain't going back to Carson City? I wouldn't mind riding with you again."

"I'm sure. Go get the horses."

The coins hadn't scattered far, most had spilled in a pile near the other bags. Scowling, Fox scooped them back into the opened bag, thinking about Tanner's father. There was something wrong with that dynamic. Matthew Tanner was not the kind of man who failed to live up to expectations. Tanner was a strong and honorable man grounded in duty, a man who gave more than he had to. If his father believed Tanner was a disappointment, then the fault lay with the father not the son. Fox almost wished she could meet Tanner's father so she could tell him how damned wrong he was and give him a piece of her mind.

An hour later she supervised the men as they tied a half-conscious Tanner to his saddle and adjusted the sling holding his arm close to his chest.

"All right, let's get on the road." Taking a string of mules, she moved the mustang to the head of line and headed toward the next landmark, a flat valley that ran past cinder cones and ancient volcanic hills.

It wasn't until after the midday meal that she let herself think how close Tanner had come to getting killed, and the shaking began.

The next few days would always be a laudanum blur in Tanner's mind. By the time Peaches stopped forcing laudanum down his throat, the party had crossed the difficult and rocky Wasatch Range and were descending from altitude.

At supper that night, he was able to recall detouring around two landslides during the day, and Fox's disgust at the loss of time. Of the preceding days, he had no memory.

"No more laudanum," he said, waving Peaches away. Everyone at the campfire looked up from their plates. "Is the gold safe?"

"Safe as a baby at its mother's breast," Brown assured him.

"You missed out on the last settlement a couple of days back. Lot of excitement there," Hanratty mentioned. "Some Utes killed and scalped a couple of men a few days before we arrived."

Peaches frowned. "They also had a warm spring just north of the place. There's a multitude of springs in this area."

"We thought about throwing you in," Fox said, smiling.

The relief accompanying their light laughter told Tanner what an ordeal the last few days had been for all of them. Especially Fox.

He drank in her face. Even with the sunset bathing her skin, she looked tired and there were new creases between her eyes which appeared dark gray tonight. To him, she was beautiful.

"You saved my life."

His comment made her uncomfortable and she dealt with it by appearing annoyed. By now he knew her well enough to know compliments hadn't come often enough that she knew how to accept them. Realizing this caused his chest to tighten with an emotion he couldn't put a name to.

"You had a fever for several days. You can thank Peaches for seeing you through."

"Thank you." He spoke to Peaches but he didn't take his eyes off Fox. Tonight was chilly and she wore her poncho and sat close to the fire. He knew what marvels lay beneath that poncho. Knew of the softness she seldom showed the world. There had been a moment, gazing into her eyes before he lost consciousness, that he'd seen the tenderness in her eyes and he'd wondered if he would ever see her again. Thinking he might not had devastated him.

"Are you strong enough for a short walk?" she asked, studying his face. Tanner suspected he didn't look too sprightly himself.

"Yes." In truth he felt exhausted but nothing could have

made him admit it. Once away from the fire, he pressed her arm to his side and asked, "How many days?"

"It's been almost a week." She glanced at his sling. "How does the arm feel?"

"Sore."

"You lost a lot of blood. And you had a fever that scared all of us."

Bits of memory came back to him. "You led my horse."

"We took turns, shifting between the mules and you."

She turned him so deftly that he hardly noticed until he saw the campfire ahead and realized she'd turned him around. "Did anything happen that I should know?"

Fox ducked her head and he suspected she was frowning. "All in all everything went smoothly."

"But?"

"There are small settlements in the area we've been passing through. Mostly Mormon settlements but a few have saloons. Jubal Brown had an incident in one of those."

Tanner stopped and forced her to face him. "Go on."

Fox shrugged beneath the hand he'd placed on her shoulder. "He got drunk and apparently instigated a fight over a woman in the saloon. To put it politely, we were asked to leave at once."

"I'll speak to him," Tanner replied, his gaze fixing on the men at the fire.

"He's already been spoken to," Fox said in a tight voice.

Her tone said it all. Tanner nodded. "And Peaches?"

"I think he's a little better."

Her tone also spoke to this issue and Tanner understood her answer was more wishful thinking than truth, which didn't surprise him. Peaches was slumped with fatigue and his dark eyes were dull.

Fox laced her fingers through his and gazed up at him with softness in her eyes. "I missed you."

"If an unconscious man can miss someone, then I missed you, too," he said with a smile. More than anything right now, he wanted to kiss her. Wanted to sink down to the spring grass and hold her in his arms and sleep without the feverish dreams. He wanted to tell her how amazing she was, tell her that he'd never met a woman like her. Wanted her to know that her courage astonished him.

Later, as he lay in his bedroll gazing up at the spangled sky, he thought about everything he owed his father. His upbringing, his education, a privileged life, his livelihood. For as long as he could remember, he had made decisions to please a man whose only flaw was that he couldn't be pleased. Whatever Tanner did, it wasn't good enough. How long did a son keep trying? How long until the debt was paid? Could he ever make a choice without first considering the effect on his father? Without wanting his father to finally offer approval?

No matter how he turned the question in his mind, the answer came up the same. His father would never accept a woman like Fox. And in truth, he doubted Fox held any interest in the world Tanner lived in. He couldn't picture her paying or receiving calls, or standing by while a household staff tended her home, nor could he imagine her rigged out in a ballroom gown.

The San Rafael Swell was impassable. It rose like a great barrier of towers, buttes, and chasms. In places the sheer red cliffs soared to two thousand feet. An inexperienced guide could waste weeks attempting to find a passage, but Fox had faced this obstacle before. Still, it pleased her that she led them directly to the hogback and the narrow opening that dropped them down into a long valley. Here the terrain leveled out and she pushed the company hard, riding long days to make up time.

Temperatures soared and in places the ground was barren. In the last couple of days the men had turned silent and surly. Finally spotting the trees that signaled the presence of the Green River was like finding an oasis in the desert.

"Lord, I am ready for some fricking shade," Hanratty said, swinging down from his horse and wiping sweat from his forehead. He led his horse to the river and knelt on the bank, splashing water on his dusty face.

"You sit under a tree and catch your breath," Fox ordered Peaches. In the midst of a coughing spell, he cast her a grateful glance, then doubled over again.

She watched him a moment, feeling her heart seize, then pressed her lips hard together and began pulling the packs off the mules. After a minute she noticed that Jubal Brown worked beside her.

"He's bad off, ain't he?" Jubal asked, jerking his head toward Peaches.

"He's been better," Fox said, separating the packs into those with provisions they needed to make camp and those with items they wouldn't require tonight.

"He needs a doctor and a month of bed rest at least."

"Well, I'll just take him to the hotel then. Get him a fine room and some pretty nurses."

"Don't go getting pissy with me. I didn't make him sick."

Fox walked away, going to the river's edge. She could tell herself twenty times a day that Peaches was improving, but that didn't make it true. A dozen times she'd asked herself if she shouldn't have insisted that he stay in No Name. It didn't help to know that Peaches would have ignored her.

Tanner walked up behind her and placed his hands on her shoulders. "There's a lady doctor traveling with the group camped up by the willows. Maybe she should take a look at Mr. Hernandez."

Fox glanced toward the other groups waiting to ford the Green River. "I'll speak to him but I can almost guarantee that he won't agree. Most likely the lady doctor would just tell him to stay in bed a month." Spreading her hands, she indicated the steep canyon walls to the north and south. "This is the only flat space for miles. I don't know why there isn't a settlement here with a place for a man to rest, but there isn't." They stood in silence, gazing at the campfires up and down the riverbanks. "He won't do it, Tanner. He's going to Denver with me and that's that. But five minutes after we reach Denver, I'll have his butt in a real bed and a real doctor on the way to see him." Her mouth turned grim. "I don't know what else to do."

After supper she asked Peaches if he felt up to a game of chess. For the first time that she could remember, he shook his head no.

"It's been a long day, Missy," he said, squeezing her hand. "We'll have a game tomorrow. If crossing the river goes well."

"It should. We'll pay the ferry to take you and the packs across. Then me and the men will swim the horses and mules."

"Tanner's not wearing the sling anymore, and he's eating again. Glad to see it."

"I'd like to see you eating more."

"You eat enough for the two of us, Missy. Always have."

They smiled at each other then Fox made him promise

again to have a chess game tomorrow before she wandered off in search of Tanner. She found him kneeling on one of the gravel bars, turning a piece of rock between his fingers.

"It's petrified wood," he explained when she asked. "And there are fossils scattered all over this area."

Fox knelt beside him and examined the petrified wood. "Hanratty was talking to one of the other groups that have been here a couple of days. He says they've found a lot of jasper and agates in these gravel bars."

"Doesn't surprise me."

"I've seen fossils before. What makes them?"

Tanner warmed to the subject and was still telling her about dinosaurs when the sun slipped behind the peaks.

"You know a lot of interesting things," Fox commented as they walked back to their fire, brushing up against each other seemingly by accident.

"So do you. We just know different interesting things." Stopping, he pulled her behind a tree and kissed her deeply, then wrapped his arms around her. "I wish there weren't so many people around."

"Me too," Fox said, her voice smothered against his neck. Lord, he smelled good.

She longed for him, burned for him. She even dreamed about him. Sometimes, when the trail ahead was obvious, she would drop back and ride behind him so she could look at the wide slope of his shoulders and the way he sat his horse. His dark hair was long again, dropping below his collar, and she liked that. Loved watching his strong thighs grip the sides of the bay. And every time he favored his sore arm, she noticed that she touched her shot-up earlobe, a discovery that made her smile.

Lifting her mouth, she tasted deep of him and shivered when his arms tightened around her and she felt the heat and hardness of his desire for her.

It would be so easy to love this man.

The thought shocked her and kept her awake long after the campfires along the river had been extinguished and the only sounds were the night music of crickets and the rustle of small animals moving through the underbrush.

In her entire life Fox had loved only two people. Her mother and Peaches. She had never imagined there could be another.

And yet, when she gazed at the craggy angles of Tanner's

strong face or looked at his hands or remembered the heat of tangled bodies, her chest tightened and she couldn't breathe right. An ache closed her throat.

She suspected that was what love was, a knot behind a person's ribs that could expand with wild miraculous joy and then clamp down into a ball so heavy it hurt to carry.

Lying there in the dark, feeling the weight behind her ribs, she reaffirmed her vow to take revenge on Hobbs Jennings and kill the bastard. Since she could have no future with Tanner, it didn't matter that she had no future at all. It would be better to cut her life short than to spend it hurting inside, wanting what she could never have.

CHAPTER 16

A warm steady rain followed them south as they left behind the book cliffs Fox had been tracking. Last night they had given up on a fire and had gone without coffee. They'd eaten cold food while rain dripped off their hat brims. Cakes of mud clung to their boots and had to be carved off with a knife before they crawled into their tents.

It was still drizzling when they woke. Mornings were never Fox's best time of day, and mornings without coffee made her snarly. She led out without speaking to anyone and stayed well ahead until Hanratty rode up beside her.

"What do you want?"

"Coffee, a couple thousand dollars, and a willing woman."

Fox flipped her wet braid over her shoulder and didn't bother turning her head. "There's a hope for one of those things if the fricking rain ever stops." Grimacing, she gave herself a mental kick. Since talking to Barbara Robb, she was trying not to swear. Trying not to stride.

"I was talking to some people back at Green River," Hanratty said. "One group is going to Denver, too, but they're heading straight east."

"Which will be a ride as easy as ours until they reach the Grand River, which is impassable on the route they've chosen and it's going to look even worse because it's flooding now." She was in no mood to justify herself and resented his implication.

"How do you know it's flooding?"

"Because it's spring." She refrained from adding "you idiot." Collecting a smidgeon of patience, she added, "The Grand drains the Colorado mountains. It runs high longer during the spring melt than other rivers."

"I want to tell you something," Hanratty said. Then he fell silent for so long that Fox finally sighed and glanced at him. He rode hunched against the rain, his gaze straight ahead.

"Well?"

"If I'd known you were looking for a man . . . I might have thrown my hat in the ring."

Fox's shoulders jerked back and she stared. "I wasn't looking for a man." Anger heated her cheeks. "Tanner and me . . . it just happened."

"Did it happen because he's got a rich daddy?"

"The gold doesn't have anything to do with anything! I've told you before, this is none of your damned business."

"If you're staying in Denver because of him, you're in for a fall." Now he straightened in his saddle but he still didn't look at her. "I'm asking you to go back to Carson City with me."

Fox's mouth fell open. After a minute she dashed rain from her eyes and looked away, frowning. "For the last time, I'm not going back to Carson City. I have business in Denver. And before you ask, it's none of your concern."

"I could wait in Denver until you finish your business."

He was making this difficult and embarrassing them both. "I don't have a hankering in your direction." Blunt was best in situations like this. "Furthermore, just so there's no misunderstanding, it's not you in particular," she said, although it was mostly him in particular, "there's not going to be another man for me."

"You're turning me down."

"Yes."

He nodded shortly, scattering raindrops. "Then it's on your head. When things go wrong, remember that you could have prevented it." Jerking savagely at the reins, he turned his horse and rode down the line of mules.

Twisting in the saddle, Fox looked back, pissed that he'd approached her in that way and also because once again he'd taken it on himself to offer advice she didn't need or want. She was still irritated when they stopped for the night and she stared across the fire at Hanratty, who stared back at her.

Peaches held his hands to the flames and sighed. "The heat feels good." He tilted his head to check the clouds. "I think it's going to rain again before we have a chance to dry out."

"Count your blessings, old man." Jubal cupped his hands around his coffee cup. "It ain't raining now."

"Well, Missy, I've been putting you off for several nights. Tonight I think I have the energy to beat you in one game."

"How about we put it off for one more night?" She ran an eye over his wet clothing and weary expression. The sooner he crawled into his tent and donned dry duds and got some early sleep, the better. "I'm not in the mood to get whipped at chess." It broke her heart that he looked relieved and didn't argue.

"Are you in a mood to take a walk?" Tanner asked, standing and stretching his neck against his hand.

With a final glance at Hanratty, she stood and walked out on the short wet grass, stopping near the horses.

"What's going on between you and Hanratty?" Tanner asked, coming up beside her.

"Nothing important."

She'd had a few hours to consider their conversation and what puzzled her most was the timing. Why would Hanratty choose to ask her to take up with him now instead of waiting until they were a day or two out of Denver? To Fox's way of thinking, that would have made more sense, to approach her when the liaison with Tanner was ending. Hanratty had to realize that she was committed for the duration of this trip.

"I had a horse this color when I was a boy." Tanner stroked his hand down his big bay's neck. "His name was Cannonball. Do you remember your first horse?"

"Oh yes." She glanced at his mouth, swallowed hard, and ran a hand down the bay's flank. Lord, she loved kissing this man. "On my first trip east, I lived with some Paiutes for a few months. When I left, they gave me a mustang. I've favored mustangs ever since."

"That's right. You said you'd spent some time with the Indians." Tanner studied her with interest. "Did they capture you?"

Fox laughed. "No. I just wandered into their camp one day, cold and hungry. They were so astonished to find a woman traveling in the wilderness alone that they invited me to stay a while. I think they thought I had magic powers or something."

"I'm astonished, too," Tanner said, meaning it. "You really crossed the wilderness by yourself?"

"I was seventeen. Too young to know that women didn't do that sort of thing."

"Seriously, why did you?" Hands clasped, they walked away from the horses.

"I'd just learned that my stepfather had stolen my life." She drew a long breath and held it a moment. "I decided I'd go to Denver and kill the bastard."

Tanner stopped and peered at her face. "Good Lord. Did you kill him?" he asked softly.

She shook her head. "I found him all right. He lived in a big mansion on a hilly street. When I got there, the place was lit up like daylight and surrounded by fancy carriages. I stood in the trees about an hour watching people going in and out, dressed like kings and queens. And I felt about this big." She held her thumb and forefinger an inch apart. "I realized I'd wasted almost a year getting there because I'd never get close enough to him to kill him. I don't know," she said, rubbing her eyes. "Maybe I could have. But I turned cowardly. He seemed so big and important, and I was . . . I don't know. But I turned around and went to Carson City where I hooked up with Peaches again." She shrugged. "Folks made a fuss about a woman making the wilderness trip twice by herself, but it didn't seem that special at the time."

Tanner took her into his arms and held her. "I'm sorry, Fox. I wish things had been different for you."

"You know what I wish I'd been able to do?" She leaned back and looked up at him. "I wish I'd seen Paris, France. If my stepfather hadn't stolen my inheritance, I would have taken a trip to Paris. Would you tell me about it? Is it really the city of lights like they say in the books?"

Between kisses and heated touches, he told her. But she didn't pay attention. Instead, she marveled at how much she thrilled to the touch of his hands and the lingering taste of his mouth. If the ground hadn't been muddy, she would have dragged him down and pulled the blissful weight of him on top of her. Since she couldn't do that, she let his deep voice enchant her, enjoying the sound of his words more than the words themselves.

"What are you thinking?" she asked as she straightened her clothing before they returned to camp.

"I was imagining you in Paris," he said, smiling down at her. "I'd love to see your face the first time you saw Versailles. Or when you entered Notre Dame."

Fox felt her eyes shining at the pictures that rose in her

mind. "I'd like to have coffee in one of those sidewalk cafes. Hold my pinky finger out like this." She mimicked her idea of a grand lady and was rewarded when he laughed. "And ride in one of those little boats and dangle my fingers in the water like the ladies in pictures do." She let her head loll back and made a trailing gesture with her hand.

Tanner caught her up in his arms and held her so tightly that the breath squeezed out of her. "Christ, Fox. I . . ." His mouth came down hard and he kissed her until her scalp was on fire.

When he released her, she blinked at him, stunned, and raised trembling fingers to her lips. "My Lord," she whispered. "Tell me what I said to bring that on so I can say it again."

"Do you suppose anyone would notice if I snuck into your tent tonight?"

Laughing, she kissed him on the chin. "Probably no more than three people." She loved it when he sighed with frustration and disappointment equal to her own.

Tanner led a string of mules and Fox rode beside him most of the next day. They talked about growing up, told funny stories on themselves, shared memories that explained and entertained. Late in the day Tanner found himself talking about the mining industry and how he'd grown bored doing a job so familiar there were few challenges left to conquer.

"What would you rather do?" Fox asked curiously.

"There's a growing market for fossils," he said, having thought about it. "I'd enjoy hunting fossils for museums."

"Why don't you do it then?" she suggested, direct as always.

The answer circled back to his father. The expectation had always been that one day Tanner would take over the business. His education had been directed toward that end and most of what he'd accomplished since had added skills that would serve him well when the time came. His father had worked a lifetime to build something for Tanner's future and the future of any children he might have. Naturally he expected Tanner to eventually head the company.

"I suspect my father will consider me going into a different line of work as the ultimate betrayal," he said, keeping his voice light. But that conversation would come, and soon. He knew he would not return to the Carson City area to pick up where he'd left off. And he knew his decision to leave the mining industry would devastate his father.

Fox glanced at him but didn't comment. There was no way she could understand the bonds of family obligation or the desire not to wound a man who had sacrificed and worked hard to give Tanner the best that a father could give. When Tanner went out on his own it would be hard on them both.

"You've told me about life as a mining engineer, what would your life be like if you were a fossil hunter?"

"Rustic," he said, smiling. "I'll live like a gypsy, moving from place to place in the west. Camping out for weeks or months during the search. If I'm fortunate enough to find well-preserved specimens, I'll solicit buyers, pack the bones and ship them. And begin the search again."

Fox's eyes sparkled with interest. "That sounds interesting. If there's any money in fossils, it sounds like a good life."

"Only you would say that," he responded, laughing. "I don't think most women would." But she wasn't remotely like most women.

Their conversation drifted to the sandstone hills around them and the towering red cliffs. Here the wind had sculpted soft sandstone into strange and wonderful shapes. Before they reached the staging area for the river crossing, they passed a hundred wind-wrought arches of amazing and magnificent proportions. As fossils were on his mind, Tanner would have liked the time to prowl the hills in search of ancient treasure. Someday it would happen.

Beside him, Fox swore then slapped a hand on her thigh as if angry with herself. She drew a breath and said, "Well, my stars. I'd hoped to get here early enough to camp by the fort, but others beat us to it."

"My stars?" Arching an eyebrow, he smiled at the flush on her cheeks.

She ignored him, her gaze on the ruins of a fort the Mormons had built and then abandoned after problems with the Utes. "We'll camp closer to the river."

"And closer to the mosquitos."

They rode past the crumbling walls of the fort, nodding to those already camped there. Tanner thought he recognized two or three parties who had been at Green River. His guess was confirmed when three men called a greeting to Hanratty and Hanratty shouted back.

Once camp was set up and the fire going, Hanratty asked if there would a problem if he had supper with the men near the fort.

Tanner glanced at the gold tucked beneath his saddle. "Go ahead."

"There might be a poker game later."

Tanner nodded. "Just be ready to go in the morning."

Hanratty looked over his shoulder at Jubal Brown. "I'd invite you in, but those boys don't trust strangers."

"Makes a body wonder how you got so friendly with them."

"It's my charm," Hanratty said with a grin. He slicked back his hair and settled his hat before he walked away.

Frowning, Tanner watched Hanratty go, taking with him any hope for some private time with Fox. Since Peaches didn't count for the two-gun rule, he couldn't leave Jubal Brown alone.

"Mr. Hernandez," he said later. "Would you care for a game of chess or checkers?"

"I think you could beat me tonight with your eyes closed." Peaches raised a weary smile. "Instead, how about we just talk some?"

"I'd like that, too. Anything particular on your mind?"

Peaches apologized for a coughing fit then said, "Do you believe in heaven and hell, Mr. Tanner?"

"I regret to say that I've never settled that question to my satisfaction."

Peaches nodded. "I do believe. But it's troubling me that the standards for heaven are set so high. Maybe too high for an ordinary man to slip through."

"Well that's just crap," Fox said, joining them. "If you can't get past the gates of heaven, then no one can. And that means it isn't a place you'd want to be anyway. Now think about it," she said, handing Peaches a cup of cold river water. "If the standards are as high as you're thinking, then there wouldn't be enough people up there to give you a game of chess." She slapped a mosquito on her neck. "When you die—years from now—Saint Peter is going to drag your butt inside with a whole lot of hallelujahs. He'll hand you some wings and a halo and the prettiest angel. Probably give you some new overalls if you ask nice."

"Is this a private conversation or can anyone join?" Jubal sat down beside Peaches. "Do you play poker, old man?"

"I don't care much for it, but I play."

"You two?" Pulling a deck out of his waistcoat pocket, Jubal riffled the cards.

"Better think about it," Fox warned. "If you play with me, I'll have everything you own in three hours."

Tanner smiled. "I've played a time or two."

"Good." Jubal moved away from Peaches to a spot where Peaches couldn't see his hand. "We'll have our own poker game."

"We'll have to play with beans," Tanner insisted. "I don't take money from employees."

"That won't be a consideration," Jubal said. When Tanner stared at him, he sighed. "Beans it is."

At one time or another, each of them had been far ahead of the others, but at the end, exactly as she'd predicted, Fox walked away with all the beans. She winked at them, then said good night and, whistling, swaggered to her tent.

"Nothing I hate worse than losing to a woman!" Jubal looked as if he might throw the cards in the river, then thought better of it and pushed the deck back into his waistcoat pocket.

Peaches's laugh ended in a prolonged spell of bloody coughing.

"It's bad, isn't it?" Tanner asked softly. "Is there anything I can do?"

"Don't know if I'm going to make it to Denver." Peaches pressed a handkerchief to his lips. "Did she tell you about her stepfather?" He'd waited to ask this question until Jubal had left them and crawled into his tent.

"Yes."

Peaches examined his expression as if searching for a reaction he didn't see.

"There's something missing, isn't there?" Tanner asked after a minute.

"It's her story to tell, except . . . I'm wondering if she'd listen to you."

"You're talking in riddles."

"I know it," Peaches said, rising, his gaze on his tent. "And I apologize. We might talk about this again."

Curiosity urged Tanner to press for an explanation now,

but he didn't. Instead he sat by the firelight, listening to Peaches cough. He, too, wondered if Peaches would make it all the way to Denver. Every day Peaches looked older and coughed more. He'd started holding an arm across his chest. No one talked about it, but they had all taken a hand in doing Peaches's chores even though Peaches protested. But the protests were half-hearted, and that concerned Tanner as much as it did Fox.

They would have crossed the Grand earlier in the day, but the party ahead of them wrecked, losing a horse and a teenaged boy to the swollen river. After a brief service for the boy, they crossed without incident. There was no understanding fate, Fox decided uneasily. Nothing fair in the way life played out.

Turning north, she led them along the east side of the Grand River, through the towering sandstone sculptures cut by wind and weather. At midday they did without a fire due to their late start, and ate jerky and cold biscuits while the horses and mules rested and grazed on tufts of sparse desert grass.

"You'll be happy to know that we're coming into the last leg of the trip," Fox said, sipping river water instead of the coffee she would rather have had. "We have almost four weeks left on your deadline, and should make it easily to Denver in that time."

"Easily?" Tanner asked, raising an eyebrow.

A thin smile touched her lips. "I'm hearing from other travelers that the Utes are quiet, especially the farther east we go. We don't have many more major river fordings. And crossing the divide isn't going to be as difficult as you're probably thinking it might be." She gave him a thoughtful look. "In fact, a man riding alone and fast could shave a week off the schedule."

"Are you suggesting I go it alone?" Tanner asked, frowning.

"I'm saying if you had to, you could." She walked a few steps away from him, her gaze on Peaches. He rested with his back against one of the sandstone arch pillars, his eyes closed. "You just follow the Grand until it cuts due north. The mountains would be tricky, but only until you crossed the divide. The pass is slow going, but you can't miss it. From there on, the roads out of the mining camps will take you down into Denver."

"I'd be lost on the second day."

"Liar," she said softly. "Your biggest problem would be the

gold. How to hide it on horseback, but we'd think of something. And you'd have Hanratty and Brown with you."

Tanner put his hands on her waist and Fox closed her eyes as her skin tightened and her breath came faster. The end was drawing near and she couldn't stand it.

"We'll cross this bridge when and if we come to it," he said, his breath stirring the hair on the back of her neck.

"I won't leave him," she said quietly. "He never left me. That time we were apart, when I went off into the wilderness, that was me taking off, not him. And I always regretted leaving him behind. I won't do it again, especially not now."

"I would never ask you to."

"I'm not saying the worst will happen. Peaches is getting better every day," she insisted stubbornly, hoping God was listening. "But just in case, I thought you should know where I stand."

"You know what I'd like?" Turning her between his hands, he dropped his gaze to her lips and Fox felt her mouth go dry. "I'd like a few hours alone with you."

His touch was like flame circling her waist, leaping to set her mind ablaze. "I think you'll like the campsite I have in mind," she whispered.

His eyes narrowed and turned almost black with intensity. "Right after supper. No waiting for darkness."

She nodded, unable to speak. When he looked at her like this, it was a marvel that her knees held her upright. She licked her lips, and heard Tanner groan. It was hard to walk away and give the signal to move out.

The afternoon passed in an eyeblink with Fox thinking about the evening to come. Every nerve ending strained toward the moment when Tanner would take her in his arms. She could hardly concentrate when they stopped for the day and began setting up camp near the canyon lip overhanging the river. A thick stand of trees thrived here, unusual for the area, mostly pine and juniper, which had carpeted the stony ground with old needle falls.

Later Fox would flog herself for being so unfocused and stupid. It didn't register that she was hearing the hooting of owls from within the trees while it was still a couple of hours until nightfall. She did notice that Hanratty helped Peaches by unloading the money mule, but she didn't attach any significance to it. She continued with her own chores until she heard Tanner admonish Hanratty.

"The bank bags go underneath my saddle. You know that."

"Not anymore," Hanratty said, raising his gun he fired in the air.

As Fox spun, she saw three men riding out of the pines and junipers and understood in a flash what was happening and who had been the source of the owl calls.

"All of you, toss your rifles over here," Hanratty said, lowering his gun to sight on Tanner.

Fury rose like a tidal wave as Fox did as he demanded. "Your poker pals, I assume?" The men reined up behind Hanratty, guns trained on her, Tanner, Jubal Brown, and Peaches.

"I warned you," Hanratty snarled. "You could have prevented this."

For an instant she had no idea what he referred to. Then she remembered and disgust pulled down her lips. She'd believed he was talking about her and Tanner when he said the trouble would be on her head and that she could have prevented it by accepting him.

"You bastard."

One of the men dismounted and walked to the bank bags. "I need some help here," he said once he discovered the weight of the bags. One of the other men dismounted while Hanratty and the remaining man on the horse covered Fox and the others.

While the first man slung a bank bag up behind his saddle, Fox assessed the situation. She was still standing beside the mules and thought she had a chance. There were too many of them to hope she could get them all, but damned if she was just going to do nothing. She'd go down fighting.

She eased back a step, then in one fluid motion, reached into the ammunition pack and withdrew the Colt she knew was there. She got off two shots and had the satisfaction of seeing the second man beside the bank bags go down and the man who had taken the first bag shout and grab his shoulder.

Before she ducked behind the mule, she glimpsed Jubal Brown bend toward the ground and come up with a boot gun. Peaches flattened out on the dirt and Tanner ran straight into flying bullets to retrieve his rifle.

The gun battle seemed to last a lifetime, but in reality it was over in minutes.

"Fox? Are you all right? Jubal? Peaches?"

"The son of a bitch shot me in my fricking leg," Jubal shouted.

Fox came out from behind the mules in time to see Peaches sit up and run his hands over his body to check if he'd been shot. Discovering he hadn't been, he pulled up and rushed toward Jubal. Tanner stood over Hanratty's body, his rifle by his side. When Fox peered through the dust and smoke, she discovered the would-be robbers sprawled on the ground. Their horses had bolted.

A long sigh dropped her shoulders. But first things first. She made sure the robbers were dead, then had a look at Jubal.

"The bullet went through the fleshy part of his thigh," Peaches announced. After stopping to cough, he continued wrapping a bandage around Jubal's leg. "I got the bleeding stopped and put on a poultice to protect against infection."

"Goddamn, I wish we had some whiskey," Jubal said, staring down at his ripped pant leg and the bandage Peaches was wrapping.

"It could have been worse. Could have hit bone and shattered your leg." Peaches looked up at Fox. "Give him what's left of the laudanum."

"I suspected something like this might happen," Fox said, kneeling beside Jubal and offering the bottle of laudanum. "But I thought it would be you."

"I know you did." Jubal managed a tight smile.

She apologized, then added, "I thought you might steal the gold for the Confederacy."

Jubal squinted up at Tanner. "I'm going to follow you right to the kidnapper's door. If there's no kidnappers, I'm going to shoot you and then ship the gold south."

"What you do after the kidnappers take the gold is no concern of mine. If something should happen to them and the gold should fall into your hands . . ." Tanner shrugged.

"Speaking of the gold," Fox said pointedly, standing. Two of the bags were where Hanratty had placed them originally, near the fire. A third bag lay a few feet away where the robber that Fox shot had dropped it. The bag had broken and coins spilled on the ground. The fourth bag was missing, tied behind the saddle of a horse that had run off and could be God knew where.

When she said as much, Tanner shook his head. "We won't have difficulty finding that horse." Fox lifted her eyebrows and he pulled a hand down his jaw. "He's leaving a trail of coins."

She dropped her head and swore for a full minute before she studied the sky. "Oh my stars" just didn't serve in this situation. "We have about an hour and a half of daylight left. Let's get started."

At Tanner's suggestion, they found the horse first to prevent further wandering. Even so, the coins were scattered along a lengthy erratic path. They removed the horse's saddle and bridle, set him loose, and tied the nearly empty bank bag to Fox's saddle. Then began the long back-bending job of following the coins back to camp, picking them up one by one. They had taken lanterns with them and needed the light before they finally arrived back at the fire Peaches had started. The welcome smell of coffee and frying bacon guided them in.

"I couldn't manage setting up a tent," Peaches apologized, the admission coming hard, "but I got Jubal into his bedroll. He's sleeping, but he's restless. Still, he's young and strong. He'll pull through just fine. So far, there's no sign of fever."

"Have you eaten?" Fox asked, collapsing on the ground. Her back ached like blazes. When Peaches nodded, she said, "Then you get some sleep, too. Me and Tanner are going to be up half the night counting these coins."

Tanner volunteered to set out Peaches's bedroll but Peaches's had already managed it. He cast them a grateful glance then stumbled off into the darkness, the sound of racking coughs trailing behind. What he hadn't managed was to haul the robbers and Hanratty beyond the light of the fire.

"I'll do it," Tanner said, following her glance.

"I'll pour some coffee and set up for the count."

Before they started the count, they ate bacon and biscuits and the last of the pickles that Peaches had been guarding.

"I wish it hadn't been Hanratty," Fox said, buttering her biscuit out to the edges. "I hate saying this, but the betrayal would have been easier to take if it'd been Jubal Brown."

"Maybe." Tanner set down his plate and stretched his shoulders. "Smelling that bacon reminded me that you haven't smelled like bacon for a time." A tired smile softened his eyes. "Did you abandon the fanny beautification project?"

Fox returned his smile. "Barbara Robb gave me some lotion that I like better. There's not much scent but it feels wonderful."

They gazed at each other in the flickering light. "I'd like to check that for myself," Tanner said in a gruff voice. "This isn't how I'd anticipated spending tonight."

"Me either," Fox said softly. It was the understatement of her life. "There'll be other nights."

But not many of them. And surely not as long a night as this one turned out to be. At the end of the count they were missing sixty coins, too many to leave behind. Exhausted and grim, they fetched the lanterns and retraced the horse's flight. At two in the morning, they had recovered fifty-five of the missing coins and gave up on the rest.

Too tired to do more than hold each other, they stood beside the dying fire and Fox wished with all her heart that their evening had gone as planned.

"Several men have died over this ransom money. You'll have scars on your arm for the rest of your life. Jubal will have scars, too. I lost part of an earlobe . . . I sure hope your father is worth all this," she murmured.

"He is, and more," Tanner said. "Fox?" He tilted her face up to him. "When my father walks away a free man, it will be because of you. I'll never forget that, and I'll make sure he doesn't either."

Unsaid words hung between them. Fox knew what words she bit off and didn't say. She wished she knew what words Tanner held back. Undoubtedly they weren't the same words she couldn't speak, but she would have liked to hear them just the same.

CHAPTER 17

*I*N the morning Tanner and Fox covered the bodies with loose rocks, pausing over Hanratty's mound once they finished. "Do you want to say a few words?" Tanner asked.

"I guess I could." Fox removed her hat and held it to her chest. "Good riddance, you bastard. Amen." She jammed her hat back on her head and walked away. "Let's go. It's going to be a long hot day."

Before midday they entered the canyon lands where shade was as elusive as water. Here the ground was stony beneath soaring red sandstone formations, and the sun reigned with merciless supremacy.

Without an experienced guide, a man could wander from dead-end canyon to sheer cliffs until he died of thirst or the sun drove him insane. Tanner looked ahead with gratitude at the red braid swinging down Fox's back. She didn't display a hint of hesitation or failing confidence. She knew where she was going and how to find depressions in the rocks where rainwater collected. The mules carried enough feed to take them to the forage along the Dolores River. She had prepared for whatever might befall them, and Tanner realized that he had been lucky as hell to find her.

Crossing the country revealed and tested character. Like Fox, Tanner had not been surprised that one of his guards had betrayed him. Fox had believed Jubal Brown was the more likely candidate, but the two seemed equal in Tanner's view. Only a few days on the road had brought him to the realization that these were men more inclined to steal gold than to protect it. He was willing to wager his last nickel that Jubal was making plans already. For whatever reason, Jubal Brown had decided not to steal the gold from Tanner, but he'd marked the kidnappers as fair game. In the end Brown would possess the gold. Maybe the Confederacy would benefit, maybe not.

It also hadn't taken long to recognize that Fox was a woman of honor and integrity. He knew the core of her character, and didn't give a damn about the unconventional life she had led. In a crisis, he would rather trust Fox by his side than any man he could name. She was resourceful, courageous, and fearless. Feisty, loyal, and beneath the bravado beat a loving heart.

This time when he looked ahead, the braid swinging across her back looked to him like a pendulum, ticking down the hours he had left with her.

That was not acceptable.

"This is the life," Jubal Brown said, watching with a smile as Fox and Tanner set up camp, the two of them doing the work previously done by five.

If Fox hadn't understood that he was in pain, she would have taken his head off. But she'd been shot in the leg years ago by a rival guide and remembered the pain of riding and walking.

"Enjoy it while you can." She pulled her collar away from her throat, wishing for a breeze. "The coffee will be done in a minute."

Even if they had camped beside a river and had cold water available, they would have preferred coffee despite the unrelenting heat. Coffee was the staple food of the west.

Stretching, Fox scanned the campsite looking for scorpions or snakes. Satisfied, she sat away from the fire and fanned her face with her hat. All the men had stripped off their shirts, and she wore hers with the ends tied at her waist and her sleeves rolled as high as her elbow. The faces and hands of the men were sunburned but she wasn't. Thanks to the lotions given her by Barbara Robb and Peaches, she'd arrive in Denver with only a light tan. Her skin wouldn't be milky white, but neither would she appear as if she were an uncouth type who'd spent her life in the sun. The realization brightened her spirits a little.

"How are you feeling?" she asked Peaches, who sat beside Jubal in what Peaches referred to as the invalid section.

"Hot, sweaty, and tired. Otherwise, I'm in the pink."

Fox had hoped the dry, heated air would relieve his chest congestion, but that didn't seem to be happening. And seeing Peaches without his shirt shocked her badly. A man who had radiated glossy brown health now appeared ashy and shrunken. She could see his ribs, and his arms had begun to resemble sticks.

"How much weight have you lost?" she asked, staring.

"Everyone loses weight on a long trek. You've trimmed down yourself, Missy." He summoned a smile. "Looking mighty fine, you are."

She thought of the chess pieces packed in a box that hadn't been opened in weeks. "Maybe we'll rest a day at the Dolores River. You could do some fishing maybe. You'd like that, wouldn't you?"

"If I didn't have to eat anything I caught." He smiled and she knew he remembered their arguments last winter about salted fish suppers. There wasn't much that either of them could mention which didn't trigger good memories.

"Where's Tanner?" Jubal asked, blowing on his coffee.

"He's looking for fossils." Fox spotted him in the distance, examining a flake of sandstone. "I'll take him some coffee then come back and check on the beans."

"Look," Tanner said when she approached. He exchanged the flat of sandstone for the coffee she extended. "That's a fern."

"It's pretty." Amazing, really. Fox could make out every leaf on the ancient frond. The leaves were as clear and well defined as the muscles on his naked chest and arms. Light perspiration had collected in the hollow of his throat and dampened the hair at his temples. Swallowing hard, she walked to the lip of the canyon and looked down.

He pushed back his hat and studied her. "I've been wondering about something, but haven't had a chance to ask."

"Go ahead." At the bottom of the canyon cliffs, late afternoon sun sparkled on the Grand River. She'd heard stories of men dying of thirst up here on the sandstone, within sight of water they couldn't reach. Since Tanner had received the arrow in his arm, she had noticed a dozen ways a man could die out here in the wilderness.

"You said you went to Denver to find your stepfather. Does he still live there?"

Fox's attention sharpened abruptly. She held her expression blank but her mind raced to find an answer that wouldn't be an outright lie. "Why do you ask?"

"Maybe I know him. Certainly my father would."

"I don't expect you to get involved in an old story."

"In other words, don't pry?"

"That's not what I said." In fact, she was wildly flattered that he cared enough to be curious. "I'm just not interested in talking about him." But thinking about Hobbs Jennings was a different story. Now that they'd entered the Colorado Territory, she spent long hours every day contemplating Jennings and brooding over how he had ruined her life. First he'd stolen her money, and a comfortable and respectable way of life. Now, because of what Hobbs Jennings had taken from her, she would never fit into Tanner's life. Jennings had stolen the only future she'd ever wanted.

The moment would be so sweet when she stared Jennings in the eyes, told him who she was, and then emptied her gun into his heart. She had been visualizing that moment for over half of her life, and had never wanted it more than she did now. Every time she looked at Tanner and thought about what might have been, her fingers curled around the trigger in her mind.

Tanner mopped his face and throat with his bandanna, watching her. "I don't believe you've mentioned what you intend to do after we reach Denver."

"Does it matter?"

"You tell me."

She read what he was thinking. "I've been to Denver several times since that first trek, and I didn't kill my son of a bitch stepfather. He's still alive," she added bitterly. Then her eyes narrowed in suspicion. "Did Peaches say something to you?"

"Not really. But I have a feeling there's something he could tell if he wanted to."

"Maybe there is," she said, sounding angry. "And maybe I even wish I could talk to you about . . . certain things. But I can't." She knew Tanner. As sympathetic as he felt toward her, Hobbs Jennings was his employer and Tanner wasn't going to step aside and let her kill a man he'd worked with for years. First he would attempt to talk her out of the killing and when that didn't succeed, he'd feel honor bound to warn Jennings.

"Fox . . ."

"There's something I'm curious about, too." This was as good a time as any to put a few questions to him, and she wanted to get his mind away from her Denver plans.

He placed the fern fossil on the ground and glanced toward camp. "What's on your mind?"

"I know you work for Hobbs Jennings, but I have a strong impression that your father is also in mining. If that's true, and if your father expects you to take over his company some day, why aren't you working with him instead of for that bastard Jennings?"

"This thing with Jennings irritates the hell out of me. What do you have against the man? To my knowledge, and I've known him a long time, Jennings is a good decent person."

"The hell he is," she snapped, walking toward camp.

"Did you know that he wholly supports an orphanage for girls?" Tanner asked, following her. "Or that he's one of the few mine owners who actually upholds union principles? Do you know that each Christmas he gives every person in Denver who needs one a free meal? Because of his civic efforts, Denver is a safer place to live."

"Yeah, I know," she said, not looking back at him. "You think the bastard is a fricking saint."

She was striding, cussing, and if there had been a drop of whiskey in camp, she would have drunk it down. Some days she did well practicing Barbara Robb's rules for respectability. Today, she was falling on her face. Too bad. Maybe she wasn't cut out for respectability. Besides, she only had to appear respectable enough to get close to Hobbs Jennings, a total of perhaps twenty minutes.

"Give me one specific reason to think differently," Tanner said, following her to the fire.

Fox lifted the lid on the beans then slammed it back down. "You're entitled to your opinion, and I'm entitled to mine." The idea of making biscuits rose in her mind then evaporated in the heat.

Grabbing her shoulders, Tanner spun her to face his anger. "You impress me as a fair-minded person in every area but this one. If you're going to malign the man, you should state your reason."

"If you were Hobbs Jennings, I'd gladly give you a dozen reasons," she said, jerking away from him. Planting her fists on her hips, she glared. "But you're not, thank God. And I don't have to justify myself to you."

He stiffened and his dark eyes narrowed. "No," he said finally. "You don't."

Fox watched him walk away, then she glanced at Peaches and Jubal who were shamelessly eavesdropping with great interest. "Not a word," she warned them both, "or you can eat sand for supper."

They obeyed her warning and no one spoke while they ate beans and bacon without biscuits or bread to sop up the juice. Fox could have made a vinegar pie to supplement the meal, but she'd been in no mood for it. When everyone finished, Tanner scrubbed the plates with sand, not speaking a word.

Jubal crossed his arms over his bare chest and raised an eyebrow at Fox. "You used to smell like bacon all the time, but you don't anymore. Now you smell sort of like milk. Why is that?"

"Just shut up and mind your own business. I'm turning in." Peaches was the only one of them to whom she said good night. She pulled a light blanket to her waist and turned her back to the fire.

She didn't know what time it was when Tanner woke her, but the sky was on fire with a million stars and Peaches snored with a resonance that told her he'd been asleep for a while.

"What is it?" she said, jumping to her feet with her gun in her hand.

"Nothing's wrong." Tanner ran his hand down the braid laying over her shoulder. "Come with me."

Her impulse was to refuse, but the back of his fingers brushing the upper slope of her breast crumbled any thought of resistance. Silently she let him lead her away from the dying embers of the fire.

"You were pretty certain that I'd come with you," she said when she saw that he'd spread a blanket on the ground at the base of a sandstone tower.

"I hoped you would." Sitting, he patted the space in front of him. Although the temperature had dropped, the sandstone held the day's heat, making the spot he'd chosen comfortable despite a cool night breeze.

They sat facing each other, their knees almost touching. Tanner took her hands. "What the hell are we fighting about?"

Fox started to answer, then closed her lips on a frown. Casting backward, she reviewed their earlier conversation. Tanner had asked a question that she hadn't actually answered, then she had asked a question that he hadn't answered, and then somehow or another, Hobbs Jennings had come into the conversation and they had exploded at each other despite knowing each other's opinion beforehand.

Her shoulders slumped and she withdrew a hand to cover her eyes. "I don't know."

"This wasn't quite as crazy an argument as the one we had about where my wife should live, but almost . . ." Gently, he smoothed a loose tendril off her cheek. "Listen, I don't agree with your opinion of Hobbs Jennings, but you were right. You're entitled to think whatever you like, and you're entitled to keep your reasons private. I won't mention him again."

It was a generous almost-apology considering Fox had raised Jennings's name, not Tanner.

"I'm sorry," Fox said in a low voice. "I've been moody and irritated lately."

"We're less than a month out of Denver."

Letting her head fall back, Fox gazed up at the winking, flashing stars. "I don't have any education to speak of," she said, speaking quietly. "I spent a lot of my growing up years disguised as a boy, working on the San Franciso wharves. I cuss, I smoke, I don't often say no to a glass of whiskey. I've lived alone with a black man for years. I've made this trip a dozen times, the only woman in a company of men. I've lived with Indians. I've killed a few men, been in fights with a few others."

She wasn't speaking to Tanner. She was listing all the reasons why she could never be accepted in his world because she needed to hear them herself. And maybe, just maybe, he needed a reminder, too.

"You saved my life. You're going to get this gold to Denver and save my father's life. The people I spoke to in Carson City have nothing but respect for you."

Unconsciously fingering her shot-up earlobe, Fox blinked at the stars. "There aren't many old guides out here in the wilderness." The risks were too great. Guides died from gunshots, snake bites, scorpion stings, bear attacks. They drowned or fell down cliffs or off horses. Indians or bandits killed them. Their eyesight failed, their limbs broke, their hearts gave out. "I have no future," she whispered.

"I think you do," Tanner said, an urgency in his voice that she hadn't heard before.

Fox placed her fingertips across his lips, her chest aching. "No." She didn't want him to say something out of pity that he could only regret. "I know who I am. I know my place."

And she knew how it would all end for her. Every now and then she got mired in the might-have-beens and struggled to find a way toward Matthew Tanner's life. But the answer was always the same. Her future had been foreordained the day Hobbs Jennings dumped her on the doorstep of her mother's cousin. Nothing would change that. For a brief time she'd been given a glimpse of happiness, allowed moments of joy that she'd never imagined. Those moments would never come again, she knew that. And what would life mean if her only joy lay behind her, never to come again? It was better to face the hangman than to live an empty life without this man.

Tonight they made gentle love beneath the brilliant night sky. They undressed at leisure, teasing each other with slow revelations and whispered promises. Lying face-to-face, gazing into each other's eyes, they stroked skin that trembled beneath exploring palms. Kissed until Fox ached with desire and whimpered his name with mindless need. And when he moved his weight on top of her—yes—and finally thrust into her—oh yes, yes—all thought fled her mind and she surrendered to a blissful tension so intense she could not contain it. Clinging to his sweat-damp shoulders, she gazed at the sky and felt herself fly toward the tiny pinpoints of light. When his head collapsed on her shoulder, she held him tight so he wouldn't see the tears in her eyes.

Tanner held her until his arm went to sleep and cramping tingles made him grind his teeth. Only then did he carefully withdraw his arm, lean his back against the cooling sandstone tower and light a cigar.

The usual mix of thoughts stirred his mind. Memories of the day's long ride jumbled with concern for his father's welfare, interspersed with the problems on the job he'd left uncompleted in the Nevada mines and the problems that would arise after his father was freed. He thought about his life in general and in Denver.

His father dined with bankers, judges, mining magnates. When Tanner was in town, so did he. Denver's society was rustic, still developing, but it existed and he and his father moved in those circles. Tanner wouldn't be in Denver three days before invitations began to arrive for soirees, musicales, lectures, balls. At this time of year there would be lavish outdoor entertainments, picnic excursions into the foothills. Calls to pay. Lectures. Dining at his club or formal dinners at the large homes of civic leaders.

Dropping his head back, he blew smoke at the dark sky. Wherever he went mothers would throw their daughters at him, lovely pastel creatures made of gossamer and fairy dust, ready to collapse in a faint at the mere suggestion of impropriety. They would gaze at him over the folds of summer fans and declare their love of nature and animals and small children. Some would display their skills at piano or singing. Others would find a reason to show him hand-painted flowers on china cups. If the young lady were of a bold nature she might resort to mild gossip when the allowable range of topics expired.

Remembering such encounters made Tanner's mind go numb. Not for the first time he wondered why a man would choose to spend his life with a woman whose honor demanded restricted conversations and actions. A woman who locked away her true self. A woman who would never give herself to a man the way Fox had given herself tonight.

Yet such women were the wives of choice for successful men with wealth and background. Pretty ornaments without dissenting opinions whose duty was to produce an heir and never to dishonor their husband's name with a breath of scandal or outrageous behavior. That was the type of wife Tanner was expected to choose.

He gazed down at Fox, sleeping in a protective ball, her rich red hair loose to her naked waist. He could dress her in silk and install her in a mansion, buy her the finest carriage in the territories, and still the people in his world would never accept her.

The problem seemed insurmountable. A man could polish a piece of granite all his life and never turn it into a diamond.

They crossed the Dolores River early enough in the afternoon that Fox suggested Peaches get in some fishing since plenty of daylight remained. When he appeared reluctant, she gave him a little push. "We'll have a fish fry for supper. Aren't you sick of beans and jackrabbit?"

"Even fish would be better than snake."

Desperate for variety, they had skinned and fried a large rattler the previous night, but ended by tossing supper over a cliff because no one could get past the idea of eating snake.

"You pick a good spot and I'll fetch your pole."

Tanner was off searching for fossils and Jubal read one of the yellow journals about famous outlaws in the west. "I wish someone would write about me in one of these books," he said as Fox passed him carrying Peaches's pole.

"You have to be famous first. And then it's mostly lies in those books. Made up to shock the rubes back east."

"By tomorrow I figure I won't need the crutch Tanner made me. Figure I can start carrying my own weight again."

"It hasn't been quite a week yet. Give yourself a little more time."

"Well, I'll be damned," Jubal said, staring after her.

Peaches was sitting on the ground, watching the water rush past, his eyes tired and muddy brown. Usually he didn't cough much unless he was moving, but he had a spell now that left him breathless. Fox studied him a moment then pulled her shoulders back. "I'll see if I can dig up some worms or find something else that will serve for bait. How are you feeling?" she asked, making it sound like an afterthought.

"Never felt better," he said looking at his handkerchief before he stuffed it in his pocket.

"Good. Glad to hear it." Keeping her mind focused on finding a fricking worm, Fox stabbed at the ground with a shovel. Near the river the ground was spongy and moist and eventually she collected half a cup of worms. "This should get you started."

Peaches walked to the edge of the river and she sat on the damp ground, hugging her knees to her chest.

"Remember that big fish you caught off the pier in San Francisco? Nobody could believe you caught it by just dropping a line off the pier. And how about the prize trout you caught in the Carson River the first summer we were there?"

"I remember a couple of big ones you caught, too, Missy." But he didn't have the energy to be specific, and he was coughing again.

For the next twenty minutes, Fox talked, sparing Peaches the need to say anything. She talked about laying in salted fish for the winter, and hanging fresh venison away from the bears.

Talked about some gypsies they'd met a long time ago who said they ate skunk, which was disgusting. No one ate skunk.

"Missy? Come here. I got something. Been so long since you caught a fish, I'll let you bring it in."

Fox saw his arms trembling, and took the pole from his hands. Turning aside, he bent and gripped his knees and coughed until she thought her nerves couldn't stand it anymore.

"It's a big one," she said, bringing the fish in, pretending not to notice as he sank to the ground. "You know, if you don't mind, I think I'd like to catch the next one myself."

"I don't mind," he said in a strangled voice.

She'd made a mistake. She'd hoped to give Peaches a few hours of pleasure, but his expression told her that she'd created a punishment. Blinking hard, she swore silently and jerked the pole savagely to sink the hook as she pulled enough fish out of the river to make a generous supper.

"This is the best fish I ever tasted," Jubal said later, savoring each bite. "Thanks, old man."

Peaches started to explain that Fox had caught all but one, but a coughing fit interrupted him. Fox jumped into the silence with a bright voice. "Yes, sir, Peaches is one of the best when it comes to fishing." She told them the full story about the big fish Peaches had caught off the pier that no one had believed.

Tanner and Jubal exclaimed in the right places, speaking in the same bright unconcerned voice that she had used. It broke her heart.

"That old man's in a bad way," Jubal said after Peaches went to his bedroll.

"No he's not," Fox snapped, fury in her eyes.

However, she decided against spending a free day on the banks of the Dolores. Peaches needed rest, but more than that, he needed a doctor. Once they came off the mesa and dropped into the valley, there would be settlements and people. Surely there would be someone who knew how to relieve consumption.

Neither Tanner nor Jubal Brown said anything, but she read the pity in their eyes. Mad enough to spit, she stamped away from the fire and went down to the river where she hurled rocks into the water for an hour, until her arm felt like it would fall off.

Fox stayed beside the river until she was sure Tanner and Brown were asleep. Before she stumbled back to camp, she threw back her head and screamed at the new moon.

"If he dies, you and I are through! You hear me, God? I'll never talk to you again in my whole fricking life! You take someone else and leave Peaches alone. Damn it! I need him more than you do!"

She waited a full minute, staring hard at the moon, then she dashed a hand across her eyes and strode away from the river.

CHAPTER 18

DURING their second day on the mesa, a small group of Utes passed, traveling in the opposite direction. Both parties eyed each other suspiciously, the Utes showing particular interest in the strings of mules, but no one spoke. That night Tanner, Jubal, and Fox rotated on night watch. Twice Tanner thought he heard odd sounds rustling among the piñon trees to the east of camp, but nothing came of it.

"It might have been Indians," Fox agreed over her morning coffee. "If so, they must have spotted you sitting near the fire with a rifle across your legs and thought better of taking a run at our mules."

After a long hot morning they reached the edge of the mesa and Tanner reined up to soak in the pleasure of the broad fertile valley below. Here, at the confluence of two major rivers, spring burst forth in full glory. Cottonwoods flared in full leaf, knee-high grass rippled in a light breeze. Drifts of yellow and purple wildflowers ran riot across the valley floor.

Something eased and then expanded in Tanner's chest. Without realizing it, he'd been looking for this place all of his life. A lush valley sheltered to the south by the mesa and on the north by soaring red book cliffs. And trees and water near the fossil fields he'd discovered in the sandstone.

More important, here was the solution to his future.

"Daydreaming isn't going to get us off this mesa and across the Gunnison River," Fox said lightly, leading her string of mules up beside him.

"A person could drop a seed down there and it would be a radish before he came home from fossil searching."

She cocked an eyebrow. "I don't see you as a radish farmer."

Shifting on his saddle, Tanner met her gaze. Today her eyes were a deep ocean blue with only a hint of gray. "I was thinking that the man's wife might grow radishes." They stared at each other. "If she had a mind to, that is. Do you like radishes?"

Fox sucked in a breath and an odd stricken expression clouded her gaze. She looked as if she might topple off the mustang. When she finally spoke her voice sounded choked, and he had to lean forward to hear. "Gossip travels faster and farther than you think. People would gossip about that radish-growing wife of yours. They would think you'd lost your mind."

"I don't give a damn." Silently, he cursed. This wasn't the time or the place for this conversation. They should have been naked in a big bed with candles glowing and a bottle of good wine close at hand.

"Well, you should care. You deserve better than being saddled with a wife you'd have to defend. Besides, a man who goes through everything you have to rescue his father doesn't throw away his father's good opinion." She jerked her reins. "And he shouldn't."

Frowning, he watched her ride away. For the first time in his life, Tanner had just asked a woman to marry him, albeit in a roundabout impulsive way, and she had rejected him. Damn it. Everything had come together in his mind so perfectly. The land . . . Fox. He wanted both more than he'd ever wanted anything.

The land he could have. Fox, he would have to work on. She had told him all the reasons why she could never fit into his world, and he had agreed. The solution was obvious now that he'd found it. He could fit into her world.

They didn't have to live in a city. They could live in a place like this valley that didn't have a layer of society waiting to pass judgment on those who didn't fit the prescribed mold. Here, she wouldn't be ostracized or made to feel inadequate.

As for him, Tanner wouldn't miss the attractions of a city. The instant he had completed his education, he'd left cities behind and had headed west to work in rough-and-tumble mining areas. That had been his preference from the first. Occasionally he'd experienced an urge for the trappings of greater civilization, and satisfied those temporary urges by heading to the nearest city for a few days of museums and galleries, good newspapers and high-scale restaurants.

The same could happen here, he thought, letting his gaze travel the length of the valley. When a yearning for culture struck, he could ride to Denver. It would be a joy to expose Fox to art and music and foods she'd never tasted, to install her in a luxurious suite and pamper her and buy her silly trinkets that would make her laugh.

Touching his heels to the bay's sides, he cantered after the others, who had already begun the descent. Once they reached the valley floor, he looked around and nodded. Eventually, roads, railroads, and culture would come to this valley. A treasure like this would not long remain undiscovered. Already a few farms had appeared. Settlements would follow, and someday a city. It would be gratifying to play a role in the valley's growth and development.

Peaches appeared beside him. "Beautiful, isn't it?"

"A man could make a life here."

"How would your daddy feel about that?"

"Disappointed." But he'd done a lot of thinking since the Shoshone had shot him. "I've spent all of my life trying to live up to my father's expectations, Mr. Hernandez. I'm through."

Peaches nodded. "Have you discussed those expectations with your father?"

He waited for Peaches to stop coughing before he answered. "Enough to know that my father made sacrifices to ensure that I'd have the education, background, and contacts to make a mark in the world. I doubt he'll place fossil hunting in that category."

Looking ahead, Peaches watched Fox ride along the banks of the Gunnison, her brow creased in concentration, searching out the best spot for crossing.

"I've never been a father, Mr. Tanner, but I think I know a little about it. A father wants his child to make sound decisions, and often that means imposing the decisions the father wants the child to make. He might feel disappointed when the child rejects his guidance, might even feel angry. But in the end . . ." His gaze softened on Fox, "a father wants his child to be happy. Even when he doesn't agree with the means of that happiness. In the end, the father will set aside his own hopes and dreams for the child and wish the child well."

"Am I one of those means to happiness that you don't agree with?" Tanner asked.

"It's a worry, Mr. Tanner, that it is. Even if the fancy people would welcome Missy with open arms, which they never will, Missy couldn't be happy frittering away her days tatting doilies and watching maids clean a house she'd rather clean herself." Sad eyes swung to Tanner. "And if you persuaded her to set aside her own goals and come here to settle down . . . well, I know my Missy. She couldn't be happy if she believed you'd disappointed your father on her account."

"You just said—"

"I know. That your father will come around. And I believe he will. But time has to pass before that happens, and during that time, angry things will be said. Missy will never forget them. She'll always blame herself for coming between you and your father. That won't make her or me happy."

Frustrated, Tanner spread his hands, his hard gaze on Fox. "Then how do I resolve this problem?"

"I'm not sure that you can." Peaches shook his head. "I'm thinking on the problem, too, and now that I know your intentions, I'll think harder. But what you and Missy want is a complicated situation."

Tanner experienced an absurd urge to formally request Fox's hand. A smile curved his lips. "You're a good man, Peaches Hernandez."

"So are you, Mr. Tanner."

Fox shouted up at them. "Bring those mules down here. The day isn't getting any younger!"

Before Tanner rode out, he glanced at Peaches. "There's something Fox said she'd like to tell me but she can't. Do you happen to know what that would be?"

"I might." Peaches pressed his handkerchief to his lips and waited for the spell to pass. "But it's up to her to tell."

Tanner stared after him. He'd expected Peaches to give him a flat-out no. He didn't like the confirmation that Fox hid something of a serious nature.

Half angry, he rode down to the Gunnison and stopped beside Jubal who was holding Fox's string of mules. Fox had ridden across the river and returned while they waited and watched.

"It isn't as deep or as fast as it looks," she said, taking off her hat and wiping her sleeve across her forehead. She jerked a thumb at Jubal. "He wants to stop here for a bath and a swim."

"We have three more weeks," Tanner calculated. Sun glistened on the sweat on her throat. He wanted to lay her in the tall grass and lick that sweat off her skin. Turning his head, he looked away and swallowed. "Is that enough time?"

Frowning, she narrowed her eyes on Jubal's grin. "We'll stay long enough for everyone to have a bath. Then we'll put in a couple more hours riding." She mustered a smile as Peaches joined them. "Does a nice cool bath sound good to you?"

"I could stand to lose a couple pounds of dust and grime."

"All right. As soon as I get that string of mules across, I'll make some coffee."

She was covered by red dust, hot, sweaty, and focused on the river crossing. Tanner's thighs tightened. She was the most magnificent woman he'd ever known. He wanted her in his bed, in his life. He didn't want a future without her.

After they forded the river, Fox set a fire and started the coffee, then she turned the animals out to forage and cleaned her gun while the men bathed. She wished there was something more complicated to do so she didn't have to think about what Tanner had said. Or how she had responded.

Lord, Lord. Unless she'd misunderstood, Matthew Tanner wanted to marry her. The shock of it had been so great that she didn't even remember bringing the animals across the river. And refusing him then riding away had been one of the hardest things she'd ever done. Hunching forward, she covered her face with her hands.

Oh, she knew he believed what he'd said. And by and large it was probably even true. Most of the time he wouldn't give a damn what people whispered about her, not out here. And in the beginning, he might not blame her for the estrangement that was sure to occur between him and his father if he married someone like Fox. But eventually, he would. How could he not?

And then there was Hobbs Jennings. Assuming, and it was a huge assumption, that she could kill Jennings without getting caught, she could never confess it to Tanner. So there would always be a secret between them. There would always be a chance that someday a posse would find her and then Tanner would learn that she'd killed a man he admired as much as he admired his father.

Dropping her hands, she stared down at the oil and rags in her lap. Slowly, she ran a finger down the barrel of the gun. She didn't have to kill Jennings.

The instant the thought passed her mind, every cell in her mind and body protested. It was not right that Hobbs Jennings should get away with stealing his dead wife's fortune and destroying his stepdaughter. The need to make Jennings pay for what he'd done was as much a part of Fox as her red braid and blue gray eyes. Hating him had kept her going during the bad times when she couldn't think of a reason for living.

How could she walk away from her hatred without acting on it? How could she live with herself knowing she could have punished Jennings but had not? If she walked away from revenge, would a time come when she and Tanner looked at each other with resentment hot in their hearts? Over time, would love flare into blame as the impact of what they had given up took root? To be together, Tanner had to turn his back on his father, and she had to abandon the one goal she had dreamed of accomplishing for as long as she could remember. A single tear dropped on the back of her hand.

That night they camped between the cliffs of the Grand Mesa and the waters of the Grand River, which they had caught up to again and would follow for several days. At supper they talked about the two dangerous sections of narrow canyons the Grand plunged through.

"Can we detour around the canyons?" Tanner asked.

Fox shook her head. "Following the river is the fastest cut through the mountains. Any other route would add at least two weeks to the journey."

Jubal looked up. "How bad is it going to be?"

"Through most of the canyons, we'll have to travel single file with only a few feet between rock walls and the water. A slip means disaster. The Grand shoots deep and fast through the canyons."

"When do we reach those canyons, Missy?"

"We'll enter the first set tomorrow morning." She peered into the dusk toward the north. "If I have this figured right, we'll reach the second set of canyons at the half-moon. That's good because there's no place in that canyon wide enough to pitch a camp. We'll continue until we come out the other side." When no one said anything, Fox drew a breath. "It's your decision," she said, speaking to Tanner, "but I'd suggest you disperse the money bags among four mules. That way, we don't risk everything if we lose the money mule."

Standing, he extended a hand. "Let's take a walk and talk about it."

Jubal rolled his eyes. "Nothing like a bath to make a man want to take a walk. Yes sir, that's what I always want to do after a bath."

Ignoring the comment, Fox let Tanner take her hand as they moved toward the deeper shadows near a sheer rock wall. Neither spoke when Tanner turned her to face him. Fox cupped his face between her palms and tried to see his eyes through the falling darkness.

"I can't grow your radishes, Tanner," she whispered. "I'd like to. But I can't. It just won't work, so don't go pushing."

He kissed her with hungry passion, ravishing her mouth while his hands roamed to her waist. "Why?"

Fox's eyelids dropped and she moaned softly. She knew that tone of voice, knew desire deepened the timbre. Already his hands had found bare skin and a shivery thrill shot through her body.

"I'd be an embarrassment to you."

Cupping her buttocks, he clasped her hard up against his erection, letting her feel the power of his need. "That's ridiculous." This time when his lips crushed hers, there was anger behind them.

Struggling for breath, Fox pressed her hands against his chest. "You say that now, but—"

He smothered her words by forcing her lips apart with his tongue and tasted deeply of her. Slowly, they sank to the ground, locked in an embrace.

"Tanner . . ." She gasped his name, wanting to say something that fled her mind as his hands slid up under her shirt and found nipples that had risen rock hard in excitement. When his thumb scraped across the buds, she arched her back and forgot everything but the tension building beneath his hands and his tongue in the hollow of her throat.

When neither of them could bear a minute longer the blaze

of desire that brought sweat to temples and skin, they threw off their clothing and fell backward on the sparse grass, unmindful of small pebbles or insects. A stagecoach could have rattled past missing them by a few feet and Fox would not have noticed. Nothing existed except Tanner rising above her, muscles rippling down his chest, his gaze holding hers.

They moved together in a symphony of their own making, and Fox was certain no other two people in the history of the world had created this magic between them. No other woman had felt what she felt for Matthew Tanner. No other man had known how to inflame a woman's sensations or how to take her to the pinnacle of joy and amazement.

Afterward, they lay on top of their clothing, letting the cool night breezes dry their skin. Fox nestled her head in the hollow of his shoulder and smiled up at the growing moon. She was happy. At first she hadn't recognized the peculiar warm lightness expanding her chest. When she did, she had laughed aloud with delight.

And she had come within a heartbeat of saying "I love you." Thankfully, she had stifled the powerful need to say the words, because once spoken, such words could not be recalled. And had she said the words she longed to speak, she would have complicated an already complex situation.

"Fox? I want you to marry me. No, don't say anything," he said against the top of her head. "Just listen a minute. You and I are much alike. We share the same values and commitments to duty, loyalty, and honor. Both of us have been shaped by the past. I want to change that and I believe you do, too. I believe we can make a fresh start and a good life right here, in this valley."

Closing her eyes, she turned her face against the warmth of his skin. He smelled faintly of river water and man sweat. "There's no such thing as a new start. People can't shake off the past like shaking mud off a boot. It's part of what and who we are, Tanner."

"I'm trying to tell you it doesn't matter."

"And I'm telling you that it does. Your father's opinion and approval are important to you, and I admire that. What son doesn't want his father's love and approval?" She waited a moment for the tightness in her throat to recede. "And there's something I have to do." Turning in his arms, she lifted to look into his eyes. "I *have* to do this, Tanner. I *have* to. If I fail, then I don't have that sense of duty and honor that you spoke of."

"Do it. I'll help you. Then, whatever this is, we'll put it behind us and look forward."

She dropped her forehead to his chin. "It can't happen that way."

"You don't have to kill him, Fox."

She stiffened in his arms. Of course he would guess.

"We can go to the authorities."

"I can't prove anything," she whispered. "My mother's cousin died. Peaches is the only other person who knows the truth. He was there the day I arrived. He saw my stepfather and he knows him by sight. Do you really think the authorities will believe the claims of a woman and a black man?" She shook her head.

"You've implied that your stepfather is a prominent man. At the very least you could create a damaging scandal."

She almost laughed. "Can you really think that would be enough?" Rolling away, she sat up and drew her knees to her chin, her eyes turning hard as ice. "Never! There were times when me and Peaches went hungry, Tanner." She thrust her hands out in front of her. "Every one of these calluses were earned by hard labor. I've been shot, beaten, humiliated. I've had to be tougher than any woman you ever met just to survive." She gave her head a savage shake. "No. Embarrassing that bastard with a scandal is not enough! I want him dead! That's all I've thought about for years and years."

"Fox—"

"I should have killed him long ago. But I let his wealth and power intimidate me. And I didn't want to pay the price. Then, right before I met you, I decided the price wasn't too high. Dying to achieve justice is not too high a price!"

"And you still feel that way?" he asked in a carefully expressionless voice.

It would hurt him to hear that she put revenge above her love for him, and it would pain her to say it. But God help her, that was the truth.

"I have to do this." It surprised her that her heart could break without making a sound. Dropping her head, she ground her forehead against the top of her knees. "I wish . . . but I have to do this," she repeated. Behind her, she heard him dressing. Glanced to the side when he dropped her clothing beside her.

"Tell me one thing, then I won't bother you with this again. If it wasn't for your stepfather, could we have worked out the rest? Could you have accepted my assurances that none of the other obstacles mattered?"

"Maybe," she said after a minute. "It would have been hard to know I caused an estrangement between you and your father."

"You wouldn't have been the sole cause."

Fox nodded before rising and pulling on her trousers. His father would be furious to learn that his plans for Tanner's future would never happen. But maybe, eventually, he'd come around.

They didn't speak again until they were almost in camp. Then Fox glanced at him from the corner of her eyes. "You never answered my question about why you work for Hobbs Jennings instead of for your father."

"The answer doesn't matter anymore, does it?" Stopping beside the fire, Tanner led her gently into his arms and held her. "Is there any chance you'll change your mind and let go of the past?"

A film of moisture blurred his face. "No." He made something impossible sound so easy. Just let it go. He might as well have asked her to simply forget about a cancer gnawing her heart.

His arms closed around her so strongly it was almost painful and he gazed into the darkness with narrowed eyes and a tight mouth. "Will you do one thing for me?"

"I'll try."

"I'm going to pay the ransom and I'll remain in Denver until I'm certain my father has suffered no ill effects. Then I'm coming back to this valley. Can you wait two weeks to kill the son of a bitch? Until after I've gone?" Now he looked down at her. "I don't want to be there for the aftermath."

Slowly, Fox nodded. If their positions had been reversed, she couldn't have borne to see him hanged either. "I can do that."

He kissed her gently then set her away from him and walked into the darkness.

Fox hadn't cried in years. She'd come close a few times, but always she'd been able to swallow back the tears. Tonight, she couldn't. She lay in her bedroll with a corner of the blanket clamped in her mouth to muffle any sound and wept for all the might-have-beens. Wept for the loss of a future she'd never been destined to have.

Traversing the first set of canyons was as difficult and dangerous as Fox had predicted it would be. For part of the challenge they traveled on damp ground a few feet from raging waters. Several times they ascended narrow rock ledges that rose high above the river.

Once, Tanner looked down and could not see the ledge beneath his horse. It appeared that his leg dangled in midair. He didn't look down again. Ahead were the mules, free of the tether line for safety's sake, and in front of them, Jubal Brown. Jubal rode frozen in a hunched position, his gazed fixed straight ahead. Peaches rode in front of Jubal, undoubtedly trying desperately not to cough, and in front as always, Fox led the way. From his position at the rear, Tanner could see only her hat, but her hat told him that she rode as always, straight in the saddle, one hand on the mustang's reins, the other on her hip. The woman was fearless, he thought. If she could face this heart-stuttering trail with her spine straight, he could do no less. Grinding his teeth, he straightened in the saddle, trusting the bay to find sure footing.

After what seemed an endless day, they emerged from the canyons into a lush low area thick with wild currants and good grass. Tanner was hot, tired, thirsty, and still tense as wire.

Jubal slid off his horse and leaned against its side, closing his eyes. "Jesus. I don't ever want to do that again."

Fox unbuckled the cinch then swung her saddle off the mustang, removed the bridle and gave him a pat on the rear before she turned him out to enjoy the tall grass. "We'll hit the next set of canyons the day after tomorrow," she said cheerfully, grinning at Jubal's groan. Then her gaze settled on Peaches and her smile vanished.

Peaches still sat on his horse, his chin on his chest and his eyes closed. A dribble of blood leaked from the corner of his mouth.

Fox and Tanner reached him at the same instant. "I'll get his boots out of the stirrups, you catch him," Fox said.

Tanner carried Peaches to the shade near a thicket of currants and wild roses, surprised by how little the man weighed. Carefully, he placed him on the ground.

"Thank you," Peaches croaked. "Feel like a damned idiot."

The next coughing attack seemed to go on forever. At the finish, Peaches fell back against a boulder, exhausted. "Can I get you anything?" Tanner asked.

"Here," Fox said, pushing past him. "Here's some cold water." Tearing her bandanna from her throat, she mopped Peaches's forehead, and the blood at his lips. After glancing at his shaking hands, she took the cup and held it to his mouth. "You're scaring me bad, old man," she said softly.

Peaches looked at her so long and lovingly that Tanner stepped backward, feeling as if he intruded on their privacy.

"Can we have biscuits tonight for supper?" Peaches asked.

Fox smiled. "If you wanted fried alligator, I'd go find you one, kill it, and bring it back here."

"Never liked alligator."

Her fingertips brushed his cheek. "I'll bet you never tasted alligator in your life. But you'll get those biscuits."

"I'm going to take a little nap 'fore supper," he said, patting her hand.

"Good. I'll wake you when the biscuits are ready. I'll even butter them for you."

"Right out to the edge," Peaches murmured with a smile.

Standing, Fox blinked hard then walked into Tanner's arms and stood there trembling, her forehead pushed against his chest.

There was nothing to say that wouldn't be a lie or that wouldn't devastate her. All he could do was hold her and try not to think about what might be happening to his own father.

"I don't know what to do," she whispered. "We're days from any settlement, any real bed where he could rest. There's nothing in the medical kit that can help him." Swearing, she pounded her fists against Tanner's chest. "I hate this, I hate this, I hate this!"

Jubal Brown came up beside them, favoring his left leg and limping. "I brought you some coffee." He gave them the cups, his eyes on Peaches. "He's not going to make it, Fox."

"Shut up! Just shut up!"

"He's got courage, that old man." Jubal pursed his lips. "He took those canyons without flinching. I thought sure as hell he'd cough himself right over the edge of the ledges." He gave Fox's arm an awkward pat. "I'll start supper."

Fox stared at Peaches, the coffee forgotten in her hand. "What am I going to do?" she whispered. "He's always been there."

Tanner wrapped his arms around her.

CHAPTER 19

THE next day was easy riding, thank God, with relatively flat terrain and only a few creeks to cross, nothing difficult. Still, Fox kept turning in her saddle to check on Peaches. He seemed marginally better today, which she prayed was a good sign. Puffs of white clouds drifted across the sun off and on so it wasn't as hot, and she called an extra rest stop in midafternoon, hoping that would help.

She knew he'd had a fitful night, waking exhausted and drenched from the night sweats, his skin a dull yellowish tint, and it looked to Fox as if he was losing hair at an alarming rate.

After supper, she sat next to him, drinking coffee and turning her face to the cool breeze coming off the river.

"How are you doing?"

"Thirsty all the time, and cold at night. Otherwise, never felt better," Peaches said.

"Well, you look like hell," Fox said, pretending she didn't notice his hands shaking as he raised his coffee to his lips. And pretending that his voice didn't sound hollow, and that his eyes weren't overly bright with a fever that none of the remedies she'd tried could bring down.

"I expect I do," he said, smiling. Then his expression turned serious. "What are you going to do about Mr. Tanner, Missy? That man loves you."

She pushed the heels of her boots into the loose shale and frowned. "He's never said so."

"You figure high in the plans he's making."

She listened to the gasping breaths he took between words

and worried herself sick. "I can't," she said while he rested from coughing. "And you know why. I have something to do. Besides, I'd just shame him." Firelight flickered on Tanner's face where he and Jubal sat over the chessboard. Jubal Brown was the only man present she could look at without feeling her heart crack.

"He knows what he'd be getting, Missy. Not your place to decide what would or would not shame a man."

"I took a vow. I'm going to see it through," she said between her teeth.

"So you're going to defy my deathbed wish and kill Jennings."

"Now don't start that deathbed crap again. Peaches, sometimes you make me plain crazy."

"You have to choose. You can throw your life away, or you can grab hold of it."

Fox turned despairing eyes on him. "Look at me! I'm no beauty."

"You are, too, beautiful." It was the first sentence he'd spoken whole, without panting every few words.

"I'm only now getting into the habit of holding my fricking fork properly. And listen to me. I swear."

"So stop swearing. If you can break one habit, you can break another."

"Peaches." Exasperation twisted her mouth. "I don't fit his world and I'd be miserable trying to."

"He's willing to meet you halfway, Missy." He paused to breathe. "In fact, he wants to live away from that world you're afraid of."

"And his father. Imagine what his father would think if Tanner brought *me* home!"

"His daddy will come around. His daddy isn't marrying you, Tanner is. His daddy doesn't get to choose his son's wife."

Fox threw out her hands. "Why are we talking about this? It isn't going to happen. Tanner will find someone more suitable, and I'll hang. End of story."

"You break my heart."

"Oh God, don't say that." Fox dropped her head. She wished he wouldn't talk at all, the cost was so great for him.

"You don't believe this, but you deserve to be happy," Peaches said quietly. "You didn't do anything to deserve that bastard throwing you away. It wasn't your fault. Let Jennings go, and choose life."

"You're doing it, aren't you?" She glared at him. "You're putting a death wish on me."

An exhausted grin touched his lips. "And I'm going to be leaning out of a cloud, watching to see what you do."

She met his eyes. "I'm going to kill him, Peaches. So help me God, I'm going to make him pay."

"Come here. Lean your head on my shoulder like you used to do when you were little. We'll watch the stars and remember things."

"I'll do the remembering, you just rest."

Fox moved under his arm, careful not to place her full weight against his chest. He tired so easily that she knew they wouldn't sit together long. After a while, she couldn't stand listening to his chest rattle and gurgle so close to her ear and she stood, pretending to be tired herself.

"We've got the worst set of canyons tomorrow," she said softly. "It's going to be a long day. From dawn until whenever we get through. We could finish in moonlight. Will you be all right with that?"

"I'm glad you brought it up. Might be best to put me last in line," he said, pressing his handkerchief to his lips then glancing into the folds. "I took a half teaspoon of salt. Seems to help with the bleeding."

She nodded, her mouth white. "Sleep well, old man."

But she knew he wouldn't. The cold air and the night sweats would keep waking him. And he'd admitted that if he didn't sleep sitting up with his back against his saddle, he felt as if he were suffocating.

Instead of joining Tanner and Jubal Brown, Fox went straight to her bedroll and rolled up in the blankets staring at dark blades of grass. Peaches. Tanner. Peaches. Tanner. How could one human heart hold so much misery?

They entered the canyon before the dawn shadows lifted, leaving camp after Peaches recovered from a frightening coughing spell. The coughing was worse in the mornings, but today had been the most violent attack yet.

While there was still room to maneuver, Fox dropped back and rode beside him for a few minutes.

"Did you take salt this morning?" she asked. He didn't speak, only nodded. "You didn't eat any breakfast."

"Mouth is sore and tender." He struggled for breath. "Hurts to swallow."

Fox stared at the mules' swishing tails. Toward the end, her mother's mouth had turned too sore to swallow. Her voice had been as feeble as Peaches's and resonated with that same odd hollowness. Fox's heart skipped a beat.

"First place we come to that has a bed, that's where we're staying. Tanner and Jubal can go on alone." She expected him to protest, but he only nodded and that's when Fox's heart stopped and she knew he was dying.

No, she'd known for a while. Now she had to admit it. Without another word, she touched her heels to the mustang's flank and trotted up beside Tanner.

"There's a place two days' ride from the other side of the canyons that the Utes use for medicinal magic. It's a series of mineral springs. If I remember right, there's a small trading post there."

"I know the place. Once we reach the mineral springs, it's familiar territory on in to Denver."

"Tanner?" She gazed at him with damp eyes. "I'm asking you to buy the trader's bed and give it to me and Peaches. You and Jubal go on to Denver. I'll stay with Peaches until . . ." the words strangled her, "until it's over."

Tanner reached out and took her hand. "I'll buy you the whole damned trading post. Take whatever you think might help."

She looked at him, loving him, her heart in her eyes, then cantered along a narrow strip past the mules and Jubal to take her position at the head of the line.

The canyons were terrible. In places the rock ledges narrowed to two feet across. They couldn't stop for the midday meal, but the moment they would have stopped became memorable because two of the mules went over the ledge about that time. Fox counted four heartbeats before the mules hit the river and vanished in the speeding, raging waters.

She thanked God it hadn't been Peaches, and then for the next eight hours she worried that one or two bags of gold coins had gone over the ledge with the mules and were now unrecoverable.

But Peaches was there at the end of the day. A yellowish

froth bubbled at the corners of his lips, and he was too fatigued to talk when Tanner lifted him off his horse and wrapped his sweat-drenched body in blankets. Tanner propped a saddle behind Peaches, and Fox bathed his face, her expression set against the sucking sounds Peaches made in his struggle to breathe.

"The ride gets easier now," she murmured. He wouldn't have to face the canyons north of the Ute springs. By then his suffering would be finished.

Fox and Tanner spun when they heard Jubal's shouts. Jubal was running up from the river as if his leg was fully healed, a large brown bear not ten feet behind him.

Instantly, Fox's eyes swung toward the saddlebags and packs piled near the tethered animals. Where the guns were. Cursing, she swept a glance across Tan-ner. He wasn't wearing his gun either. And Jubal was headed straight toward them, bringing the bear with him. If Jubal brought that bear to Peaches, Fox vowed to shoot him before she shot the bear. Assuming she could get to the weapons.

Apparently Jubal realized what he was doing and veered off. And the bear stopped, distracted by a slab of bacon that Jubal had laid out beside the fire for supper.

"Stay here," Tanner ordered, already hunched over and moving into the darkness, heading toward the packs with the weapons.

Fox swore then looked down at Jubal who had circled around to them and now sunk to the ground holding his shot-up leg and muttering curses. "I'm going with him."

She caught up as Tanner pulled his rifle out of the pile of gear. Fox found her own an instant later. The bear rampaged through camp, slashing at bags, snuffling near the fire. His huge paw swiped forward and a shower of gold coins arched in the firelight before the ripped bag fluttered into the flames.

They fired at the same moment then fired again until the bear went down and stayed down. Slowly, Fox walked forward, scowling at the devastation the bear had caused in such a short period. Loose flour, salt, and sugar lay thick on the ground. Utensils were thrown around the site, most now dented. The leather had been ripped across Tanner's saddle.

But what she focused on were the hundreds of loose coins gleaming in the flicker of firelight. She was so sick of worrying about those coins, picking them up, counting them.

Every muscle ached from the tension of getting through the canyons. For the last two hours she'd been thinking about a quick supper and then sleep. But that wasn't going to happen.

"Well," she said into the silence. "I was wondering if the mules that went over the ledge were carrying any of the money bags. I guess not."

Tanner looked as angry and weary as she was. "I swear I know every individual coin by sight." He stretched his neck and rolled his shoulders back. "I'll pick them up. You tend to Peaches."

"I'll check on him then come back. It'll go faster with both of us working at it." She shook a cramp out of her leg and nodded to Jubal. "Might as well get some fresh meat out of this. How about you fry us up some bear steaks?"

By the time Jubal had cut and cooked the steaks, Fox and Tanner had collected the coins near the fire and widened their perimeter. Since the bear had ripped open two bags, over twelve hundred coins had spilled on the ground. They filled the dented pots.

Calling on reserves of energy that were running perilously low, Fox carried a steak into the darkness to where Peaches lay and sat down beside him.

"Not hungry," he said between labored breaths.

"You have to eat something," she coaxed. "It's been almost a week since we had fresh meat." Hoping the scent would entice him, she waved the plate under his nose, but he turned his face away.

She tried to persuade him to try just a few bites, but he waved her off with a weak gesture. Standing, she pulled up the blankets he'd tossed off and kissed his hot forehead.

"How is he?" Tanner asked when she returned to the fire.

"How do you think he is? He's dying," she snapped. Then she looked at the pots of coins they had yet to count and remembered Tanner's father might already be dead. "I'm sorry," she muttered, sitting down. The hunger she'd felt since midday fled and she pushed away her own plate and lit a cigar, blowing smoke at the flames. "Tell me something. Instead of trekking these fricking coins halfway across the country, why didn't you just get the coins in Denver once you got there?" The question had been puzzling her for weeks.

"The kidnappers specifically directed me to bring the coins. The exchange will take place somewhere between the mineral springs and Denver." When Fox stared at him, he shrugged. "That was in a second telegram."

"What else was in that second telegram? Why didn't you mention it?"

"There was nothing else of importance. I didn't mention it because I didn't want you thinking we had more days to get there."

She considered his answer. They had started with three months to reach Denver. But the kidnappers would appear before they reached the city, so they'd had three months to reach a shorter distance than Fox had believed.

"I'm angry that you didn't tell me." But she was too tired to argue. "I guess I can understand why you didn't." He'd built in a safety factor of a few days.

Jubal rose up on one hip, reached under him and withdrew a gold coin. He flipped it into one of the pots. "This gold has been a pain in the ass. Is your old man worth it?"

"Yes." Tanner glanced at Fox and she knew he remembered her asking the same question.

"So we're going to meet up with those kidnappers face-to-face," Jubal added, his interest sharpened. "Guess that settles the question about what the money is really for."

"For the last time, this gold isn't for the Union." Tanner's gaze went hard. "And yes. We're going to meet with the kidnappers."

A slow smile spread across Jubal's face. "I might be leaving this little group sooner than expected. No sense me going on to Denver if there's no gold to protect."

"Once I have my father back, I don't care what you do."

"Well," Fox said reluctantly, "sitting here isn't getting those coins counted."

"We aren't going to count them this time," Tanner decided, shifting his gaze to the pots of coins. "We'll sew new bags then call it a night."

"The kidnappers . . ."

"The kidnappers get whatever we have. I don't see them quibbling over a few hundred dollars."

She held his gaze. "It's your call. I'm willing to do the count."

"Not tonight." Holding her gaze, he spoke to Jubal. "Go to bed."

"I'm too tired to—" Fox said after Jubal had limped away without a word.

"So am I." He patted the ground and slipped his arm around her when she moved next to him.

They leaned on each other, smoked, and watched the flames die to embers. Before the light flickered out entirely, they each sewed a new bag for the coins then filled them.

"I love you," Tanner said, looking down at the new bank bags.

"I love you, too." Fox ran her hands up his back, feeling the tense muscles along his spine and the knots in his shoulders. She felt half dead with exhaustion.

"We're going to work it out, Fox. I don't know how, but we will."

"Maybe." She didn't believe it. But if there was an answer, they wouldn't find it tonight. Her brain felt like pudding. She was too exhausted to be amazed that they had finally said the words.

In the morning, it was clear that Peaches could not go on. When Fox brought his coffee, the cup was too heavy to lift to his lips. She held the cup to his mouth, then wiped his chin and sat beside him.

"It's going to be a dry day." And the thin mountain sunshine would be hot. Holding the coffee between her palms, she watched the early sun paint a rosy glow over the snowcapped peaks surrounding them.

"You and me," she said after clearing her throat, "we're going to stay here a few days. Rest up."

"Tanner . . ." Whatever he said next was lost in a fit of weak coughing.

"Tanner knows the way from here. He and Jubal might stay with us for a while, or they might go on alone." She shrugged, and gave him another scalding sip of coffee when the coughing ended. "You'll have to do without biscuits though. The bear tore up the flour sacks."

"A bear?"

Her heart sank. The stink of the bear and the noise he'd made plus the shots . . . Peaches either had been unconscious or his mind wandered. She told him about the evening's events.

"That man sure does love his daddy," Peaches said when he heard about them picking up coins again. "The animals?"

"The horses were rearing and the mules kicking. They had an agitated night, but the bear didn't get to them."

"That's good," he murmured, closing his eyes.

"I'm going to set up your tent so you'll have some shade."
She looked around. "This is a good place to rest a while. We've
got water and good grass. We can see anybody coming out of
the canyons. Won't be any surprises on that account. And we've
got enough fresh bear to feed a village."

"Dying's not a dignified process, Missy." He wouldn't look
at her.

"What's that mean?"

"I soiled myself."

Tears jumped into her eyes. The end was closer than she
could stand to believe. "Hell, Peaches. You wiped my fanny a
time or two, guess I can wipe yours. It's not like I haven't seen
a man's butt before." She thought a minute. At least she could
do it in privacy. "I'll set up the tent and find you some fresh
pants. You just rest a bit, and I'll take care of things real soon."

"I love you, Missy," he said looking up at her.

"I know. I love you, too, old man."

And then she walked away fast, heading past the fire and
back toward the canyon rocks. She was going to explode inside.
Was going to splatter salt tears and heart's blood. When she
reached the canyon walls, she beat her fists against the rock and
kicked at it until blood ran down her wrists and she would have
broken every toe but for a good pair of boots. When the rage
was spent, she sank to the ground and covered her face with
bloody hands, sobbing with grief.

The pink had turned to gold on the high peaks when she finally dropped her hands. And a pair of familiar boots stood beside her.

"How long have you been here?"

"A while," Tanner said.

A wet bandanna dropped into her lap and she covered her
face and swollen eyes, breathing in the scent of cold river water. Sitting beside her, Tanner gently took the bandanna and
wiped blood from her hands, careful with the wounds on her
knuckles.

"I'm staying with you."

"You don't have to."

"I know where we are now. Only ten or twelve days out of
Denver."

"That's if nothing happens to delay you."

"I'm staying."

Shaking hard, she flung herself into his arms and held on as if

Tanner were the only thing that anchored her to the earth. "It isn't fair! Goddamn it!" Then she remembered leaving Peaches in soiled clothing and struggled to rise. "I have to set up the tent."

"Jubal's doing it."

"And I need to find Peaches some clean—"

"Already done." His arms closed around her and he guided her head to his shoulder. "Just rest a minute. Then we'll move Mr. Hernandez into his tent."

Fox melted into his strong body and held on until she stopped shaking. She wished she could stay there forever.

Jubal had positioned the tent so Peaches could see the river and the mountain peaks rising jagged against a clear blue sky. A light breeze drifted through the open tent, but it was still hot inside. The heat didn't bother Peaches, he kept the blanket wrapped around his body, but Fox felt a trickle of sweat leak from her temples and zigzag down her cheek. She brushed it away and continued reading aloud.

"Missy?"

Marking the sentence with a finger, she glanced up. "Are you thirsty?" The spare coffeepot was filled with cool water at her side.

"I'm putting my death wish on you."

She swore softly. "You have to take it back. I'm going to kill Jennings, Peaches, and that's that. The only thing you'll accomplish with that death wish is to make me feel guilty all the rest of my life." Which wouldn't be long, but still . . . "I'll feel like I let you down."

"You will have. Can't mince words now."

She hit the ground with her sore fist. "Now this isn't fair, and you know it!"

"I'd be honored if you named the first boy Jamie."

"Jamie?" She stared. "Good God. It never occurred to me that you had a name other than Peaches."

"If it's a girl, I'd be real pleased if you named her Maria."

"That was your mother." She dropped the book and threw out her hands. "Why are you saying this? If there's one thing I can imagine even less than trying to picture myself as a wife, it's trying to imagine myself as a mother!"

"Never seen a challenge you couldn't get on top of." Gasping and panting, he leaned against the saddle and closed his eyes. "If you don't mind, I'd like to speak to Mr. Tanner now."

"Well, I do mind. But I'll fetch him."

Irritated, she stomped out of the tent and found Tanner checking the horse's hooves. "He wants to see you," she said, jerking a thumb over her shoulder.

"How are you holding up?" Tanner asked, settling on the ground beside Peaches and placing his hat alongside him.

"I've felt better." Peaches raised a hand to cover a series of bubbling coughs. "Arms and legs swollen like sausages," he murmured, shaking his head. "Need to tell you Eugenia's story."

Eugenia? Tanner hid a smile. "I know most of it."

"Good." Closing his eyes, struggling to breathe, Peaches rested a minute. "Maybe she'll listen to you. Don't let her kill Jennings."

Tanner stiffened. "Jennings?" he said in a flat voice.

"Hobbs Jennings. Your employer. Figured if you knew that, you'd try hard to stop her. Know you admire the man."

Tanner's mind raced, rushing back over everything Fox had told him and her puzzling hatred of Hobbs Jennings. The pieces fell into place.

"Her mother was Delphinia Foxworth," he said, thinking it through.

Peaches nodded, his head barely moving. "Got to stop her."

Tanner stared out the tent opening. Fox and Jubal Brown sat beside the fire, drinking coffee, not talking. Her braid had come partially unraveled and red strands lifted in the breeze. Faint circles bruised her eyes.

"It can't be Hobbs Jennings," he said in a low rough voice. "Hobbs Jennings would never steal a nickel. He would never, not ever, throw away a child."

"He did. I was there, Mr. Tanner. Saw the bastard. Heard him introduce himself to Miz Wilson, the cousin of Fox's mother. Saw him leave a little girl on the porch and ride away in his fine carriage without a backward glance."

Tanner lowered his forehead into his hand. His mind rejected what he was hearing, but the pain in his gut told him it was true. During the long minutes that passed in silence, he suddenly understood lifelong puzzles.

"Fox can't kill Jennings," he said flatly. "If I can't change her mind, then I'll have to tell Jennings that she's coming after him."

"Hoped you'd say that." Peaches turned his head and wiped

froth from his lips off on his sleeve. "Nasty business, this dying," he apologized. "Do whatever it takes to save her from hanging."

Shock paralyzed him. He sat beside Peaches long after the old man had slipped into a semiconscious fitful sleep, staring out of the tent at Fox. Eugenia Foxworth. He had known there was a child, a little girl, but he couldn't recall if he had ever been told her name.

The sun was past the midday mark when he finally emerged from Peaches's tent and walked toward her.

"Come with me," he ordered in a rough voice. "We have to talk."

CHAPTER 20

TANNER led Fox to the canyon wall where he'd found her earlier, and halted beside the bloodstains on the rock.

"What is it?" she asked anxiously, trying to read his expression. "Is Peaches—?"

Tanner's hands clasped her shoulders. "My full name is Matthew Tanner Jennings."

The announcement wasn't close to what she had expected and her mind skipped past it, waiting for whatever would follow. His hard expression told her to go back.

Fox ground her teeth in exasperation. Matthew Tanner Jennings. Slowly, comprehension widened her eyes and she jerked out from under his hands, shocked and unable to speak.

"My mother was Caroline Tanner. When I went to work for Jennings Mining and Mercantile, my father suggested I use Tanner as a last name and I agreed. I could do my job better and with more cooperation if I wasn't known as the boss's son. Moreover, the men would speak freely. I'd be able to identify problem areas before those problems became serious."

"Peaches told you about Hobbs Jennings," she said, working it out. For a second her mind refused to grasp the implication of what he was saying. Then she reeled backward, staring with wild eyes. "Oh my God. Hobbs Jennings is your father!"

"I don't have the answers, Fox. I don't understand how the man you know meshes with the man I know. But Hobbs Jennings is a good man."

"Shut up!" Her scream echoed down the canyon. Bending

at the knees, she swallowed back a rush of vomit. His father. Oh God. "I need to think a minute."

The late-afternoon heat radiated off the rock, making her feel dizzy and sick inside. Tanner was Hobbs Jennings's son. It couldn't be true. Straightening abruptly, she studied his face, searching for Jennings in the shape of his brow, the craggy angle of his jaw. But too many years had passed. She didn't remember or didn't want to.

"There was a son," she whispered, rubbing her temples. "I never met him. He was back east somewhere." Now she knew he'd been in Boston because Tanner had told her. He'd been living with an uncle, going to school.

"If my father did this, Fox, it's tortured him."

"Good! I wish it had killed him!"

Tanner's lips thinned and he turned stony eyes toward the river. "There's a portrait he keeps on his desk and has for as long as I can remember. A little girl of about five or six. I've always assumed she was one of the girls from the orphanages he supports."

"It sure as hell isn't me, if that's what you're implying. Your father has no reason to want to remember me. My mother wasn't buried yet before he'd dumped me on Mrs. Wilson's doorstep and walked away. He stole my money and never gave me another fricking thought! That's what a good man Hobbs Jennings is!"

"I can't believe that." Turning, he faced the sunwashed rock stained with Fox's blood.

Fox felt like attacking the wall again. "I've picked up coins until my back was screaming in pain. I've killed men, I've been shot up myself." Her fingers flew to her torn earlobe. "I've been half baked by the sun, and half frozen in snow. And all to rescue the bastard who ruined my life! I don't believe this!"

"And I'm paying you to go to Denver and murder my father."

They squared off, facing each other with rock-hard eyes and tense bodies.

"Don't do it," Tanner said softly.

His revelation and the enormity of what he asked drained the fight out of her, leaving her limp and trembling. "And then what? We go off and live happily ever after?" She shook her head violently enough that her braid flipped over her shoulder. "One day I'd look up at you and hate you, Tanner. I'd think about him living in that big mansion enjoying a life he stole.

Maybe I'd think about you and the fancy education that my inheritance paid for. I'd think about me and Peaches eating out of waste cans behind San Francisco restaurants while you were on a Grand Tour of Europe. Paid for with my mother's money that should have been mine."

Tanner's shoulders twitched and he swore for a full minute. "If my father did this, then every privilege I grew up with should have been yours. Is that what you want to hear? All right. If my father did this, then it's true."

"*If* he did it? *If?*" She barely restrained the urge to lunge at him and claw his eyes out. "You *know* he did! My mother fell in love with a man who had no fortune, but she didn't care because she had money enough for them both. Do you remember the time before you had all those fricking privileges?"

The flicker in his gaze told her that he'd been a child, but old enough to remember.

"And suddenly, the money troubles ended, didn't they?"

Tanner didn't answer, but she knew what he was thinking. He'd been told his father inherited after his new wife and her daughter had died.

"Oh Christ." Turning in a circle, Fox stamped her feet and hit her thighs with her fists. "It's not your fault." Leaning forward, she covered her eyes and pressed her forehead hard against the warm rock.

Now she knew why he had brought her here. The dried blood on the wall reflected her anguish over Peaches. Tanner wanted to remind her what he would feel if she killed his father.

If ever there had been a slim hope that she and Tanner could find their way to each other, now it was gone. If she killed Hobbs Jennings, Tanner would never forgive her. If she abandoned her vow and let the bastard live for Tanner's sake, she would end up hating Tanner for condoning what Jennings had done. And that's how she saw it. If Tanner didn't believe that Jennings should pay for his crime, then Tanner condoned it.

When the hangman slipped the noose around her neck, Fox would thank him.

She knew Tanner had walked away although he hadn't spoken. His absence was like a void at her back. After trying to piece herself together, she followed, bowed by a mix of emotions that battered her like swinging clubs. Head down, she walked into his back.

Tanner turned and opened his arms. Fox scowled upward, read his expression, and her face went slack. She knew. Fighting like a mad woman, she struggled to shove past him, but he held her, pulling her back against his chest.

She could see into Peaches's tent straight ahead. Jubal sat inside the tent, holding Peaches in his arms.

"He's gone," Jubal said quietly. But Fox heard.

She gripped Tanner's arms so hard that later she realized she'd gouged deep nail marks in his skin. "Did he . . ." Oh God, oh God. Halting, she licked saliva into her mouth. "Did he say anything?"

Jubal looked at her over Peaches's head on his shoulder. "At the end, he was talking to a child, it sounded like. Seemed like he thought the world of that child."

Fox sagged against Tanner, silent tears strangling her. Her chest hurt. When she could breathe again, she wiped her nose and jerked back her shoulders then walked forward.

"Get out of that tent. I need to hold him for a while."

She wrapped her arms around Peaches and held him until it was almost dark, singing in his ear, all the lullabies she could remember. Singing to drown out the sound of digging. Singing to send him on his way to the pretty angels and the new overalls.

They buried him at dusk. Before the men lowered Peaches into the earth, Fox tucked his chess set inside his blanket. Then she asked Tanner to cut off the lower six inches of her braid, and she laid that inside his blanket, too.

When it was done, Fox watched with dull eyes as Tanner fashioned a cross out of two wooden spoons and pounded it into the ground at the head of the mound.

Jubal took off his hat and cleared his throat. "I guess he was about the best black man I ever knew."

"Rest in peace, my friend." Tanner bowed his head.

Fox crushed her hat against her chest and blinked hard. "Wait for me," she whispered. "It won't be long."

Not caring that Jubal could see and overhear, she walked into Tanner's arms and wrapped her arms around his waist. "I need you. Can we forget about the rest for tonight, and just . . . you know?"

Without a word, he lifted her and carried her away from the fire, walking in the opposite direction from the canyon walls.

Closing her eyes, Fox wrapped her arms around his neck and breathed the scent of him. Earth, horses, sweat, wood smoke. Peaches must be smelling the same thing, she thought, because this was how heaven must smell.

When Tanner laid her down on a blanket spread across the lush river grass, she realized he had anticipated her need. Lying where he'd placed her, Fox stared up at a black sparkling sky, and wondered if it was true that a person's soul became a star.

"Don't move," Tanner said softly, kneeling beside her. His fingers opened her braid. "Just lie there and let me love you."

She watched his face as he undid the buttons on her shirt and pulled off the rope that cinched her trousers. Every line at the corners of his eyes and mouth was known to her. She could have drawn the exact shape of his lips and the stubborn angle of his jaw. She knew the feel of his skin beneath her palms, knew the silky tickle of his chest hair under her cheek. She knew his strength and his tenderness. She knew all this, but she hadn't known his real name.

When they were both naked, she rolled toward him, warming herself against the cool night air with the heat of his body and the fire of needing him inside her.

Tilting her face up, Tanner kissed her, gently at first, not rushing. He didn't touch her body until she caressed him first, then he stroked her with infinite tenderness until he felt her tremble and heard her moan his name. And then he kissed her with growing urgency, licking and suckling at her breasts, combing his fingers through the damp hair between her thighs. Kissed her until she gasped and thrashed beneath him. Stroked and teased and touched until the world receded and she was wild and half mad with desire.

When he came into her, she clung to him, unaware of the tears that flowed silently to pool in the hollow of her throat. She loved him. Loved him so hard and deep that it hurt inside. Loved him like a dream so real it was a shock to wake and discover it never was and couldn't be. She loved him so much that she would rather die than live a life without him.

Afterward, they lay in each other's arms, lost in the joy of each other. Then Fox sat up suddenly and grabbed the edge of the blanket, yanking it forward to cover her breasts and bottom.

"You're my brother!"

The moon illuminated his shock as Tanner also shot upright and stared. "Good God. You're my sister!"

"No, wait." Fox thrust out a hand and drew a deep breath. "Hobbs Jennings is your father, but he's only my stepfather."

"We aren't related by blood."

Fox clapped a hand over her eyes. "Thank God. For a minute there, I thought . . ."

The insanity of their situation washed over her and she fell back on the blanket, breathless with great gusts of laughter. "Oh my Lord!"

Tanner dropped beside her, laughing until the tension and emotion of the last few days ran out of them. At the end, Fox pressed against him and his arms closed around her.

"I'm sorry, Tanner. With all my heart, I wish things were different. I wish there was a future for us."

"There could be."

But the lack of conviction in his tone told her he didn't believe it. He'd reached the same conclusion as Fox. He couldn't live with a woman who had killed his father. She couldn't live knowing she'd let Hobbs Jennings go free without paying for his crime.

They dressed in silence then held hands on the way back to the campfire. Immediately Fox's gaze swung to the spot where Peaches's tent had stood. Jubal, bless him, had removed the tent and packed it away.

Turner pulled her close. "I'll have to tell him."

"I know," she said in a low voice. "Do what you have to do."

It didn't matter. Hobbs Jennings could surround himself with a dozen bodyguards, and she'd still get him. Give her a rifle and a split second with a clear shot, and the bastard would die.

They held each other with a hint of desperation, as if they both knew there would not be another night like tonight. From now on Hobbs Jennings would stand between them. It was one more thing the bastard had to pay for. Now he'd stolen the last two weeks of her time with Tanner, where she could have found enough joy to see her through to the scaffold.

"If I could find a way that I could live with . . ."

Tanner placed a finger across her lips. "I know."

They stood together, tangled in an embrace until their eyelids drooped with exhaustion. Even then they could not part.

Slipping to the ground, Tanner rested his back against one of the packs and near dawn fell asleep with her head on his chest.

The shock of discovery had dissipated, replaced by an icy stone of anger that knocked against his chest. How could his father, a man he believed he knew, have stolen his wife's fortune and then thrown away a child? What kind of man committed those crimes?

His arms tightened around Fox and he rested his cheek on her hair, inhaling her scent, listening to the soft whisper of her breath. Fury closed his throat. Every instinct demanded that he protect this woman and avenge the wrongs done to her. Nothing could change her past and the injuries done to her; his love for her insisted on justice.

But the man who had ruined her life was his father. A man Tanner respected and loved as deeply as he loved the woman in his arms.

Christ. Easing a hand away from Fox, he rubbed his forehead as if he could erase the jumble of emotions hammering inside his head. Love and loyalty tore him into two pieces.

Fox hadn't realized how slowly they had been traveling. Without Peaches to adjust for, the pace picked up considerably and they made good time, riding hard from dawn to dusk. They reached the mineral springs in one day instead of two.

The following morning they entered the canyons cut by the Grand north of the mineral springs. Jubal cursed, muttered, and made dire predictions, but a perilous and tense day passed without incident.

The next day, deep into the mountains now, they left the Grand and followed the Eagle River east, climbing steadily into pine forests and stands of shimmering aspen. The air freshened and cooled. Each day Fox saw foxes, bobcats, deer, or mountain sheep.

Spring came late to the mountains, but had arrived in full glory. Blue and white columbines looked for sun on the forest floor. Wild purple lupin grew thick near the river, and carpets of low white phlox vied for space with great drifts of bright yellow dandelions.

At night their campfire smelled like pine, and the warmth was welcome at high altitude. Fox had returned to wearing her poncho even during the sunny part of the days. They had begun to watch for movement in the trees, waiting for the kidnappers to make themselves known.

"I'm guessing they'll approach at the top of the pass," Tanner said that night, warming his hands around a cup of coffee. "That's where I'd do it."

Jubal nodded agreement. "The timber will be thinner. They'll hear us coming long before we see them."

"Do you expect trouble?" Fox rode with her rifle and slept with her Colt. After the incident with the bear, none of them allowed any space between themselves and a weapon.

Tanner shook his head. "They want the gold. If my father is alive, I'm guessing the exchange will proceed smoothly."

Jubal agreed. "But if your father isn't present, then they're killers. We shoot them before they get us."

"I guess we'll know the day after tomorrow. That's when we'll reach the summit."

Fox missed Tanner so much that she couldn't look at him across the fire. She burned for him, ached for him. During the first days after Peaches's death, they had ridden beside each other, filling in the details of their pasts, like figuring out where he'd been at the time she'd made the first trek across country to find Hobbs Jennings. She'd told him how the newspapers in Denver had printed her name wrong, identifying her as Eugenia Fox instead of Foxworth. The name had stuck.

Tanner had smiled. "Fox suits you."

"I never felt like a Eugenia," she'd confessed.

Later that same day Tanner had talked openly about the strains within his relationship with his father, speaking as if his thoughts were more for himself than for her.

"If my father stole your inheritance, that could explain his high expectations. Perhaps he needed me to succeed at the life he'd provided to justify what he'd done."

Fox said nothing while he worked it out in his mind. Every time Tanner said "if" his father had ruined her life, her hackles rose and she gripped her reins tighter. But in her heart, she understood his reluctance to accept the truth. She could never have believed that Peaches was guilty of a similar crime.

Except Peaches never was, and Hobbs Jennings was guilty as sin.

"Every time I disappointed him, he must have wondered if what he'd done was worth it." Tanner rubbed his knuckles across his chin, and his eyes glittered. "Damn him. There's no justification. None." He spoke as if he'd spent many hours struggling to find a reason, anything that might vindicate his father.

After Fox had reached her limit of understanding, she'd ridden ahead, grinding her teeth and wondering at the whimsies of a fate that could throw them together.

And now, tomorrow or the next day or the day after that, she would come face-to-face with Hobbs Jennings for the first time since he'd abandoned her on Mrs. Wilson's doorstep. She'd seen him during those times she'd been in Denver, but always from a distance, and he didn't know what had happened to her. For all Jennings knew, she was as dead as he'd claimed she was all those years ago.

Well, he'd know different soon. After Tanner told him that Fox was alive and gunning for him, Jennings wouldn't sleep another night. He'd be looking over his thieving shoulder until he finally saw her there. Except she didn't plan to shoot the son of a bitch in the back. No, she wanted him to see her and know who she was. She wanted to look into his eyes when she pulled the trigger.

The going got tougher the higher they climbed. Boulders as big as a stagecoach littered the slopes as if thrown from a giant's hand. Fallen logs lay like huge matchsticks flung on the ground, slowing the animals to a careful walk. One of the mules went down with a broken leg and Tanner had to shoot him. They took the essentials from the animal's pack and left the rest behind. They were close enough now that they could do without all but the bare necessities.

That night they sat around the fire, faces pink with cold and shoulders slumped with weariness.

"The old man couldn't have managed this," Jubal commented scanning the patches of snow surrounding their campsite.

"No," Fox said, rubbing some heat into her cheeks. "Are you still planning to go join up with the war?" She hadn't thought about the war in weeks. Didn't much care about it.

"I haven't ruled it out exactly. But a few other possibilities have turned up. Maybe I'll head to Mexico. Find me a hot tamale and settle down." He let the steam from his coffee bathe his face. "How about you?"

"I've got some things to do in Denver," Fox answered vaguely.

"Are you going back to the mines outside Carson City?" Jubal asked Tanner. "Or going off to look for fossils? What are your plans?"

Surprisingly, Tanner opened up and talked about the valley off the Grand mesa. Quickly Fox realized he was actually speaking to her. Looking into the flames, she listened as he spoke about the life a man could build in the valley. The house he would design and the apple trees he wanted to grow. In her mind she recalled sunlight sparkling off the river and the tall cottonwoods winding down the length of valley. Remembered the smell of early spring and fertile earth. Radishes that could spring out of the ground before a man came home from fossil hunting.

Putting down her coffee, she walked away from the fire and crawled inside her tent.

Like the men, Fox rode with her rifle across her lap and continually scanned the trees on either side of the trail. The expectation that today they would encounter the kidnappers made her jumpy. The old familiar anger raged in her chest, worsened by the knowledge that she would help rescue Hobbs Jennings from his ordeal, if the bastard was still alive.

She wanted him to be alive. She wanted to be the one who killed Jennings and she wanted him to know why. On the other hand, part of her hoped he was already dead and she would not play a role in saving him. Part of her wanted the kidnappers to have killed Jennings and thereby solved the problem between her and Tanner.

The hair stood up on the back of her arms and she frowned, sensing the moment draw near. Tanner and Jubal felt it, too. Both rode up beside her, faces hard and alert.

Fox spotted a red bandanna tied to a tree limb at the same moment Tanner said, "Up ahead."

They were ready. Tanner led the money mule. The other mules followed the horses, not realizing no one led them. Fox touched the Colt at her side, removed her gloves and slid her fingers down the stock of her rifle. The weapons were right; her mood was right.

"I'm thinking they're just beyond the rise," Tanner said tersely. His eyes glittered like dark stones above a tight jaw.

Fox glanced at him, knowing his thoughts had jumped

ahead. In minutes he would discover if his father was alive or dead. Everything they had gone through to get here came down to the next few minutes. She tilted her head and listened hard, but she heard nothing except the sound of their animals and her own steady breathing.

They topped the rise and Fox spotted Jennings at once, sitting on the ground with his arms bound behind him, his ankles tied in front. His head had dropped, chin on chest, and he appeared to have difficulty breathing the thin mountain air. She had a quick impression that he was bruised and filthy before she pulled up on her reins and examined the trees behind Jennings.

There were three of them, mounted on Indian ponies poorly positioned behind the stunted trees that grew at this altitude.

"We can take them," Jubal said quietly. "Your call."

"No." Tanner stared at his father, watching his chest rise and fall in shallow breaths.

Fox couldn't read Tanner's expression or the emotions that flashed in his gaze. Anger, contempt, relief followed by a stare that said he was looking at a stranger.

"Once this is over and they've moved out," he said to Jubal, "they're yours if you want them. Not now."

A voice shouted from the trees. "Throw down your guns and bring the mule to the edge of the trees."

Tanner rode forward. "I'm bringing the mule. All the money is in the bags. But we're not throwing down our guns."

Fox overheard low voices arguing. "They're about as Indian as I am," she muttered to Jubal.

"We're not looking for trouble," Tanner shouted. "Take the money and go." He led the mule to the spot they had indicated.

Nothing happened. From the corner of her eye, Fox watched Tanner move the bay away from the mule and head toward his father, his expression hard and tight.

Then a man rode out of the trees dressed in a Ute war shirt, a feather knotted in his hair. He wore a Union soldier's trousers and his face was painted blue and yellow. If the moment hadn't been so tense, Fox would have laughed at his ridiculous attempt to impersonate an Indian. Instead she focused on the rifle pointing at her and Jubal and her fingers tightened on her own weapon.

"Don't nobody move," he shouted. While Fox and Jubal stared back at him, he dipped, caught the mule's lead and returned to the trees. Within minutes the kidnappers had moved away from the clearing and dropped below the rise.

Jubal spit in disgust. "If that ain't a let down! We come all this distance for what? Five minutes during which nothing happens." A string of cuss words poured out of his mouth.

"They didn't insist on counting the coins," Fox said, as disgusted as Jubal. "There could be rocks in those bags for all they know right now."

"I've had more excitement visiting my grandma."

"Maybe you'll find some excitement hunting them down," Fox said, her eyes fixed on Tanner cutting the ropes that bound his father's arms. She couldn't look at Jennings. Her hatred was so intense that she itched to shoot him here and now.

"Probably not much. Did you see them? Amateurs. Getting that gold is going to be like stealing from a blind man. Hell, they're going to leave a trail a mile wide, plus the mule will slow them down. Stealing the gold is going to be so easy, it's insulting."

Grinning, Fox turned to him and thrust out her hand. "You're one of a kind, Brown. Good luck to you."

He gripped her palm and returned the grin. "Luck to you, too, ma'am. Aside from the time you beat me up, it's been a pleasure riding with you."

"Wish I could say the same," Fox replied, and they both laughed.

Tanner helped his father to his feet and wrapped him in an embrace, feeling the tremble that rippled through his father's body. For the first time he thought of his father as frail, the image disturbing and sad and utterly different from the brutish figure he'd been imagining since he'd learned the truth.

"I knew you'd come. I told them."

"Is anything broken? Are you ill?"

"By and large, they treated me squarely." He supported himself by holding on to Tanner's arms while the circulation returned to his legs and arms. "I want a bath, a shave, clean clothing, and a real bed." He stared. "I've never been so happy to see anyone in my life."

Almost a year had elapsed since Tanner had last seen his father. He'd forgotten the sadness in those expressive eyes, so like his own. Now he suspected the source of that sadness. "I'll get you to the closest mining camp with a real hotel," he promised.

Despite his anger and sense of urgency, he would wait until

his father had rested and begun to recover from his ordeal before confronting him. Then, Tanner and Fox would . . . he looked over his shoulder and spotted Jubal tying the loose mules back on the tether line, wearing the look of a man eager to be on his way.

Fox was gone.

CHAPTER 21

As there was no longer any time pressure Fox didn't rush the final leg of the journey into Denver. Undoubtedly Tanner would take his father to the nearest mining camp to rest from his ordeal, so she bypassed the camps and pushed on to Idaho Springs.

What had begun as a rough collection of tents and dugouts had boomed into a gold and silver bonanza town since her last trip east. Tents, wooden shacks, and a growing number of substantial buildings lay strung out along a narrow canyon bottom. Wagons, carts, stages, and horses congested the road through town and the excitement of hope and actual strikes sparkled beneath the dust spun up by wheels and hooves.

Fox chose a two-story hotel with a weathered front that looked cheaper than the brick palace on the corner. The room she rented was small but the bed felt like a piece of heaven after sleeping on the ground for nearly three months.

She tossed her hat toward a row of hooks and stowed her saddlebags beneath the bed, then she tugged off her boots and fell fully clothed on the quilt, sighing deeply when her head sank into a feather pillow. In minutes she slept soundly enough that she didn't open her eyes until noon of the next day.

First thing after pulling on her boots, she ate a big breakfast of ham, eggs, potatoes, and biscuits smothered in cream gravy, washed down with a pot of sugared coffee. Next she went to the bathhouse and ordered the works, a private cubicle, fluffy clean towels, scented soap and shampoo. It seemed a shame to dress her freshly scrubbed pink self in the same travel-stained clothing she'd worn so long, but it would only be for a brief while.

Throughout the remainder of the afternoon she explored what stores were available in Idaho Springs, pleased to discover she could buy the items she needed.

Her first acquisition was a tapestry bag in which to place the other items she intended to purchase. Starting from the ground up, she bought lady boots and a hook to button them. Next she collected stockings and garters, a cotton shift and drawers, and, after much indecision, an embroidered corset with wooden stays. A saleslady labored long to sell her a crinoline, but Fox wasn't yet ready for that contraption. She settled for several stiffened petticoats to plump out the wide percale skirts that came next. Then two shirtwaists followed by a summer mantle.

And of course she had to have little lace hankies and gloves and a wrist bag and hairpins plus a decent comb with all the teeth present. She curled her lip and passed on smelling salts but allowed the saleslady to exploit a secret weakness and sell her a small bottle of rosewater that she had absolutely no use for.

"You'll need earbobs," the saleslady suggested.

"No, I don't."

The saleslady peered at her missing earlobe then promptly moved her to a display of bonnets. "You must have a good bonnet," she insisted. "If your house is on fire and you can choose only one item of clothing to save, choose your best bonnet. A good bonnet can make or ruin your ensemble."

Fox shrugged, tired of shopping for items that impressed her as necessary to her plan but were grossly uncomfortable. "You pick one out."

The saleslady selected a summer-weight bonnet trimmed with tiny ruffles and a spray of violets that matched her new mantle and the ribbon trim on her skirt. Fox didn't suppose that she herself would have thought to match the colors.

As she paid for her purchases, shocked by the prices of lady items, the saleswoman studied her. "Part your hair in the center and wrap it into a clever bun on your neck." She sighed and shook her head. "Well, at least into a bun."

After dropping her packages at the hotel, Fox walked down to the trade lot and sold her rifle and the mustang for a good price. Before she left, she wrapped her arm around the mustang's neck and stood with him a while thinking how far they had come together. She was happy about the price he'd fetched, but it was never easy to sell a good horse, or a good rifle. Unfortunately, she couldn't ride a horse in her lady getup, and the rifle wouldn't fit into her tapestry bag.

To end the day, she selected the quietest saloon and ordered the whiskey she'd been thinking about since her last drink in No Name with Barbara Robb. The liquor hit her stomach like an explosion of hot metal, and three glasses later she understood why some drunks cried. Her spirits sank to the sawdust floor.

Peaches was gone. She kept listening for his voice, but he wasn't going to speak up and tell her that she'd had enough whiskey and it was time to go home. Never again. And if he was leaning out of his cloud watching, no doubt he was pissed because she'd spent the day readying herself to dishonor his dying wish.

"Damn it." The man at the bar to her right looked her way, taking in her raggedy hat, old poncho, and travel-stained trousers and boots. She glared him down, half hoping he was spoiling for a fight, but he turned back to his glass.

That was probably a good thing since there was no one to patch her up afterward if she got banged up fighting. There was no one to look out for her. No one who knew where she was now or gave a damn. There was no Peaches, no Tanner.

Thinking about Tanner made her feel lower than dirt and raised an ache in her chest, but she couldn't help herself. Where was he? In some mining camp with his father? Or had he taken a stage that had passed through Idaho Springs while she was sleeping or buying lady clothes? Had he given her a single thought since she had ridden out of his life? What had he told his father about her? And the dumbest question of all, if Tanner saw her all tricked out in her lady clothes, would he laugh or would he think she was beautiful?

Beautiful, ha. What the hell was she thinking.

Before she climbed into bed that night, Fox stiffened her spine, summoned her courage, and made herself look into the cloudy mirror above the bureau dresser.

The reflection wasn't what she'd expected or hoped for, to be more accurate, but then it never was. However, she didn't look as bad as she'd dreaded either. She wasn't sunburned or peeling. Her cheeks weren't raw and chapped and neither were her lips. When she opened her freshly shampooed braid, it flowed through her fingers all shiny with lamplight. Maybe it was just whiskey-thinking, but she decided she'd probably succeed in posing as a respectable woman for however long it took to get close to Hobbs Jennings and kill him.

Curious, she parted her hair in the center and pulled it back from her face. Careful examination led to the conclusion that she was too pink and too freckled to be beautiful. Too cool-eyed and spit-in-your-face stubborn.

But Tanner had seen her as beautiful, and damn, that hurt. One man in the whole fricking world believed she was beautiful and wonderful and had wanted to spend his life with her. And who did he turn out to be? The son of an immoral, thieving, no conscience, conniving, backstabbing, son of a bitch.

She dashed a hand across her eyes, wished she could kill Hobbs Jennings right now, then fell into bed.

In the morning, togged out in her new lady clothes, Fox climbed aboard the stage bound for Denver.

Denver had grown by leaps and bounds. Residents pouring into the area had planted trees along what Fox remembered as bare dusty streets, and there were even city ditches to provide the convenience of nearby water for the new plantings.

The number of large mansions didn't surprise Fox, but the multitudes of smaller homes did. Many were fashioned from brick or stone, built to endure. Leaning from the stage window, she gaped at three-story office buildings, restaurants with awnings shading the doors, shops with polished windows and gold lettering. Denver was a genuine city.

While the stage waited for a herd of rangy cattle to clop down First Avenue, Fox hopped out and purchased a newspaper from a boy on the corner. She glimpsed Hobbs Jennings's name before she folded the paper under her arm and climbed back into the crowded stage.

Soon enough she spilled out of the coach with the other passengers, glad to be finished with squeezing among them and breathing hot sour air. Rolling the cramps out of her shoulders, she took stock of her surroundings, but nothing appeared familiar. She had to ask the man inside the post house for the address of the Jennings Mining and Mercantile Company and then request a recommendation for a modest hotel near those offices.

Happily, she discovered the Alphonse Hotel was situated

only a block from what was already being referred to as Denver's business district. In what she took to be a nod from fate, the hotel sat within easy walking distance of Jennings's office.

This time, after looking her over, the hotel clerk assigned her a better room than she had received in Idaho Springs when she'd entered the lobby fresh off the road. This room had wallpaper—ugly, but more pleasing than bare walls. A pitcher of water stood ready beside the washbasin, and someone had placed silk carnations in a vase before the vanity. The man who carried up her tapestry bag opened both windows to the smell of dust and cow dung, but the breeze was welcome.

Then he asked if she wanted a bath sent to the room, carefully looking aside as he put the question. Such an idea had never entered Fox's mind, that she could have a bath in her room.

Also looking aside and stupidly blushing, she allowed that she would indeed like a bath. "And a beef steak with fried potatoes," she added, waiting for him to say that was not possible. But he only nodded. So she added, "And coffee with sugar. And cake! It should have thick frosting."

She could learn to love hotels, she decided, setting out her new comb and old brush alongside extra hairpins. This kind of luxury was worth the extra money. Of course, in the past, she'd never had extra money. But now she had a pocketful from the sale of the mustang and her rifle, and a limited time to spend it.

Only one cigar remained from her stash and she smoked it while soaking in the tub and reading the newspaper.

Hobbs Jennings's disappearance was solved, the newspaper announced in large headlines. Accompanied by his son, Matthew Jennings, Mr. Jennings had returned to Denver yesterday afternoon following a harrowing ordeal with kidnappers. The amount of the ransom was hinted but not revealed. Officials predicted they would soon have the kidnappers in custody.

Fox rolled her eyes and thought of Jubal Brown, then read that Mr. Jennings was exhausted and weak but basically unharmed. Hobbs Jennings predicted he would be in his office by Tuesday at the latest and assured the public that Jennings Mining and Mercantile would resume business as usual.

Fox flung the newspaper across the room then leaned back in the tub and drew on her cigar. The bastard led a charmed life. He'd drawn three kidnappers who were such novices they had treated Jennings like a prince instead of killing him as more experienced thugs would have done. If Fox had been running that show, at the very least Jennings would have needed more than a few days to recuperate.

Tuesday. Narrowing her eyes, she formulated a plan. She'd give him until Friday afternoon to deal with well-wishers and business associates and whoever else might crowd into his office after a three-month absence. Then his charmed life would end.

Not until the tub and service tray had been removed did Fox remember that she had promised Tanner she would wait two weeks before she put her neck on the line for a noose. But that had been before he knew his father was the man she intended to kill. She doubted there was a chance in hell that Tanner would leave Denver knowing she was going after his father. Besides, if she was going to defy Peaches's death wish, what did a promise to Tanner matter? It wasn't like she was trying to reserve a spot in heaven. That wouldn't happen. And Tanner wasn't going to say, "Yes, you murdered my father, but it's all right because you kept your promise to wait two weeks before you did it."

Now that she'd worked out her plans, Fox had expected to drop off to sleep without a qualm. Instead, she lay in bed staring at the windows and thinking about Tanner. His face rose in her memory, his saddle brown eyes soft with a smile. There were so many memories of the surprise and joy he'd given her. But the image that broke her heart was the tender expression he'd worn when he'd looked in her eyes and talked softly about a man's wife growing radishes if she had a mind to.

Fox pushed her face into the pillow trying to smother the images that reeled through her thoughts. Tanner, face tight with concentration, leading a string of mules across the creek. Tanner, looking into her eyes as he made love to her. Tanner, taking his turn at the fire, flipping flapjacks. The look and feel of his hard body, the sound of his deep voice in her ear. "Oh Tanner," she whispered, her voice cracking. "It isn't fair. You should have been another man's son."

It drove him wild. Tanner knew she was in Denver, but he couldn't find her. He'd checked all the public stables, searching for the mustang and then he'd hired a dozen men to canvass private stables owned by the hotels. The last two days had driven him to the desperation of riding the streets looking for a faded poncho and a long red braid.

He'd posted guards around his father's mansion, armed with her description, and he'd assigned a couple of men to watch the doors of the company offices.

After signaling the waiter in his club to bring another drink, he raked his fingers through his hair. She couldn't just vanish. Denver had a few thousand residents, but the city wasn't so large that a woman as striking and memorable as Fox would fade into the population without someone taking note.

She was here somewhere, he could feel her.

He loved her and, damn it, she loved him. If she would just agree to sit down with him and with his father, surely they would find an answer that could give them a future.

Dropping his head on the back cushion of the club chair, Tanner closed his eyes. Until the moment he had questioned his father about the past, he had continued to hope there was a mistake, a set of unlikely coincidences that had led Fox to believe Hobbs Jennings was her stepfather and that he'd stolen her inheritance.

But everything Fox had claimed was true. During the course of a night-long conversation intensely painful for them both, his father had admitted the long ago crime. And so many puzzles had been solved. Finally he understood the pain and flashes of torment in his father's eyes. And he understood that nothing Fox could do would punish his father as deeply as his father had punished himself. That punishment changed nothing. But maybe if Fox knew the price his father had paid in self-hatred and recrimination, maybe it would be enough. She wouldn't forgive any more than Tanner could forgive. But . . . maybe it would be enough.

He had to find her before revenge destroyed the two people he loved most. If she would just talk to his father, if she could bring herself to do that much, just maybe they could get through this.

Staring into space, he listened to the clubhouse clock ticking down the minutes. Whatever would happen was going to happen soon.

"Good afternoon," Fox said pleasantly, modestly dropping her gaze away from the young man at the desk. "Is Mr. Jennings in?"

"Do you have an appointment?" The name on a brass plate said Claude Piper.

"No, but I was assured Mr. Jennings would see me. I'm so-liciting donations from businessmen in support of children without mothers."

Mr. Piper put down his pen and studied her as thoroughly as Fox had ever been studied. Face flaming, she wondered if her Colt was outlined by the fabric of the bag looped over her wrist. As his examination continued during what seemed like an eon of silence, Fox fidgeted and tried to decide what she would do if she couldn't get past the obstacle presented by Claude Piper.

"And your name is?"

She felt positive that he stared at her bag. "It will be sufficient if you inform Mr. Jennings that I represent the Motherless Children's Society." She forced her lips into a wooden smile and ques-tioned the wisdom of presenting herself as a respectable young lady even if doing so was certain to garner newspaper attention and the public exposure of Jennings's crime. If she'd chosen to come here as herself, the moment would have been easier. She would have kicked Piper aside and pushed into Jennings's office. By now the bastard would have been standing at the gates of hell.

Mr. Piper rose behind his desk. "I'll only be a moment."

Having waited twenty years, she decided another minute or two didn't matter. It was surprising, however, that Jennings had hired only two men to guard his building, and that she had walked right past them. Tanner would certainly have informed his father that she was coming. Did Jennings believe the threat was idle? That she lacked the nerve to actually kill him? Her gaze turned stony. If so, that would be his last mistake.

Immediately she wished she hadn't thought of Tanner. Not now. He would be devastated by what she was about to do. Whatever else Jennings was, he was still Tanner's father and Tanner cared deeply about him. Fox wished that didn't disturb her so much.

"Follow me, please." Mr. Piper stood beside the entrance to a short hallway paneled in honey-colored pine.

Fox squared her shoulders and pressed her lips into a thin line. Her pulse increased and her skin tingled with electricity. She had waited so long for this moment.

Smiling tightly, she followed Piper down the hallway and into a commodious office crowded with bookshelves, paintings, and rugs in muted colors of burgundy and blue.

"Mr. Jennings will be with you shortly." Mr. Piper gave her a long stare, then shut the door behind him.

Irritated at having to wait, Fox walked to the windows and scanned the mountains she had so recently crossed. Snow hung on the distant peaks, reminding her that she wouldn't live to see another winter. She'd never cared for winter anyway.

Turning slowly, she glanced at the clock on the fireplace mantel, then examined Jennings's large mahogany desk. And jerked backward in shock. Two framed portraits faced Jennings's desk chair. One depicted Tanner as a boy, and the other was unmistakably Fox. Reaching a gloved hand, she held the portrait to the window light, her mouth dry.

This was the child's face she expected to see in the mirror, slightly mischievous and smiling on the verge of laughter. Clear blue gray eyes and a smiling rosy mouth beneath a tumble of red curls. She didn't recall sitting for this portrait, but she remembered the white pinafore and the little string of pearls.

"That is the daughter I should have had," a voice said behind her. "Not a day passes that I don't regret her loss."

Fox whirled, dropping the portrait and gripping her bag. Finally, she stood face-to-face with the man who had occupied her thoughts more than any other.

The years had not been kind to Hobbs Jennings. She knew for a certainty that he was twenty years younger than he appeared. Once his hair had been as thick and dark as Tanner's. Now the thinning strands were white. He no longer stood tall and elegant. His back hunched as if he were in pain, and he leaned heavily on a cane. What shocked most was the deep sadness in his dark eyes. Fox had never seen a man with sadder eyes.

She fumbled with the drawstring on her bag. "I've come here to—"

"I know why you've come, I've been expecting you," he said quietly, sinking into his desk chair with a heavy sigh. "And I know who you are."

"Tanner told you." She had known he would. Standing across the desk from Jennings, she aimed the gun at his forehead.

"I would have known you in any case, dear Eugenia. You're the spit image of your mother, did you know?"

The comment was so unexpected that it swept the ground from under her, and brought an unexpected and embarrassing rush of tears to her eyes. There was no one else alive who remembered her mother, just this man.

Confused and angry, Fox adjusted her grip on the butt of

the gun and finally lost an argument with herself. Unable to speak above a whisper, she couldn't resist asking, "I don't remember any more. What did she look like?"

"Your mother was lovely, as slender and elegant as a reed. Her eyes were blue gray, and her hair as red as yours." A ghost of a smile pleated the wrinkles scoring his cheeks. "She was graceful but strong, wise and courageous and loving." Shifting sideways in the chair, he fixed his sad gaze on the mountains. "I wasn't much of a match for her. She had wealth and position, I didn't. But Delphinia didn't care about those things."

"You betrayed her trust, you bastard!" The gun leveled at his head shook in her hand.

"Yes, I did." He turned back to her, his old man's voice steady. "Since the night Matthew told me that you would appear, I've tried to think what I would say to you. I could tell you that without Delphinia I didn't have the funds to keep my son in school, but that's only part of it. I wanted the life Delphinia had shown me." His knotted hands laced together. "Nothing I can say will explain that time in my life. There is no justification whatsoever. I betrayed Delphinia's trust, and I changed your life irrevocably." Hunching forward, he drew a hand across the pain in his gaze. "Matthew told me that you and your friend ate food out of garbage bins. There's nothing I can do or say to change that. I would give everything I own if there were."

Fox's eyes burned from staring, acid churned in her stomach. "You didn't just change my life, you bastard. You destroyed it!"

The Colt felt heavy in her hand. Was Jennings stalling? Hoping Mr. Piper would return with a dozen henchmen? No. He'd said he expected her. Claude Piper knew who she was, too.

"You won't believe this, but I ruined my life, too." Bending, he picked Fox's childhood portrait from the floor and held it in his hands. "I spent years searching for you. But by then Mrs. Wilson was dead and no one knew what had happened to you."

"Your life was ruined?" He was right. She didn't believe it.

"Once I thought of myself as a good decent man. But I learned that I wasn't. I'm not. That knowledge has permeated my life, soured everything I've touched. I haven't been the father I should have been. I pushed Matthew to achieve impossible heights to justify what I'd done, so I could tell myself my crime had been worth betraying your mother's trust. I've lived alone since . . ." His voice trailed. "I've done some things with the money that I hope Delphinia would have approved of. But trying to use your mother's money well didn't change what I'd done to get it. It didn't change what I'd done to you."

"It was *my* money you stole!"

"That was the greatest crime of all. Abandoning a child."

Her heart pounded against her rib cage and the gun wobbled in her hand. Her mother had loved this weary tormented man. Tanner loved him.

"I'm going to kill you," she said, gritting her teeth. His remorse didn't touch her. It was too late.

"I know."

But he'd done nothing to protect himself. He'd known she would come but he had not instructed Mr. Piper to block her from his office. The sheriff wasn't waiting. He hadn't pulled a gun from his desk and shot her first.

Hobbs Jennings waited in calm resignation, gazing at her with eyes filled with anguish by the guilt that drove him to keep a portrait of a little girl on his desk. This man would not regret dying. Death would come as relief from living with a past that shamed and haunted him.

"I am the justice you've been waiting for," she whispered, hating him.

Hobbs Jennings placed her childhood portrait next to the portrait of Tanner as a boy, then he looked up at her. "I'm sorry, Eugenia, for the terrible wrong I inflicted on you and for betraying the trust of a woman I loved. Sorrier than you could ever imagine. You deserved so much better."

"You're damned right I did."

Fox leveled the gun and fired.

CHAPTER 22

*T*HE door to the office burst open and Mr. Piper rushed forward, skidding on one of the rugs.

"It's all right, Mr. Piper." Hobbs Jennings opened his eyes and drew a breath. "Continue about your duties."

Claude Piper's eyes widened on the smoke curling from the gun in Fox's hand, then swung toward the shattered window behind Hobbs Jennings. Swallowing hard, Mr. Piper nodded and backed into the hallway.

Once he had gone, Fox's knees collapsed and she sank into the chair facing Jennings's desk. She dropped the Colt on the floor then covered her eyes.

"I hate you more than any person I have ever known," she said, her voice shaking. "I've hated you for so long that I can't remember a time when hating you wasn't part of me. I can't find words strong enough to express how much I regret not killing you. But I can't do it. I don't understand why . . . but I can't."

Part of the reason had to do with the people she loved. Her mother, Peaches, and Tanner. Another powerful reason was knowing if she killed Hobbs Jennings, she would be doing the bastard a favor.

"So what happens now," she asked after the silence between them had grown heavy. "Will you call the sheriff?"

Jennings roused himself from gazing at the two portraits on his desk. "Actually, I was considering buzzing Mr. Piper and requesting tea. Do you drink tea?"

"Lord, no. I don't drink that stuff. Coffee's acceptable, but whiskey would be better. This has been a confusing, upsetting, whiskey damn drinking kind of day." She glared. "Thanks to you, I'm not a refined tea-drinking woman. Whiskey's my choice and I can drink most men under the table." Her chin jutted and her gaze challenged him to express disapproval.

"Then something good came out of this." Jennings managed a small tired smile. "I see why my son loves you."

His words sent a jolt to her heart. Tanner. There would be time to think about him later.

During the wait for Piper to fetch whiskey and glasses, which arrived in a crystal decanter and etched glasses, Fox stared at Hobbs Jennings. Never in a lifetime of trying could she have imagined that she would end by sharing a glass of whiskey with a man whose death she had dreamed a thousand times.

Jennings lifted his glass to her but Fox didn't return the salute. "Why?"

"I don't know," she answered after a long hesitation. "I guess I love your son more than I hate you."

Something odd was happening in her mind and chest, something cracked and broke free. She hoped Peaches was watching, wished she could tell him that he had been right. The past couldn't be changed. It was time to let go of old wrongs, old bitterness. Hobbs Jennings had punished himself more than a quick death ever would have. She wondered if Peaches had guessed that.

And there was another truth. If Fox had grown up in a grand mansion surrounded by servants and finemannered friends, she would have missed so much.

She would never have known the smell of morning coffee boiling over a campfire. Or the splash of cold river water on her face. She wouldn't have watched deer and elk in the wild, would never have traveled the country in the way she had. She wouldn't have experienced the satisfaction and, yes, the pleasure of labor and earning her own way. She wouldn't have been independent or self-reliant. Worst of all, she would never have known Peaches. If she had lived the life she might have had, she would not be who she was. She would be someone else entirely.

But sitting here now, drinking whiskey with the haunted old man she came to kill . . . Fox understood that she liked herself fine, just as she was.

A hard knot fell away from her heart, crumbling as the anger drained out of her body. She had been so angry and so filled with hate for so long that for one panicky moment she tried to hang on to those feelings, then she exhaled slowly and feeling lighter by the minute, she let them go.

Tears glistened on her lashes and she swallowed hard.

"Did Tanner tell you how many times we picked up those gold coins?"

"He told me about the outlaws you two chased down."

"Did he tell you about getting shot by an Indian?"

"Lord, no." Asking her to relate the story, Jennings refilled their glasses.

Fox glanced at the ceiling, imagining she heard Peaches laughing his heavenly butt off. It would have tickled him to see her trading stories with Hobbs Jennings. "Well, we'd stopped at a Mormon fort. Might be the place that served buttermilk." She made a face and shuddered. "I don't recall. Anyway, we helped chase off a party of Utes, but a couple of them snuck into our camp to steal our horses, and—"

It wasn't going to be easy. The deep need to kill Jennings receded more every time she looked into those sad eyes, but Fox doubted she could ever forgive him. If the familiar hatred should rise again, she would remind herself that whatever he was, Hobbs Jennings had raised the finest man she'd ever known. She would try to respect him for that one thing.

By the time she finished the tale and one or two more, the sun had sunk toward the peaks, and they sat in shadows.

"There's much we have to discuss," Hobbs Jennings said quietly. "I hope we'll talk again and you'll allow me to know you. But right now, there's someone waiting and pacing the floor. He's turned this town upside down searching for you."

"You aren't the only problem between us," she said, looking down at her empty glass. "I don't fit in his world."

Jennings regarded her with a thoughtful expression. "Whose opinion do you value? That of people you'll never meet and never know? Or Matthew's opinion? Matthew doesn't care what people might think of you. He's willing to accept you exactly as you are."

Oh Lord. The person whose opinion she cared least about agreed with Peaches, the person she'd cared the most about. Sudden tears stung the back of her eyes.

"Instead of worrying about you fitting into Matthew's world, or him fitting into yours," Jennings said gently, "perhaps you can create a world that's right for the two of you."

Damn all. It was something Peaches might have said. And Peaches would have made it sound just as possible.

"Tanner cares about your opinion . . ." she whispered.

"Eugenia? Nothing would please me more than to see you both happy."

"Thank you." Fox blinked hard. "Not that I care whether you're pleased or not," she added hastily.

"I hope someday you will." Standing, he gazed at her with those heart-wrenching, dark eyes. "We've both waited a very long time for today. Welcome home."

Without a word, Fox spun and walked out of the room. She didn't want him to see her cry.

Someone had to know where she was. Or maybe she'd changed her mind about killing his father and headed back to Nevada. No, she wouldn't abandon a goal almost as old as she was. Tanner swore in frustration.

The only thing he'd done since returning to Denver was search for Fox and think about her. A redheaded woman who wasn't afraid of anything, a woman unlike any he'd known before. A woman he loved enough to do whatever it took to have her beside him forever.

Pacing the length of his parlor, he combed his mind for a hint of where she might be. What was she thinking now? When and how would she go after his father? He knew in his gut that he could change her mind somehow because that had to be true. But he couldn't think of anywhere else to look for her. He'd exhausted all the possibilities.

A pounding on the door interrupted his thoughts. He peered at the clock but couldn't read the time since he hadn't yet lit the lamps. He wasn't expecting anyone. The pounding continued and he waited in annoyance, then recalled that he'd dismissed the servants for the evening.

"Damn it." Striding into the foyer, he pulled open the door, prepared to send away whoever he found there. But a beautiful young woman stormed past him in a swish of skirts and a waft of rose scent. "Fox? My God, is that you?" He couldn't believe his eyes. She was the loveliest creature he'd ever seen.

"It's me, all right," she said, rounding on him and jabbing

him in the chest to punctuate her words. "Like father, like son. If one of you isn't stealing my money, it's the other."

"What?" She wouldn't be here if she'd killed his father. A slow grin of relief and joy spread across his face. She had come to him. "I don't know what you're talking about, but I know I want to kiss you until you scream."

"Our deal was that you pay me half up front, and the other half when I dragged your butt into Denver." The finger poking at his chest became several fingers unbuttoning his shirt. "You didn't pay me."

"Good Lord. You're right. I forgot about it until this minute." Sweeping her into his arms, he kissed her forehead, her eyes, her cheeks, the corner of her lips.

She licked his earlobe, and his thighs tightened painfully. "I suppose you're going to claim that the money you owe me is upstairs in your bedroom." Her arms wound around his neck and she grabbed him, kissing him hard, kissing him until they both were gasping.

"That's exactly where my money is," he said hoarsely. "Do I take it correctly that you didn't kill my father?"

"I didn't kill him," she said, not sounding happy about it. "You and me, we've got some family problems to work out, namely that I may occasionally still want to kill that bastard, your father. On the other hand, he has a way about him."

"I want to hear every detail about what happened . . . later." Tanner slung her over his shoulder and gave her fanny a long caress, remembering fondly when that fanny had smelled like bacon. He started up the staircase. "I hope you aren't tired, I promise you, this is going to be a long night." Stopping midway up the stairs, he threw back his head and shouted. "I love you, Eugenia Foxworth soon to be Jennings."

She smacked his back with her fists. "Not Eugenia, damn. And not Jennings. Can't we be Tanner?"

"We can be whatever you want us to be!"

Kicking open his bedroom door, he set her on her feet beside the bed and lit the lamps. He wanted to see her as he undressed her, wanted to see and touch and taste every piece and part of her. Good God, she was beautiful. Glowing. Radiant. Cupping her face, he gazed into the face he loved so well. "You aren't going to change your mind, are you?"

"About not killing your father?"

"About loving me."

"Oh Tanner." She touched his lips with a trembling finger. "I'll love you forever, until we're as old as those fossils you're going to find. I'll keep your house, grow your radishes, and raise your babies. I'll fight your enemies and try to love who you love. Or at least tolerate him."

He hadn't wept since he was a child. The hot sting behind his eyes surprised him. Then he laughed as she hopped up on the bed, sent her bonnet flying across the room and shook the hairpins out of her magnificent hair, letting it shimmer and fall to her waist. She arched an eyebrow and crooked a finger. "Come here and I'll show you how much I love you. That will never change. Never. Truth is, I can outdrink you, outshoot you, and outlove you."

"You can outshoot me, but you can't outlove me," he said, loving her so hard he couldn't breathe.

She smiled and opened her arms, her eyes soft and shining in the lamplight. "Let's find out."

He suspected it would be a contest they'd be waging when they were old and holding each other in the bedroom of the house he would build for her. They were about to embark on the greatest journey of their lives. When he took her into his arms, he knew the journey had begun.